TANGLED LIVES . . .

Dr. Michael Carrington—selflessly dedicated to surgery and ruthlessly demanding the same dedication from everyone else, until a tragedy changes his life. . . .

Nedra Scott—aloof, beautiful, gentle and *almost* Mrs. Michael Carrington. . . .

Dr. David Savage—the rich young gynecologist who thinks himself a "god," proves it by abusing women. . . .

Susan Thomas—the stunning nurse who hopes to marry a rich doctor, and disastrously sets her heart on David Savage. . . .

Dr. Joseph Merrick—a successful family man whose seething hatred for David Savage is matched only by his passion for Pamela Gibson. . . .

Pamela Gibson—an actress with the kind of problem that could put Joseph Merrick in jail. . . .

Aaron Metz—a terminal cancer patient with a battle to wage—against his only living daughter. . . .

Dr. Keith Johnson—a promising young resident who risks his career for a night of "on-duty" kinky sex. . . .

The Surgeons

**Shirley Hartman &
Walter P. Ellerbeck, M.D.**

PYRAMID BOOKS ▲ NEW YORK

All service ranks the same with God—
God's puppets, best and worst are we;
there is no last or first.

—Robert Browning

Chapter I

. . . friday

Jesus, thought Dr. Michael Carrington as he waited for the red "Don't Walk" light to change to green, this neighborhood really is going to hell.

He had pressed the pedestrian signal button only moments before and knew from experience that he had some minutes to wait. Bemusedly he stared at the structure on the opposite side of the moderately busy intersection. The Marin Medical Center was dull gray brick, and the dim 6:00 A.M. morning light made it seem even more depressing than it would appear a few hours later when the Los Angeles sun had burned off the morning mist and fog.

Why, thought Carrington, does every hospital seem to have a shroud of impending crisis settled about it?

Basically Marin Medical Center was an old building, although from time to time, as expansion demanded and Medicare financed, new wings had been added and certain remodeling had been attempted. Even now the newly installed wide glass entrance door gleamed almost obscenely from the otherwise ancient and dull façade.

A block away, a wino lurched from between two buildings and walked diagonally across the intersection with dignified drunken disdain for the traffic. Dr. Carrington glanced from the drunk to the light. Still red. Twelve years ago, when he had first set up his offices in the medical complex directly across from the hospital, it had been a good neighborhood. Things had certainly changed. Only last month, there had been two attempted rape cases involving nurses going off duty at the end of their three to eleven shift. A minor mutiny had been averted when the hospital instituted a policy of having an armed guard accompany each shift change across the street and back from the parking lot. A hell of a note. No wonder the hospital was having difficulty recruiting competent nurses. Other doctors had moved their offices to Century City or Beverly Hills and applied for rights at one of the "in" hospitals. But as Mike appraised the ugly eight-story structure, he realized it was a damned fine hospital, and besides—it was home.

The light finally changed to "Walk," and Mike strode briskly across, approaching the entrance. As his tall, muscular body broke the electronic beam, the door swung open into the brightly lit lobby.

Mary McCullough looked up sullenly from the card rack, where she was arranging the alphabetical list of patients, and watched Dr. Carrington cross the deserted lobby to the newspaper stand, insert a dime, and remove the morning paper. As he turned, he was oblivious to a near collision with a utility man steering a power-driven floor polisher, intent upon buffing the tile to gleaming sterility. Mary watched the doctor enter the Admitting Office and emerge almost immediately with the typed list of his patients currently in the hospital.

She half smiled, spitefully, remembering an incident only a few weeks ago when, through some clerical error, one of Carrington's patients had inadvertently been omitted from the list. He had made his rounds that morning, had been called for minor emergency surgery, dashed to his office to keep appointments, and had come back at 6:00 P.M. for evening rounds, working from the same list. He had been on the freeway, dogtired, halfway home at 7:30 P.M. when he realized that he had missed seeing a patient because of the error. The hospital was still talking about the scene that had followed. Wouldn't any normal surgeon simply have seen the patient the next morning, turned on the bedside

8

charm, and made a logical excuse for the skipped visits? Most of the doctors Mary knew through her job as chief admitting nurse at Marin would have done so. But Carrington had turned around that night and come back. Big deal! Who did he think he was—one of the Knights of St. John?

Mary continued to watch covertly as Mike walked slowly through the lobby, scanning the list. She tensed as he passed her without raising his eyes and headed toward the bank of elevators.

Dammit, she thought, who does he think he is? Viciously she pushed the button opposite his name on the large board listing the staff doctors. A green light came on, attesting that one Dr. Michael W. Carrington was now on the hospital premises.

Susan Thomas, the young blond admitting nurse who was just beginning her second morning on the job, watched curiously.

"Who's that?"

"God. Who else?" snapped Mary. "He refuses to turn on his signal light because he says the board is in an awkward spot and he has to walk all the way around the desk to do it!"

Susan watched his retreating figure, measuring the width of his shoulders, estimating his probable bank balance. "He's kind of cute."

Mary stared at her coldly. "That, my dear, as you'll soon find out, is Dr. Michael Carrington. He's one hell of a surgeon, and he fills more beds in this hospital than any other five doctors combined. But cute he is not! And before you ask—he's forty-three, got that tan playing on his boat, the *Non Nocere*." Noticing Susan's raised eyebrows, "That's Latin. It means 'Do no harm.' I think it's from Hippocrates or somebody. I'm not sure." She thought for a moment. "I guess they preach it in medical school. As far as the patient's concerned, if you can't help, at least, do no harm."

"Sounds reasonable," Susan grinned.

Mary shrugged. "And again—before you ask—he's a

bachelor. But forget it—every nurse in the hospital has made a play for him. He's not buying."

Both of them watched, with different emotions, as Mike stepped into the elevator and pressed the button for the eighth floor. His fingers drummed lightly and impatiently against his side as he waited for the mechanism to slide the door shut.

"Doctor Carrington. Doctor Michael Carrington."

Hearing the page, Mike slipped out of the elevator just as the door began to close, walked to the admitting desk phone and picked it up.

"Doctor Carrington," he snapped.

The filtered voice of a telephone operator came through. "Doctor, I have a call for you from Emergency. Just a moment." And then—

"Jeff Melburn, Doctor. I know you're not on call for us, but we've just gotten in a guy from an automobile accident. In shock. I'd appreciate it if you could look at him."

"I'll be right there."

Although Mary and Susan had self-consciously busied themselves with the tasks at hand during the brief conversation, again their eyes followed Mike as he walked past the admitting desk, along the short hall behind it, and through the swinging doors leading to the Emergency Room.

Once past the doors, Mike entered an L-shaped corridor lined with chairs and presided over by a female clerk seated behind a desk. Even at this early hour, activity had begun. He gave only a brief, disinterested glance at the very pregnant black girl holding a blood-stained towel over her right wrist. A few chairs removed from her was a middle-aged man and a teen-aged boy. From their similar features and coloration, it was likely they were father and son. The youngster sat quietly, calmly staring at the ugly barbed fishhook which protruded from the fleshy area at the base of his thumb. The father, now and then glancing at his boy's injured hand, looked as if he might be sick at any moment.

At the admitting desk, an elderly man in a raveled

blue sweater was complaining of severe abdominal pains while the clerk calmly filled in the necessary forms.

"May I have your Medi-Cal card, please?" she asked.

Mike sighed inwardly. The Medi-Cal card—with its all-important stickers—the wampum of the modern hospital.

Christ, we've come full circle, he thought as he pushed his way through the second set of swinging doors. A sick Sioux Indian enticed the services of the tribe's witch doctor with beads and bits of colored cloth. Now the "beads" were little yellow gummed pieces of paper that guaranteed the hospital would be paid.

Entering the Emergency Room, Mike quickly surveyed the situation. Three of the four curtained-off beds lining the wall were empty. The fourth was occupied by a Mexican child, perhaps six, maybe seven years old. One of the Emergency Room nurses was gently sponging blood from his face and arms as Dr. Francis Bolker, Marin's pediatrics resident, began his examination. Nearby, a Los Angeles patrolman stood questioning a young Chicano woman with a very old face, obviously the mother of the injured child.

Just beyond, the automobile-accident victim lay on a hospital gurney. Jeff Melburn, the Emergency Room doctor, bent over him intently, drawing blood. Two policemen, a sergeant and his younger partner, stood nearby. The sergeant spoke.

"While you're at it, Doc, I need a tube of blood for alcohol content. He ran the stop at Third and Western and clipped this Olds—"

Dr. Melburn nodded curtly, cutting him off. "You'll get it."

Mike watched Jeff with professional admiration. Dr. Melburn was just out of training, about twenty-eight years old, longhaired, with a neatly trimmed beard. Mike grinned. It must have been a slow night, because Jeff's green scrub pants and tunic bore the unmistakable, disheveled look of having been slept in. Mike paused as Jeff expertly removed the syringe. Jeff was worth every cent of the surprising five thousand dollars a month the hospital paid its Emergency Room doctors. It was a rough assignment of from eight to twelve hectic hours a day, often longer, the doctors catching sleep when they could. And an Emergency Room doctor had to be *good*—able not only to apply the vital lifesaving techniques but to diagnose expertly under pressure. He must know exactly what steps to take, what specialist to call.

As Mike continued to wait, he noticed Eva Niles, the night supervisor, and Betty, the Emergency Room nurse, carefully cataloging the victim's valuables. Checking, double-checking, and checking each other. They inventoried the contents of the wallet—especially the identification, the credit cards—counted the currency and loose change, and listed the jewelry—the ring, wristwatch, cuff links, and tie tac. Then, finally sealing the envelope, each signed it.

Beside them on the desk in a neat pile were the patient's clothes. Even from where Mike stood, he could see they were of good quality. The jacket bore the distinctive label of "Carroll's," one of Beverly Hills' most expensive men's stores. And the shoes were undeniably Gucci.

At least, thought Mike, this won't be a "labor of love"—a term the doctors used when an emergency case was obviously an indigent—no money, no insurance, no Medi-Cal sticker, no means to pay for services. Not that it affected the quality of medical help given. As far as Mike was concerned, a life was a life, and rich or poor, a person had the God-given right to live every day, every hour, every minute that medical science could provide. But this guy was obviously able to pay, and it kind of made up for all the times Mike and other staff doctors went into a difficult five- or six-hour operation, knowing in advance there would be no compensation.

As Mike approached the patient, the sliding doors to the parking lot opened, revealing a police ambulance and several squad cars. The two ambulance attendants entered, recognized Carrington, and glanced at each other in satisfaction. They were well aware that Jeff could not admit a patient to the Medical Center, and if he were unable to find a staff doctor to do so, the patient, after receiving emergency treatment, would have to be taken to County General Hospital. Carrington's presence assured them that the additional trip would be unnecessary.

Dr. Melburn handed the syringe of blood to Betty and she began filling numerous tubes bearing various colored caps. One of the ambulance attendants extended a clipboard for an official signature. Now aware of Mike's presence, Jeff tilted his head in greeting as he scribbled his signature on the receipt and proceeded to fill Carrington in.

"Automobile accident. Drunk . . . bumped his head . . . abdominal pain . . . I've called X-ray for a portable machine. Blood pressure eighty over sixty. Getting better, was lower before the plasmanate was started. Pulse a hundred and forty."

Mike nodded, glancing automatically at the two IVs already running—plasmanate and Ringer's Lactate. He looked down at the Foley catheter as Jeff continued.

"Urine flowing okay, no blood. Unresponsive when brought in, starting to talk a little now."

"Any idea who he is?" asked Mike.

Betty handed a violet-stoppered vial to the police sergeant. He nodded his thanks. She joined Mike and Jeff.

"I.D. says George Selkins, Roxbury Drive, Beverly Hills," she volunteered.

Mike ran his eyes over the patient. About forty years old, definitely drunk. You could smell it—and the fact that he evidenced no fear, no apprehension, no interest in his injuries, was indicative of intoxication. Mike approached him.

"Morning, I'm Doctor Carrington. Let's see what we've got here." Methodically he started with the patient's head—eyes, ears, nose, mouth, moving the jaws.

13

No apparent problem. Suddenly Selkins jerked his head away.

"Now just a damned minute. If I'm going to be in some fucking hospital, it's not going to be this one. And I want my own doctor. You get Dr. Kentner!"

"No problem, Mr. Selkins," Mike said soothingly. "Just as soon as we know it's safe to move you, you can go to any hospital you want."

Selkins seemed slightly placated, but not willing to leave it at that. "All these tubes . . . all this shit about—"

His grumbling was cut off by sudden vomiting. Betty appeared magically with a pan, wet towels, and a red rubber tube about thirty-five inches long and three-eighths of an inch in diameter.

"A number eighteen Levine tube okay, doctor?" she asked.

He nodded as she began to lubricate the tip of the tube. He knew Betty from previous cases and liked her. She was typical, thought Mike, of almost every Emergency Nurse he knew. Bright, attractive, young, and aggressive. Willing to work twice as hard as the regular nurses and take the inevitable abuse from drunks, overdosed kids, and harrassed doctors for the extra pay Emergency commanded.

As Betty finished lubricating the tube, Mike spoke gently to the patient. "We have to put this tube into your stomach, Mr. Selkins. I know you're not going to like it, but it won't hurt and—"

Selkins stared at the tube and shook his head violently.

"No way!"

From experience, Mike knew that some people were happy souls when they drank. Others became belligerent. He had long since learned that the combination of alcohol—too much alcohol—plus injury and fright often produced the latter. And he had also learned how to deal with it. You met fire with fire. Rough and unsympathetic as it seemed, he knew he had to be direct, firm, meet Selkins head-on to avoid an interminable, time-wasting argument. He automatically changed his tack.

"Look, buddy, you may not realize it, but *you are hurt*—and these things we're doing are important to keep you living."

Betty tried to insert the tip of the tube in Selkins' nose. He pushed her hand violently away. His exertion precipitated another bout of vomiting. Mike deliberately came on stronger.

"This is no bullshit," he said evenly. "You need that tube! It's no fun, but then neither is dying!"

The shock value of Mike's words had the desired effect, and Selkins lay passively as Betty expertly inserted the tube through his nose, into the stomach, and attached the other end to tubing that went to a glass bottle attached to wall suction. That done, she gently proceeded to clean up the patient and the mess.

The mop-up job completed, Mike continued his examination. Picking up a stethoscope from the nearby tray, he listened to the heart, then for breath sounds on both sides of the chest. So far so good. He palpated the abdomen and was rewarded by a wince and a groan. Going back to the stethoscope, Mike listened intently for some moments. No sounds, no gurgles from the abdomen—just ominous silence. Big trouble here, he knew. On to the legs now, flexing each one . . . then the feet. They were warm, with good pulses. No artery or nerve was disrupted, Mike noted with satisfaction— motion and sensation were intact.

The police sergeant had been busy getting the patient's I.D. from Betty and filling out his report. He sensed Mike had just about completed the preliminary examination and moved in.

"Mr. Selkins, I'm Sergeant Farnsberg. Can you tell me where you were coming from and—?"

Mike spoke curtly to the police officer. "Not now, sergeant. There'll be plenty of time once he's been admitted, and he'll be in better shape to answer questions!"

The sergeant seemed about to argue the point, then nodded and withdrew.

Jeff turned away, hiding a grin. If Carrington hadn't interceded to stop the questioning, he would have done so. Not that interrogation at this point would have done the patient any harm. It was a matter of personal survival.

In his first month or so on Emergency Room duty, he had been naïve enough to allow law-enforcement personnel to question patients in his presence—and then found himself constantly subpoenaed to testify as a witness in the ensuing court cases relating to the accident. At first he had reminded himself that it was his duty as a citizen, but then, as he was served time after time, usually spending a full day in court on each of the many cases, waiting to corroborate testimony, realizing he had nothing of importance to add, the impossibility of the situation had slowly dawned on him. So, being a bright young man, he soon made it his business to make sure that he could honestly report to the District Attorney's office or to an interested lawyer that he had heard nothing. Occasionally, as he watched Sergeant Schultz in reruns of *Hogan's Heroes* on television recite his famous line—"nutting! I have heard *nutting!*"—he chuckled at the resemblance. It didn't endear him to the legal hotshots but, he reminded himself, his profession was medicine—not law. He realized now that Carrington employed the same tactics.

Mike caught Jeff's half grin of conspiracy. I'd really like to know him better, Mike thought fleetingly. Heard somewhere he's married . . . maybe invite them down to the boat. . . . And he just as quickly discarded the idea. Too dangerous.

Already there was gossiping among the older staff doctors of the hospital—disgruntled physicians wondering why Mike got so many of the Emergency patients. Ugly little hints of possible kickbacks and payoffs. Mike bristled just thinking about it. Didn't the sons of bitches *know* why he got so many of the calls? He was *there*—actually in the hospital—when many of the calls came in, while the complainers were out on the fourth hole of the golf course. If he wasn't actually in the hospital, he

16

could be there in minutes. Also, he never bitched about a middle-of-the-night call, when Jeff was desperately searching for a staff doctor. He'd make admitting arrangements by phone and get his ass down to the hospital immediately. Hell, Jeff knew that Marin Medical Center, because of its contract with the city, had to keep careful records of its Emergency Room operation: fatality ratio, number of cases referred elsewhere, patient complaints. Mike made Jeff look good and—all other things being equal—Jeff returned the favor with a "fat case" occasionally, even when other doctors were available.

Besides, Jeff wouldn't be there long. As soon as he piled up enough loot to establish himself in private practice he'd be long gone—and another young, ambitious doctor would take his place.

His thoughts were interrupted by the appearance of the burly young patrolman Mike had noticed earlier questioning the mother of the injured boy. The officer peered around intently, slightly bewildered, a little concerned. The sergeant filling in the report on Selkins glanced up.

"Hey, Pembrook! What's the matter—lose something?" he kidded.

Serious, concentrating, Officer Pembrook ignored the bantering tone. "Yeah," he announced. "Did any of you see a young Mexican woman . . . about five feet one, maybe a hundred and five pounds, dark hair—"

Interrupting, the sergeant's partner surveyed Pembrook's six foot three, muscular frame with a wide grin. "What happened? Did she overpower you and get away?"

In spite of themselves, Jeff, Mike, and the nurses laughed. Pembrook blushed uncomfortably. "Aw, come on. She's the kid's mother. She was crying and all. She asked me to get her a cup of coffee, and when I came back she was . . . well, she was gone. Just disappeared, that's all. No one even saw her leave."

The sergeant had been aware of the earlier activity at

the other end of the room. "Well, the kid's still here, isn't he?"

Pembrook nodded. "Yeah, but she's been gone quite a while . . . and nobody can find her. And I don't know if charges will be filed against her or—"

"Relax," the sergeant suggested. "She probably went to the powder room. She's not going to blow without her kid."

Before the discussion could be continued, two X-ray technicians arrived, wheeling the portable equipment. Carrington met them at the door and indicated Selkins.

"I'll want X-rays of the skull, chest, and abdomen," he ordered. "In the meantime, I'll get this guy a bed in the Intensive Care Unit."

He turned back to Jeff. "Electrolytes and liver function studies—be sure to get them."

"Already done," Jeff countered, with a slight, deferential bow. "Blood gasses, too."

"Good deal," Mike acknowledged. "Oh, and antibiotics—we'd better give him a gram of Keflin, via IV push." He turned his attention once again to Selkins. "And I'll call your doctor now."

As he started to leave, Mike turned back and sharply addressed the X-ray technicians. "And I'll be upstairs to look at the X-rays in *five minutes!*"

The technicians nodded resignedly. They knew Dr. Carrington.

As Mike emerged from the elevator on the eighth floor, he went directly to the phone in the X-ray waiting room. Sitting down, he dialed "9" for an outside line, then "411" and waited for the information operator to answer. He sighed, unfolded the newspaper and began to scan the headlines. Knowing from experience the delay and the frustration he could expect from trying to make this one, simple call, he detested wasting the precious minutes it could consume. But it was unavoidable, he knew, and the morning ritual of buying the newspaper was his insurance against losing his temper.

His estimation of the progression of the phone call was right on the button.

"Information," announced the nasal voice at the other end of the phone.

"Could you give me the number of Doctor Kentner in Beverly Hills, please?"

"Kentner," repeated the operator. "How is that spelled?"

"K-E-N-T-N-E-R," Mike recited, automatically becoming immersed in one of the news items.

"What is his first name, please?"

"Arthur."

"And do you know the street, please?"

"Afraid not," Mike replied cheerfully, still reading.

"Just a moment, please," and interminable minutes passed, then finally, "This is a doctor you are calling, sir. Did you want his home number or his exchange?" the operator asked.

"Exchange please." It was a code of honor among physicians to call each other via exchanges—never at home. Otherwise, too many times a wife might answer, volunteer her husband was not there, but he could be reached at his office or the hospital. And should the indiscreet caller insist that he had just tried unsuccessfully—that the doctor was at neither place—marital suspicions and fireworks erupted, often ending in an unpleasant scene, and occasionally divorce. Calling the service was a simple precaution each doctor extended his colleagues.

Mike punched another button for a new line, dialed "9" and the number he had been given. Another long wait.

"Doctor Arthur Kentner's exchange," a bright voice announced. But before Mike could speak, the voice continued, "I'll be right with you"—and clicked off.

Mike shrugged slightly. It was par for the course. They had invented vaccines against smallpox, cholera, polio. If someone could come up with a serum to prevent unnecessary delays, it would save a helluva lot of lives. He turned to the sports section and was able to

19

read several articles before the operator finally came back on the line.

"Doctor Arthur Kentner's exchange. Can I help you? The office doesn't open until nine."

"Yes, this is Doctor Michael Carrington. I'd like to speak to him—"

"What is your telephone number, doctor?" she interrupted.

"I'm at Marin Medical Center, and—"

"Is there an extension?"

"No," Mike explained tiredly, "you'll have to page me."

"Is this an emergency?"

"Yes," said Mike, "it is."

"Just a moment," and before he could say anything further, she had clicked off again. It was Mike's private conviction that answering services gave each prospective employee an intelligence test. If their IQ tested fifty or under, they were automatically hired. He turned back to the newspaper and began filling in a few scattered words of the crossword puzzle. Eventually, she came back on.

"I am unable to reach Doctor Kentner at the moment, but I will have him call as soon as I am able to reach him," she announced cheerfully.

"Just tell him I may have to operate on his patient, George Selkins," Mike instructed.

"I'll give him your message, doctor."

"Thank you," he said wearily as he hung up the phone.

Society doctors, snorted Mike under his breath as he headed toward the X-ray Department. He knew of Dr. Kentner—hell, who didn't? Probably, he thought, if I turned to the amusement or society sections of the paper right now, I'd see his photo escorting some half-dressed starlet to the latest charity benefit premiere. Kentner was handsome, suave, sophisticated, a quack and a butcher. Unfortunately, thought Mike, a medical diploma hanging in an office did not a doctor make. Mike knew of several specific instances where Kentner's ineptitude and disinterest had produced fatal results. Only a few weeks ago, the beautiful wife of a prominent industrialist had died of a massive cerebral accident which only a few hours before Dr. Kentner had diagnosed as a tension headache. He had prescribed a codeine compound, and had left for the celebrity tennis tournament at La Costa. Kentner was widely photographed as one of the eight honorary pallbearers at her funeral.

As Mike made his way down the deserted corridor of the X-ray Department, his thoughts were shoved aside by the appearance of Dave Thurmond, the chief X-ray technician. Dave was about thirty years old, with a wry, irreverent attitude that belied his crisp efficency. He greeted Mike in his usual slightly sarcastic manner.

"You're late this morning. It's already light. Where've you been? And what patient of yours can I stick in front of all the other patients today?"

Mike grinned. "We'll get around to that. But first I want to see the X-rays on the dude from the Emergency Room."

"The films just came up—they're still in the processer." Dave looked at his watch and shook his head in mock sympathy. "You're going to have to wait a whole hundred and eighty seconds to see them. Sorry about that."

Mike gave an exaggerated sigh and turned to the Procedures Board on the opposite wall where the scheduled patients for the day were listed.

"Well, while we're waiting—you know I *would* like to get Mrs. Whitlock up first, I'm worried about her. And then, if you can manage it, there's an upper G-I on the man in 308, a Mr. Campion . . . I would appreciate it, Dave. I think I'm going to be around the hospital a couple of hours, and it sure would save me time this afternoon."

Dave threw up his hands in disgust, but before he could answer, the X-ray developer situated in the alcove across from them began spewing out film. Both men crossed quickly and started picking up the negatives, carefully checking the labels for the patient's name to make sure no slipup had occurred.

Mike put the first one up on the view box and scanned it. Behind him, Dave peered at it too, more concerned with the technical quality of the film than with a medical diagnosis.

Mike looked at the four skull X-rays, each taken from various positions and angles, for only a few minutes before passing on to those of the chest. Again, he glanced at each one only briefly. When he got to the abdominal X-rays, however, he peered at each for several long minutes before speaking.

"Is your friendly neighborhood radiologist around?"

Dave nodded. "Sure. Doctor Reichner is the only one who gets in as early as you do. I think he's in his office reading the films taken last night."

Mike gave a half wave of thanks and started to leave. Dave called him back, indicating the X-rays Mike held.

"Christ, don't take those to Reichner without a jacket. You trying to get us all crucified?"

The technician hurriedly picked up a folder and wrote Selkins' name and hospital number on it and watched until Mike had inserted the X-rays. Reichner was a tyrant on many matters that concerned his department, but he was rabid in his insistence that films be immediately put in folders and kept there. Hundreds of X-rays were processed every day and were handled many times. Should a patient's X-ray find its way into someone else's file, there could possibly be serious consequences if the error went unnoticed. Of lesser importance was the fact that once a film had gone astray in such a manner, locating it represented a Herculean task, and it was probably lost forever.

Mike understood and thoroughly agreed with Reichner's dictum, but couldn't resist needling Dave. It was practically a way of life between the two of them.

"Picky, picky," he muttered audibly and, still grinning, headed briskly to an office a short way down the corridor. He stuck his head in the door.

"Got a minute?"

The middle-aged, gray-haired doctor sitting behind the desk made a quick gesture with his head, and Mike went in and flipped the first two groups of X-rays on to the giant view box which occupied the wall behind Reichner's desk. As he mounted them, Mike explained.

"This is a guy, maybe forty or forty-five . . . auto accident this morning . . . drunk."

Reichner twisted in his chair and carefully examined the X-rays, one by one. He had almost finished before Mike spoke.

"The skull and chest look all right to me."

"I'll buy that," Reichner agreed.

"Now, what do you make of these?" Mike inserted the abdominal X-rays alongside the others. The radiologist was forced to stand to view them. He studied each film without speaking—then went back to one taken of the patient in an upright position. He stared at it for some time before finally voicing his opinion.

"A little small bowel air . . . no air fluid levels. Doesn't mean much. No free air. Tube in the stomach. Right psoas shadow . . . a little blurred. Spine intact."

Reichner shook his head and started pulling down the X-rays. He sat down, carefully stacked the films and tucked them inside the jacket, finally laying the folder on a corner of his desk where someone from his department would routinely collect it.

"Looks like you'll have to break down and examine the patient," Reichner said casually. "No magic diagnosis here."

Mike smiled good-naturedly, recognizing the subtle dig. "You know," he said, "I just might do that."

As Mike retraced his steps from the X-ray Department, he noticed that the corridor was no longer deserted. Six or seven patients in wheelchairs were already lined up, waiting their turn—and several outpatients were being ushered into rooms where they could exchange their street clothes for hospital gowns. He noted with satisfaction that his Mr. Campion was at the head of the line. As he approached the elevator, the door opened and an orderly pushed out a chair bearing Mrs. Whitlock. She was wanly attractive, about forty-seven years old, and her eyes brightened on seeing him.

"Good morning, doctor."

"Morning, Mrs. Whitlock," Mike said warmly. "I've ordered a few additional tests after X-ray—and I'll be down to see you a little later."

She nodded gratefully. Mike held the elevator door open for a moment before entering and was gratified to see Dave direct the attendant to wedge Mrs. Whitlock's chair in directly behind the patient from 308. Spying Mike, Dave gave a mocking, military salute.

As he pressed the button for the sixth floor, Mike whistled softly. He knew he sometimes bugged the X-ray Department with his special demands. But, hell, medicine wasn't a popularity contest. Let the other doctors routinely order their X-rays and get the results the following day. A little friendly pressure exerted here could save him many precious hours later. Diagnosis and treatment could be started sooner, and often he could even save a patient the expense of an extra day of hospital care.

Mike was still whistling as he stepped out of the elevator on the sixth floor, made a sharp right turn, and pushed open the large door marked "Intensive Care Unit." Below that was a small sign: "Absolutely No Admittance—Ring for Nurse."

Inside, the room was carpeted and decorated in bright colors. A middle-aged woman, actually a licensed vocational nurse, manned the large main desk, behind which the complicated electronic equipment monitored the vital signs of the patients in the ten glassed-in units which comprised the ICU. Each patient could be physically observed from the desk, and each was hooked up to an EKG unit which blipped a warning at the slightest change. Mike glanced at his watch—6:47 A.M.—then looked beyond the desk into the deluxe conference room behind it.

Six women sat around the table. The two night nurses were conferring with the four morning shift nurses who

24

were about to start their duty—bringing them up-to-date, patient by patient, on what had happened during the night.

"Is Mr. Selkins up yet?" Mike asked the LVN.

"No, not yet, doctor," she replied.

Mike hid his annoyance, picked up the phone, dialed "328," and asked evenly, "Has Mr. Selkins left the Emergency Room yet?"

"We've been short of orderlies, doctor. He's just being wheeled to the elevator," was the reply.

"Thank you."

Mike once again settled himself on a stool opposite the desk and idly began scanning the crossword puzzle, filling the words in with his pen. He chuckled. He had heard somewhere that the height of egotism was doing a crossword puzzle in ink. He stopped as his eyes rested on an ad just above the puzzle. It advertised a used-car lot, and the bannerline urged prospective customers to "HURRY – HURRY – DON'T WAIT!" A sudden whimsical thought struck him. He wondered if accident victims realized how timing often dictated whether they lived or died. What would happen, he wondered, if the medical profession took out an ad in the morning *Times*. Mentally, he began composing it. Let's see . . . "HURRY – HURRY – DON'T WAIT! Don't wait until 6 A.M. to have your accident. Have it at 3 A.M. or 10 A.M. or 4 P.M. 6 A.M. is a no-no if you want a chance to live." Six in the morning was the death hour, he admitted to himself—and it just couldn't be helped. A patient arriving at a hospital between 6:30 and 7:00 was jeopardized in so many ways. First of all, there just wasn't enough help. The night shift was about to leave and didn't want to get involved—the day shift had not yet arrived. Most of the doctors were enroute, and the various vital functioning departments of the hopsital had not yet been roused from their nighttime lethargy.

He suddenly put his paper down and addressed the woman behind the desk. "I'll want to do an abdominal tap as soon as the patient arrives."

She looked at him for a moment, slightly flustered,

then ran to get one of the nurses in the conference room, relaying Carrington's request. The nurse nodded and immediately left the meeting, bustling about to gather the equipment and instruments he would need.

Mike reached over the desk and picked up a release form. He dated and noted the time on it, then proceeded to fill in the blanks on the form. "I"—Mike penned in the name "George Selkins"—"hereby give Dr."—Mike filled in "Michael Carrington"—"permission to perform upon me"—he hesitated, then finally wrote, "an abdominal tap with irrigation." He stared at the words, intrigued with the thought which had just struck him. Six months ago he would have written "abdominal paracentesis." But with the current rash of malpractice suits and controversial court cases, it was imperative that the patient could never honestly say that he had not understood the procedure involved. And just to be sure, Carrington would verbally explain the procedure to him, in front of witnesses.

Mike glanced up as the door finally opened and the orderly wheeled in Selkins. He watched as they proceeded to one of the units and were joined by a nurse who would help transfer the patient to the assigned bed. Mike suddenly got up and walked toward them.

"Wait a minute. Let's tap him right here. Maybe we can save him a move. If he has to go to O.R., we'll just leave him on the cart."

From across the room, the patient had appeared to be lying passively and Mike had judged that he was only semiconscious, but as he approached, Carrington was quick to notice the victim's flash of apprehension at his words. The alchohol he had ingested was finally wearing off.

"Now just one goddamned cotton-pickin' minute," Selkins suddenly exploded. "What's with the rush act? I've got something to say about this. All of a sudden you're talking about operations and taps . . . and I don't even know who you are! How in the hell did I draw you, anyway. Are you a real doctor or just an intern around here?"

26

Mike realized that, rudely as he'd put it, Selkins had a point. In his concern for the victim's physical condition and the urgency it demanded, he had overlooked rudimentary courtesy. The patient's anxiety was understandable.

"I'm sorry, Mr. Selkins. Downstairs it was pretty hectic and I didn't have a chance to explain. I'm one of the staff surgeons, and you drew me because I specialize in abdominal surgery."

"Surgery? Jesus," Selkins said as he expelled his breath. "What happened? I don't remember a thing. The last I knew I was just driving along and then, zilch—ambulances, stretchers, cops. What's wrong with me? How bad am I hurt?"

"That's what we're trying to find out," Mike replied. "I suspect internal hemorrhaging, but I want to do a tap to make sure. You won't feel much. There'll be a little prick and a slight sting from the Novocaine, then I'll insert a needle to see if you're bleeding inside." He gestured to a nurse who hurried forward with the release. "Will you sign this for me, please? It's permission to do the test."

Selkins watched as Mike extended the release form and pen. He made no gesture to take it.

"Look, Doc, I don't want to be a bastard. But I don't know this hospital and I don't know you. Did you get Doctor Kentner?" Selkins demanded.

"I called," Mike explained. "His exchange is trying to find him." He saw the reluctance in the victim's eyes. "Mr. Selkins," he said sincerely, "I'll do my best for you, but if you'd like another surgeon to see you, I'd be more than happy to get one up here."

"I don't want somebody pulled from a hat," Selkins protested. "I want somebody I know—somebody I trust."

"I'll check with Doctor Kentner's service again." Smothering a sigh for the precious wasted moments, Mike went to the nursing station, picked up the phone, and began to dial. The nurse who had been hovering in the background to witness the consent form signature

27

leaned over and daubed away some beads of perspiration that had formed on Selkins' forehead. He was beginning to hurt—to hurt a lot.

"You don't know how lucky you are," she whispered confidentially. "Doctor Carrington operated on my husband. He's the best . . . the best there is." Selkins' eyes followed her as she bustled about the room and finally returned, just a few steps behind Carrington.

"Sorry. No luck. They still haven't been able to find Doctor Kentner," Mike said shortly. "I left another message, but—" He shrugged. "Look, is there any other doctor you know . . . one you'd like me to call?"

"I don't know. I . . . I just can't believe all this is happening," Selkins muttered.

"I understand," Mike said sympathetically, "but believe me, Mr. Selkins, you are seriously hurt. And this test has to be done, regardless of who does it, and time is important." Mike ran his eyes worriedly over the patient. He could sense a rapid deterioration in his condition.

It was true. Selkins shifted slightly and attempted to raise himself on one elbow and was hit with a shock wave of pain in his abdomen so intense that he sank back with a groan. Mike automatically took his wrist and counted the much-too-rapid pulse beats. Selkins noticed the concern in the doctor's face. Through pain-glazed eyes, he stared up at the man attending him. He was young. He was strong. He seemed genuinely worried. The cut of his suit bespoke the fact that he was successful in his profession. Selkins had noticed the natural air of authority, the fact that both here and in the Emergency Room, when this man spoke, the others jumped.

He didn't want to die. But he didn't want to trust his life to strangers. He wanted a familiar face, he wanted reassurance. He wanted . . . he wanted this not to have happened at all. Panicked, he realized he felt worse, infinitely worse, than he had felt five minutes before. He looked up and met Dr. Michael Carrington's eyes watching him steadily. He had an intuition that this man was competent, that he would expend his best effort, that Carrington was the best, maybe the only chance he had. He forced a bravado he didn't feel.

"Fuck Art Kentner! When it comes right down to it, I wouldn't let him operate on my poodle. Gimme the paper and let's get this over with."

Mike held the release in a position where it could be signed without disturbing the running IVs. "You probably won't hear from friend Kentner until after nine," Selkins muttered as he wrote. "He'd rather die than give up breakfast at the Polo Lounge." He handed back the pen and closed his eyes.

"But he's not the one in danger of dying—is he, doctor?"

Carrington knew that Selkins finally understood the gravity of the situation and was afraid . . . very afraid.

From his outward appearance, no one could have suspected the agitation Mike felt as he made his way back to the Admitting Desk on the first floor. The abdominal tap performed on Selkins had come up positive—he had inserted the needle through the abdominal wall, and the aspirate he had withdrawn had been blood. That was bad enough, but there were other complications.

Mary McCullough watched with guarded apprehension as he approached. Here we go again, she thought. Mike wasted no time with pleasantries.

"I've got a four-plus emergency, and I need the first operating time I can get."

"Two o'clock this afternoon. That's the best I can do. It isn't my fault. . . ." Why was she always on the defensive with Carrington? she wondered. "It's a very heavy day and—" He interrupted.

"I know that. I'm just booking it with you because that's what the rule book says. I'm going up to see Kate Grady now. We're going to have to bump somebody. Just list it and I'll talk to the O.R."

"If you want to bump somebody," she reminded him, "I'm going to have to talk to Doctor Merrick."

He stared at her for a moment. "Don't sweat it. After I talk to Kate, I'll call him myself." He stalked back to the elevators, leaving Mary glaring behind him.

Mike watched the floor lights above the elevators, indicating that the middle one was on its way down. He was seething with annoyance. Marin Medical Center had ten operating rooms, but only enough nurses were hired to utilize five of them. With the use of computers, Executive Cost Accounting geniuses had finally concluded that using five O.R. rooms eight hours a day was tremendously more economical than running ten operating rooms four hours. He searched his mind for the saving which had been listed in the financial bulletin explaining the situation to the staff surgeons. A couple of thousand dollars a day, anyway. Mike wondered if Selkins would be impressed.

On his way up to the eighth floor, Mike braced himself for the coming confrontation with Kate Grady, the Operating Room Supervisor. Kate was between fifty-five and sixty years old, with more salt than pepper in her hair, and her rimless glasses gave her the appearance of someone's benevolent grandmother. But there any similarity ended. He wondered if she knew that the staff surgeons called her "Nails Grady—as in "hard as . . ." Every O.R. Supervisor Mike had ever known had been an iron-nosed bitch, a female able to cope with the demands of every egotistical surgeon who thought his case was the most important in the world.

The difference with Katie, though, thought Mike, was that the whole time she was saying, "No way . . . forget it . . . there's no space . . . it can't be done," she was weighing the actual imperativeness of the situation from a neutral point of view. If she judged in your favor—and she was seldom wrong—the whole time she was saying "No" she was bustling around, juggling time, space and personnel to accommodate the emergency.

She watched Mike walk toward her.

"Hi, Kate," he offered.

30

Without replying, she turned and walked away from him, her actions unmistakably screaming, "Get lost, buster. I've no time for you and your constant emergencies." Mike called her back.

"Look, honey, I've got a forty-year-old businessman downstairs, fresh from an automobile accident, with a positive belly tap. Now that doesn't sound too bad, does it? The hooker is that five minutes after I tapped him, his blood pressure fell out. Now either something let go in that belly from the accident—or I nicked something with that needle. I need time—and I need it now!"

Mike felt better now that he had voiced his concern to someone. There was only a slight probability that he had done damage during the tap—but it was possible—and he agonized over that possibility.

Kate sensed his anxiety, too, and, for a change, gave him no static. He knew she was mentally running through the O.R. schedule.

"All the rooms are full, and everything is already underway," she said quietly. "There won't be any breaks for several hours. The only way is to open another room, and I really don't have the help. I've got a nurse out with the flu, so that means one girl is already circulating two rooms." She paused for a long moment. "But I guess we haven't any choice. We'll just have to spread ourselves thin. I can scrub myself, but that will mean two more rooms with one circulator, and all hell's going to break loose."

Mike looked at her questioningly. She grimaced and indicated Operating Room Two with her head.

"Guess who's in there, up to his arm pits in an exenteration? None other than our little darling, David Savage."

"You mean the prima donna might have to think ahead five minutes to figure out what he's going to need?" Mike muttered sarcastically.

"Not a chance," Kate muttered. "Think? He'd rather do his war dance any day."

Dr. David Savage was very good in his field of obstetrics/gynecology—and a real sonofabitch. He was conceited, self-centered, overly demanding, and unbelievably foul-mouthed. The O.R. nurses were vehement about their reluctance to work with him. Not that any surgical nurse objected to an occasional four-letter word—they had heard them all. At best, an operating room was a tense situation. But Mike had inadvertently eavesdropped on a fragmentary conversation only a few weeks before. Martha, one of their best scrub nurses, had been standing with another girl.

"You know," she had complained bitterly, "if things start going wrong, I don't blame a doctor for coming out with an 'Oh, shit,' or something like that. I've done it myself. But this morning Savage just looked at me and snarled, 'Get out of the way, you fucking bitch'— and that's something else again."

"You don't have to take that," the other girl had said, outraged. "If I were you, I'd fill out an incident report and turn it in." Martha had nodded.

"I think I will. I wonder if a nurse ever told a doctor to just go to hell?"

"Probably," her friend had giggled, "but I wouldn't recommend it."

Their conversation had not particularly surprised Mike. He knew Savage. About thirty, tall, blond, muscular, extremely good-looking. In fact, like many OB–GYN men, he had chosen his specialty because he *was* physically attractive to women, which was good for business. He was certain that the nurses, his patients— in fact, any woman—found him so attractive that he could do or say anything that gratified his sadistic nature.

On the other hand, Mike had to remind himself, the surgical procedure Savage was performing was a difficult, tedious, complicated—even horrendous—operation, involving the total removal of a woman's uterus, bladder, and rectum. It was done for advanced but still localized cancer. Once removed, it was necessary to build new stomas, or outlets, for the urinary tract and bowel on the abdominal wall—and nobody could do the procedure better than Dr. Savage. He

32

would have his hands full, but he'd still find time to make it more difficult than necessary for his surgical team.

When a surgeon was assigned hospital privileges at Marin Medical Center, he filled out a card for each and every surgical procedure he was likely to do, listing in advance the exact instruments and supplies he preferred and would need. These cards were updated regularly as new medical and technical advances dictated, or if the doctor's preferences changed. Such a card was an invaluable guide for the circulating nurse who equipped the room in advance. Naturally, as unanticipated situations arose or procedures had to be changed, the circulating nurse would have to augment these supplies during the actual surgery, but the basic card kept these occasions to an efficient minimum.

The system worked pretty well—except for Dr. David Savage. He delighted in being totally inconsistent. After the circulating nurse had equipped his room in advance with everything listed on his card for the procedure involved—and, from experience, had even gone a step further by anticipating every piece of equipment or instrument he might conceivably demand—he luxuriated in constantly snapping a request for a special pair of scissors, a newly advertised clip, a seldom used suture—and being obscenely abusive when they were not immediately at hand.

Besides the anesthesiologist, a minimum surgical team was made up of the surgeon, his assistant, a scrub nurse, and a circulating nurse. Once the first three entered the sterile field surrounding the patient, they could not leave. It was up to the circulating nurse to be on hand to get from the cabinets lining the walls anything that might be needed but was not already available on the table in the sterile field. It was an important, demanding duty, for even if the surgeon was consistent and cooperative, the girl was constantly busy. On those occasions when, as today, the O.R. was shorthanded and the circulating nurse was forced to work two operating rooms instead of one, most of the surgeons were cooperative and understanding about the inconvenience and delays.

Except for Dr. David Savage. He took such a situation as a personal affront and insult and retaliated by pacing and cursing—his childish shouts for attention often drifting into the adjoining rooms.

Mike glanced up as Kate hurried back to the desk. "Okay, so we open another room," she said. "Be ready in about thirty minutes. We've got to clear it with Doctor Merrick, though, and Super Chief isn't always easy to find at this time in the morning."

Mike knew she wasn't being totally irreverent in her reference to the chief of surgery. She disliked Merrick the man: picky, intolerant, self-centered, vocal in criticizing the faults of others yet blind to those same traits in himself. Nevertheless, she was fully aware that Merrick the surgeon was competent, able, and truly caring about the needs and problems of his patients.

"Look, doll," he said, "you spend your time getting that room ready. I'll spend my time getting him." Mike picked up the phone and dialed Merrick's exchange.

"Doctor Joseph Merrick's office."

"Doctor Merrick, please."

"Doctor Merrick isn't in at the moment. I'll try to reach him. What is your name and phone number, sir?"

Oh, Christ, thought Mike. Not again. He was not in the mood, nor did he have time to play games now. He spoke sharply.

"Look, this is Doctor Michael Carrington. I am a staff surgeon at Marin Medical Center. I have to talk to Doctor Merrick *right now*. If he's at home, I have the number and I'll call him myself. Or is he in the hospital? Do you know where he is?" he demanded.

"Well," said the operator, slightly intimidated, "I believe he's already at the hospital. At least, that's where I would try first."

"It's not his operating day," Mike reminded her crisply.

"But . . . but he's usually in a meeting at the hospital on Friday mornings," she stuttered.

"Should have thought of that," Mike replied, hanging up. Going to another line, he dialed the hospital operator.

"This is Doctor Carrington. Page Doctor Merrick for me, and if he doesn't answer immediately, try the Executive Board Room!"

He kept his hand on the phone as he heard Dr. Merrick paged. A brief interlude, then paged again. He waited. Suddenly the phone rang. He picked it up instantly.

"Doctor Merrick here."

"Joe? Mike Carrington. I've got a forty-year-old man, fresh from an auto accident, with a positive belly tap, and he's suddenly gone into shock. I've already talked to Kate up here, and she can open an extra room, but we need your approval."

There was a moment of silence before Merrick spoke. "Did this one come from the Emergency Ward again?" he asked.

Mike decided to ignore the sarcasm. A man's life was at stake. "Yes, he was brought in about six o'clock this morning."

"You're not on call for Emergency this month," the chief of surgery said sharply. "How come you got the patient?"

"Joe," Carrington explained tiredly, "when I came in this morning, they were looking for any surgeon they could find."

"You and I are going to have to talk about all these Emergency referrals," Merrick announced accusingly. There was another pause. Then: "You've got your room. No problem . . . this time!"

No problem . . . I only wish that were true, thought Joseph Merrick as he hung up the phone. The chief of surgery was of medium height, perhaps five feet ten inches, and although sixty years of age, he appeared much younger. His wavy hair was full and dark, lightened at the temples with just a suggestion of gray, but his comparatively youthful appearance was marred by deep-set facial lines, the product of years of frowning. And he was frowning as he walked slowly back to his seat. In his self-appointed role as watchdog of the hospital, he felt ordained by God to keep everyone on the right track. Yes, he thought as he sat down, he'd look into the matter of Dr. Carrington and all those emergency cases.

The large, elongated Executive Board Room was some forty-two feet long by fifteen feet wide. Except for the small corner console with the phone where Merrick had taken Mike's call, the only other furniture was a well-designed table extending almost the full length of the room. This was banked by ten leather upholstered swivel chairs on each side and one at each end. The area was handsomely carpeted and draped.

Merrick glanced around at the other men attending the meeting of the Executive Medical Board. Present were the chief of staff, the vice chief of staff, the administrator of the hospital, and representative members of all of Marin Medical Center's services—Gynecology, General Practice, Internal Medicine, and Pediatrics— along with a young male secretary.

Dr. Whitney Palmer presided at the head of the table. The chief of staff was a huge man, well over six feet and weighing in at close to two hundred and thirty pounds the last time he had ruefully braved a scale. He had been arranging the contents of a manila folder in front of him, and as Merrick settled comfortably in his chair, he peered over his gold-rimmed glasses and spoke quietly.

"Well, gentlemen, now that Dr. Merrick's back with us, let's return to the matter at hand—Doctor David Savage."

He stopped for a moment as he sifted quickly through the papers before him. Although there was an air of easiness in the room, it was an official meeting, and Dr. Palmer presented the business at hand with the required formality.

"In addition to the grievances filed on the incident reports we've already discussed, there are several others

36

here which, I think, merit our attention. We have a report by Miss Pauley."

He glanced about the table, and several of the members nodded. They all knew Catherine Pauley was in charge of the fifth floor and was one of the best nurses in the hospital.

"She states," Palmer continued, "that on March eighth, Doctor Savage wrote similar orders for three patients on her floor—blood pressure, pulse, respiration and rectal temperature—*every thirty minutes* until the order was discontinued by him. Since there was no apparent reason for concern, she felt Doctor Savage's orders stemmed from a personality conflict with her and were therefore strictly punitive."

Dr. Kelly, from Internal Medicine, who considered himself the hospital's wittiest member, leaned forward, resting his elbows on the table.

"I don't imagine it made the three patients too happy, either," he put in wryly.

There was a brief flutter of conversation between the others as they discussed the implications of the grievance. They all knew that anything discussed in that room was privileged and that they could speak absolutely freely. Dr. Palmer regained their attention.

"We also have here an incident report from Mrs. Reardon on the night shift in the lab. She complains that during the entire past month Doctor Savage has written all his blood count orders for six A.M. Under 'possible reason,' she has noted, 'personal vendetta.'"

Dr. Valdez, a G.P., spoke up. "Why would he order for six instead of the normal seven in the morning? After all, he knows she couldn't possibly manage that in the last hour of her shift."

Before Palmer could reply, Dr. Gerstine from Pediatrics leaned forward and got their attention. "Look, maybe I can shed some light on this. As you know, before Judy and I were married, she worked on the fifth floor, and she still yaks with a lot of the gals from time to time—and the white underground is hot and heavy with rumors about Dave."

The doctors focused on him with interest. The white underground was the name for the very real, extremely accurate pipeline that unofficially passed information along from nurse to nurse. Speculation . . . gossip . . . rumor . . . facts—nothing escaped them, and their information was exasperatingly up-to-the-minute.

"Judy and Cathy are good friends," Gerstine went on. "From what Judy was told, everything was fine on the fifth floor until Savage asked Cathy for a date. She hates his guts and politely told him 'Not a chance.' He ignored her refusal and said he'd pick her up at seven thirty. She thought he was kidding—she really did. Well, when the door bell rang that evening, she opened it and there he was. According to Judy, he was furious that Cathy wasn't dressed, ready to go, and panting for the sight of him. It ended up in a real shouting match. She told him to leave—and leave he did, slamming the door so hard that Cathy was tempted to bill him for cracked plaster. Our boy's got quite a temper."

He shook his head. The other doctors shifted uncomfortably. Dr. Lyons, the assistant chief of staff, fiddled with the pencil in front of him.

"Maybe the same thing happened with Mrs. Reardon. She's a widow, and a cute little thing. There are probably other cases we don't know about . . . which haven't been reported. Most of the nurses are afraid of him . . . and any rebuff, well, he makes life tough for them. Savage fancies himself a divine gift to the female sex."

Dr. Palmer withdrew two additional sheets of paper. "There are also formal complaints here from two of his patients, or perhaps I should say ex-patients," he said quietly. "A Mrs. Hallman says that while she was here at Marin, she questioned some medication Savage prescribed, got into an argument with him, and he told her to find a new doctor and stormed out."

Merrick straightened in his chair, his concern evident. "My God, that's desertion. That's a basis for legal action."

Every physician in the room knew that precedent had been set in court cases which prohibited a doctor from abandoning a patient. Five days' written notice must be given, thereby assuring a patient of uninterrupted medical assistance during the time it would take to locate and enlist the services of a new doctor. Palmer waved away Merrick's agitation.

"Oh, he covered himself. Before Mrs. Hallman checked out, she signed the 'leaving against medical advice' form. But she was so mad she would have signed anything."

"It's still risky, and damned unethical," Merrick fumed. "What he does in his office is his business, but what he does here—"

"The second letter," Palmer interrupted smoothly, "is addressed to me from an Elizabeth Bowers. Miss Bowers writes that she started having problems when she was about twenty-five, some five years ago, and during that time she has been to several gynecologists. It's a very long letter, but what it boils down to is that she feels very strongly that Doctor Savage took entirely too long doing a pelvic examination on her."

Dr. William Fulton, from Gynecology, who had made no comment up to this point, reacted explosively.

"Jesus! A thirty-year-old spinster. It was probably the thrill of her life! Now listen, before we give any credence to this, let's find out what day it was done, and what nurse was in there with him. See if she remembers anything out of line." He paused. "And even that wouldn't mean much, considering how the nurses feel about Savage. Say what you will about Dave, he's a top gynecologist, and I just can't believe he'd mix business with pleasure."

Palmer nodded thoughtfully. "You're probably right. She closes the letter by saying he also charged her too much." He put it aside decisively. "We'll just send her one of our standard 'disgruntled patient' letters, attach a carbon to the complaint, and file it as a matter of record."

Another representative from Gynecology, Dr.

Maughm, just recently appointed to the Executive Medical Board, had been staring reflectively at a cigarette smoldering in an ashtray nearby. He suddenly leaned forward to snuff it out.

"Everything we've heard so far," he began hesitantly, "anything of any substance, that is, seems to relate to Doctor Savage's personality. He *is* a hell of a doctor. I can sincerely say I've never met anyone better in his field. Don't you think—"

Dr. Palmer interrupted, his tone kindly but firm. "Dr. Maughm, if these other gentlemen will indulge me, I'm going to take a few moments to acquaint you with the facts of life. *Every* staff physician at Marin Medical is a hell of a doctor. Tolerating anything less than total competence would be unthinkable. This hospital has a fine reputation and, without a doubt, it offers the best medical care available anywhere in this country. But times have changed. We no longer have to worry about filling beds. Our biggest concern is to have a bed for every patient who needs one. Our next concern—crass as it may sound coming from the hallowed throat of a dedicated man of medicine—our next concern is money. Marin Medical Center must operate on a financially sound basis. Because, face it—red ink means no hospital." The doctors around the table listened, mesmerized. Most were aware of the facts, but they had never before heard them verbalized.

Palmer went on. "Now, this city—this country, in fact—is full of doctors in every field, and many of them would like privileges here because of our reputation. They are all competent specialists. They each might approach a similar problem a little differently, but in the long run every one is technically able to perform the procedures necessary for the patient's wellbeing with uniformly fine results. Now let's take, for example, three surgeons—A, B, and C. Perhaps one is slightly better than the other two. He's faster, his fatality ratio is lower, his infection rate is nil, but in the long run all three are competent. Looking at it from a profit angle, which one will best serve Marin?" Dr. Maughm started to interrupt and was waved to silence.

"The one who has the personal ability to get along, who will become part of the team, the one who will not make waves, the one who will not cost the hospital unnecessary dollars."

Louis Taylor, Marin's administrator, entered the conversation. "If a nurse quits in a huff because of a real or imagined insult from a doctor," he explained quietly, "replacing her costs us money. If an employee or a patient complains, simply investigating that complaint—right or wrong—wastes dollars. If we're sued, even if there's no basis for that suit—it costs us money to defend. And if we lose—god, if we lose—it's disaster time."

"It sounds to me like Doctor David Savage is a disaster walking around waiting to happen," Dr. Kelly observed.

Dr. Valdez cut in, addressing his remarks to Dr. Maughm. "What Doctor Palmer is trying to say is that basically we don't care if a doctor has the combined healing powers of Jesus Christ and the Mayo Brothers; if he causes problems, we don't want him. We can't afford him. He can be the greatest physician in the world, but he's temperamental . . . well, let *Time* magazine write up his amazing exploits in medicine—they can have him. And the hell of it is, Doctor Palmer's absolutely right!"

Dr. Maughm nodded sheepishly. "I understand your point. All I meant was . . . well, don't you think if somebody talked to Doctor Savage maybe he would quiet down and all this would just blow over?"

"Well, hold on a minute," Dr. Merrick suddenly interjected, reaching into his attaché case and removing a memo. "I'm not sure we want it to blow over. I've seen this coming for a long time, and I don't think Doctor Savage is . . . what you did you say? . . . a combination of the Mayo Brothers and Jesus Christ. I asked Joan in Medical Records for a compilation of statistics on Savage. He's done almost no obstetrics. What he has done is a surprising number of therapeutic abortions."

Fulton found himself staring. He knew that Merrick was a punctilious man, perhaps overly concerned with facts, figures, ratios, charts, and minute details. But he was surprised at the obvious time and effort the chief of surgery had extended in this case. He had come fully armed for attack. Fulton realized he had underestimated Merrick. Okay, let's have it out, thought Fulton, as he addressed his question pointedly to the chief of surgery.

"How many major cases did he do last year?"

"In the twelve months ending February first of this year," replied Merrick, consulting his notes, "he did one hundred sixty-eight gynecologic procedures."

"Any deaths?" Fulton shot back.

"One—" began Merrick. Fulton interrupted.

"And that was late in the postoperative period—in a woman with advanced cancer. Pretty enviable, considering the magnitude of the surgery he's doing on some of these women. You can't show me one general surgeon with that kind of record." Fulton waited only a moment before continuing. "Is his infection rate out of line?"

Merrick shook his head and started to reply, but Fulton ignored him.

"Do his patients stay in the hospital longer than expected?"

Merrick, obviously angry at Fulton's tactics, simply stared at him as he continued.

"Look, Joe, I know the answers to these questions. He's part of my service. He's a good surgical technician, and you're going to have a hell of a time trying to discredit him on any medical basis."

"But all these abortions—" Merrick stared at the figures in front of him.

"Listen," Fulton shot back, "Savage didn't write the law. And since they changed it in California, abortion has been a pretty popular operation. As long as he's following the rules, you're not going to be able to make much out of that one either."

"For Christ's sake," Merrick snapped, getting up and pacing behind the table, "you're making it sound like I'm out to get this guy."

"Now, calm down, Joe," Fulton said softly, easing back in his chair. "I just don't want it said that the brand of gynecology practiced at this hospital is anything but A-one." He turned to Palmer. "Maybe Dave has a disruptive personality, but you try coming at him medically and there'll be trouble. Oh, you could maybe dig up one or two cases over the years, but—"

He stopped, deliberately dramatic, resting his eyes for a brief moment on every single doctor seated around the table before going on. "Gentlemen, we all live in glass houses. I ask each one of you to think very carefully if, at one time or another, you haven't made one or two errors you'd rather forget than advertise."

There was dead silence in the room as they reflected on the truth of Fulton's words. Without exception, they had all made mistakes. Mistakes not blocked from memory but carefully tucked away—removed from view and everyday consciousness, yet serving as guides to avoid repetition.

Palmer eyed the doctors sitting about the table, correctly guessing their thoughts, and finally gazed at Fulton with admiration and respect. Damn, he thought, he's a good man to have on your side. But the chief of staff was not lulled by Fulton's eloquent rhetoric. He broke the silence.

"Well, we can't just sit on these other complaints. We've got a hospital to run. The floor nurses hate Savage's guts—I've heard a lot of stories that aren't in this file. The pharmacy staff detests him. The O.R. nurses dislike him so much Doctor Merrick tells me there's trouble even getting someone to scrub with him. You know what the laboratory thinks—that's right here in this file, at least one example of it. And Doctor Reichner in X-ray? His department would celebrate if they never saw Savage again. Talk about personality problems—this guy's got them. And if we don't do something about it, we're going to have a hospital with nobody to run it. The day is long past when the doctor's word was law. He's just one part—granted, a damned important part—of a great big machine called a hospital. We've got to make Savage shape up—or get rid of him."

He pondered a moment and then looked squarely at Fulton. "You've had some good things to say about him. It's obvious that the first step is for somebody to have a little talk with him. Seems to me you're the man to do it."

"Now wait just a minute," Fulton protested. "My kids have an expression: 'Let it all hang out.' So right here in this cozy little room, gentlemen, let's tell it like it is. David Savage's father is vice chairman of the Board of Trustees of this hospital. And from the time Dave was a kid, his father insisted he was going to be a doctor. He got him out of scrapes all through medical school, bought him a practice, crammed him down our throats here at Marin. And while sonny-boy may be a problem to us, papa is one hell of an important man in this town!"

"I don't give a good goddamn who his father is," Merrick erupted. "I agree with Doctor Palmer. Something has to be done."

"Well, you're not electing me the patsy," Fulton said with finality. "In the words of another great man, 'I do not choose to run.' " He shook his head slowly. "Jesus you two guys really hate him, don't you?"

Whitney Palmer broke in quickly. "Now, Bill, slow down. Nobody hates anybody . . . but we've got a hospital to run. Right, Joe?"

"Right," Merrick said.

Wrong, Merrick thought. Outwardly it didn't show, but Dr. Joseph Merrick had a quirk in his personality. He was not like normal men. His life was incomplete without someone to hate, pursue, and, hopefully, destroy. He was currently without a victim, but he'd had his eyes on two likely prospects: Dr. Carrington and Dr. Savage. There was much in their disfavor. They were both young, physically attractive, and too successful too soon. Somehow the machinery of hate in Merrick's soul could not run in two directions at one time. He felt suddenly content. On the basis of what he had heard at the meeting, he had made his choice: David Savage. Or perhaps fate had made it for him.

David Savage! He was easy to hate. The supercilious young son of a bitch! Shouting orders, throwing temper tantrums, acting like he owned Marin Medical Center! And he, Merrick, had been there—working, laboring, striving for the good of the hospital—for more than a quarter of a century.

The hate machine was picking up speed. Merrick felt almost excited as his mind reached for further justification. In particular, he was remembering an episode that had occurred just last February. A patient had come to him complaining of a vaginal discharge. Merrick had made his examination, noted some inflammation of her uterine cervix, suspected a cancer, and had taken a biopsy. Then he had prescribed appropriate treatment for the minor infection that was present and told her to return in one week for re-examination. Just two days later, he had noticed her name on the operating room schedule. Evidently, she had marched straight from his office to see Dr. Savage. With his usual steamroller tactics, Savage had immediately admitted her to the hospital, taken a biopsy right there in her room, carried the specimen to the pathologist himself, and demanded a frozen section be done while he waited. The next day, when the permanent slides confirmed the diagnosis of carcinoma-in-situ, Savage had already scheduled her for surgery. The report on Merrick's biopsy lay in an unopened envelope on his desk. The chief of surgery had followed the usual protocol and the diagnosis had reached him in the morning's mail.

Curious, Merrick had dropped in to see his ex-patient. With tears of accusation, she relayed Dr. Savage's diagnosis of cancer, comfirmed by the surgery. There had been no use explaining that he had done the same tests and would have reached the same conclusion, that a week's delay was inconsequential, that it

45

was far more important not to frighten a patient until he was sure of the diagnosis. Who else on the floor had heard her angry words? "I could tell when I was in your office you didn't know what you were doing," she had shouted accusingly. *"You* just gave me some salve. I could be dead because of you! Doctor Savage saved my life!" Her door had been open. Damn David Savage!

Another episode a few weeks later had really rubbed salt into his still open wound. The elevator operator where he had his office had come to him with what proved to be appendicitis. He had operated on her and she had developed a minor wound infection after the surgery. One morning when he was in her room, with the floor nurse assisting him, he had reassured her that it would heal with no problem. The patient had cheerily volunteered that she wasn't a bit worried—because Dr. Savage had told her the same thing. While Merrick was still reeling from that, she asked: "Would some antiseptic soaks help? I think it was Betadine that Doctor Savage suggested when he was here." Taken aback, Merrick questioned her further and was blistered by her reply.

"Oh, Doctor Savage comes in each morning. We're old friends. I used to work in his building. And I have such faith in him."

"If you have such faith in him," Merrick had snapped, "why didn't you go to him in the first place?"

"Oh, I would have, but he was out of town."

Had he imagined the look on the floor nurse's face? Had it really been a smile?

These two episodes had hurt. They were enough to bruise the pride of any physician.

Hell, yes, he could hate David Savage. He could despise him! And when Dr. Merrick despised, he specialized. Carrington could wait. Dr. David Savage was his target. If it took a lifetime, he'd destroy him!

Merrick felt a strange elation and wholeness as his schizoid anger grew. He reveled in it; he wallowed in the prospect of hating—and it was with a visible start that Whitney Palmer's words brought him back to the present. He hadn't missed much, he guessed.

"We have a hospital to run and David Savage is getting in the way," the chief of staff was saying. "Maybe he can't help it. From all I've heard and what I've read and what you fellows have told me . . . well, I seriously wonder if he wouldn't benefit from a little psychiatric care."

"Are you going to tell *him* that? Or are you going to tell his father?" Fulton shot back sarcastically.

"It's going to be tough, but somebody has got to tell somebody something," Merrick insisted, afraid that the matter might be dropped.

"I can see the buck coming to a stop here at the head of the table," sighed Palmer. "But I think this calls for more than a little chat in the hall. With your permission, I'd like to write him a letter from the Executive Medical Board, asking him to meet with a special committee composed of myself and the last three chiefs of staff."

There was immediate assent and relief from most of those present. They were off the hook on this one.

"Let's get on to the next matter," intoned Dr. Palmer.

But Merrick heard no more. He had been chief of staff before Palmer. He'd be at that meeting. Already he was rehearsing what he would say. The crusade of hate had begun.

In the doctors' dressing room adjoining the surgical suite, Mike went down the row of fifteen lockers, one by one, searching for an empty compartment. It was one of the small irritations and frustrations of his life. The regular anesthesiologists and four resident surgeons who worked every day claimed permanent lockers and kept the keys with them, therefore, only four or five lockers were available for use by the staff surgeons. The cheap bastards! What could a dozen more lockers cost? But then, where would they put them? Mike wondered. The dressing room was already so crowded you could hardly move. For some unaccountable reason, he recalled the executive director's office. It was five times the size of this tiny room. But which was more important, Mike fumed, the comfort of one executive director or that of twenty or so surgeons? Just as he was giving up hope, Mike finally found one locker unoccupied and gave a grunt of elation. Maybe he was living right after all.

He quickly removed his suit, shirt and tie—then hesitated. Normally he removed only his outer clothing, but if an operation turned out to be particularly bloody, it was possible to get soaked clear through. He didn't know what to expect with Selkins, and with sudden decisiveness, he shed his shorts and undershirt, too, before donning the green scrub pants, tunic, shoe coverings and surgical cap. Just before putting his street clothes in the locker, he removed his wallet from the jacket and tucked it into his sock. The lockers were cheap and flimsy, and there had been a couple of unfortunate incidents recently that justified this precaution. He turned the key and dropped it into his tunic pocket, then took off his ring and watch, glancing at it in the process.

Approximately twenty-five minutes had passed since he had received Merrick's okay on the operating room. As he placed the jewelry in his pocket with the key, he snorted derisively. Where was the green Sir Galahad that movies and television series depicted? He wondered—that surgeon who saw the patient, made an instant diagnosis just by gazing at him, dramatically whisked him to a waiting, fully staffed operating room, and began surgery within minutes after arriving on the scene?

He thought back over the nitty-gritty details that had occupied him for the past half hour. Before he had left the ICU after the abdominal tap, he had ordered additional blood to be drawn from Selkins for immediate coagulation studies, called Special Services to do an electrocardiogram, and had instructed the nurses to get two units of blood up immediately, warm them, and begin transfusing the patient—one unit in each arm.

After the go-ahead on the room, he had phoned an

Anesthesiology Group and determined that their backup man, Ray Trent, was available and had left word for them to locate Trent and have him call. Luckily the head of the Group was already in the hospital, so getting his necessary approval to utilize Trent was comparatively easy. And when his call was returned, Mike knew his luck was holding. Ray lived just a short distance from the Medical Center, could be there in fifteen minutes, and true to his word, had arrived and was already with Selkins in the O.R.

He had overcome the problem of finding an assistant by tracking down Keith Johnson, one of the hospital's resident surgeons. Keith admired Mike professionally and personally liked him, and even though he was swamped with Emergency Ward duties, he had eagerly agreed to assist. He would be up within minutes.

Then, satisfied that his surgical team was complete, Mike had dashed back up to X-ray for a final look at Selkins' abdominal films on the chance he had missed something. He hadn't. He knew Jeff had ordered a blood cross match in Emergency, but Mike had personally called the Blood Bank to make sure that a sufficient supply was actually on hand. He'd want four units ahead at all times, he had cautioned them—as he used one, they were to cross match another. He had checked to make sure that the electrocardiogram he had ordered on Selkins was attached to his chart. It was. He had located a heart specialist in the hospital to read it and confirm that it was normal.

Prominently attached to the chart was a Standard Consent Form which Admitting had typed up. It had to be signed. So Mike made a quick call to Emergency to determine if they had been successful in reaching Selkins' wife. They had—she was on her way to the hospital. Mike then had checked with Admitting and was told that Mrs. Selkins had not yet arrived. He left word to have her wait in the lounge adjoining the ICU. He'd see her immediately after surgery.

Mike knew he dared not wait for Mrs. Selkins' arrival. He signed the Standard Consent Form and made a mental note to have Keith cosign it later. Across the bottom he had noted, "Patient unable to sign due to medical condition. Immediate surgery imperative."

As he began the prescribed ten-minute scrub ritual at one of the basins, Carrington mentally reviewed the results of the tests he had just received by phone from the lab. In the short time available, they had completed all but a few—and those weren't particularly important to the actual surgery. The missing information would be vital in preventing complications in Selkins' postoperative care, but they could wait.

Prothrombin time, a measurement of liver function and one parameter of blood coagulation . . . bleeding time . . . platelet count . . . the P.T.T. . . . and all the other really crucial test results—the ones that actually concerned the surgical procedure—had all come back normal, Mike remembered with satisfaction. Selkins apparently had everything going for him.

The scrubbing finished, Mike headed for Operating Room Number Six, arms extended in front of him, elbows bent, hands high, to prevent any water from his forearms running down to his now sterile hands. Pushing the door open with his knee, he walked to the scrub nurse, who handed him a sterile towel. He dried his hands, then his arms, being careful not to let any of the towel which had touched his arms contaminate his hands. Even though they would be protected by gloves, it was necessary that his hands be sterile. It was not uncommon for a glove to break or be cut during surgery.

The girl held a sterile gown in front of him, enabling him to insert his arms through the sleeves, while the circulating nurse secured the ties in back. Then the gloves—the nurse holding the right one, thumb towards him, so he could slip his hand in with ease—then the left. Aware that his assistant had not arrived, she handed him another sterile towel to cover his hands while he waited.

Mike watched as Ray Trent inserted the endotracheal tube. Selkins was ready to be prepped and draped. As the circulating nurse swabbed the abdomen with an antiseptic solution, the scrub nurse readied the linen she would use to drape the patient so that only the surgical field would be exposed.

The door was pushed open, Keith Johnson came into the room, slightly breathless—and the gowning and gloving ritual began again. The resident surgeon was tall and lanky, black, with his modified Afro hair style now crushed under the surgical cap. In Mike's opinion, Keith was one of the best young surgeons he had come across. They practiced the same brand of medicine, and most important, Keith *cared*. From previous conversation, Carrington knew that emotionally Keith was still trying to find himself. On one hand, he was anti-establishment—during his vacations, he worked in the ghettos and communes, closely identifying with the problems of his black brothers and the hippies. On the other hand, he wanted all the things the establishment could provide—wealth, status, recognition of his talents, a stable home and family.

Mike was well aware that three minutes ago there had been no sign of Keith outside. He grinned behind his mask.

"Pretty fast ten-minute scrub," Mike observed innocently.

"I," said Keith, his eyes twinkling, "can do the fastest ten-minute scrub in town."

This was not as irresponsible as it sounded. As resident surgeon, Keith had probably been involved in at least four surgeries during the past twenty-four hours, scrubbing each time. The disinfecting solution used had at least a twelve-hour residual effect, and Mike knew that Keith's hurried scrub before this operation accomplished the sterility that was necessary for the well-being of his patient. In fact, a full ten-minute scrub done often over a short period of time could be detrimental. The strong solution and rough brush might irritate the skin and cause tiny lesions that could be a breeding ground for germs that would threaten the patient. In medicine, as in all other fields, there were rules to be followed and rules to be broken.

They stepped up to the table, Mike taking his place on Selkins' right, Keith going to the opposite side of the table.

"'Sorry I was late. You wouldn't believe the night I've had," Keith sighed.

"I'd believe it," Mike said, turning his attention to the anesthesiologist, Ray Trent. "Ready?" Trent nodded his okay to proceed with the surgery.

The scrub nurse handed Mike a scalpel and he made a long midline vertical incision that penetrated to the fascia. As both men busied themselves stopping a few major subcutaneous bleeders, Keith continued.

"And then, at the last minute, the 'Peds' resident wanted me to see a beat up kid he's admitting from the Emergency Room."

Mike dropped the original scalpel in the used instrument tray and was handed another by the nurse. When in medical school, they had preached this procedure—to use a new, sterile scalpel for deep cutting in case the skin harbored any residual bacteria. He doubted the present validity of this commandment, but old habits died hard. He cut into the tough fascial layer under the skin that surrounded muscle. Keith attached a retractor to hold the incision open for easy access. Both were aware of the bluish color under the peritoneum, the thin, transparent layer that lines the entire abdominal cavity. Mike glanced at Keith.

"Mexican kid?" he asked. "I think I saw him when I was there this morning."

Carrington liked general conversation during the less stressful periods of an operation. To the uninitiated, the casual dialogue and off-color jokes that invariably went on during critical surgery might seem shocking, but those involved realized that such talk and an occasional laugh kept everybody loose and relaxed—and that was important.

"Yeah," Keith nodded. "Ricky Sanchez. Second time he's been here this month. Last time somebody beat the

52

shit out of him, Mama said he fell while roller skating around the kitchen table. And the kid was too terrified to open his mouth. And it wasn't the first time—some of those bruises were old."

"Jesus," Mike groaned. "Can't something be done about these child abuse cases?"

Keith shrugged. "We feed whatever we find to Marin's social worker. If the evidence is solid enough, she contacts the police. At least the cops are starting to take an interest. But it's damned hard to prove and everybody knows it. Usually the kid is kept for a few days, patched up and sent home. Until he's beaten again. Then the parents take him to the Emergency Room of a different hospital, so there's no running record. And it's repeated and repeated until the kid is permanently injured or maimed—or dead. Unless he's lucky."

During the conversation, both doctors had lifted the underlying peritoneum, and Mike used another scalpel to incise the raised portion. Even through the small opening, it was obvious that the bluish color previously noted was caused by old, clotted blood. Using a pair of Metzenbaum scissors, Mike rapidly extended the peritoneal incision the full length of the surgical wound.

All extraneous conversation halted now as they concentrated upon the operation.

Using his cupped, gloved hands, Mike quickly scooped out the blood and clots into a waiting basin supplied by the scrub nurse, and an immediate search was begun to determine the source of the bleeding.

In the meantime, Keith was using a Richardson retractor on his side of the wound, holding it up so it would be easier for Mike to depress the viscera with his left hand while his right hand searched the upper reaches of the abdomen where the spleen lay. It was immediately apparent to him that no injury existed in the spleen that could have produced the degree of hemorrhage he saw before him. He'd check it again later. He shifted his attention to the liver, and on the far right encountered a gaping, musky, clot-filled crack in its right lobe. Keith shifted the retractor to the right side of the incision to allow direct viewing. Mike gently scooped away additional blood clots, careful not to disturb the fracture. There was no continuing free bleeding, he noted.

Rapidly placing warm, moist packs against the damaged areas, he turned his attention to the rest of the abdomen. One of the great mistakes that could be made in treating an abdominal injury, Mike knew, was to assume that the first injury seen accounted for the whole problem. It was mandatory to look for any other possible sources of hemorrhaging before zeroing in on the obvious one.

He minutely inspected the small bowel. There was no apparent injury. It was then lifted, covered with warm packs, and held toward Mike's side of the table, enabling him to inspect the blood vessels in the back of the abdomen, the left kidney, and the left colon. No problem. The small bowel was then displaced toward the left while Mike similarly inspected the structures in the back of the right side of the abdomen. There was no evidence of bleeding from any of these areas, and the large bowel itself appeared intact, as were the kidneys.

Satisfied that there would be no continued hemorrhaging from another source, Mike turned his attention back to the liver, assaying the extent of the damage and planning the surgical treatment that would be necessary.

As Mike examined it, the problem was evident. Selkins must have plunged against the steering wheel with considerable force at the time of the collision. There was a partial detachment of about one-fifth of the liver; the jagged fracture, or crack, was clearly visible. Since this area was cut off from its main blood supply and was, essentially, dead tissue, it would be necessary to remove the damaged portion surgically by extending the injury through the full thickness of the liver and completely detaching it.

"Padded clamp," Mike snapped, extending his hand. He had it instantly. "And I'm going to need lots of clips," he cautioned the scrub nurse.

The clamp was a large one, about ten inches long,

softly padded, designed so that it would compress without injuring. Mike carefully placed it across the portal vein and hepatic artery, shutting off all blood flow into the liver. Gently he evacuated the huge blood clot that filled the fissure and quickly began breaking through the remaining liver tissue by finger fracture, carefully pinching through the mushy substance. Had he used a scalpel, cleanly excising the damaged portion, there would have been massive bleeding, and it would have been impossible to locate each vessel to stem the flow. By finger fracturing, he was able to halt each time he came to a strand, stretch it slightly, and attach a metal clip before cutting through it. The slight retraction then pulled the clip closely to the side of the undamaged portion, where it would remain as a part of Selkins' anatomy forever. The procedure was repeated time after time. Sometimes Mike clipped, and sometimes Keith, depending upon who had easier access. They worked silently and swiftly, well aware of the danger of leaving the large pressure clamp on and depriving the liver of blood for longer than necessary.

Finally the damaged lobe was completely free, and Mike removed it, dropping it into the basin that the scrub nurse held ready. A quick glance assured Mike that no additional clipping was necessary and he began to insert wet packs against the raw edge of the liver. That done, he removed the large pressure clamp, permitting blood to flow once again into the gland. He straightened momentarily, the tremendous tension and stress at least temporarily alleviated.

He began slowly removing the packs, occasionally clipping a bleeding vessel now evident because of the restored blood supply. He shot a look at Keith.

"So what about Ricky?" he asked.

As he spoke, he removed the remainder of the packs, noting they were relatively blood-free. As Keith replied, Mike once again carefully examined the stomach and duodenal area to make sure there was no injury he had overlooked.

"Well, maybe a little luck has come the kid's way.

55

This time there were witnesses," Keith related, a note of satisfaction in his voice. "About four o'clock this morning, some of the neighbors heard Ricky screaming and were willing to get involved enough to at least look out the window. The stepfather was beating the shit out of the kid again."

While he was listening, Mike took the omentum, an apron of fat and vessels that usually lies over the small bowel, and placed it against the raw edge of the liver. Deftly taking a few stitches between the omentum and the capsule of the gland, he made sure it would stay in place. He paused as the nurse handed him a scalpel.

"Stepfather?"

"I guess so. Who knows?" Keith replied with disgust. "Maybe Mama's married, maybe he just lives there. The neighbors didn't know . . . said he just shows up now and then. Anyway, there he was in the front yard, about as drunk as you can be and still stand up, chasing Ricky around with this wooden mop handle, landing about one blow in ten—but still landing them. Probably a good thing he was drunk. The kid's pretty agile and the old boy missed a lot, or Ricky would be in worse shape than he is. Well, to make a long story short, one of the neighbors finally got annoyed enough to call the police. Get this: He told the cop it was the noise he was complaining about, that normally he was a good neighbor and made it a policy not to interfere, but he was getting sick and tired of never getting a decent night's sleep. He had to go to work, he told them, and he worked hard. The evening before, he told the police, it had been a barking dog that had kept him awake half the night."

Mike made an incision, approximately one inch long, in Selkins' skin just below the ribs. Then taking a large, heavy Mayo clamp, he inserted the point into the slit and, with one hand protecting the vital area beneath it, drove it through the abdominal wall with a powerful thrust. Spreading the clamp to make the hole larger, he took three soft rubber drains and fed them into the clamp, pulling the ends through the wound to the outside.

"Christ," Mike said, without looking up, "where does the kid live?"

"Some barrio down on the east side, I think. Minding your own business there is a way of life, a matter of survival. Well, by the time the police arrived, the old man had taken a powder, just disappeared. So they loaded Mama and Ricky into the car and brought them here."

Mike sewed the ends of the drains to the skin, then arranged the opposite end in the space where the liver had been removed. They would, he knew, lead any blood, bile, and serum that collected to the outside where they could do no harm.

The conversation about Ricky Sanchez again came to a halt as Mike made one final, meticulous inspection of the entire abdomen to make absolutely certain that no other injury had occurred. His terrible nagging fear that the needle he had used for the abdominal tap might have caused damage had been unfounded and he experienced a vast feeling of relief.

"Any problems?" Mike asked the anesthesiologist. "How's he doing?"

"Everything's on an even keel," Trent assured him.

"Sponge count," Mike said to the nurse, as he preceeded to irrigate the abdominal area with copious amounts of a saline solution which had been heated to body temperature and which had the same salt content as Selkins' body.

"Sponge count correct," the nurse reported.

Now Mike applied an abdominal suction device, removing the saline solution from the cavity. In all simplicity, this had been a washing and cleansing procedure. Any blood, clots, or bits of liver that were missed would eventually have to be absorbed by the patient's body, a prime cause of postoperative sickness and fever.

"I'll need number 30 steel wire," Mike advised the nurses. Keith grimaced. He knew it was the strongest closure available and would cause the patient the least trouble. But it was hard to tie and absolutely square knots must be made, with the short ends bent downward so as not to irritate the patient later. The assistant surgeon knew that as Mike sewed, he would tie, and unless the steel wire was handled extremely cautiously, he would sustain shallow but painful and irritating finger cuts. Some surgeons would elect to close with other material which would be easier and swifter for them, he knew. But not Dr. Carrington. In this case, steel wire was to the patient's advantage, and like Mike, he wouldn't have it any other way.

As the routine of closing began, the two men worked almost like a choreographed team. "Did they ever find Ricky's mother?" Mike asked curiously. "When I was in Emergency, she had disappeared and—"

"Naw," Keith interrupted. "She never came back. She's not at the house, either. The police checked. Either she took off with her boyfriend or she's frightened and is deliberately making herself scarce." Keith frowned. "People like that don't deserve to have kids. And this time," he finished triumphantly, "I think we can make a pretty strong case."

As they finished closing the skin over the wound with nylon monofilament, Mike requested a final sponge count, which was confirmed. The surgery over, he picked up Selkins' chart from the anesthesiologist, and the two doctors headed back to the locker room.

As he passed through, Mike checked the back of the door to the operating room he had just left. Five telephone messages had been taped there—calls which had come in for him during the surgery. He glanced at them briefly before tucking them into his tunic pocket. Keith headed for a locker, removed his surgical gown, and slipped a white lab coat over his greens. Mike walked toward the small dictating booth at the rear of the room.

"You know," Keith remarked, "that little Sanchez kid's really gotten to me."

Mike paused. "I don't see many children in my practice. Do you get many cases like this in Emergency?" he inquired.

"Too damned many. At least a couple a month." Keith hesitated. "You know, I wonder how long it'll take before it stops making me sick to my stomach."

Mike moved away. He didn't have an answer.

In the dictating booth, Mike sat down and picked up the phone which was automatically connected to recording equipment in a central steno pool where his operative note would be transcribed. This was a mandatory procedure which had to be done immediately following each and every operation. He began.

"This is Doctor Michael Carrington," he dictated. "Operative note on George Selkins, that's S-E-L-K-I-N-S, Hospital Number 8B374. Date of operation 4/27. Preoperative diagnosis: acute abdomen due to blunt trauma. Postoperative diagnosis: fractured liver. Name of operation: partial hepatectomy. Risk—"

He hesitated. Each surgeon was required to indicate his prognosis for the patient. The standard ratings were "excellent," "good," "fair," "poor," or when the case warranted it, something even more pessimistic. Take your choice: "lousy," "terrible"—any word that accurately described the physician's opinion. It was a general practice—and every surgeon Mike knew did it—to rate the risk one step lower than the doctor honestly felt was true. It stemmed from the fear of embarrassment which would result should a surgeon, after optimistically and officially going on record with an "excellent," lose his patient.

"Risk," Mike repeated, "fair." He then concluded with a brief summary of the surgery—what had actually been done.

The operative note finished, Mike reached for George Selkins' chart, which lay on the desk nearby. He started scribbling furiously. "Measure vital signs hourly" . . . "nothing by mouth" . . . "connect Levine tube to low suction" . . . "connect Foley catheter to gravity drainage, measure output hourly" . . . "measure all intake and output" . . . "gently turn from side to side hourly, otherwise bed rest." Then he wrote orders for IVs, medications, and dressing changes.

Every surgeon had his idiosyncrasies for writing up charts. And Mike had developed a formula which served as a doublecheck against any omissions when he was hurried, tired, or preoccupied. He called it his DE-LAPP system. His orders must cover, he knew, Diet, Elimination, Laboratory Tests, Antibiotics, Pain, and sleeping potions. The final "P" stood, in his mind, for Peculiars—any specific orders, other than routine, that would apply to that particular patient. For him the formula worked well, and it was very seldom that a nurse was forced to call him for lack of covering orders.

Mike exchanged his surgical gown for a clean one and headed for the Recovery Room to check on Selkins. He handed the chart to Marjorie, one of the four nurses on duty, and moved to his patient.

The nurses in Recovery were among the best in the hospital, especially skilled in the techniques required immediately after surgery, that period of time between the patient's removal from the surgical suite and the time he awoke. Carefully and without delay, Marjorie read the chart Mike had given her. She was primarily concerned with three things. First, could she read his writing? She could. Second, were there any glaring omissions or questions which she might be forced to call and clarify with him later? Not that she could see. And third, she checked for any treatments or medications that he might have ordered which should be started immediately.

As Mike approached Selkins, he noted that a nurse's aide was already monitoring the patient's blood pressure. He took Selkins' pulse, at the same time professionally running his eyes over the man. Pattern of breathing okay, good color, no blood in his urine. Pulse eighty. He personally checked the Levine tube to ascertain that it was sucking properly, then inspected Selkins' feet. They were pink and warm. The nurse's aide spoke.

"Blood pressure one hundred over sixty."

Mike nodded. That it was low did not especially concern him. The pulse was good and the condition of the feet indicated that the heart was pumping blood to the extremities—a fact as important as the actual blood pressure reading.

Just before he left, he inspected the dressing to make sure it was dry. Mr. Selkins is doing very well, he thought, with extreme satisfaction.

Now to placate Mr. Selkins' anxious, waiting wife.

Mike had just punched the elevator button on the eighth floor when Dr. David Savage emerged from the locker room and glanced down the hall. Sensing the elevator's imminent arrival, Savage increased his pace and was halfway there before he heard himself paged. He turned back, picked up a phone and identified himself.

"Doctor Savage?" asked a feminine voice, "This is Doris Pierce in the Administrator's Office. I have a letter here for you. Could you—"

"I'll be right down," promised Dave. He replaced the phone and managed to join Mike just in time to enter the elevator. Mike pressed the button for the sixth floor and looked questioningly at Savage.

"One," he said, and as Mike pressed the appropriate button, "Keeping you busy?"

"Haven't even made rounds yet," Mike admitted ruefully.

Before the small talk could continue, they stopped at the seventh floor and Susan Thomas entered. She smiled tentatively at both doctors. Mike nodded pleasantly as she stepped past him to stand at the back of the elevator. Savage turned and openly assayed her, deliberately running his eyes from her blond hair, down her short white uniform and shapely legs—and back again. The elevator stopped at the sixth floor to let Mike out. Savage continued his appraisal as he commented.

"Susan Thomas—Admitting's newest asset. Right?"

She was flattered, and her smile brightened. "Right."

"How about having dinner with me tonight?"

Susan blinked. He sure doesn't waste time with pre-liminaries, she thought. "W-e-l-l—"

"Cut the coy crap," Savage snapped. "Yes or no?" He glanced at the light on the indicator panel. "You have three floors to decide."

Susan continued to stare at him, taken aback, as they glided to a stop at the first door. The doors opened. Savage shrugged and started to step out.

"Yes," Susan gasped, finally gathering her wits. Savage gave a small smile of satisfaction, wedged a toe against the door to keep it from closing, reached in his breast pocket and withdrew a slim, leather-grained notebook and pen. He looked at her questioningly for a moment.

"Well?"

Susan returned his gaze blankly. Savage snapped his fingers.

"The address. C'mon, I'm running late."

"Oh. The Wilburn Arms. Uh . . . 1628 North Wilburn. That's two blocks off of—" But Savage had removed his foot, permitting the door to close.

"Seven thirty," she heard him say, before the elevator resumed its trip to the ground floor.

Dave replaced the notebook and automatically adjusted his tie before opening the door to the Administrator's Office. Miss Pierce, busily typing a letter, glanced up and smiled.

"Good morning." She picked up an envelope which was propped against the daily calendar on her desk, stood, and handed it to him. Savage assessed her. About ten pounds overweight and wearing a wig. Not for him. He liked them lean and natural. He glanced at the sealed envelope which was marked "Personal—Confidential," grunted his thanks and left.

As he walked down the hall, he ripped open the letter and started to read it. He stopped abruptly, visibly shaken, then glanced up and down the corridor, concerned that he might be observed. The hall was deserted. He started the letter again, from the top, reading the words with growing annoyance and indignation.

April 27

David R. Savage, M.D.
3629 North Doheny Drive
Los Angeles, California

Dear Dr. Savage:

Several complaints concerning your conduct in the hospital and with hospital personnel have been reviewed by the Executive Medical Board.

By their unanimous vote, you are requested to meet with a special committee appointed by the Board to discuss these matters. The meeting will be held at 8 A.M., Tuesday, May 1st, in the office of the administrator of the hospital.

Please confirm your ability to be present by noon of Monday, April 30th.

Sincerely yours,

Whitney Palmer, M.D.

Chief of Staff
Marin Medical Center

The pompous bastards, Savage raged inwardly. They sit on their fat asses in their air-conditioned board room while I'm breaking my balls curing cancer If it weren't for me, Marin's OB-GYN department would be just another bumbling, second-rate service devoted to bringing a bunch of babies into the world that their feckless mothers don't want, anyway—with some routine hysterectomies thrown in for good measure. Doesn't the Board realize that I perform surgery that no one else can do? That I save the *lives* of these neurotic hysterical females? Besides, I've done a lot for this hospital, he thought as his indignation mounted. I've put in time at their stinking clinic—been part of their stupid teaching service. And for what? Damn Palmer and Merrick—and the administrator, too—damn their souls in hell for even listening to the ramblings of irresponsible broads.

Suddenly he double-checked the letter. Shit, he thought, Wouldn't you know? They *would* pick Tuesday morning. That was the weekly GYN breakfast, and he always looked forward to them. The affair would be pretty dull without him. Yes, they'd miss him, by God. He was the star of those get-togethers, regaling the others with his excruciatingly funny stories and awing them with the details of his most recent surgical triumphs. Savage momentarily toyed with the idea of informing the Board that the date they had specified was not convenient—but then he reconsidered.

No, it would be worth missing the breakfast to have the opportunity of telling the Board what they could do with the imagined complaints against him. And those bitchy nurses—it had to be the nurses—he'd take care of them. He crumpled the letter and stuffed it in his pocket. Damn them all to hell!

Mike had been only half aware of the interplay between Savage and Susan on the elevator. His mind had been on the coming meeting with Mrs. Selkins—and it still was—as he momentarily paused at the door of the lounge adjoining the ICU.

His eyes rested on the woman seated on the couch. Obviously Mrs. Selkins. Although somewhere in the vicinity of forty, she was striking. Her short hair—dark brunette and frosted—was fashionably cut, and her pink suit was perfectly tailored. Her attractiveness was only slightly diminished by the fact that her makeup had obviously been hastily applied and failed to camouflage the red that rimmed her eyes. Her fingers fiddled nervously with the handle on the beige purse resting in her lap as she listened earnestly to the elderly, well-dressed, distinguished gentleman seated beside her.

Mrs. Selkins glanced up, suddenly aware of Mike, got up and hurried toward him. Mike took a few steps, covering the distance between them.

"Doctor, is my husband all right? What happened to him? Can I see him?" Mike steered her gently back to the couch, seated her, and pulled up a nearby chair. He nodded to her companion, but addressed his words to the woman.

"I'm Doctor Carrington, Mrs. Selkins. I've just finished surgery on your husband. To begin with, he's all right. But he was seriously injured . . . lost a lot of blood . . . and has had a major operation. He's going to be a sick man for several days."

"What kind of surgery, doctor? How badly was George hurt?"

"We had to take out part of his liver—it was fractured in the accident." Mike was alert to her anxiety and answered the obvious question before it was asked. "But he's got plenty left to live a long life with if he gets over this surgery."

"*If?*" the woman gasped. "Doctor, he'll be all right, won't he? For God's sake, tell me the truth. I have to know When can I see him?"

Mike knew that in her state of agitation she was only half hearing him. He deliberately ignored the first question.

"As far as seeing him is concerned, I'd suggest you wait until this evening. He'll be heavily sedated, but you can look in on him for a minute." Mike desperately wanted to be absolute in his assurance to this woman that her husband would be fine, but law suits were based on such replies. Should anything unexpected or unforeseen happen during recovery after he had been too definitely optimistic. . . . He deeply resented the cruelty that possible malpractice suits enforced upon him.

"But doctor, I—"

Carrington inwardly cringed at Mrs. Selkins' understandable persistence, but was saved from being forced to reply by her companion.

"Now, Marion, you heard what he said. Everything's going to be fine." He moved closer and placed an arm about her comfortingly.

"Oh," she gasped, suddenly aware. "Oh, doctor . . this is Robert Bradley, our attorney."

Michael acknowledged the introduction and quickly surveyed Bradley. Tall, maybe sixty-five, gray-haired, with a closely clipped, small moustache. His clothes were conservative and expensive. His casual intimacy with Mrs. Selkins indicated that he was a family friend as well as their legal counsel. Bradley smiled slightly, sensing Mike's curiosity at his presence.

"I think I should explain, doctor," he said easily. "After Marion got the call from the hospital, several unfortunate incidents occurred, and she—"

Distraught, Marion interrupted. "It's been a horrible morning. Just ghastly. And I'm afraid I made things worse. Oh, God . . . I don't know what to do. It was like a nightmare." She got up suddenly, walked to the window and stared out, trying to compose herself. Both men watched her silently, then Bradley spoke.

"Marion . . . I think we should be absolutely honest with Doctor Carrington. He may be able to help." He paused. From the window, Marion slowly nodded her approval without turning around.

"Marion was asleep when the call came from Emergency that George had been injured," Bradley went on. "All she could think was to get dressed and hurry down here. As she was getting into her car, some hotshot reporter who monitors police reports showed up, confronted her and demanded a statement. Naturally she was confused. She didn't know any of the details then— only that her husband had been injured—but the reporter didn't believe her. He started shooting a lot of questions at her: Hadn't she missed her husband? Did he often stay out all night? Did he have a habit of drinking? How did she think it would affect his image at the Academy? How did she feel about the little Harris boy?"

Marion turned from the window, tears streaming

down her face. "Oh, doctor. When he told me about that poor little boy, it was such a shock. I started to cry. And then this photographer who was with him jumped out of a car and started snapping pictures and . . . well, I know I said things I shouldn't have . . . things that might be damaging. I . . . I don't even remember what I said. But I did have sense enough to call Bob here, and he was afraid there might be more reporters outside the hospital so—"

Bradley noticed Mike's utter confusion, and interrupted quietly. "Are you aware of any of the details of the accident, doctor?"

Mike shook his head.

"First of all," Bradley explained, "George Selkins is the owner and dean of the Greenglen Academy for Girls, in Bel Air. You've heard of it?" Mike hadn't, but he nodded anyway. Bradley continued. "Then you know what a fine school it is, catering to the young daughters of some of the movie stars, the socialites, the best people in Beverly Hills."

Marion interrupted again. "Oh, Bob, did I tell you George's secretary called me? Just as I was leaving. A television crew was already up there, interviewing the students, getting some of the parents' reactions. There will probably be withdrawals, and they didn't know what to do, and I didn't know what to tell them, and—"

"There's nothing we can do, Marion," Bradley consoled her. "It'll all work out." He turned back to Mike and went on.

"A Mrs. Victor Harris was driving the car that George hit. She had taken her husband to work—he's on the early shift—had just dropped him off, in fact, and was heading back home. She had her five-year-old son Billy in the front seat next to her. When the collision occurred, Mrs. Harris had her seat belt on and suffered only superficial injuries, but the boy . . . well, it seems he was kneeling on the front seat, looking out the back window and—"

Bradley looked at Marion, wanting to spare her, but knew he had little choice. "Billy was thrown against the dashboard and has substantial head injuries. I don't know the medical details, but from what I can find out, he is still in a coma. And the doctors who are caring for the child feel that he could be permanently"—he paused, searching for the proper word—"retarded."

Marion started to sob, and Mike quickly stood up. "Mrs. Selkins, would you like a cup of coffee? I think it might help." She nodded and Mike made his way to the corridor to relay his request to a passing nurse. Bradley followed him out.

"Doctor Carrington, while we were waiting for you, I phoned my office to have them get a copy of the police report. They called me back. According to the investigating officer, George may have been intoxicated at the time of the accident. Is that true?"

Mike hesitated a moment, then nodded. "There are indications," he admitted.

Bradley shook his head. "That means criminal charges of felonious injury." He paused, then said thoughtfully. "We'll be hearing from the Harrises' attorney, you can bet on that. George has substantial insurance coverage—up to a million. But juries lately have been extremely sympathetic and generous in permanent disability cases, especially when the victim is young and bright. And it's a cinch their lawyers will take pains to paint Billy Harris as the smartest and most promising five-year-old in town."

Mike nodded. Only that morning, one of the news items he'd read concerned a similar case—with the award of a huge sum, plus substantial monthly support payments, potentially amounting to over twenty million dollars.

Bradley sighed. "I'm afraid the Selkinses are facing tremendous uncovered personal liability, a possible unending drain on their resources for the rest of their lives. I haven't mentioned the subject to Marion, but she indicated that the reporter did." His shoulders slumped dejectedly. "You know, it's too bad. George has a drinking problem, but they're actually awfully nice people—and they really love each other."

As the nurse returned with the coffee and entered the lounge, Mike and Bradley followed her in. Marion Selkins was still staring out the window. She turned.

"Doctor Carrington, I want the very best for George. You'll get him a private room, won't you? And I want special nurses. I want someone with him every minute."

"No problem with the room," Mike said slowly. "I've already taken care of that."

He paused. Private nurses. It was the old question. Somehow people felt they assured a patient the ultimate in care. Exactly the opposite was true in the case of someone critically ill or injured. In Mike's opinion, private duty nurses couldn't begin to touch the super-efficiency and knowledge that the young, in-touch, floor nurses possessed. With the nursing shortage and the higher wages, every available R.N. worth her salt was working on the floors. Generally, only old, unable-to-cut-it nurses were available for private duty. There were exceptions, of course. Some competent nurses just didn't want to work full time or didn't like floor nursing, but they were rare—the exception, not the rule.

Certainly private nurses had their place. If a patient were suicidal or in any way psychotic, they were mandatory. And once a patient was sufficiently recovered, if his financial position permitted such luxury, private nurses were companionable and attentive, catering to every whim, focusing all their attention on their single charge. But often they were merely very expensive baby-sitters. The real danger, in the case of a critically ill patient, was that once private nurses were assigned, the regular floor nurses felt relieved of responsibility. Mike remembered too many times visiting a critically ill patient in the middle of the night and finding the private nurse, wrapped in a blanket, sound asleep, oblivious to the condition of her charge.

"As far as the private nurses," Mike said persuasively, "let's wait awhile before deciding. As I said, Mr. Selkins will be heavily sedated for a few days. I can assure you he'll get excellent care in the meantime."

Marion started to protest, but Bradley interceded. "Let's trust the doctor, Marion. Let him decide."

Marion reflected for a moment, then nodded, but immediately turned to another subject. "Doctor, you won't let any reporters bother George, will you?"

"The hospital automatically protects its patients, Mrs. Selkins," he assured her.

"And the police. I don't want them questioning him, either," she insisted.

"Nobody is going to bother your husband until it's medically safe," Mike said quietly. "I'll see to that. But the law's the law, and I have to obey it, too. When he's better, he's going to have to talk to the police." He understood her concern. "I'll be happy to call you or Mr. Bradley when the time comes, though, so you can be present if you want."

"I'd appreciate that, doctor," Bradley replied. "Be sure to let me know."

Marion suddenly buried her head in her hands. Mike knew she was close to the breaking point. Bradley encircled her in his arms.

"Take it easy, Marion. Try to pull yourself together. After all, your husband's life has been saved. Right?"

She pulled away from him and stared at the carpet for a long moment. Then she said evenly: "Wrong. My husband's life has been ruined!"

Mike headed back to the eighth floor, the truth of Marion Selkins' words ringing in his mind. Before he had left, he had done all the right things: reassured her regarding her husband's progress, offered her a sedative, urged her to call him should she have questions or desire information. But the certainty that his necessarily measured tone of reassurance had fallen far short of comforting her haunted him.

He glanced at his watch grimly. Almost eleven—and he hadn't started his rounds yet. If he didn't get going, he'd be competing with the luncheon trays. He'd just look at the X-rays on Mrs. Whitlock and Mr. Campion so he would know the results before seeing them. Then he'd start, as was his custom, visiting each of his patients, working from the top floor down.

For the third time that morning, he walked down the corridor toward the X-ray Department. He was almost there when he heard the page.

"Doctor Carrington. Doctor Michael Carrington."

Mike retraced his steps, picked up a phone, and within a few moments heard the soft, cool voice.

"Mike?"

Just the sound of her caused a shiver to course through him, and he noticed that his hand holding the phone was shaking slightly. Two days had passed without hearing Nedra's warm, low, intimate tone . . . two days had been wasted without running his hand over her smooth, silken flesh. Two days that had seemed a lifetime of hell. And it was a hell he had deliberately brought on himself. An exercise in egotism . . . in stubbornness. He had vowed he would not call her. If their relationship was to be resumed, it must be on his terms. It must be she who made the first move. He had to have the upper hand. He was, he admitted, a bastard, pure and simple.

What in the hell was wrong with him, he wondered. The doubts and misgivings he had experienced as a result of the last time they were together—they were normal, maybe justified. But not even to call her? What was this insane, childish game he was playing? Had the sea of misery in which he floated and worked so anesthetized his emotions that he felt no remorse in causing pain and misery to someone he loved? Loved. The word shocked him. He realized now he had always avoided it. For the past two days he'd been convincing himself that Nedra was no different from the many other girls he had slept with before he'd met her. But he couldn't remember the others—not their faces, not their bodies.

He closed his eyes. He remembered the way Nedra's eyebrows grew, the tiny indentation on her cheekbone from a childhood bout with chickenpox. Her high, upthrust breasts with their rosy nipples were a vivid image . . . her flat stomach, the slightly jutting hipbones,

71

one perhaps a half-inch higher than the other. The triangular patch of soft, blond pubic hair—the taste of it, the smell of it. The clean stretch of her thighs. God, Nedra was part of him! She was his sanctuary. She was the only thing in his working world of blood and torn flesh and amputations and tears and death that kept him from losing touch with the shreds that kept him a human being.

And he had knowingly . . . willingly . . . with steadfast determination . . . used every ounce of willpower to keep from calling her. He needed time, he had assured himself. Time.

"Mike?" He realized his thoughts had used up several moments and his silence had made her unsure that he was on the line.

"Hi." He hesitated uncomfortably. "Nedra—"

He had expected hurt, perhaps recriminations, accusations—at the very least, a frostiness. But her voice was normally low and warm and matter-of-fact as she interrupted.

"Mike, I was just watching the news on television, and they had some film of an auto accident this morning—a little boy was badly hurt. They said the driver of the other car had been taken to Marin. Were you involved?"

He realized she had used the news item as an excuse for calling him. God bless the television stations and their newscasters, one and all. He went along.

"I just finished operating on him. He'll be fine. But his wife—"

"I know. They had a picture of her, too. She looked so dazed and confused . . . and alone."

He searched for something to say. What words, what apology, could mitigate his selfishness of the past two days? But in the time it took to seek them out, Nedra continued.

"They also had something about a child abuse case there."

"Yeah, the Sanchez kid. I heard about it. Keith drew that one," Mike said shortly. "It's a lousy world."

"I'm sorry," she said softly. "I'm beginning to know what you meant about crying."

Mike wanted to pour out his love for her, but the nursing station was teeming with activity. "Nedra, look," he lied guiltily, "I've picked up the phone a dozen times to call you, and every time something happened and I—"

"Forget it. I understand." There was a pause. "Mike, are you free tonight?"

"Honey, I'm sorry," he groaned, "but it's the fourth Friday of the month and that means the County Medical Association Meeting." He was suddenly sickened at his own words. What was the meeting compared to Nedra? "Look," he said hurriedly, "I'll skip it. Where can I meet you?"

It was Nedra's turn to hesitate. "I'd forgotten about the meeting. Aren't you chairman of the fee committee? You have to go," she decided.

He wanted to hug her for her thoughtfulness and consideration. "Hey, why don't I get someone to cover me this weekend?" he blurted out anxiously. "I'll pick you up tonight after the meeting . . . it'll be over by eleven. We'll spend the night on the boat and get an early start Saturday morning."

"Sounds wonderful," she said softly. "And I have an idea. Instead of wasting all that time picking me up, why don't I meet you at the hospital after the meeting, and we can head directly for the marina from there?"

"That would be great! I'll have to come back here anyway. Look, when you get here, park your car in the lot across the street and have me paged from the lobby. We'll drive back together Monday morning."

"Right. See you," she said.

He paused before hanging up. "Nedra? God, I'm glad you called."

"Good," she said softly. "I'm glad, too. I thought I had blown it," and hung up.

Nedra. He had met her at the Marina Yacht Club on a Sunday night. He had dropped in for a quick martini, but the place was a madhouse, packed with the boating crowd rehashing the just completed Ensenada race. He was about to leave, reluctant to brave the noisy maelstrom, when the owner of the boat moored next to his had spied him and insisted on buying a drink. Trapped, he had joined the group.

He had noticed Nedra immediately. Cool, serene, watching the childish gaiety about her in an almost detached fashion. Her dark blond hair was pulled back and tied with a scarf, pony-tail fashion. Mike judged her to be about thirty-five, and only fantastic bone structure would allow a woman of that age to dare such severity. The white pullover sweater over the navy slacks accentuated her coppery tan and clear skin.

As he finished his drink and rose to leave, she stood up also. He was surprised to see that she was only a few inches shorter than his six feet. The incessant chatter and hailing back and forth across the room had caused introductions to be overlooked. The girl smiled.

"I'm Nedra Scott," she said quietly. "This looks like it could go on for hours, so if you'd just see me to my car . . . I have a living to earn tomorrow."

"Michael Carrington," he smiled, "and I'd be delighted."

Nobody seemed to miss them as they left. While they waited for the parking attendant to bring the cars around, Nedra surveyed him with interest.

"Do you come here often?"

"No, at least not up until now. But I have a feeling that with a little encouragement, I would make it a regular thing."

She laughed easily and shrugged. "I don't come here at all. I'm not really one of the boating crowd."

"Oh? What do you do?"

"I'm a painter. Seascapes are my 'thing' right now. I was in Ensenada doing some sketching, met that crazy crowd in there, and found myself talked into hitchhiking back with them on their boat."

Mike withdrew a pack of cigarettes and offered her one. She shook her head. He looked at her with sudden awareness.

"The Scott Seascapes! Right? I've seen your work. A couple of months ago, in that LaCienega Gallery."

She nodded.

"Lady, you *are* a painter . . . a very good painter."

She shrugged. "What's your line of work, Mister Carrington?"

"Cutting and sewing."

She looked slightly surprised. "A tailor?"

"Surgeon."

The attendant had arrived with her car, a late-model light tan Grand Prix. Mike held the door as she got in, as the boy headed for his Mark IV in the section of the lot reserved for club members.

"Good night, doctor," she murmured, as she shifted the car from "park" to "drive."

"Wait a minute," he asked. "Do you have a card?"

"Oh, are you interested in seascapes?"

"No, but I think I'm interested in you."

She hesitated only a moment, reached into her handbag and handed him a card. Wordlessly, she drove off.

Later they often laughed over the banality and highschoolish quality of that encounter. Nedra admitted to being an amateur in the art of pickups. After the death of her pilot-husband in the latter stages of the Vietnam war, Nedra had immersed herself in her work, accepting dates only from old friends.

Mike didn't care to reveal much about his own social life. Like any eligible bachelor, he had more of a problem fighting off predatory females than searching for dates. There had been a string of spasmodic, superficial affairs, all following the same pattern. When he felt the physical need, he wandered into one of the singles bars, crowded with the young girls who inhabited the many "swinging" apartment complexes at the beach. Average time of conquest: about eight minutes. He slept with a girl a few times and then dropped her. He recognized the normal physical need—but additional emotional entanglements were something to be avoided.

He made it a policy not to date nurses from the hospital. After his twelve- or fourteen-hour day at Marin, their shoptalk, their gossip, their sameness would bore the hell out of him, he knew. He also realized it would be difficult to have a professional doctor-nurse relationship with someone he had laid the night before. Other physicians managed it, but he was unwilling to take the risk.

The affair with Nedra had been going on for about eleven months—almost a year—some kind of record for him. He *had* called her for dinner about a week after their initial meeting and found her pleasant, uncomplicated, and fun to be with. It had been a short step from an occasional dinner or movie to the bedroom.

The attachment had simplified his life. It had given him stability without responsibility—and that suited him fine. If Nedra was going to be tied up on business, she let him know in advance. She dated no one else. He could drop in unexpectedly and she would be there—cheerful, delighted to see him. They ate together two or three times a week, and it was tacitly understood that dinner meant bed privileges afterward. Sex with each other was the best they had ever known.

And so the relationship continued. There were no complaints from Nedra if plans had to be canceled at the last minute due to unexpected hospital crises. They seldom socialized with other couples. The few times they had tried becoming involved with others, a last minute unscheduled surgery had fouled up the evening. Besides, Nedra knew Mike was uncomfortable with strangers in a social situation, and she was also reluctant to foist his uncertain schedule and changeable moods on her friends. So most of the time they were alone together, watching television, taking drives, or on the boat. Nedra was a natural sailor, and within a short time he had taught her practically everything there was to know about a sailboat—she could crew as well as any man. Sometimes, if Mike's schedule permitted, they spent the entire weekend on the *Non Norcere,* sailing to

Catalina or heading for the various meccas of the yachting crowd that dotted the coastline north and south of Los Angeles. There had been no problems.

Until two days ago. Wednesday. It had been a gorgeous day—warm and breezy—and Mike had been able to get away early. They had taken the boat out around two in the afternoon and simply cruised, idly heading north past the rocks where the brown pelicans roosted. Mike watched as Nedra sketched the great birds, capturing their alternately awkward and graceful maneuvers. At dusk, they headed back to her apartment for dinner, and it was evident that she had gone to great pains to make the meal very special, to prepare and serve the things he liked most—veal Parmesan, the green noodles, even his favorite Lambrusco wine.

Afterward, he could hear the rattle of the dishes as she tidied up while he settled into a chair, absorbed in the seven o'clock news on Channel Two. He was unaware that she'd left the kitchen until she quietly walked up behind him, put her hands over his eyes, and laid her head next to his.

"Hey, you really interested in this program?" she whispered.

Smiling, he reached up and captured her hands in his. "Not really. Any special reason you asked?" She put her arms around his neck, her mouth close to his ear.

"Mmmm, maybe." She kissed his temple and slid her hands inside his shirt, letting them lie against his chest. They lingered there until he turned his head and kissed her arm where it crossed his shoulder. Taking her wrists in his hands, he led her to the front of the chair.

"Come around here. I like to see who I'm kissing." She flicked off the television set, sank to her knees and, smiling softly, put her head in his lap. He undid her hair and let it fall. So beautiful, so fine, so Nedra, he thought. Mike lifted her chin and held her head up toward his. She was so warm, so willing, her eyes so filled with love, as he leaned forward to kiss her. Suddenly

77

her warmth was intensity, but despite her response, the kiss lingered. Throwing her head back, she pulled him to the floor and kneeling, they pressed together from knees to mouth.

Passionate but loving words were whispered as she rubbed his back and he kissed her neck. As she began to unbutton his shirt, the smile on her face was almost impish. When she pulled her sweater over her head, her full breasts were taut. She had not been wearing a bra and the even skin color, the lack of a tan line, made her firm, lithe body all the more beautiful to him. Pulling her back toward him, they both felt the stimulation of bare flesh in contact. He kissed her softly on the mouth, the neck, and then he nestled his face in her breasts. He felt her body arch and heard her whisper his name with an urgency born of desire.

He was fully stumulated and without a word he stood and turned down the lights. She started to stand, but kneeling again, he pulled her back to him. Her arms were over his shoulders, her head next to his.

"The bedroom, Mike, let's—"

With a boyish grin, he lay back and pulled her on top of him. It was plain he had no intention of going anywhere, that the floor was to be their bed that night.

She responded all the more willingly, clinging to him, answering his every movement. Few words, but much feeling passed between them as they undressed each other, and there on the floor, they began to live their passion. Nedra led him, her tender words and soft caresses calling him on like the instruments in a beautiful symphony, a concerto of complete and utter love, each note anticipating the next, each body calling forth from the other the next motion. In the final breathless moments, her body clung to him and answered and loved. Mike collapsed over her, his head on her chest. She cradled his face against her breasts. Her lips formed the words "I love you . . . I love you . . . I love you," but no sound escaped. A strand of her hair strayed next to his face, pressing against his cheek, and he took it between his lips, tasting the fragrance. He lay there, lost in that dream world that comes halfway between sleep and wakefulness.

From beyond this warm sense of contentment he was feeling, he heard her speak. It was as if she were a long way off, but her words came creeping into his consciousness, one by one.

"Michael . . . I . . . want . . . to . . . get . . . married."

He lay there for just a moment more and then rolled away from her, lying on his stomach, his head buried in his arms. He could feel Nedra's eyes on him, he was aware of her tension, her expectancy of a reply—but he didn't know what to say. Thoughts tumbled through his mind like the entrapped snowflakes in a paperweight— coming from an unseen source, going nowhere. Mike knew what he felt, but he didn't know what he wanted. He knew he cared about Nedra and enjoyed being with her. He looked forward to their times together with unbelievable anticipation.

"Mike," he heard her repeat, "I want to get married."

He lit a cigarette and plopped into a chair. Staring silently at the growing ash, he was aware that she had shifted slightly so she could see his face as she reached for the sweater to cover her nakedness.

Mike wanted his freedom. He liked his life exactly as it was. Marriage was a partnership. His life as he now knew it was a monarchy. His will, his wants, his pleasures, were absolute. He wanted it to stay that way. Marriage. The word had the sound of a trap springing shut on a wild animal. Abruptly he stood up and sighed for what he was he was about to lose.

"Marriage is out, Nedra. Surgery is my whole life. Instead of a home and kids, I chose a career. I can't have both. I don't have time," he lied. "So don't ask me to choose between you and the hospital. Don't ask me—because you'll lose." He was experienced enough to know that once the issue of marriage was raised, their relationship could never be the same. They could not go back to the way things had been. It was better to end it, so he added, "I love being with you, making love to you, but I don't think I've ever really loved anyone."

He ground out the cigarette and began dressing. Nedra turned away from him, and her voice was muffled when she spoke.

"I think I'll get rid of the apartment and move to New Orleans."

He recognized the subtle attempt at emotional blackmail and resented it.

"Why New Orleans?" he snapped cruelly. She turned to face him now, and he saw tears welling up in her eyes. "And Jesus, don't start to cry. Don't ever cry. I hate it."

She looked at him quietly. "Don't you ever want to cry, Michael?"

Fully dressed, he was once again Dr. Michael Carrington, a solitary man seemingly in full control of his emotions. He turned and stared at her for a moment. . . .

"God only knows how many times," he said, and gently closed the door behind him.

He hadn't been able to get her out of his mind since. For forty-eight hours she had flitted in and out of his thoughts—danced behind his eyelids—her remembered smile and words and gestures had stabbed at him like burning splinters.

For two days he had deliberately pushed her image away with a vague uneasiness. Each time he'd passed a telephone, he had fought the overwhelming desire to call her. He'd get over her. *He'd never get over her!* Was he actually mortal enough to love somebody? Yes. Oh, God, yes! *He loved Nedra!* He wanted her. He needed her. He wanted her with him the rest of his life. He wanted to marry her! And he'd tell her tonight!

He glanced at his watch. Eleven thirty. He had office appointments beginning at one in the afternoon and was booked solid. So, he calculated grimly, he had exactly an hour and a half to make hospital rounds, to see fourteen patients, chart their progress and write new orders—an average of six minutes for each. Well, with a little luck, and a good tail wind, he could do it.

It was almost three thirty when Susan Thomas arrived home after her shift at the hospital.

She climbed the short flight of steps leading from the street to the entrance of the Wilburn Arms with deliberate slowness, scrutinizing the building with obvious distaste. It was an old section of town, still good, but on the very fringe of an area where Mexicans and blacks were gradually taking over. It was as if the inhabitants of the neighborhood, alert to the danger, made a special effort to manicure their tiny lawns and shrubbery meticulously, but despite such endeavors, the seediness of the buildings was barely camouflaged.

Susan momentarily inspected her reflection in the glass door before entering. Her natural blond hair, her wide green eyes, gave the impression of soft naïve femininity. Nothing could be further from the truth. Actually her lovely, almost childlike features hid an iron-willed determination. She knew exactly where she was going.

From the time she started nurses' training, Susan had not looked upon it as a career, but rather as a means to an end. In short, she intended to marry a rich doctor. Why not? Nature had been extremely kind to her, and she had the calculating mind that would make it happen.

In the lobby, Mary McCullough was just collecting her mail from the long row boxes which serviced the building's tenants. She paused as she glimpsed Susan at the door and reflected on the affection she felt for the younger girl.

Mary and Susan's mother, Lorrie, had been friends all through school—a closeness which had been sustained through Lorrie's marriage, the subsequent birth of Susan, and the divorce from her husband. The women were often together, and Mary had watched Susan grow from an adorable baby to a beautiful young woman. When Lorrie had died several years before, Mary had felt a sense of love and responsibility that she had never before experienced.

She had been delighted when Susan elected to become a nurse, subconsciously basking in the realization that the young girl was emulating her, and when Susan had expressed discontent with her job in a San Fernando Valley hospital, it had been Mary who urged her to apply for a job at Marin Medical Center and had pulled a few strings so her friend could work with her in Admitting. Mary had taken the girl under her protective wing, even securing an apartment for her at the Wilburn Arms, where Mary had lived for the past nine years.

Susan opened the door and hid the little shudder of distaste she experienced each time she crossed the lobby. Not that it wasn't clean. It was, well . . . tacky. The dark green walls, the lighter green ceiling, the worn and faded carpeting grated on her. She was destined for something better; she deserved it.

"Hi." She smiled at Mary and checked her own mailbox. She groaned inwardly. Bills, nothing but bills. Saks, Magnin's, Robinson's—it was tough on her salary, but she looked upon the expensive clothes she bought as a necessary investment in attaining her ultimate goal.

"How'd it go today?" Mary asked.

"Couldn't have been better." Susan started up the stairs, then stopped and turned back.

"Hey, Mary . . . can I borrow your steam iron? I want to wear my jersey stole tonight, and it's a mess. Forgot to hang it up last time."

"Sure," agreed Mary. "I'll get it for you. Big date tonight?"

"Yes," Susan answered shortly, hoping Mary wouldn't press for details, but knowing that she would.

"Anybody I know?"

Susan hesitated. Here it comes, she thought. "Doctor Savage."

On the steps behind her, Mary came to a dead stop. Sensing it, Susan turned to face her.

"Oh, Susan, no! After all you've heard? After all I've told you about him?" Determined, Mary started up the stairs. "Well, you can just call him . . . tell him you think you've picked up a flu bug or something."

82

Susan stood her ground, blocking the way. They might as well have it out now. "I intend to keep my date with Doctor Savage," Susan said. "I've been out with weirdos before. I can take care of myself."

Mary felt almost nauseated. "Susan, for goodness sake, think! You've talked to the other girls . . . you know he's sick. Why him? Why David Savage?"

"Because he asked me. And he's rich!" She flared, voicing her frustration. "Do you think I intend to live like this? In this rundown haven for spinsters who haven't any choice?" Mary winced at the insensitive cruelty of the words, as Susan went on. "Do you think I want to drive a 1967 Chevrolet the rest of my life? Work at a rundown hospital where I'm not even a human being—just a glorified maid? I'll tell you what I want! I want a house in Trousdale; I want a Bentley; I want a houseboy to serve me breakfast; I want lunch at the Bistro . . . and I want a husband! And I'll get them. Believe me, I'll get them. Any way I can!"

"Susan!" Mary was taken aback by the girl's vehemence. She stared at her for a moment and then her gaze softened. Susan looked so vulnerable, her lovely face belying the conniving harshness of her words. A product of an unhappy broken home; it had to have left its mark. Mary deliberately willed her voice to be casual. "I wouldn't know, but I've heard love's pretty important, too."

Susan caught her lower lip between her teeth for a moment. "Look, Mary, sure I want love," she admitted. "Doesn't everybody? But remember my family? Mother was in love, and after the divorce, I was the one who watched her grow more scared and older and lonelier every day. She even died alone. All alone! And do you know why? Because I was out working, trying to keep bread on the table." She swallowed a sob. "Oh, Mary, I don't want that to happen to me. Almost every night, when I'm in bed, I have nightmares about it. I get up, and turn on the light, and sit and stare at the empty, unmussed other side of the bed. Sometimes I don't think I can stand it. What I said before about working at the hospital wasn't true. I don't mind it. I like the feeling that I'm helping people, I really do. But when I see those women, those girls, who come in all alone—alone and so terrified—carrying their own overnight cases, nobody with them, nobody caring whether they live or die, I just shrivel inside." Tears glistened beneath her long, blond lashes. "I'd be a good wife, Mary, I honestly would. Anything my husband wanted from me, I'd give. I'd make him the happiest man on earth. And all I'd ask in return was security, for him to just be there, to hold my hand when I needed him." Her voice dropped to a whisper. "To love me as much as I'd love him. I want love . . . and I want kids, lots of them. Believe me, I'd be mother of the year. It's all I think about." Mary watched Susan's eyes turn agate-hard again. "But I can love a rich doctor just as easy as I can love some poor slob. And believe me, that's the way it's going to be!"

Mary started to protest, then stopped. Who was she to criticize Susan? She knew who she was—she was all the things that Susan didn't want to be.

But, oh, God, David Savage!

Susan flew up the steps to the second floor. As she reached the top, Mary called to her.

"Susan, wait!"

Bristling, the girl turned and stared at her.

"I'll get you the iron."

Ashamed, Susan nodded and waited while Mary entered her apartment and emerged a few seconds later.

"Thanks, Mary," she said, taking the iron. "And I'm sorry. Don't worry. Believe me, I'll be okay."

Mary nodded, unconvinced, but desperately trying not to reveal it. As Susan started up the steps to her room on the third floor, Mary couldn't help herself.

"Be careful," she blurted.

"You betcha," Susan called down airily.

It was four thirty in the afternoon, and Mike had just about finished his office appointments. His two nurses, Celeste and Jennifer, had been efficiently shuttling patients in and out of the three treatment rooms, and when the phone rang, it happened to be Jennifer who took the call.

"This is Mrs. Comstock in Admitting at County General Hospital," the woman identified herself. "We have a patient of Doctor Carrington's here—an Aaron Metz. Just brought in . . . was coughing up blood and fainted. Our doctors have examined him. He has good blood pressure, is stable, and can be transported. Will Doctor Carrington accept him?"

Jennifer asked the caller to hold on a moment and quickly thumbed through a file. Then she sought out Dr. Carrington and relayed the message. "The only problem," admitted Jennifer, puzzled, "is that we don't show him as a patient."

"Metz," repeated Mike thoughtfully. "Aaron Metz. The name rings a bell, but—"

He searched his memory for a few moments and it suddenly came to him. Aaron Metz, the elderly waiter at Harrington's Steak House, a restaurant he frequently patronized. He always tried to get a table attended by Aaron, for his service was impeccably professional. Mike recalled the brief snatches of conversations between them from time to time. How the subject had come up, he didn't know, but he remembered Aaron once telling him that he had started his career as a busboy at a restaurant in Vienna when he was only fifteen and had later immigrated to the United States. Another time, after Mike had praised him on some subtlety of good service, he had volunteered the information that he had been servicing tables for fifty years. Mike had always tipped him lavishly and had gone out of his way to be pleasant. He hadn't really thought about it, but Aaron must be over sixty by now.

"Sure, we'll take him," decided Mike. "Check to make sure that there's a bed available, and then have them send him by ambulance. Have Marin's Admitting call me as soon as he arrives."

A quick call to verify that a bed could be made ready for Mr. Metz, and Jennifer got back to Mrs. Comstock.

"Good," the other woman said, "we'll send him right over."

Jennifer fully understood Mrs. Comstock's relief, for she had worked at County General for a short time. The Emergency Room there was unbelievably hectic—beds, gurneys, cots and chairs everywhere, and victims were brought in at an incredible rate. If a patient expressed a desire for, or volunteered that he had a private physician—and was able to be moved—the personnel instantly exerted every effort to implement the transfer. It simply meant that a few extra square feet that were now occupied would be available for the next patient.

When the call came from Marin that Mr. Metz had been admitted, Mike had only one patient in the office still waiting to be seen, and since it was a routine postoperative examination that would take only a short time, he delayed seeing Mr. Metz until he had finished.

It was close to a half hour later when he made his way to Marin's fourth floor to pick up Mr. Metz' chart before seeing him. The head nurse on four-south was in a state of agitation.

"Doctor Carrington, what have you done to us?"

Mike looked at her with genuine surprise as she continued. "You've got to have a talk with Mr. Metz."

"What's the problem?" Mike asked absently, as he surveyed the patient's chart. Blood pressure normal, pulse normal, temperature normal, he noted automatically.

"He's . . . well . . ."

Mike looked up at her sharply.

"He's been masturbating," she blurted out, embarrassed, "ever since he got here!"

Carrington gazed at her blandly, picked up a stethoscope and wordlessly walked into Room 409. Aaron Metz looked smaller and much older than Mike remembered, and he realized the crisp red waiter's jacket had hidden the wrinkles and scrawniness that the hospital gown now revealed. His almost bald head, fringed with white, lay limply against the pillow. His eyes were closed, the blue-veined lids almost transparent. Mike touched his shoulder.

"Hello, Mr. Metz. It's good to see you again," he said softly.

The elderly man had obviously been dozing and as he awoke, his glance moved dazedly about the room. Immediately his hand slid under the sheet toward his genitalia, the frantic movements of his fingers clearly apparent under the thin covering.

Gently, almost tenderly, Mike turned down the sheet and raised the gown. Mr. Metz had removed his shorts and his hand was deep into them.

Mike caught a glimpse of what appeared to be the corner of a dollar bill. He looked closer. Aaron Metz had pinned a substantial amount of money to his shorts for safekeeping—Mike estimated almost a hundred fifty-dollar bills—and was obsessed with the ritual of making sure it was still there. Quietly, Mike re-covered the patient and again addressed him.

"Mr. Metz?"

Aaron's vacant eyes focused on Mike as he struggled to orient himself. "Doctor? Doctor Carrington?" he asked hesitantly.

"Right here," Mike said, taking the dry hand.

"I'm sorry, doctor," the old man apologized hoarsely. "I remembered your name but . . ."

"But what," prompted Mike.

"I didn't know if you took care of waiters."

"You bet I do," Mike assured him. "Now, I understand you coughed up some blood. A lot, or just some streaks?"

"Well, it seemed like a lot to me," Aaron replied.

"Do you smoke?"

"Cigarettes? Sure," the old man confessed, "started smoking when I was just a kid."

"How many?"

"Oh, less than a pack a day, I guess. Used to be more, but I've cut down."

"How much weight have you lost?" Mike probed.

"Who weighs," the old man chuckled. "A scale I

don't have. My clothes seem a little looser, maybe. Lately, being around food all day, serving people . . . when the time comes to eat myself, I don't have much appetite."

Mike helped Aaron to a sitting position and, with the stethoscope, listened to his back. A couple of little wheezes on the right side, not much else. He listened to the heart, thumped the chest, and noticed that the right diaphragm was a little higher than it should be. That, plus the hoarseness could be significant. Gently, he laid Aaron back down and felt his abdomen and liver.

"Well, it looks like we'll have to get some X-rays and blood studies, Mr. Metz." Mike knew that Aaron's vital signs were okay, but he felt suddenly protective of the old gentleman.

"Do you feel strong enough to go to X-ray in a wheelchair?"

The man nodded, closed his eyes and slid his fingers back beneath the covers—to assure himself once again that nothing had happened to his money.

Mike walked slowly back to the nursing station. He began writing orders for a complete blood count, a biochemical profile, a VDRL, urinalysis and chest X-rays. The head nurse watched, wordlessly.

"You know, Agnes," he casually commented as he continued to scribble, not looking up, "you have a dirty mind."

She gasped, but before she could protest, Mike went on, his attention innocently riveted on the chart. "Mr. Metz is not masturbating." He made several lengthy notations before continuing. "He is merely counting his assets!"

He let her stew in bewilderment as he completed the chart, then explained. As he progressed, she began to chuckle. She was still giggling as she picked up the phone and called Admitting. They would send someone up to count the money—it would be double-checked—then a receipt given, and the currency would be deposited in the hospital's vault for safekeeping.

88

When Mike left to make his evening rounds, she was still laughing as she related the story to another nurse.

Susan spent three hectic hours after her confrontation with Mary. She washed her hair, rolled it on curlers, set up her portable dryer, and utilized the necessary forty-five minutes under it carefully enameling her nails with the newest shade. Then a warm, leisurely bath. A quick cleanup of the small apartment—stuffing things in drawers, in closets, behind furniture. Neat, she wasn't. In the kitchen, while the iron heated, she gingerly prepared a cocktail dip, careful not to mar her long, exquisite nails. As she struggled with the concoction of sour cream and onion soup, she wryly consoled herself: single girls make dips, married ladies give dinner parties.

She dressed carefully, slipping into a long royal blue sheath with a dotted blue and white chiffon overshirt. The low V-neck revealed just enough, she decided, as she carefully applied the finishing touches to her makeup. The fact that Savage had not shown her the courtesy of indicating where they might go, so she could dress accordingly, nagged at her. She shrugged. She had a philosophy that covered the situation. She dressed as if she expected to be taken to Chasen's—and it was a rare date who, after seeing her, had the guts to suggest a hamburger at a drive-in.

A few minutes after seven, she set out the dip on the coffee table, surrounded it with corn chips and placed a tray with ice, Scotch, and glasses nearby. She hoped Savage was a Scotch man, because that was the only liquor she had on hand. That done, she put an album of Sinatra classics on the stereo and sat down to wait. And plan the strategy of the evening. She was fully conscious that he would try to seduce her. She giggled aloud at her mental use of the word. Maybe she was more Victorian than she realized. Anyway, she pondered, shall I go to bed with him on the first date—or play a little hard to get? She weighed the pros and cons without coming to a decision—there was something to be said for either course of action.

When Dr. Savage appeared at the door a few minutes past seven thirty, she smiled fetchingly and invited him in.

"Sorry, doll, I've got reservations. You look great. Let's get going."

Susan hurriedly picked up her bag and stole, stopping to click off the stereo. She glanced at the dip ruefully. It ought to be covered, she thought. The hell with it. Let it turn brown and crusty—who cares?

She was pleased when they drove into Nacio's Restaurant parking lot. It was one of the "in" restaurants of West Los Angeles, constantly mentioned in the film and society columns. Dave was obviously a regular customer, and the captain greeted him by name and showed them immediately to a comfortable table. Susan glowed. Savage really was nice. She discounted the scene in the hospital elevator. Like any doctor, he had been rushed and preoccupied. While they had Margaritas, he kept her entertained with amusing anecdotes and tidbits of gossip about his recent cases and patients. The food was superb; the Flamenco entertainment excellent.

Halfway through dinner, Savage suddenly spied an acquaintance at the bar, got up abruptly and walked across the room to greet his friend. Almost half an hour passed before he returned. Susan fiddled with her food, her silverware, her water glass, growing more and more uncomfortable. Then he rejoined her, sat down, bolted his food—and before she had finished her coffee, he rose, indicating they were to go. She was upset at his rudeness, but was determined not to show it.

As they were leaving, a well-known television character actor who was waiting for a table hailed Dave as he passed. During the lengthy, lively discussion between the two men, Savage didn't bother to introduce Susan, and she had no choice but to stand there, a smile frozen on her face, looking and feeling like excess baggage.

When they finally got to the parking lot and entered his Jaguar, Susan's mind was racing. Well, here it comes, she thought—get set for the seduction pitch. She had to decide, she told herself, yes or no. Dave drove north wordlessly, past Wilshire, Sunset, heading for the Hollywood Hills. They were almost at his apartment before Susan realized that he wasn't even going to be subtle about it; he wasn't even going to ask; he took it as a foregone conclusion that she was ready and willing. She fought her growing anger and humiliation.

The doorman on duty at the luxurious apartment building where they stopped opened her door and went around to the driver's seat to garage the car. Susan got out and was suddenly aware that Savage was some ten paces ahead of her, moving toward the elevator. She hurried to catch up. The door opened immediately at the pressure of his finger on the button. She preceded him in.

"It's been a marvelous evening, honey," he said as they rode to the top floor. "I can't remember having a better time."

Susan was silent. He certainly was sure of himself, she thought resentfully. Now was the time to assert herself. Right now. Then she shrugged inwardly. Her confidence that she could charm him, tame him where others had failed, returned to her. Things would still work out. Once alone with him, he'd see her worth. And what the hell, she thought, I've gone this far. What have I got to lose—certainly not my virginity.

But it didn't help her disposition when Savage stepped out of the elevator ahead of her and again strode down the hall, leaving her trailing behind him. He opened the door, and as she stepped inside, she gasped. It was a fabulous apartment, expertly decorated in whites, beiges, browns and bright touches of yellow and tangerine. She stood motionless, drinking in the panoramic view beyond the floor-to-ceiling glass wall that stretched the entire length of the living room. The apartment actually seemed to float in space, and the city lights appeared to stretch forever, the blues, reds and greens of neon seeming to vie with each other and with the stars in brightness and design. She could make out some of the major boulevards—LaCienega, Fairfax, LaBrea and Crenshaw—their accentuated lights cutting

91

a brighter swath through what seemed, at this height, a giant, decorated Christmas tree.

While she gazed entranced, Savage walked across the room to the bar and made himself a drink. The fantasy Susan had been enjoying—the picture of herself sharing all this—dimmed, and she stared at him unbelievingly. He really didn't intend to offer her one, she realized. He had put ice and bourbon in *one* glass, and was filling it with soda. He glanced back at Susan and motioned to a door leading from the huge room.

"The bedroom's in there. Go ahead, I'll be along in a minute."

As he turned his attention back to his drink, he missed her sudden indignation. Damn him! He had repeatedly ignored her throughout the evening, and she had suppressed her resentment, always feeling that a little patience and a lot of charm on her part would get her to her goal. But this final degradation freed all that restrained anger. He was treating her like a whore! She felt physically ill. Stunned, she slowly made her way across the room and wordlessly perched on an arm of the couch directly behind him. Several minutes passed before he became aware of her.

"What are you waiting for?"

"Dave, just take me home." Her tone was even and her words were exactly spaced. He slowly put down the glass. For an instant, his features became ugly as he glowered at the thought of this stupid girl whose capriciousness threatened to disrupt his plans. To him, Susan was nothing. Nothing but a piece of tail—and at the bottom of his agenda for the evening he had planned a good, lusty fuck. He took a deep breath, and bit by bit, piece by piece, the mask of charm fell back into place. When he turned, his smile was ingratiating.

"Ah, come on, honey, what's the matter?"

Dazed, her hurt eyes remained riveted on the single glass, the only visible evidence of the continual debasement she had suffered. He realized his transgression and rectified it. Picking up the tumbler, he carried the drink to her.

"Here you are, doll—bourbon and soda, just the way you like it," he said convincingly, offering her the glass. "You know, I guess maybe I'll make myself one, too."

As he had hoped, the possibility that she had mistaken his original intention threw her off balance, and she took the drink automatically. He hid a grin as he went back to the bar and mixed another. It was going to work out. Indulge her with a little talk, and lead her to it slowly. It wouldn't take all that long.

"You know, Susan, we didn't get much of a chance to talk tonight, and I've got an idea. There's a French restaurant in the valley that's intimate and quiet. No hustle or bustle. Great food. And we'd have a chance to just be together." His drink now in hand, he turned on the stereo and as he sat down in an armchair facing her, he continued. "It would be a nice evening. We'll have to do it soon."

She was still leaning on the arm of the couch.

"Come on, honey, you look uncomfortable. Drink your drink. Sit down and relax."

Never taking her eyes from his face, Susan slid from the arm to the cushion of the couch. Tense, back erect, she listened, but she was not at ease, and her bourbon remained untouched. He measured her mood. He knew enough to keep talking, but it was going to take more than words. He pretended to feel in his pockets for a cigarette—and finally shrugged. He shifted adroitly from one subject to another and, still talking, stood up. He had to be near her and add the element of touch, but he had to get there smoothly, naturally. She must be unaware of his deliberate maneuvering.

"I've been trying to cut down, but bourbon always makes me want to smoke. How about you?" Silently she shook her head. Still talking, he walked to a cigarette box on the table behind her, took one, but did not light it. Returning, he paused alongside her and lightly touched her hair.

"You know, the first thing that attracted me to you was this beautiful blond hair." Sitting on the arm of the couch, he gently rubbed the back of her neck. Encouraged that she did not object, he continued, his voice no longer conversational, but soft and intimate. "But it's not just your hair. There's something special about you. You've got class." His hand slipped over her shoulder. "You're one of the most beautiful girls I've ever met." His fingers traced along the deeply cut V-neckline of her dress, then slid inside and cupped her breast.

"Knock it off, Dave." She jerked away and stood up. This time the violent temper that was David Savage, the temper that he had been curbing, burst forth. He stood.

"Look, Susan," he spat at her, "cut out the coy crap. It bores me. You didn't waste any time saying yes to going out with me. What do you want—a six month courtship before you sacrifice your body? What in the hell did you expect when you came up here?"

Even though she recognized the truth of his accusation, it didn't excuse his crassness.

"I'll tell you what I thought—"

"Christ," he interruped, "if you ever had a thought in that stupid blond head of your ours, it would die of loneliness. Now cut out the comedy and get in the bedroom. That's what we're here for. You know it and I know it!"

"No way, Romeo," she snapped. "I want to go home."

He stared straight at her, his eyes glinting with anger. "You teasing little cunt! You want to go home—go find yourself a cab!" He had taken a few steps back toward the bar before Susan erupted.

"You bastard!" she hissed between her teeth. "You lousy bastard! What in the hell makes you so special— can you shit vanilla ice cream or something?"

He stopped and turned, livid. Susan was oblivious, her anger causing her voice to shrill.

"I've heard about you," she taunted. "You think you're so goddamned hot. You! Big deal! Well, I've got a bulletin for you. I haven't missed much. The girls in the hospital say you're the lousiest screw in town!!"

Without warning, but with tremendous force, he backhanded her across the right side of her face. The impact was so great it stunned her, and she stood teetering. The second blow—a vicious punch to her midsection—was unexpected and she sagged, crumpling to the floor, the back of her head striking the corner of the ornately carved coffee table. Savage stared down at her in white-hot fury for a long minute, then he strode past her to the bedroom on the opposite side of the apartment and entered, slamming the door so hard that the entire room shuddered.

Susan lay where she had fallen, waiting for her equilibrium to return. Her teeth had cut into her lips from the blow, and she tasted the warm blood in her mouth. Automatically she groped in her small bag for a tissue and held it to her lips. The side of her face throbbed painfully, and she could already feel the tightness of the swelling beginning. She stood up, swaying slightly, holding on until her balance returned.

Then she hurried out of the apartment.

Mary arrived about fifteen minutes early for her 11 P.M. to 7 A.M. shift, and the minute she got behind the Admitting Desk, she dialed Susan's home number. The girl had not returned by the time Mary left for the hospital but, after all, she reasoned, you could hardly expect her home by ten o'clock. No answer this time, but she'd keep trying.

She was just hanging up the phone when she saw Dr. Carrington enter. She glanced at the clock—ten till eleven. Doesn't he ever sleep, she wondered. Why fight it, she shrugged, and before Mike was halfway across the lobby, she pressed the button opposite his name.

Mike hummed softly. The past four hours had been pleasant, but not especially productive or stimulating. He had gotten to the County Medical Association meeting shortly after six thirty, socialized with some of the members over a drink, then had gone in to dinner with his group.

He was presently assigned to the Fee Complaint Committee, a body which concerned itself with persons who felt they had been charged too much for a medical service. When a letter was received by the Association, the facts were evaluated to determine if there appeared to be legitimate grounds for complaint. Then an administrative assistant sent a copy of the letter to the doctor involved and asked for an explanation. Most of the time, a quick reply was received, notifying the Association that the physician had settled the problem with his patient—another way of saying that the billing had been adjusted voluntarily to a more realistic figure. Occasionally a doctor would reply, defending his billing by pointing out unusual circumstances that justified it: a particularly difficult procedure, excessive demands on his time, unmentioned complications. At that point, both the complaining patient and the defending physician were asked by the Association to sign arbitration agreements. In other words, that they would both abide by the decision handed down by the Fee Complaint Committee. That accomplished, the Committee investigated all facets of the situation and openly discussed a solution at the monthly meeting, finally arriving at a decision—of which the doctor and patient were notified. It was a valuable but, unfortunately, not a widely known service to the community.

Tonight's meeting had been routine, and Mike felt he could have used the time to better advantage—like, for instance, being with Nedra. He was, however, a member of the organization and supported it wholeheartedly. It set standards of practice that benefited both patients and doctors.

But it had run on longer than he had anticipated, and he realized he had only ten minutes or so before Nedra would arrive.

He had called Dr. Phillip Veech earlier and had made arrangements to sign over his patients to him for the weekend, but Mike wanted to leave orders as far ahead as possible, to minimize any problems that Veech would be facing.

He got off the elevator on the seventh floor, where Selkins had been transferred to a private room, and picked up his chart. Pulse, urine output, temperature, blood pressure—all okay. Mike breathed a sigh of relief. Selkins, of all his patients, was in the most critical condition, and he appeared to be doing well, but he'd better be sure. He walked a short way down the hall and entered the room. He approached the bed quietly, the only illumination being the soft night light, but as he neared, Selkins turned. He was sedated but not asleep.

"Doc?" he groaned.

"Evening. How you doing?" Mike turned back to put on the overhead lights now that he knew the patient was awake.

"Hmmm, pretty good. I hurt . . . but it was worse before the shot." His speech was halting, but coherent.

"You're doing fine, Mr. Selkins. I just happened to be in the hospital and thought I'd look in on you." Mike took his pulse, then examined the dressings. They had been recently changed and were relatively dry. Just some blood-tinged fluid along the drains. No bile. Better than Mike had expected.

"Doc, this damned rubber thing," Selkins said, pointing to the Levine tube. "When do I get rid of it?"

"It's a safety valve, Mr. Selkins, and believe me, at this point it's better than vomiting. We'll take it out in a day or two. Just bear with it for a while."

Mike turned to leave and had almost reached the door before Selkins called him back.

"Doc, he mumbled, half asleep. "Wanted to ask you . . . am I doing okay down there?" he indicated the area below his waist and Mike knew that, like many patients, Selkins was haunted by the fear of a colostomy.

"You're fine," Mike hastened to reassure him. "Nothing was removed but a piece of your liver. In a few days, everything will be working like before."

Selkins nodded and closed his eyes.

Mike hurried to the eighth floor and shuffled through the stack of unread X-rays that had accumulated. He found the ones he had ordered for Aaron Metz and glared at them for several minutes, his eyes glued on the shadow readily apparent in the right lung. The right diaphragm was raised, indicating a paralysis of the phrenic nerve. The mass he observed was a tumor, almost certainly malignant and surely inoperable.

Damn, he thought as he angrily pulled the films down, that's it for poor Aaron.

Each time Mike encountered a situation such as this, he felt a personal affront, a sense of loss, of impotence—as though an enemy had challenged and defeated him. He could extend Aaron's time slightly with drugs and X-ray therapy, but in the end he'd lose. And Carrington didn't like to lose!

Mike was positive that he had correctly interpreted what he had seen, but he could take no chances. On his way to the fourth floor, he debated the diagnostic procedure to use to verify his analysis. He could, of course, take out a lymph node for pathological examination. But even though the operation was no big deal, he hated to put the old man through it. He elected, instead, to do an induced cough procedure, whereby sputum could be obtained and subjected to a Pap test, and when he reached the nurses' desk he wrote orders accordingly.

From there he went from floor to floor, one eye on the clock, checking charts and writing orders to cover the weekend.

Nedra glanced at the clock on her dashboard as she pulled into the parking lot across the street from the hospital. Five minutes to eleven, she noted with satisfaction. She'd timed it just right! She eased her car into a slot between two others, close to the adjoining building, and snapped off the car lights. Checking that the right door was locked, she swung out of the car and reached into the back seat to retrieve the small overnight bag she would need for the weekend. She sensed, more than heard, the rapid, stealthy footsteps behind her, and quickly straightened. Before she could turn, a burly arm hooked around her throat, eliminating any possibility of a scream. At the same time, she felt the violent attempt to wrench the purse from her hand. Instinctively she tightened her grip on the handbag and kicked backward with all her might. The soft deck shoes she wore contacted with something solid, and she heard a slight grunt as the arm about her neck loosened momentarily. Twisting away, she was able to half turn to face her attacker.

She saw the glint of light on metal only moments before she felt the sharp stabbing pain in her upper abdomen. She slumped against the car in utter surprise, and was hazily conscious that her purse was jerked from her numb fingers. She slid slowly down the fender to the ground and crumpled on her side. She lay for a moment, slightly annoyed that she had obviously fallen in a puddle—her sweater was wet. She made a giant effort to move where it was drier, but her muscles would not obey. Damn, she thought, I'm going to be late. And everything went black.

Most of the nurses parked in the well-lighted area adjoining the hospital, but the overflow was forced to park in the lot across the street.

A few minutes before eleven, Jamie, one of Marin Medical Center's Security Guards, made his way to the Admitting Desk in the main lobby. Although he was armed, it wasn't apparent, and except for the small patch on his shoulder, he could have been taken for a young, brawny, black college athlete in his gray slacks and blue blazer. He joked with Mary as he waited for the departing nurses to assemble so he could escort them across.

"Hey, Mary. Did you hear the story about this guy who went to heaven, and as soon as he was fitted with his wings and halo he was told to join all the others in the assembly room? So he went in and sat down, and it was just beautiful—flowers, birds singing, violins playing, all that jazz. And suddenly two huge bronze doors opened and this tall, imposing figure came through dressed in a green gown and mask. So this cat pokes his elbow in the ribs of the dude next to him and whispers, 'Who's that?' 'Oh, that's God,' the other answered. 'Sometimes he likes to play doctor.' "

Jamie laughed uproariously at his own joke, and

Mary chuckled appreciatively. That punch line reminds me, she thought, I'd better try Susan again.

By now, three nurses had joined the guard at the front desk, giggling, talking, discussing plans for the coming weekend.

"This everybody?" Jamie asked.

There was a chorus of replies of "guess so," "probably."

"Well," decided Jamie, "then let's go." He turned back to Mary, who was frowning with displeasure at the lack of response to the phone's tenth ring. "If anybody else shows up, have them wait. I'll be right back."

Still chattering, the group hurried across the intersection and entered the parking lot. The girls made for their respective cars as Jamie surveyed the lot with professional care. Everything quiet. Suddenly there was a gasp and a shriek from one of the girls. Jamie heard her whisper, "Oh, my God."

He hurried toward her. The other girls hesitated a moment and gathered at the spot where the first girl stood staring, her eyes riveted on the ground.

Jamie bent over the inert figure and groped for his flashlight. Its beam revealed a woman lying on the ground, a sticky splotch of blood on the front of her white pullover sweater. As his beam traveled to illuminate her face, a bubbly sigh escaped her lips. Jamie straightened.

"Wait here," he snapped. "And don't touch her. I'll get Doctor Melburn in Emergency." As he started away, his eyes glanced over the shadowy parking lot and back to the three nurses huddled around the figure on the ground.

"No," he said decisively, "I'd better stay." He indicated one of the older nurses, the most composed of the three. "Jacky, you go. Tell them to bring a stretcher."

Jacky nodded and ran back toward the hospital. He glanced at the girl on the ground. "And Jacky," he called after her, "You'd better tell them to hurry!"

The Emergency Room at eleven o'clock on a Friday night was jammed, as usual. Jacky flew through the crowded waiting room, past the clerk, and burst through the doors to where Jeff was bandaging the badly cut forearm of a man who had been involved in a barroom brawl.

In practically one motion, Jeff indicated that Betty should complete the bandaging, shouted to an orderly to bring a stretcher, and was halfway across the street before Jacky had finished.

As soon as they arrived, Jeff checked the victim for possible broken bones. Finding none, he helped Jamie and the orderly get the girl on the stretcher. Losing no time, they transported her across the street to the Emergency Room.

"Get out a Code Ten," Melburn snapped at Betty. As she picked up the phone to comply, Jeff and the orderly gently began cutting off the woman's clothes.

"Code Ten, Emergency Room . . . Code Ten, Emergency Room."

The voice coming over the speakers was deliberately casual and matter-of-fact, camouflaging the urgency of the announcement—making it seem routine to the ears of the hospitalized patients and the uninitiated.

Mike was still seated on a stool, writing orders. He rose hurriedly, automatically, then hesitated and glanced at the clock over the nurses' station. Nedra was already late and would probably be there any minute. She'd be upset if he got involved in anything that would spoil their plans.

A Code Ten was broadcast at least once a day in a hospital as large and as busy as Marin. Usually it was followed by a room number—occasionally, as in this case, by a department. It signaled for help with resuscitation. It meant that a patient was dying or was dead—dead in the sense that breathing or heart action had stopped. But even so, there was always a few minutes' leeway before the brain would die from oxygen lack and death would be really complete. Each hospital had its own nomenclature, but a Code Ten at Marin was a

101

red alert to everyone with any kind of medical skills to respond at a dead run.

Success depended on speed and manpower. A Code Ten at noon, for instance, when the hospital was teeming with doctors and specialists, resulted in a small army of skilled personnel pounding to the room. It was not unusual for two or three surgeons, several cardiologists and anesthesiologists, plus a horde of internists and nurses to appear within seconds. No one ignored the plea for help, and often so many specialists flew to offer aid that it boiled down to the fact that those who actually administered resuscitation techniques were the ones who were nearest and would run the fastest. The surplus stood by for a moment until they were certain they would not be needed, then dissipated to return to other duties.

But ten after eleven! At this late hour, Mike realized, he was probably the only staff surgeon in the hospital. Again he thought of Nedra's displeasure, but his indecision was short-lived. It would be immoral not to respond, and she would understand. He ran to the stairwell. Taking the steps three at a time, he consoled himself. Nine chances out of ten, it was a heart attack. It usually was . . . and that would require a specialist in cardiology to assume primary responsibility for the care of the patient if resuscitation were successful. Unless it was a case requiring general surgery, his chances of becoming the admitting doctor and being tied up half the night were less than 10 percent. But he could at least lend his services on a first-aid basis. It should only take a few minutes.

He could hear someone pounding down the stairs behind him, but he did not waste time to see who it was. He sprinted to the Emergency Room and reached it just in time to see Eva Niles, the nursing supervisor, rush in ahead of him.

Mike burst through the door and stood paralyzed, unbelieving. It couldn't be Nedra! It couldn't be . . . but it was!

Betty was struggling to insert a large-bore plastic IV

102

needle in Nedra's limp arm—struggling unsuccessfully because the veins has already collapsed. She tried again and again with desperate urgency, knowing that the victim's only chance hinged on the ability to get an IV into her—fast, and running wide open.

Eva Niles, who had entered just before Mike, hurried to get plasmanate and a saline solution to have ready the moment Betty was successful.

It had been Keith Johnson pounding down the steps behind Mike, and he entered the Emergency Room right on his heels. The resident surgeon plunged through the door and stopped, partially blocked by Carrington. Keith shot him a puzzled look and pushed past, grabbing a cut down tray. His first glance had relayed to him the difficulty Betty was having, and with one quick slash of a scalpel, he cut into Nedra's ankle, laying bare a large vein. Simultaneously, Betty stopped her fruitless efforts and hurried to the foot of the table, inserting the IV line in the ankle and hooking it up.

Eva quickly wrapped a blood-pressure cuff around the girl's arm while Jeff bent over her with a stethoscope, monitoring the heart beat.

Out of the corner of his eye, Dr. Melburn was aware of Mike, and began routinely filling him in. "Guard found her in the parking lot—she's practically bled out—stabbed in the upper adbomen, with a belly full of blood."

"No blood pressure at all," Eva reported.

"Heart beat's fast as hell . . . getting weaker all the time," Jeff noted. He straightened and backed off slightly as Betty hooked the victim up to the portable electrocardioscope. The undulating line was weak and erratic.

Mike still stood rooted to the spot, watching the familiar ministrations as if they were part of some strange, incredible nightmare.

Then, like a sleepwalker, deliberately willing the placement of one foot before the other, he approached Nedra. Gently withdrawing the sheet that covered her, he stared at the small, innocent-looking slit just to the left of the middle of her abdomen. A few drops of crimson still oozed slowly from the wound. He stared with horror at the distended belly that made her almost look pregnant. He refused to admit to himself the certainty that his parcticed eyes and trained mind diagnosed: the stab wound had caused a massive hemorrhage, perhaps even severed the aorta; the huge bulge was the accumulation of Nedra's life's blood.

Unbidden, his hand moved to Nedra's face and tenderly removed a smudge of dirt from her forehead. Her lids fluttered.

"Mike?" she whimpered, almost inaudibly.

Her head turned slightly to the side, facing him, and her lips formed the words "help me," but no sound escaped. Then the muscles of her face relaxed and were still.

"Get a board under her," Mike shouted to the orderly, and with maniacal energy placed his hands, one over the other, above Nedra's heart and began pumping rhythmically—furiously—his eyes glazed, unconscious of anyone around him. If I can get blood to her brain, he repeated to himself, over and over and over.

Jeff allowed himself only a moment of confusion and then quickly and expertly inserted an endotracheal tube. Basically he knew their efforts were futile, but Dr. Carrington was the senior doctor in the room, and all past training and conditioning dictated that he was not to be questioned. Gently, he raised the victim's eyelids. The pupils were fixed and fully dilated. He knew the battle was lost before it had really begun.

"She's dead," he announced ruefully. "You can squeeze that heart all night, but there's no blood in there to pump. She's bled to death."

Mike continued, unhearing—up, down, up, down— as if the demons of hell were prodding him. The others in the Emergency Room glanced about uncomfortably, unwilling to meet one another's eyes.

"Doctor Carrington . . . she's dead!" Jeff said softly but sharply.

Mike straightened and stood staring at the inert form,

then moved to the electrocardioscope. It registered only a flat, unwavering line. The perspiration that ran down his face mingled with the tears streaming from his eyes. He started to take a step toward her, caught himself, and stopped. He stared at Nedra for a long, last minute. Then, without a word, he walked slowly from the room, the tears still rolling down his cheeks.

Chapter II

... saturday

Mary was an emotional wreck as she ran up the three flights of stairs to Susan's apartment. She had tried phoning intermittently throughout her entire shift, trying one last time before she left, a little past 7 A.M. She had no way of knowing that, from midnight on, Susan had been at home, staring at the phone morosely, deliberately letting it ring. She knew it would be David Savage or Mary, and she had no inclination to talk to either.

Mary knocked at the door sharply, waited, and rapped again. She was just about to give up when the door was cracked open.

"My Lord, Susan," she chattered, giving vent to the vast relief she felt, "I've nearly been out of my mind. Why didn't you answer the phone? Did you just get home? Susan? Susan, what's the matter? Are you all right?"

"I'm fine. Just leave me alone. Maybe I'll come down later." The girl's words were thick and she spoke with difficulty.

"Susan, let me in!"

The door opened a little wider, and Mary pushed her way inside. She gasped at what she saw.

The right side of Susan's face was blue and grossly swollen, the skin stretched taut and shiny over the blood clots beneath it. Her right eye was spongy, almost shut,

106

and ringed by a huge black bruise, her lower lip was dry and cracked, puffed out to twice its normal size. As Mary stared horrified, Susan raised the ice bag she held in her hand and placed it gingerly on her cheek bone. Without another word, the young girl walked across the room and lay on the sofa. Mary followed her in, shutting the door behind her. She was seething.

"I guess I don't have to ask what happened? Savage?"

Susan nodded. "Super doctor strikes again."

"The time has come," announced Mary, "to pull the plug on our slugging gynecologist." It was a struggle for her to maintain the flip and airy tone, but she knew it was her best bet for communicating with Susan. Actually, she wanted to cradle the girl in her arms. "The first thing Monday . . ."

Susan sat up, grimacing at the effort. It was impossible for her to hide the pain she felt. "Mary," she hissed between her teeth, "for once I want you to mind your own business. Somebody, some day, will lead the crusade to get David Savage—but it's not going to be me!"

Wide-eyed, Mary started to protest, her righteous indignation causing her to sputter. Susan cut her off, spacing her explanation evenly, as one might instruct a slow-witted child.

"Look. So maybe I'm dead right. And that son of a bitch Savage is dead wrong. But if I make trouble for him—any kind of trouble—no doctor in this town will come within a mile of me, much less ask for a date. I don't want anybody to know about this. Do you understand?" Mary was silent. "*Do* you?" Reluctantly, Mary nodded. Susan sighed with relief and for the first time realized the comfort derived from her friend's presence. "Please, Mary, stay with me for a while. Would you put some more ice in this for me?"

She extended the ice pack, and Mary moved toward her to take it. Up close, the bruises looked more serious, the face more misshapen, than she had originally estimated.

"Susan, I think you should see a doctor—I really

do." Mary went to the refrigerator and removed an ice tray. Susan grunted from the couch.

"Just where will I find a doctor on a Saturday morning?"

"I could call Doctor Merrick," Mary suggested, returning with the replenished compress. "He'll be at the hospital now, making rounds."

Susan sat up violently. "Mary, didn't you hear a single thing I said?"

"Doctor Merrick and I are old friends," Mary countered defensively. "I was in Admitting when he first started at Marin. He was young and bright and gracious—and I liked him. I made sure his patients got upstairs faster, that they didn't have to wait, that they were called first. And that they got the best rooms. I still do. And he knows it. He'll be anxious to return the favor. Besides, Susan, you work at Marin. You're a nurse. Doctors take special care of their own. You know that. You can trust him." She pressed her case. "We could make up some story. He wouldn't have to know the truth." She shot a concerned glance at the younger girl. "I really think you should see him. What if something's broken?"

She saw the quick flash of panic in the girl's eyes as she suddenly got up, went to the bathroom and peered into the mirror for some moments. Mary took advantage of Susan's fear.

"Let me call him. I can handle it."

Susan walked slowly back into the room. After eight hours of ice packs, her face did not seem improved. If anything, the pain and discoloration were worse. Begrudgingly, she nodded. Before she could change her mind, Mary picked up the phone and dialed Marin Medical Center. Dr. Merrick was soon on the line.

"Doctor Merrick, this is Mary McCullough from Admitting. I need a favor."

"Morning, Mary," Merrick said warmly. "What can I do for you?"

"You know Susan Thomas, doctor, she works with me in Admitting. Well, we're close personal friends . . .

have been for a long time. Anyway, last night she had an accident—" Mary momentarily hesitated, the lie coming hard for her, "and took a fall. Her face is pretty badly bruised, and I'm afraid something might be broken. I wonder if you could take a look at it?"

"Sure thing, I'll be happy to see her," Merrick replied. "Why don't you come now? I'll meet you in Emergency."

"Doctor," Mary floundered, feeling like a fool. She took a deep breath and blurted out the words. "It sounds silly, but Susan is very embarrassed with the way she looks—the bruises and all—and she'd rather not run into anyone she knows."

There was a moment of silence on the other end of the phone. "Well, let's see," Merrick said smoothly, "I've about finished rounds and I was going across the street to catch up on some paper work. Why don't I meet you at the office. There's no one there today and—"

"Oh, thank you, doctor. That would be fine," Mary acknowledged hurriedly. "We'll see you in about half an hour."

During the short ride downtown, Mary felt nothing but sympathy for Susan, who sat hunched in the car, obviously miserable and in pain. She had draped a gauzy scarf about her hair and neck in a valiant but futile effort to hide her bruised features.

Joseph Merrick was waiting in his office when Mary and Susan arrived, and he greeted the two girls cordially and informally.

"How about some coffee? It's instant, and I can't guarantee it . . . made it myself." He instinctively felt minutes allowed for pleasantries might relax her and, in the long run, make his examination easier.

As they sipped the coffee, Merrick and Mary indulged in a few tidbits of hospital gossip. Susan sat silently, not joining in the conversation, staring at her untouched coffee. Finally, he looked at her with a smile.

"Okay if I take a look?"

She nodded and reluctantly removed the scarf. Gently he tilted her face, noting the bruises, the completely closed and swollen eye, the cracked lip. As he carefully felt the areas involved, he questioned her.

"Do you have a headache?"

"No," Susan replied.

"Double vision?"

"No."

"I know it hurts, but can you open your right eye for me?"

Merrick watched intently as Susan tried—but nothing happened. "I can't," Susan finally admitted.

"Okay," Merrick said cheerfully, dismissing its importance. He was careful not to let the concern he felt register in his voice, but he had been quick to notice that each time Susan replied to his questions, only the left side of her mouth had moved. Granted, the right side was puffed and sore, but it would not completely account for her manner of speaking.

"I think we'd better get some X-rays," he said, matter-of-factly. He saw the quick glance Susan flicked at Mary and continued as he filled out the requisition. "At this time of the morning, it ought to be pretty deserted over there—it being Saturday and all—but I'll give them a call to make sure they take you right away. I know you don't feel like waiting." He handed the yellow form to Susan. "Just give this to them, and I'll be over. I'll see you there as soon as the films are ready."

"Thanks again, Doctor Merrick," Mary said softly. "You know I appreciate it." Susan said nothing.

Susan's silence continued as she and Mary crossed the street, entered Marin Medical Center, and proceeded to the eighth floor. Natalie, an old friend of Mary's, was working X-ray reception, and it was obvious that Dr. Merrick had called, for Susan was immediately whisked to a waiting X-ray cubicle. Mary chatted with Natalie for a few minutes and then went to the waiting room. She felt a surge of gratitude at Dr. Merrick's consideration and tactfulness when she realized they were permitting Susan to wait in the privacy of the X-ray room, away from any curious eyes.

110

A short time later she saw Merrick stride down the halls and head for the chief radiologist's office. It pays to have friends in high places, she thought.

Unlike Carrington, Merrick used his position as chief of surgery and the status it entailed to relieve himself of the necessity of dealing with underlings. He didn't bother with the X-ray technician. He confidently entered Dr. Reichner's office and sat down.

"Morning, Eric. How's it going?"

Dr. Reichner nodded pleasantly and turned his chair, giving Merrick the benefit of his full attention.

"We have a Susan Thomas who works in Admitting. I've just ordered facial and skull X-rays on her. Are they up yet?"

Reichner picked up the phone, punched the button for the Light Room and relayed the inquiry.

"Just one," the voice on the other end reported.

"Would you bring them here, please," Reichner ordered and hung up the phone. As the two men waited, Reichner removed a pack of cigarettes from his desk, put one between his lips and extended the pack to Merrick, who declined. The radiologist lit the cigarette, inhaled and cleared his throat. Small talk did not come easy to Merrick, but he tried.

"Well, Eric, how's the golf game? Still playing every week?"

Reichner stared ruefully at the smoke spiraling from his cigarette and then at the littered desk piled high with papers.

"Nowadays the only exercise I get is coughing."

Both men were still chuckling as the assistant brought in the folder of films. They stood in front of the view box as Reichner slipped the negatives into it and focused his attention on the facial X-rays.

"Broken zygoma—no doubt about that." His fingers traced an obvious fracture of the right cheek bone. He peered at the skull X-rays and shrugged. There was no apparent abnormality, but both doctors knew that because of the many overlapping bones, skull fractures were often indiscernible, especially those at the base.

111

Merrick stood looking at the skull films for some moments after Reichner sat down.

"When I examined her," he said slowly, still staring, "it was hard to tell with all the swelling in her face, but I think she has some seventh nerve paralysis. If it's a basal skull fracture, or the temporal bone. . . . Well," he said decisively, "I'll get a plastic surgeon down here right away—and just to play it safe, a neurosurgeon, too."

Reichner nodded. "Good idea. Nice seeing you, Joe."

Merrick made a quick phone call to Admitting from the reception desk, then walked down the hall to the room where Susan was waiting, mentally rehearsing the kindest way of imparting his diagnosis. She was a beautiful girl—of that he was well aware—and obviously vain. He thought of the old refrain, "Her face is her fortune." But the game playing was over. He had to tell her the truth—part of it, at any rate—and he had to enlist her cooperation.

She sat quietly in the room, the scarf once again carefully placed, partially concealing her face. As he perched on the corner of the table, he noticed that she shifted slightly so the undamaged portion of her features was in his line of vision.

"Susan," he said gently, "the X-rays show a fracture of your cheek bone." He winced at the panic she displayed and hurried on. "Now you're a nurse, and you know that a plastic surgeon can repair it. It's done every day. I'll get you the best there is, you can be sure of that. Just trust me. In the meantime, I've already arranged for a private room. I knew you'd prefer being alone. Now just relax and leave everything to me. As soon as you're settled I'll be up to see you."

He took Susan's cold, clammy hand in his own. Like Cerberus, the three-headed dog of Greek mythology who guarded the entrance to Hades, Merrick was fanatically serious about his job of screening the morals and actions of all connected with Marin. And like the legendary hound, his nose was attuned to sniff out mysteries, half-truths, intrigues. The scent was strong. He knew Mary well, well enough to suspect the uneasiness she had displayed. Susan's desire for secrecy concerning her injury alerted his curiosity even more. The crusading zeal which pervaded his personality made further questioning imperative. He simply had to know the truth.

"Susan, just one thing. Over the phone, Mary told me you fell. From the position of that break, it just couldn't have happened that way. Now I don't want to pry, but for your own good I have to know how it occurred."

That was an out-and-out lie, and he knew it. From a treatment point of view, how it happened made no difference. Susan lowered her head for a moment and sighed.

"All right, Doctor Merrick. The truth is . . . last night I had some friends in. A couple of the fellows brought bottles and we had a few drinks. After they left, I was straightening up. I leaned over to put some glasses away in this little cupboard under the sink and, well, I got kind of dizzy." She forced a giggle. "I'm really not used to drinking, and . . . well, I sort of lost my balance, and there was this drawer that I hadn't shut, and I banged my face against the corner. I really felt dumb, and, anyway, I asked Mary not to let on what happened. You know how the nurses here exaggerate everything. They'd turn a few drinks into 'Susan's Lost Weekend,' and being new at the hospital and all—"

Merrick patted Susan's shoulder sympathetically and mercifully cut off her rambling. "I wouldn't worry about it, my dear," he chuckled. "All of us have one too many once in a while."

Dr. Merrick was an uncommonly curious man, but Susan Thomas was an uncommonly good actress.

An orderly appeared at the door.

"Will you take Miss Thomas to 411?" Merrick instructed. Then he turned back to Susan. "I'll fill Mary in so she won't worry, and she'll probably be back to see you this evening. Is there anything you want her to bring?"

Susan shook her head before being wheeled down the hall to her room. Merrick searched out Mary. Her anxiety and concern were apparent.

"It was a good thing you insisted that she come in, Mary," he complimented her. "She has a broken zygoma, and I'll make arrangements for a plastic surgeon to get on it immediately." He decided not to mention the paralysis problem until he was sure. "She's in room 411, and I told her you'd be back tonight. She said she didn't need anything, but you might throw a toothbrush and a robe or something together." The woman nodded with mixed feelings. She was appalled at Susan's injury but relieved that she was in Merrick's good hands. "Oh, and Mary," the doctor said kindly, "she told me the truth about how it happened."

"I'm glad," Mary sighed. "She made me promise not to. You know, I begged her not to go out with Doctor Savage."

Merrick kept his face expressionless, hiding the quick stab of excitement. What did Savage have to do with this?

"Where did it happen," he asked casually, deliberately implying full knowledge of the situation.

"Well, she didn't say," Mary admitted, "but I guess in Savage's apartment. I'm sure he wouldn't hit her in public!"

Merrick rode down on the elevator with Mary as far as the fourth floor, where he wrote routine orders to cover necessary tests and medication for Susan. From there, he proceeded to an unoccupied office on the first floor. He sat at the desk, unconsciously humming a discordant tune. Had words been put to that melody, they would have been: "Okay, David Savage, I've got you now, you son of a bitch." He pulled the phone toward him and contemplated it. His mind was racing. His first call was to the nursing station on the fourth floor.

"I've just admitted a Susan Thomas—Room 411.

Withhold all sedatives until you hear from me!" he snapped.

"Yes, doctor," the nurse responded automatically. "Uh, doctor . . . Miss Thomas is extremely nervous and upset, and seems to be in considerable pain. She's been crying since she got here, and—"

"You *do* understand my order, Mrs. Rosen?" Merrick asked pointedly.

"Yes, doctor."

He'd relieve Susan's emotional and physical suffering in due time, Merrick thought. For the moment, the fact that she was tense and high-strung was an advantage he did not care to relinquish.

He turned his attention to the next order of business, mentally running down the list of top plastic surgeons. Dr. Raymond Augustine immediately came to mind, but Merrick quickly discarded the idea. Dr. Augustine was an excellent young surgeon whose reputation had recently been enhanced by several breakthroughs he had contributed to the field of plastic surgery. His results were outstanding. But he had become too successful too fast, due to his unusual ability and medical journal recognition and publicity, and Dr. Merrick personally resented that success. He optioned instead for Dr. Paul Seaton, equally good, less flashy, and the brother of a general practitioner who had recently, and for the first time, referred a surgical case to Merrick. Bread cast upon waters often returned buttered, Merrick reminded himself. He called Seaton, filled him in on the medical details, and elicited his promise to see Susan early in the afternoon.

The selection of a neurosurgeon was no problem. Dr. Whitney Palmer was the best—and, of course, was also chief of staff at Marin Medical Center. He couldn't do better than that, for Susan or for himself. He had no trouble reaching Palmer, and again was gratified that the doctor could be at the hospital within a couple of hours. He was careful to make no mention of Savage's involvement to either Seaton or Palmer.

115

Before heading back to the fourth floor to see his patient, Merrick allowed himself the luxury of sitting for a few moments, doing absolutely nothing except congratulating himself on a good morning's work.

Susan lay in the hospital bed, looking battered and vulnerable in the harsh light. Her hands nervously twisted a Kleenex and Merrick gently extricated the shredded tissue from her hands and offered her a fresh one.

"Everything's set, Susan," he announced cheerfully. "Doctor Seaton, the plastic surgeon, will be in to see you right after lunch. And I've asked Doctor Palmer to look in on you, too."

"Doctor Palmer? . . . Doctor Whitney Palmer, the neurosurgeon?" Susan gasped apprehensively.

"Just a precaution," Merrick assured her soothingly. "Now, Susan," he said, his voice noticeably sharper, "let's start being honest. You know, hospital records are official documents, and it's very unwise to lie. Tell me, after Savage hit you, did you fall and bump your head?" He watched intently for her reaction.

"Savage?" the girl mumbled defensively. "What's he got to do with this?"

"Come on, Susan, knock it off. Tell me about Savage."

"I don't know what you're talking about."

"All right, I'll give it to you straight," snapped Merrick. He continued with measured, intentional cruelty. "You've got big trouble, and you're going to need help. And you're going to need a friend. The cheek bone's no big deal. That can be fixed. But I think Doctor Palmer is going to confirm that you have seventh nerve damage. You're a nurse, you know it could mean facial paralysis—maybe temporary, but maybe permanent." He deliberately disregarded the horror and mounting fear her expression mirrored. "You're in a private room— private rooms are expensive. It won't be fully covered by your insurance. I can force Savage to help you financially."

Susan was shaking her head, willing herself not to listen. Merrick suddenly softened his tone. "No one has to know, Susan," he said quietly. "Just you and me. I'll take care of everything. Trust me. Just be honest. It's important. David Savage hit you, didn't he?"

She stared at him, cornered, utterly frightened. Slowly, as if in a trance, she finally nodded her head. Merrick felt light-headed with elation.

"Why did he hit you, Susan? Tell me."

"He propositioned me . . . I refused . . . we had an argument."

"And he hit you. Right?" Merrick pressed.

Susan nodded.

"Say it, Susan, say it. Say 'David Savage hit me'!" Merrick insisted.

"David Savage hit me," Susan recited, as if by rote.

As he turned to leave, her shuddering, convulsive sobs filled the room. Merrick did not look around. He went to the nursing desk.

"Mrs. Rosen," he said quietly, "I believe Miss Thomas is slightly hysterical. You'd better get in there. I think 10 mg of Valium will do the trick." And he slowly wrote the necessary order.

Chapter III

... monday

On Monday morning, Dr. Michael Carrington crossed the lobby of Marin Medical Center with leaden feet. He inserted a coin and removed the newspaper, then stood for a moment, glancing at the front page. A brief follow-up story occupied the lower right-hand corner. "Artist's Assailant Still at Large," the headline proclaimed. "Body of Nedra Scott to be Sent East for Burial." Mike didn't remember much of the past weekend—only that he never felt more alone in his whole life. It was hard to pick up the strings of his normal routine, but he had patients who were depending on him. Somehow he would get through the day. But he missed her—God, he missed her!

He headed for the seventh floor and picked up Selkins' chart. A nurse had clipped a note to it: "Patient very distraught and nervous, needs sedative." Well, he thought, the same applies to the patient's doctor. Straightening his shoulders, he headed for the room.

Mike could smell trouble almost before he pushed through the door. Selkins did not look at him as he entered. The man was concentrating all his efforts on picking at the bedclothes, his hands unceasingly involved in plucking some imaginary flotsam from the blankets.

"How are you this morning, Mr. Selkins?" Mike asked.

"I'd be a whole lot better if you'd get them out of here," Selkins replied cryptically.

"Who is 'them'?"

"All these strange people who keep coming in and out," Selkins said darkly. "One even had a monkey with him—dirty, filthy creatures. I can't stand them."

Mike slumped slightly and leaned against the door. Oh, shit, he thought, that's all I need this morning. A classic case of delirium tremens. Well, he'd been warned that George had a drinking problem, but he hadn't really expected this. He stood for a moment, indulging in a mental argument. Shall I give him a sedative, he debated, or do I give him what he wants? He suddenly shrugged. This was no time to be a reformer. Let Mr. George Selkins battle his alcoholism all by himself when he was healed and home. The inevitable hallucinating, the abusiveness to everyone around him, and especially the thrashing about which would result by withholding alcohol at this stage could be harmful in light of Selkins' recent surgery. Complications at this point were something that Mike could do without.

"Get a bottle of five percent alcohol," Mike instructed the nurse behind the desk, "and hang it up to run 100cc an hour. I'll be back to see how our friend Selkins is doing in a little while." He wrote the covering order.

On the fourth floor, he thumbed through the chart on Aaron Metz and wasn't surprised that the sputum test results weren't there. After all, it was Monday morning. He took the precaution of turning to the crossword puzzle before he even picked up the phone, dialed the laboratory and asked for pathology.

"This is Doctor Carrington. Do you have the Pap smears on Aaron Metz?"

"What was the source of material?" the voice queried.

"Sputum."

"Just a minute, doctor . . . hold on."

Mike concentrated on the crossword puzzle. One across . . . "choose" . . . six letters. He filled in the word: S-E-L-E-C-T. Now, one down . . . "penetrate or pierce" . . . four letters. His fingers shook slightly as he penned in the letters: S-T-A-B. Suddenly he folded the paper and pushed it aside. Pathology came back on the phone.

"The slides are here, but the doctor hasn't read them yet."

"Well, would you show them to him?" Mike asked politely.

"Glad to. Can we have him call you back?"

"I'll come down," Mike informed her. "I'd like to see them, too."

Carrington took the elevator to the laboratory floor and entered the pathologist's office. Balding and middle-aged, his shoulders permanently stooped, Dr. Dorfmann had an owlish look. Hunched over his microscope, he barely glanced up as Mike entered.

"These Pap smears on your Mr. Metz are about as positive as they can get," he said quickly. "There are great big clumps of malignant cells that leave no doubt about the diagnosis at all. This is squamous cancer. You want to look?"

Mike nodded and Dorfmann moved aside. Under the highpowered magnification, Carrington could see the clusters of large, flat cells with oversized, irregular, deeply stained nuclei. This confirmed his diagnosis, and the X-rays indicated that the tumor was beyond the help of a surgeon.

Carrington pondered the situation. Aaron Metz was a dead man, but his death could be delayed by X-ray treatments and one of the most important break-throughs in treating cancer, chemotherapy. Basically it involved dosing the patient with fancy drugs which would poison all the body's cells, but since cancer cells were more vulnerable, they could be destroyed—or at least their growth retarded—while the normal tissues would recover from the insult. Dr. Malcolm MacPherson, Mike knew, was probably the most skillful chemotherapist in the Los Angeles area, and the two men had worked together on previous cases. As soon as he and MacPherson got together, they'd talk to Dr. Reichner about X-ray treatments as well. Mike's hand was reaching for the phone to call MacPherson when he heard the page.

"Doctor Carrington. Doctor Michael Carrington."

He identified himself, and a feminine voice came on the line. "Doctor Carrington? This is Edith Frankel, Aaron Metz' daughter. How is he?"

The hardest thing about the career Mike had chosen for himself entailed the breaking of bad news to patients or their families. He always bled a little. Once the family had been told and it was necessary to disclose a hopeless prognostication directly to a hospitalized patient, Mike merely waited. When the fussing started, when the sophisticated and unexpected treatments were begun, invariably the patient sensed something wrong and asked him the key question. By the time it was put into words, somehow that patient had already half accepted and was partially reconciled to the frightening confirmation of his fears. In the case of relatives, he made it a policy never to discuss it by phone. Carrington suggested a personal meeting and again, in the interim preceding the conference, found that the family had prepared themselves for the worst.

"It's a fairly complicated situation, Mrs. Frankel," Mike countered smoothly, "and one that I think we should sit down and talk about."

"Doctor, I really don't have time to come down there right now. How is Papa?"

"I'd be happy to meet you in my office this afternoon," Mike suggested, ignoring the direct question.

"Look," Mrs. Frankel said testily, "I'm probably going to be busy all day. Do you know what's wrong with Papa or don't you?"

"Yes," admitted Mike. "We have a diagnosis."

"Well . . . what is it?"

It's not going to work this time, Mike realized. He sighed. He had no choice. "Your father's lung X-ray shows a shadow that looks pretty ominous. And I've just been reviewing some slides of his sputum with our

121

pathologist. There's no doubt that he has lung cancer, Mrs. Frankel. And not only that, from the X-rays, we can see that it's not one that can be benefited by surgery."

There was a gasp at the other end of the line as the implication of his words registered. "My God, doctor, he's been working every day! He's always been so healthy. He's never had a sick day in his life! You're not telling me that my father is going to die?"

"What I'm telling you," Mike said patiently, "is that he has a bad problem, but there is a great deal that can be done for him."

"Like what, doctor?" Mrs. Frankel persisted.

"Like X-ray therapy. And certain drugs which are available and will make the tumor regress."

"The drugs . . . will they cure him? Will he be all right?"

"No," admitted Mike wearily, "they won't cure him. But he'll probably live longer, Mrs. Frankel. Oh, your father will have some nausea during the treatments, but we can control that. And then we can reasonably expect him to live a normal, productive life for a while."

"For a while," she repeated slowly. "How long is 'for a while'?"

"That's hard to say," Mike answered guardedly.

"Well, *about* how long?"

"You have to realize that these treatments work differently on each person, and differently on each tumor. Some people can be benefited for as long as a year; others, only for a couple of months."

"That's all? That's all the time he has?" she said with disbelief. "He's dying?"

"I'm sorry, Mrs. Frankel," Mike said gently. "We'll do what we can, but eventually the tumor will cause his death. But I'll have the daily treatments started. And—"

"No," Mrs. Frankel said slowly. "No, I just can't see putting Papa through all that. Especially when you say it might be only a couple of months."

"But it also might be a year," Mike pointed out.

"There's really no way to predict, believe me. We just have to do our best by him."

Mike believed the ensuing silence was caused by Mrs. Frankel's attempt to digest the information he had imparted. It was not precisely true. Once Edith had gotten over the initial shock of the unexpected news concerning her father, her mind had been racing. She and her father had never been particularly close. Not that there was animosity between them, but once her mother had died and Edith had married, the filial responsibilities had ebbed to an occasional phone call, a birthday card, and a Christmas gift. Aaron had his life; Edith had hers. She wasn't particularly proud of having a waiter for a father. Aaron took great pride in his personal and financial independence, occasionally mentioning that he had managed, by hard work and frugality, to accumulate over sixty thousand dollars from his wages and tips. Edith felt her face flush with guilt at the thought, but she and her husband, Ed, had been counting on that money. The news of her father's unexpected affliction pained her, but the thought that his estate might be decimated by useless medical treatments hurt her almost as much. When she finally spoke, her tone was coldly decisive.

"You are not to start that therapy, doctor."

Mike was slightly taken aback. In his many years as a surgeon, he had been accustomed to expect odd and offbeat reactions. When faced with bad news, some people laughed as an outlet for their emotions . . . some cried . . . some were silent . . . some had a morbid desire to discuss every detail . . . some refused to accept the inevitable . . . some blamed and damned God. But Edith Frankel's reaction was strange, at best.

"Why don't you want it done?" Mike asked curiously.

"Papa always said he didn't want to be a burden to anyone," Edith said piously. "If he said it once, he said it a hundred times. 'I don't want to be a burden.' "

"Perhaps I haven't explained this well," Carrington

123

suggested. "Once your father has completed the treatments, he'll probably be able to live a fairly normal life. Toward the end, there'll be weakness and debility, but at that time he'll be hospitalized and—"

"No treatments! Do you understand?" Edith interrupted icily. "If there was a chance, it would be different. Papa belongs to me. He's mine, not yours! He's going to die—and I want him to die with dignity!"

"Whether or not we start therapy is his choice—not yours," Mike snapped. He had sensed the insincerity and was seething.

"We'll see, doctor," Edith Frankel said quietly. "We'll see." The gentle click as she hung up the phone terminated the argument.

You bet we'll see, Mike thought grimly. He was puzzled by Mrs. Frankel's unstated motives in demanding that medical treatment be withheld—but it didn't matter. He was fond of Aaron, but more than that, death to Mike was an opponent to be held at arm's length, by fair means or foul, until the last possible moment, until every glimmer of hope was snuffed out.

For many years, he had secretly counted himself among the small group of medical heretics who endorsed euthanasia in certain isolated instances. Mike found it sickening to prolong what he considered quasi-life when a patient's brain was gone, to keep a pain-wracked shell of a body alive by every artificial means that science could devise when there was absolutely no hope. The accumulation of huge medical bills which would burden the survivors for the rest of their lives simply to sustain the functioning for months, even years, of a vegetable that had once been a human being was, to him, obscene. The growing popularity of "living wills" whereby individuals expressly forbade extended artificial means to prolong their lives was proof of the public's growing awareness. But the legal implications as it applied to physicians were still dim. As yet, few doctors were willing to become the instrument of death, regardless of how blessed that death might be.

But when a patient, even though terminal, was comparatively pain-free and retained the capacity for enjoying the remaining time alloted, Mike viewed withholding treatment as tantamount to murder. He could not save Aaron's life. He could prolong it and exert every effort to assure his patient's comfort and happiness to the best of his considerable knowledge and ability. That was what being a doctor was all about. In such cases, he was like a Knight Templar, battling every dragon that threatened his patient's well-being. If Edith Frankel elected to become one of the fire-snorting adversaries, so be it!

After calling Dr. MacPherson with the request for the specialist to see Aaron, Mike headed for the old man's room. In the corridor, a few feet from the door, he could hear the television and the chortles of amusement. Mike entered and stood a moment. Aaron's eyes were glued to the screen, a wide grin lighting his face, as he watched the antics of Laurel and Hardy in an old movie rerun. He glanced up at Mike and immediately turned the volume low.

"Good morning," he said cheerfully. He nodded toward the screen. "Those are two funny fellows. You know, I haven't enjoyed myself so much in a long time."

"How are you feeling this morning?"

"Oh, a little weak, maybe, but otherwise hunky-dory. A little girl in pink brought this to me this morning." He indicated the book propped open across his knees. It was one of the racier novels by a popular author. "Doctor!—the things they write about nowadays!" he said in a shocked whisper. "But it's good . . . it's good!" he hastened to add.

Mike grinned.

"You know, Doctor Carrington," Aaron said softly. "For the past fifty years I've just been sleeping and working, working and sleeping. Thanksgiving, Christmas—all the times other people spent with their families, when everybody else was enjoying themselves, I was working. So who's complaining? People have to eat. But you know what happened this morning? Aaron

Metz retired! I've got a little apartment down in Venice—nothing grand, mind you, but I've fixed it up nice. And what's an old man all alone need with a bigger place? But I've got a little money, doctor, and I'm going to enjoy it. Maybe go to the ballgame, see a play occasionally, eat out and for a change let someone serve me!" He held up his hand as if somebody might try to stop him. "I've made up my mind."

Mike smiled. "I think that's a great idea, Mr. Metz."

"So . . . doctor . . ." The old man gazed at him quizzically.

"We've pin-pointed your problem," Mike said quietly. "A lung tumor—and Doctor MacPherson is going to stop in this morning to see you. Then we'll talk about it."

Through experience, Mike had found it more satisfactory to impart bleak information a little at a time, to let it sink in gradually. As he left the room, Aaron waved at him and immediately turned up the audio on the television set.

"Doctor Carrington. Doctor Michael Carrington."

The page intruded again, and Mike went to the phone.

"Mike? Mike Carrington?"

Mike tried to place the girl's voice. It was remotely familiar. Or was it? He couldn't be sure.

"Yes, this is Doctor Carrington."

"Mike! Gosh, it's good to hear your voice. This is Jeannie . . . Jeannie Brinker! Do you remember me?"

"Jeannie!" Mike whooped. "Where in the world are you? Are you in Los Angeles? What are you doing here? Lord, it's been a long time!"

"I've been in L.A. about three months now."

"Well, why haven't you called, for goodness sake? My office number is listed."

"Oh, you know," Jeannie chuckled. "Small-town girl and famous, bigtime surgeon. I wasn't even sure you'd remember me."

Remember her? Almost everybody had a Jeannie

Brinker in their lives, thought Mike. The Brinker and Carrington families had been next-door neighbors for years. The Brinkers' brood of five kids and Mike and his brother had all played together from cribs on. They had gone to the same school, the same summer camps, had occasionally double-dated, and had even kept in touch all through college. Of all the Brinker kids, Jeannie had always been Mike's favorite. Even though she was about five years younger, the two had regularly gone to movies together, bowled, swam, sipped Cokes, talked, shared confidences. There had never been a romantic attachment between them, but they had thoroughly enjoyed each other's company. What Mike most remembered about Jeannie was her irreverent and unpredictable sense of humor, her bubbling good nature, and most of all, the weird magnetism about her that seemed to attract the unusual, the humorous, the unbelievable. Things seemed to happen to Jeannie that just didn't happen to anyone else.

"What are you doing here in Los Angeles?" asked Mike.

"Guess what? I got married. About three months ago. Back East. Do you believe that? Isn't it a hoot? You can imagine what the small-town cats had to say about it. Do you remember Imogene . . . Imogene Corman? She met me on the street. 'What does a thirty-seven-year-old bride wear?' she asked me. 'White? . . . or elastic stockings?' "

Mike chuckled. "So who's the lucky man?"

"Johnny—I'm Mrs. Johnny Mendosa," Jeannie bubbled. "He's Spanish, Mike. And you'd never guess where I met him. Would you believe . . . Spain? Well, I did. I was on vacation. I had taken this dumb tour . . . and we were in Cordoba, this whole group of us, and everybody went to the bullfights. Well, the only way I was about to watch something like *that* was if I could talk them into giving the bull a sword, too. So I wandered away from the group. How was I to know the tour was going to leave for Madrid directly from the bullfights? Anyway, they did. And I was stranded in

Cordoba without any luggage . . . and the hotel had given up my room . . . and I couldn't get a ticket out to anywhere . . . and I couldn't find my traveler's checks. Then I noticed this man in the lobby . . . just watching me and smirking like you used to do when I did something really dumb and got into trouble. So he asked me how he could help, and could he maybe buy me a drink. Normally, I would have said no, but I thought, What the hell, what else can happen?" She suddenly stopped, genuinely embarrassed. "Oh, Mike, I'll bet you're busy. First I have the nerve to call you at the hospital, and then I go off chattering like a sixteen-year-old. I'll bet you standing up to you're armpits in somebody's open incision."

Mike laughed out loud for the first time in several days. She hadn't changed a bit. "Don't stop, Jeannie. Believe me, I'm not busy. Just go on and tell me the rest."

"You sure? Okay . . . well, where was I? Oh, yes. Johnny bought me this drink and told me that his family owned a big ranch just outside of town, and they had plenty of room. I told him I wasn't that kind of girl. I didn't believe him at first, but there really *was* a mother, a father, five sisters, three brothers, not to mention assorted aunts and uncles. I think I talked to every one of them on the phone, including his three-year-old nephew, before I agreed to go out there and take advantage of a spare room. Well, we all hit it off . . . and one thing led to another. I spent the whole rest of my vacation there. I guess I'm the only gal who was taken home to meet the family *before* the engagement!" Jeannie paused, catching her breath, then continued tenderly. "Johnny was just visiting his folks. He's an engineer at an aircraft factory here. And you know what's funny? He's the same age as I am, and he'd never been married before either." Her voice changed again. "Hey, Mike, what about you? Are you married?"

"No," Mike said shortly. His thoughts flew to Nedra. God, how he wished he could say yes . . . yes, he was married. Only after her death had he fully realized how much he had loved her.

"How come?" Jeannie probed.

Mike ignored the question. "You know, we've got about twenty years of catching up to do, and I'm anxious to put my stamp of approval on Johnny. When can we all get together?"

Jeannie hesitated. "Soon, I hope. Mike, this wasn't exactly a social call. Like I said, I've only been here a few months, and I don't have a regular doctor. Johnny's as strong as a horse, and he doesn't have one, either. I know you just do surgery, but I thought maybe you could recommend someone."

"Sure thing," Mike said heartily. "What's your problem?"

"Female trouble," she said, slightly embarrassed. "I've been bleeding off and on for the past two weeks, and last night I started *really* hemorrhaging. It stopped, but then this morning. . . . Well, I'm in bed now, with my feet up, but, well . . . I didn't know anybody could lose so much blood and still have the strength to talk a doctor's ear off."

"Jeannie, if it's that bad, let me get you a bed here at Marin. You'll probably need a D and C."

"A D and C? What in the world is that?"

"Dilatation and curettage," Mike explained. "It merely means scraping the inside of your uterus. Nine times out of ten that's all there is to it. I'll make the arrangements. Can you be here . . . oh, say, around two o'clock?"

"I guess so. All I have to do is call Johnny and throw a few things in a bag. But, Mike, I don't know . . ." she trailed off.

"Take the word of a big-city doctor," Mike assured her, "gynecology is a very big part of general surgery."

"Okay. Thanks, Mike. I'll be there by two."

"Good. We'll be ready for you," Mike said and hung up.

At just about the same time Mike ended his conversation with Jeannie, Edith Frankel jockeyed her Cadillac into a parking space and hurried across the street to Marin Medical Center. Since her phone call that morning, she had made several decisions. After she had told her husband of her father's affliction, between them they had mapped a course of action.

Both were convinced that Aaron had approximately three months left to him. Better that her father should be comfortable at home with them where they could watch him and exert control. Left in the hands of the doctors, both were positive that needless tests and fruitless treatments would result in ultimate ruination of their future hopes. There wouldn't be a nickel left.

Convincing her father to live with them would not be easy. Edith had come to the conclusion that the best way to accomplish this was to minimize his illness in their coming conversation, to be cheerful and decisive.

She marched up to the Admitting Desk like a soldier entering battle, identified herself, and demanded the number of her father's room. Once she had reached the fourth floor, her heels clicked on the shiny floor, heralding her coming. She swept into the room. Aaron glanced at her in surprise.

"Edith—?"

In lieu of a kiss, she placed her cheek momentarily against his, at the same time peremptorily clicking off the television.

"How do you feel?" She didn't wait for an answer. "Better than I do, I'll bet. I would have been here sooner, but God, what a morning I've had." She collapsed heavily into the chair. Tense, nervous, and uncomfortable, she began to babble, as many people do when faced with the realization that they're in the presence of impending death.

"I was just walking out the door on my way down here when I spied that damned dog from next door digging a hole in my rose bed. Right by the new scarlet floribunda that I'd planted. Over eight dollars I paid the nursery for it, not counting the fertilizer. Well, I went back in and phoned the neighbor and gave her a piece

130

of my mind. I told her I didn't care if it was the first time in a year their gate had been left open and the creature had slipped out. Then she had the nerve to accuse me of turning the hose on her cat last week. Imagine! Thinking I'd turn a hose on their cat. Anyway, that'll teach it to stay off my patio. So I told her the next time their dog barked, even one yap, I was going to file a formal complaint, and she could expect a visit from the police. I know my rights. As I was saying to Ed, why anyone would want a pet, I don't know—but if they're going to have one, they can damn well keep it home!"

Aaron had made no attempt to interrupt his daughter. Experience had taught him that he might just as well relax until she ran down. She loved him—he knew she did. And she was concerned about him. It was just that his daughter had a habit of allowing her own problems to take precedence. She always had. As Edith momentarily paused for breath, Aaron saw his chance.

"Edith, it was nice of you to come—and all the way from Brentwood, too."

"I've come to take you home," she announced.

"Home? What's with home? Doctor Carrington didn't—"

"We'll just forget about Doctor Carrington, Papa," Edith said firmly. "He's not a very good doctor." As she spoke, Edith got up and began moving about the room, rummaging through drawers, carelessly piling Aaron's clothes at the foot of the bed, checking the bathroom. "Don't you worry," she said soothingly, "Ed and I are going to take care of you. As soon as we get you home, I'll run down to the beach and close your apartment."

"Edith, my tongue should fall out before I'd hurt you, but if Doctor Carrington told you I can leave, I don't want to go home with you. When have we seen each other? Two, maybe three times a year?" He raised his hand, cutting off her protests. "It's not your fault, but . . . Edith, we're strangers."

"Papa," Edith cried, going to him. "Don't say that.

Ed and I love you. We want you with us." She stopped long enough to blot her eyes with a tissue, and then continued opening drawers.

Aaron shook his head. "Put the clothes back, Edith."

She hesitated, considering. "All right, maybe it's best you stay here for just a day or two. We'll get another doctor—a specialist—somebody who won't insist on this therapy nonsense that Carrington wants to try. Like I said, he's not a very good doctor. After I talked to him this morning, I called Doctor Feiner, who's a friend of Ed's. He's a dermatologist, but he knows all about lung cancer, and he said—"

"Cancer?" Aaron was stunned.

Edith winced, stricken at her slip. It hadn't occurred to her that her father had not yet been told, and she hastened to cover the revelation as best she could.

"Everything will be all right. Ed and I—"

"Cancer?" Aaron repeated.

"I'm sorry, Papa," Edith said gently. "I thought you knew. Doctor Carrington told me this morning, and that he intended to start therapy. But I won't let you go through with it, Papa. Dr. Feiner says sometimes it doesn't work—"

"But sometimes it does?" Aaron pressed. Edith's silence was the admission Aaron needed. He was still reeling. "Cancer! So if I've got cancer . . . if I'm maybe going to die anyway . . . this therapy . . . well, what have I got to lose? What's the harm?"

"Papa!" The words came out as an anguished wail. "It's painful . . . and—"

"Expensive?" he finished gently. Edith turned away, but not in time to hide the color rushing to her face at her father's correct assumption of her motives. Damn my tendency to blush, she thought. It had plagued her all her life.

Aaron looked at her, slowly shaking his head. Despite his own fear at the dreaded and unexpected diagnosis, he spoke with affection and understanding. "Edith, Edith," he said softly. "Even as a little girl, so impatient, so stubborn. You and Ed—you've got a big house, new furniture, a fine car. You're my only child—my only heir. You'll get the money—sooner or later. Would it be so terrible if it were a little later than sooner?"

Before Edith could reply, Mrs. Rosen, the head nurse, came to the door. "Mrs. Frankel? Could you come to the desk for a moment?"

Edith hurried after her, relieved to escape the necessity of a reply to her father's question.

Two young men in white—one blond, one red-haired—stood lounging at the nurses' station, a wheeled stretcher nearby. Mrs. Rosen went behind the desk.

"I understand you ordered an ambulance for Mr. Metz, Mrs. Frankel," she said, glancing through the chart, "but I can't seem to find a discharge order." She carefully went through the papers again, then picked up the phone. As she started to dial, she spied Dr. Carrington rounding the corner of the corridor and hung up the phone.

"Doctor Carrington," she called. He walked to the desk. "I was just about to call you. This is Mrs. Frankel, Mr. Metz' daughter. She has an ambulance here to take her father home, and it seems you neglected to write a discharge order. At least, it isn't here."

"An ambulance? To take him home?" Mike said disbelievingly.

"I told you, doctor," Edith said smugly. "No therapy!"

"Wait here, Mrs. Frankel," Mike snapped, and strode into Aaron's room. Disregarding his request, Edith was right on his heels, aghast at the possible consequences of Carrington's apparent determination. The old man lay in bed, gazing pensively out the window.

"I don't know what's going on, Mr. Metz, but—"

"Doctor Carrington," Aaron quietly interrupted, "do I have cancer?"

Mike's jaw muscles tightened as, for a moment, he stared steadily and accusingly at the woman on the other side of the bed. As her blush confirmed her guilt, he sighed and turned back to his patient. It wasn't that

133

Mrs. Frankel hadn't had the right to tell her father, but he suspected that neither tact nor kindness had been employed. Still, he could not completely absolve himself. Once he had told her, he should have forestalled this unfortunate occurrence by being explicit with Aaron about the diagnosis, using words which could not be misunderstood, and at the same time, following those words with ones of hope and reassurance. Better late than never.

"Yes, you do," Mike admitted earnestly. "But there's a great deal we can do to help you. I just saw Doctor MacPherson downstairs and he's going to meet me here shortly so we can explain the X-ray and chemotherapy treatments."

"But I heard they don't work," Edith said defensively.

Mike ignored her. "Mr. Metz, I can't give you any guarantees, but if you were my father, I'd want you to have them. But the decision is yours. If you want to leave, I can't stop you. Your daughter's here with an ambulance. All you have to do is sign a release."

"Doctor, how long do I have?" Aaron asked.

"I don't know, Mr. Metz, I honestly don't know."

Aaron stared out the window for another long moment. "But the treatments will prolong the time I have left?"

Mike nodded. "Probably."

"Will it hurt?"

Mike shook his head. "You may have some nausea, but you won't have any pain."

"No pain—even right up to the end?"

Mike shook his head again. "No pain, Mr. Metz. That much I can promise you."

Aaron addressed his words to Carrington but looked pointedly at Edith. "Doctor," he said, "I want every week, every day, every hour, every minute you can give me. I have a lot of time to make up. And I want you as my doctor."

Mike clasped his shoulder. "Thank you, Mr. Metz. I'll do my very best for you."

As Mike started to leave, Aaron spoke to his daughter. "Go home, Edith," he said gently. "I'll be all right." He clicked on the television set. "The Dodgers are playing the Giants in about ten minutes."

Mike walked back to the desk, studiously ignoring Edith, who was still on his heels. "Mr. Metz is *not* discharged, Mrs. Rosen." His voice was deliberately geared to be sure Mrs. Frankel heard. "He has decided to stay in the hospital and undergo therapy. And from now on, Mr. Metz is not to have visitors unless I personally clear them."

The two private ambulance attendants had been perched on the edge of the stretcher, aware of the unusual drama, watching the adversaries as one might watch a Ping-Pong match. At Carrington's words, the blond attendant got to his feet and approached the desk.

"Well, what are we supposed to do?" he asked plaintively.

Mike whirled on him, knowing that he was venting his spleen on an innocent, but unable to help himself. "I'd suggest you both toddle back to wherever you came from, and take your stretcher with you."

"What about the bill? Who's going to pay for this?" the attendant countered.

"Meet Mrs. Frankel," Mike snapped, indicating the woman beside him. "She called you. I'd suggest you make arrangements with her."

Edith Frankel confronted Mike, her face white with fury and frustration. "You haven't heard the last of this, Doctor Carrington. You made a fool of me in there. I love my father, and I don't want you as his doctor. I hate to do it, but I intend to go to court and prove him incompetent and sue to be appointed conservator of his estate and person. Then we'll see just how long you're on this case!" She suddenly flashed him a charming smile, the prelude to a complete and surprising reversal. "Come on, doctor, let me take Papa home. After all, there's nothing in this for you—nothing whatsoever. Why don't you just send us a bill? We won't question your charges."

"Mrs. Frankel," Mike said through gritted teeth, "you go straight to hell!"

He watched as the color once again drained from her face. She spun away from him and hurried down the hall. She stood at the elevator, engaged in a heated argument with the blond ambulance attendant, as the other hurried to catch up with them, dragging the empty stretcher behind him.

Mike had three calls to make, and he wasted no time. First he called his attorney; he wasn't sure of his legal ground in a case such as this. Mike briefly explained the situation to his lawyer, outlining what had transpired. He wondered what his decision would be if he was legally advised to back off. But he was destined never to find out.

"Do what is medically proper, Mike," his attorney advised. "Don't listen to the daughter. Screw her. If it comes down to that, it'll stand up in court."

Mike breathed a sigh of relief and made the second call—to one of Marin's staff psychiatrists. He requested a psychiatric examination of Mr. Metz, with the subsequent written report to be made officially part of the patient's records. There was no doubt in his mind that Aaron was lucid, sensible, sharp as a tack, and that the psychiatrist would confirm it. If Edith Frankel was serious regarding her threat of court action, that documentation would be important evidence in protecting Aaron and disallowing her claim. It was the least he could do for Mr. Metz.

He thought back over the recent, unpleasant incident. Edith Frankel had committed two gross errors in judgment. She had elected to wage battle on Mike's home ground—in the hospital—where he had absolute power as far as the well-being of his patient was concerned. And she had underestimated what one human being, with nothing to gain, was willing to do for another.

Finally, Mike phoned Admitting to arrange a bed for Jeannie Brinker . . . no, Jeannie Mendosa. He was looking forward to seeing Jeannie again. He wished it were under better circumstances.

Mike dashed back to the seventh floor to look in on George Selkins. Now that his body was getting the alcohol it craved, the man was relaxed, blissfully sleeping. Mike watched the slow drip of the IV. He'd order the alcohol solution tapered off—a little at a time—and see what happened.

He got back to the fourth floor just in time to see Dr. MacPherson enter Aaron's room. He hurried to join him.

It was after one before Carrington and MacPherson had resolved all the details concerning Aaron Metz. Dr. MacPherson had examined him and they had both been careful to explain fully the planned treatments, making sure the old man knew exactly what was to be done and what he could expect. They realized that fear of the unknown, the unexpected, was far worse than facing realities. They left Aaron a little subdued but undaunted, and headed for Dr. Reichner's office to make arrangements for the X-ray therapy. That finished, Mike invited MacPherson to lunch in the doctors' dining room.

As they entered, they encountered Dr. Joseph Merrick, who was just leaving. He greeted Malcolm MacPherson effusively, and the two men chatted for a few moments. Then Merrick turned to Mike.

"Everything going okay?" Mike nodded. "Any problems, let me know. Always anxious to help." He put his arm about Mike's shoulders solicitously, as he turned back to MacPherson. "Mike is Marin's busiest and most popular surgeon. Don't know what we'd do without him." In his own mind, Merrick's words were absolutely sincere. Now that he had chosen David Savage as his target, there was no room for ill will toward anyone else. With a fatherly pat on Mike's arm, Merrick left the room.

Why, thought Mike, as he sat down at a table with MacPherson, can't I warm up to Merrick? Most of the time he had been cooperative and helpful, but Carrington could not shake off the suspicion that Merrick's charm was superficial, a façade that barely covered the true man—cold, envious, deceitful, an opportunist.

137

There was nothing tangible upon which to base his unkind judgment, he knew. Paranoid, he labeled himself, disgustedly.

It was two thirty before they finished lunch. Mike called Admitting from the cashier's desk and ascertained that Mrs. Medosa had checked in and had been assigned room 512. He headed for the fifth floor.

"Jeannie! Sit up, and let me hug you," he sang out as he burst into the room. The girl made a few unintelligible grunts, pointing to her mouth. Her lips were grimly clamped on a thermometer. Mike laughed, removed it from her mouth, glanced at it and placed it on the table. He lowered the bars on one side of the bed and they met in a great bear hug, giggling like children.

"Let me look at you," Mike gasped, disengaging himself.

The twenty years had been kind to Jeannie. She had matured, but her light brown curly hair, close-cropped, attractively framed a face that was still unblemished and shiny. She wore no makeup except a dab of pale lipstick, and her blue eyes sparkled with the vivacity that Mike remembered. He pressed the button on the side of the bed and elevated her to a comfortable sitting position, then settled himself in the low chair by the window.

"Now," he said with a smile, "let's talk about you."

Before he could continue, the head nurse on five—an older woman, crisply efficient—entered the room.

"Mrs. Mendosa," she said crossly, "I've told you once before about the side rails. You are *not* to lower them. And you *must* keep the thermometer—" She suddenly spied Carrington and flushed. "Oh, doctor, I didn't see you there."

"Temperature's normal, Mrs. Kowalsky," Mike said shortly. "Will you excuse us?"

She nodded, picked up the thermometer, and hurried from the room.

"Yeeck," Jeannie exclaimed. "Kowalsky! I guess maybe I shouldn't have told her my new Polish joke, right?" She paused, and then said earnestly, "Mike, I don't think she likes me. I don't think she has a sense of humor."

"What happened, Jeannie?" Mike asked, his eyes twinkling.

"Well, when I first got here, she came in—you know—with that little form they fill out." He nodded. "The first thing she asked me was if I had false teeth or any removable bridges, and I told her no. She looked at me suspiciously and said, 'are you sure?' Gosh, Mike, just because I'm thirty-seven doesn't mean I've completely deteriorated. So I told her yes, I was sure, but if it would help, I could find a couple of loose fillings she could have."

Mike exploded with a booming laugh. Jeannie looked at him innocently.

"Then she asked if I had brought any of my medication with me." She paused. "I guess she got a little upset when I offered her the Dentyne gum and artificial sweetener that I carry in my purse."

"C'mon, Jeannie." Mike was still chuckling. "She's just doing her job. She's a good nurse."

Jeannie shrugged. "She intimidates me."

Mike went through Jeannie's medical history. There wasn't much—a few childhood diseases, but generally she'd been hale and healthy. He examined her quickly and professionally.

"There's no doubt a D and C is in order," Mike told her. "We'll schedule it for late this afternoon. I've got lots to do, but I'll see you later."

"Mike!" The agony apparent in her tone stopped him cold. He turned back to her.

"I'm terrified," Jeannie admitted. "I've never been in a hospital before."

"It's no big deal," he assured her. "You'll be given a light, general anesthetic. While you're asleep, we'll go in and gently scrape the uterus—and the hemorrhaging will stop. You can probably go home tomorrow."

"That's all there is to it? That's the end of it?" she pressed.

He hesitated. "We'll send the tissue to Pathology—it's routine, just a precaution."

"When Johnny and I got married," she said evenly, "his wedding present to me was a three-bedroom house in the valley. Like I told you over the phone, Johnny's from a big family—and so am I—and we're used to having kids around. I know it's kind of late for me to have a family, but I could maybe have one—even two, if we work at it."

Mike was aware of the point she was making. "Name the first one after me," he said easily, and walked quickly from the room.

Carrington spent the next couple of hours in his office, signing insurance forms and catching up on correspondence. It was a little before five when he went back to the hospital and headed straight for Jeannie's room. She had already been sedated, but she smiled at him groggily.

"Hi. You always did have a habit of being on time. I thought maybe I'd get lucky, and you'd forget you had this appointment."

He grinned. "Not a chance."

"Mrs. Kowol . . . Mrs. . . . whatever her name is . . . she took my cigarettes away," Jeannie mumbled drowsily.

"S.P." he assured her.

"Southern Pacific?"

"No, standard procedure. They'd just as soon you didn't burn the hospital down." He lit a cigarette and held it to her lips. She took a couple of half-hearted puffs and lost interest. Mike extinguished it in the tray. "Got to go scrub now, honey. They'll be coming for you in a few minutes. Don't worry about a thing. I'll see you upstairs."

The D and C went smoothly, and the entire operation was over in ten minutes. Mike stared at the tissue he had removed from the uterus as he gave it to the nurse. It was red, of course, but with an ominous, yellowish hue.

"Get that downstairs right away," Mike instructed

the girl. She nodded. The minute he left the operating suite, he personally called Pathology.

"This is Doctor Carrington. I'm sending down some tissue on a Mrs. Mendosa. Will you be sure that it's processed with today's batch? I'd like to have the slides first thing in the morning."

"Will do," the girl in the laboratory confirmed.

Before starting his evening rounds, Mike stopped in the Recovery Room for a final check. Jeannie had reached the mumbling stage, he noted, as he took her pulse. She'd awaken soon and be taken back to her room, where she'd be sedated to enable her to sleep through the night. He'd see her in the morning.

As he released her wrist, Mike felt a wave of nausea and weakness engulf him. It surprised him. It was like nothing he'd experienced before. The self-diagnosis was not long in coming. During the hectic day, he had allowed the miseries of others to supercede his own. Now that he was finished at Marin, he had only one place to go. Back to his empty apartment. And Nedra wouldn't be there. Ever again.

Chapter IV

"Miss Pierce, has Doctor Savage arrived yet?"

Louis Taylor, Marin Medical Center's administrator, spoke into the intercom, glancing as he did so at the desk clock which indicated exactly 8 A.M. Taylor was in his early forties, crackling with energy and efficiency, and was extremely qualified for his job. He was dressed expensively but soberly, a nicety which his annual salary of fifty thousand plus encouraged and permitted. He had majored in hospital administration in college and had worked at various jobs in medical facilities throughout the country before assuming his post at Marin. While his forte was cost accounting, everything that affected the efficient operation of the hospital concerned him and he was, therefore, involved in the upcoming meeting with David Savage. Miss Pierce's voice filtered through the speaker box.

"Not yet, Mr. Taylor."

"Well, as soon as he arrives, let us know."

Taylor had relinquished his seat behind the desk to Dr. Whitney Palmer, who would chair the meeting, so he rejoined the other three men lounging informally on the long, L-shaped sectional couch which faced the desk. They were all former chiefs of staff of Marin Medical Center. Dr. Donald Bruckheimer and Dr. Howard Welker sat relaxed, engulfed in a discussion and analysis of the previous day's stock market activity. The third man—Dr. Joseph Merrick—glanced at his watch and replaced his coffee cup on the table in front of the couch with a bit more force than necessary. The chief of surgery seemed inordinately keyed up this morning for some reason, Taylor noticed.

"Attention, please," the voice over the loudspeakers intoned. "There will be a GYN conference and breakfast in the auditorium—eight A.M. this morning."

The administrator's office was soundproof and the announcement did not intrude there, but it reached the ears of Dr. David Savage, who was about halfway through changing the dressing on his exenteration patient. He paused momentarily and glanced at his watch, then unhurriedly completed the procedure. He chatted with the woman for a few moments and then leisurely strolled to the nurses' station. There he perused the chart for some minutes, and slowly wrote the progress note, making it a little longer, perhaps a little more detailed than was customary for him.

He meandered to the elevators and went to the men's room on the first floor. As he entered, Dr. Fulton was standing at a basin, drying his hands. He looked up in surprise.

"Jesus, Dave, what are you doing here? It's after eight. They'll be waiting for you in the meeting."

"As long as they designated me guest of honor," Savage said airily, "I have to look the part." He leisurely combed his hair and frittered away a few minutes more adjusting his tie.

"Look, Dave," Fulton said urgently, "I'm not supposed to talk about this, but . . . well, do yourself a favor. Go in there and just listen. No matter what they say, keep your mouth shut. Don't antagonize them. Let them butter up their egos, and everything will work out in the long run."

"Thanks, Bill," Savage responded with a grin. "See you."

When he finally entered the administrator's office,

Miss Pierce smiled, suggested that he sit down, and announced him.

Inside, Merrick reacted explosively. "Thirteen minutes late," he announced. "If you multiply that by the hourly rate each of us usually charges, Doctor Savage has just cost us quite a few bucks!"

Palmer ignored the outburst and, via the intercom, requested that Savage be asked to join them. The doctors voiced or nodded their greetings, except for Merrick, who pointedly abstained. Dave hesitated for a moment, then chose and settled into a side chair at the corner of the desk where he could face the others.

"Doctor Savage," Palmer began immediately, anxious to set the tone, "to begin with, we want you to understand the purpose of this meeting. We are not here to criticize. Everybody in this room contributes to the success and well-being of Marin Medical Center, and we're all concerned with certain problems that prevent it from running at maximum efficiency. There are areas in which we all feel that you can be of great help to us. And that, basically, is what we want to talk about."

Savage was pleasantly surprised and slightly taken aback. He had girded himself for battle, and relaxed slightly at Palmer's words.

"I'm sure I can help, gentlemen," Savage acknowledged magnanimously. "I've always done everything I could to make this a better-functioning hospital. I've been an active member of the teaching staff, and I've worked in the clinics."

"Yes," Palmer agreed, "we are aware of that, and we appreciate it."

There was a moment of heavy silence as the chief of staff glanced uncomfortably about the room. It was obvious that he could expect no help in broaching the unpleasant discussion that was inevitable.

"There have been numerous incidents, however, Doctor Savage, on the floors and in the operating rooms in which you have been involved, which we deem as . . . well . . . detrimental to hospital morale."

"I think," said Savage sharply, "before we go any

144

further, you'd better tell me exactly what incidents you're talking about, Doctor Palmer!"

"I'd really rather not go into specifics. I don't think it would serve any purpose. Let's just say that your comments, your actions, your attitude, have caused considerable resentment in the operating rooms and among the floor nurses. The lab personnel, just about everybody in the hospital, in fact—even some of the doctors—have complained. We felt you might not be aware of it, and that it was unintentional, and that if we brought the matter to your attention—"

"Now wait just one damned minute," Savage interrupted. "That brush you're painting me with is pretty broad. And I don't like it. I think we'd better talk about some specific instances. In fact, I insist on it!"

Merrick had been sitting quietly, regarding Savage with barely concealed distaste. He took advantage of Palmer's reluctance to continue. "I think he's right," Merrick snapped. "I think we *should* talk about some specific instances."

"Well," Palmer said, resigned at being trapped, "there's the matter of ordering lab tests to be done at six A.M. instead of seven. That's quite an imposition on the night crew, and there's no apparent reason why they couldn't be done as a matter of routine along with the tests ordered by everyone else."

"I'm glad you brought that up," Savage declared. "Sure I order a lot of tests at six instead of seven. Because if I order for seven, they won't be picked up until nine, and they won't be done until noon, and they won't be reported until evening. Get this through your heads. I take care of sick patients. I need those tests, and I don't have time to call all day to see if they're done. If you had a hospital laboratory that was efficient, that could get the work done right, and on time, I wouldn't have to be hampered in my treatment of patients. But since you don't, I use any means I can devise to get my results early. It's up to me to decide what's important—not them."

Dr. Howard Welker spoke. He was short, portly, and

extremely mild-mannered. He was an internationally acclaimed orthopedic surgeon who specialized in operating on hands—always a complicated and delicate procedure. "I can understand an occasional emergency, Doctor Savage, where your logic would certainly make sense. But every patient can't be so critical as to necessitate or justify the early-test routine. Couldn't you limit your special demands on the lab to occasional instances, and handle the majority of your tests like everyone else?"

Savage spun to face him. "Look, Doctor Welker, curing cancer is not like straightening a pinkie. My patients are sick. I'm not like everyone else!"

Merrick inwardly marveled at the man's insensitivity. In one sentence, Savage had managed to alienate Welker by denigrating the man's work. "Did I understand you to say Doctor Savage, that you are not like everyone else?" Merrick asked pointedly.

"That is correct, doctor."

"Well, let's go to another matter," Palmer said hurriedly. "We have a report that you ordered vital signs every thirty minutes on three patients on the same floor over one twenty-four-period. The condition of at least two of those patients didn't warrant it."

"Someone has to keep the nursing staff of this hospital on its toes. Let me tell you a little story, gentlemen," Savage said quietly. "Last month, I called the hospital to check on a patient I was very concerned about. It was late—about midnight—and it was a touch-and-go situation. I asked four-south how Mrs. Ross was doing. Do you know what answer I got? 'She's sleeping, doctor.'" Savage's voice rose to a yelp. "'She's sleeping!' Hell, she could be sleeping and *dying*. When I ask how a patient is, I don't want to be told she's sleeping. I want the vital signs: pulse, temperature, respiration, blood pressure, urine output—and I want them fast!"

Dr. Bruckheimer looked around, bewildered. "I still don't see what that has to do with ordering vital signs on three patients every thirty minutes—"

"I made my point," Savage said smugly. "That's what

146

it had to do with it. When I call or come on the floor now, the information is ready for me." He looked around the room accusingly. "If you want my opinion, instead of sitting around here, what you ought to be doing is recruiting more efficient nurses. Pay them more if you have to, but get some help that's a little bit better than these empty-headed broads who think that a white uniform makes them a nurse. Anyway, the orders I write are my prerogative. The only way to handle the nurses you have now is to make things a bit unpleasant for them occasionally. It keeps them on their toes."

"And that's your general philosophy regarding women, doctor?" Merrick prompted smoothly.

Savage nodded. Dr. Palmer resumed, visibly upset.

"Doctor Savage, what you don't seem to understand is that there are some things you do, and some things you don't do. Certain words you don't use, regardless of the provocation. It's a matter of . . . well . . . of being a gentleman. And that brings up another subject. You don't storm out on a patient because of an argument and instruct her to find a new doctor. No one knows better than I how aggravating a patient can be, and Lord knows there are times when the temptation is great—but it just isn't done."

"Doctor Palmer," Savage retorted, "I remember the incident to which you're referring. That woman was an unreasonable bitch. She'd had five gynecologists in six months. I made the correct diagnosis—and I prescribed the correct treatment and medication—and she questioned my judgment! There's no reason in the world why I should waste time arguing with a woman, when I can use that time to heal sick patients."

Merrick said quietly, "Your language brings up another point, doctor. Whether that woman was a bitch or not, there are, as Doctor Palmer pointed out, certain words that just shouldn't be used. You realize, of course, that we are having difficulty getting nurses willing to scrub with you?"

"Well, of course I'm demanding." Savage admitted arrogantly. "My surgery is demanding of me. You don't

147

have enough operating room nurses, and the ones you have aren't worth a damn. If I'm going to do difficult operations, I need competent help, and this hospital is not providing it. Most of the problems at Marin are created by its lax approach to medical care. You say we should all work together—well, I'm for that. And the first thing you can do is start hiring additional nurses, hopefully more competent than the ones you have."

"You're right, we need more help," Merrick said harshly. "And what has happened? We've lost more girls through your abusive treatment and foul mouth than we could ever hope to recruit. Get one thing straight, doctor. This hospital can run without you—but not without them!"

The room was silent. To a man, they were shocked at Merrick's bald threat which promised to turn what up to now had been a relatively gentlemanly discussion into an alley fight. Savage was first to recover.

"Well," he sputtered. "I may have been a little harsh once or twice, but I've never reacted in any way that wasn't justified by the situation."

Merrick suddenly stood up and approached Savage, stopping only a few feet in front of him. "Really, Doctor Savage?" he sneered. "That's interesting. I have a patient up in Room 411 who had the poor judgment to go to dinner with you last Friday night. I'm not sure she'd agree. She has a swollen face, a broken zygoma, and may have to live with permanent facial paralysis the rest of her life. She is an employee of this hospital and that makes us, in a degree, responsible for her. She was a young, vibrant, beautiful girl. Now she's a pitiful neurotic, ugly nothing! Unfortunately, she didn't realize that *you are not like everybody else . . . that you enjoy being unpleasant to women because it keeps them on their toes*. And I'm sure if she had realized that *you never react in any way that isn't justified by the situation,* she wouldn't have refused to obey when you ordered her to go to bed with you! She didn't suspect you'd beat her face to a pulp!"

David Savage stared at Joseph Merrick, utterly

148

shaken. "Susan?" he stuttered. "Are you talking about Susan?" The words themselves were an absolute admission of guilt.

Whitney Palmer watched the duel between the two men with disbelief. "Doctor Merrick," he asked sharply, "are you referring to Susan Thomas, the girl you asked me to see? Are you inferring that Doctor Savage—"

For once, Merrick completely ignored the chief of staff. His eyes continued to bore into the face of David Savage, who sat stunned, gradually becoming aware of his great jeopardy in this inquisition.

"She did fall down," he said slowly, giving his thoughts a chance to rally. "But I had no idea she was hurt. I had no idea she was injured when she fell."

Merrick savored his moment of triumph and moved in for the kill. "She fell down, doctor," he said succinctly, *"because you hit her!"*

"That's a goddamned lie," Savage blustered. "If you're going to use the out-and-out lie of some little Admitting Room nurse against me, you leave me no alternative but to see my lawyers." And with that he stormed out of the room.

For a moment, the silence was so complete that it seemed like a vacuum. Then Merrick moved back to the couch, sat down, and calmly lit a cigarette. Palmer stood up slowly.

"Joe, are you sure of your facts? There's no mistake?"

"She told me," Merrick said smugly. *"David Savage hit me*—she used those very words."

While the drama was unfolding in the administrator's office, Mike made his morning rounds, starting at the top floor and working down. He departed from his usual routine, however, by deliberately skipping the fifth floor. He had but one patient there—Jeannie. And she had cancer. Pathology had confirmed his fears—the tissue was malignant. Even though he intentionally willed himself not to dwell on it, the fact kept bouncing back into his brain. Jeannie had cancer. Not Jeannie! It

149

couldn't happen to Jeannie! He wouldn't let it! Knock it off, he told himself sharply. A doctor isn't God! A doctor is only a puppet—a puppet of God's will. You fight, but you can't really dictate who will live; who will die, Mike reminded the rebellion within him. You can't stipulate who'll be sick; who'll be well. But in Jeannie's case, he sure as hell was going to try. Not that he didn't try for all his patients. Mike always did his best. But somehow, this time, he was going to influence that God, whether through prayers or his skill. Or maybe he'd just pull on those puppet strings a little harder. Nothing was going to happen to Jeannie!

What he would have given if he'd been able to save Nedra! Every day he utilized his considerable skill to save strangers. Bums . . . drunks . . . people he didn't especially like . . . people he didn't even know . . . people who had brought their troubles on themselves by tempting the odds in so many ways.

And then, Nedra. That's what had been so horrible. What good had his highly perfected art, his dedication, been to her? Doctors were surrounded by death every day. It should become commonplace, but it never did. Losing a loved one was especially terrible for a physician. For most people, there was immediate grief, but the experience was so rare that the impact, the full feeling of loss didn't really present itself until hours, or maybe even days later. But for him, at the actual moment of Nedra's death, the completeness, the finality, the all-encompassing totality of loss had been immediate and crushingly apparent.

He had to tell Jeannie, of course, but he'd wait awhile. Mike procrastinated until midmorning. Then, knowing he had several minor surgical cases scheduled for the afternoon, he could postpone it no longer.

Jeannie was sitting up in bed, cross-legged. She had exchanged the hospital gown for one of her own, a fluffy buttercup-yellow print with a matching bed jacket. The wide grin she wore was equally sunny. Mike returned her smile.

"Well, now, how do you feel?"

He sat in the chair beside her, and she swung her legs over the side of the bed to perch on its edge.

"Oh, Mike, I feel wonderful, just like you said I would. It was silly to fret the way I did. Do you have any idea how worried I was? You can't imagine all the horrible things and possibilities that went through my mind. I really didn't believe you, but I feel marvelous."

He opened the newspaper, feigning an easy and relaxed manner. "The show at the Music Center has been extended two weeks," he commented. "Have you seen it?"

She shook her head. "Hey, you said I could go home today. When? This afternoon?"

He continued reading for a moment before looking up at her. "I said you could *probably* go home. . . if there weren't complications."

Her eyes widened and never left his face as she got back into bed, drawing the sheet and blanket over her as if they offered some desperately needed measure of comfort and security.

"And are there . . . complications?" she breathed.

Mike lowered his eyes once again to the paper on his lap, unable for a moment to meet her gaze. Normally he imparted a diagnosis in a certain progression: what it was . . . what would be done . . . followed by an optimistic assurance. In this case, he reversed the sequence. And for once, he would be positive in his promise of her ultimate well-being. There was no possible law suit here.

"You're going to be fine, Jeannie. You have my word on that." He wished he was as sure as he sounded. "You believe me, don't you? But it's going to be necessary for you to have an operation. And you can count on going home seven or eight days after that."

Mike casually dropped his eyes. All of his training and experience had taught him it was better to have the patient ask specific questions than for him to volunteer information. They asked only what they wanted to know, often subconsciously ignoring unpleasant or frightening implications. It enabled them to digest the

151

information a little at a time, which was psychologically desirable. He waited—and waited—and finally glanced up. Jeannie was just staring at him, looking like a small child who had just been slapped and didn't know why. He was forced to continue.

"You're going to be all right," he assured her again, "but the tissue from your uterus—" He paused and deliberately took a different approach. "What was causing your bleeding, Jeannie, was a malignant growth. Fortunately, it's the kind we cure all the time. But that cure involves a hysterectomy."

"A hysterectomy?" Jeannie struggled to keep her voice even, but the tremble was perceptible. "Oh, no, Mike, there's got to be another way . . . X-ray treatments, maybe?"

"Sometimes we use X-ray or radium treatments before doing a hysterectomy, but not as a subsitute for the operation. By itself, it's not a sure cure, and I wouldn't let you risk it." His voice softened. "There's nothing to be gained by going that route anyway. I know what's on your mind. X-ray treatments would result in certain sterility, too. There's no substitute. We've got to go ahead with the best possible treatment—and that's a hysterectomy."

He waited for the tears, even hysterics—but they didn't come. She merely stared at her hands, unconsciously twisting her wedding ring.

"Oh, Mike, Johnny and I love each other so much . . . so much that there's lots of love left over. We have so much to offer a child. If I could have just met Johnny ten years sooner, we'd have those extra rooms filled with kids by now."

There was a discreet tap on the door, it cracked open, and a head popped in and caught Mike's eye.

"They told me I couldn't come in because the doctor was here. But I'm the adventuresome type, so you can throw me out if you want. I'm Johnny Mendosa." He grinned as Mike waved him into the room.

He was medium height, stocky, not handsome by any means but not unattractive. The masculinity of his olive

152

skin and shock of dark hair was softened by huge brown eyes that glowed with warmth and sensitivity.

"You're Doctor Carrington. I've heard a lot about you." He spoke with an almost imperceptible Spanish accent. His handshake was strong and firm. He turned to Jeannie. "I decided to skip eating today, take a long and leisurely break, and spend the entire time with my wife. How does that strike you?"

For the first time, tears streamed down Jeannie's face. Sudden concern replaced his smile and he hurried to her, gathering her in his arms. "Baby, baby," he crooned. "What's the matter?" At those words, Jeannie's sobbing increased, her breath coming in tormented gasps. Johnny glanced at Mike in bewilderment.

"I'll be back a little later," Mike told them, and discreetly started to leave.

"Mike, please stay—don't go—please." Hearing the torment in Jeannie's voice, Mike paused.

"Look, will somebody tell me what's going on?" Johnny demanded. "Honey, what's the matter?"

"Johnny," she blurted, "they found . . . they found a malignancy—" Her sobbing cut off further words.

"My God," her husband whispered. He pulled away slightly and stared at Carrington.

"She's in no danger. The malignancy can be cured. It's a type of surgery that's done every day," Mike assured him.

"A hysterectomy?" It was Johnny who said the word. Mike nodded. "Well, honey," Johnny went on, clasping Jeannie by her shoulders and moving far enough away so he could meet his wife's eyes, "it's not the end of the world. Just thank God it was found in time."

Jeannie stared at him. "Do you understand? Do you know what a hysterectomy means, Johnny? No kids. No kids, ever!"

"Sure I know. Look, we both wanted kids. And now we can't have them. And I'm sorry. But six months ago, we didn't even have each other. And in another six months, I might not have had you. I'd rather have you—just you—than ten kids and any other woman in the world!"

"But that big house, all those rooms, it'll be so empty," Jeannie reflected.

"Darling." He pulled her forward and kissed her forehead gently. "It'll never be empty—not for me. Not as long as you're there." He turned to Carrington. "When should it be done, doctor?"

Mike hesitated. "Well, waiting won't make it any easier. I'd like to schedule it for tomorrow morning."

"That will work out fine." He turned to his wife. "Right, honey?"

She nodded. "Lord, I love you," she said simply.

Mike started to leave, then suddenly turned around and clasped Johnny's hand, his eyes congratulating him and mirroring the admiration he felt. "I'll come down and talk to you right after the operation in the morning," he promised. "Why don't you wait for me here in Jeannie's room?"

Johnny nodded.

Mike walked to the nurses' desk to write the orders for the surgical prep. He glanced up at Mrs. Kowalsky. "Would you call down to the kitchen and order up another tray? I think Mr. Mendosa would like to have lunch with his wife. And I only wish the food could be served on plates of solid gold. They deserve it. They're quite a couple."

The office of the president of Sutter Studios was magnificent. There was no other word to describe it. Deep-piled, off-white carpeting covered the floor and extended over a raised platform at the far end of the room. On this dais, an ornately carved, eight-foot desk was placed, and genuine walnut paneling surrounded the shelf upon shelf of leather-bound feature and television scripts of past productions. The off-white walls were enhanced by numerous casually arranged original paintings by Utrecht and Chagall, their delicate colors highlighted by soft beams of indirect light. The antique furniture gleamed with a rich patina.

154

With all that, the setting was unable to dwarf the tall, thin, hawk-faced man who sat behind the huge desk in an oversized chair, talking on the phone. He hung up and drummed his long fingers on the arm of his chair for a moment, then turned his attention to a neat stack of contracts on the desk and began signing them.

Frank Savage. His enemies called him The Barracuda; his friends and the stockholders of his company called him Genius; Marin Medical Center's Board of Trustees called him Vice Chairman; and Dr. David Savage called him Dad.

Many articles and biographies and profiles had been published on the life and fortune of this tycoon of the motion picture industry. In general, they all told the same story, with slight discrepancies here and there, depending upon the veracity or gullibility of the author. Many years ago, according to the studio's official press releases, Frank Savage had managed to secure financing from a personal friend in the Bahamas. In the more lurid tabloids, it was hinted the source of that money was the baccarat tables of the many casinos there. Nevertheless, he had utilized that capital and produced a very low-budget western, using unknowns in the starring roles. The film had caught the public's fancy and the dollars had poured in at the box office. It was a good picture, with exceptional talent, and Frank had hired the best press agent in the world to publicize it. The result was three Academy Award nominations for the film's stars. When other producers had attempted to jump on the bandwagon and capitalize on the popularity of those actors by signing them for productions of their own, they found they were all under long-term, personal management contracts with Frank Savage.

It was a logical step, of course, to open a licensed talent agency so that these stars whom Frank had created, and who were now among the most popular in the country, could work for others and provide him with a 10-percent fee. And to his credit, he managed them carefully, building their reputations, studying each script submitted, advising them with an astuteness that made his stable of stars the favorite of producers, studios and the moviegoing public all over the world. Gradually, during the next few years, certain established performers switched their loyalties from their former agents to bask under the banner of Frank's aegis. At the same time, he was constantly scouting new young talent, and his percentage of success at making these youngsters into stars was phenomenal. Before long, the talent agency known as Savage and Associates was counted among the top three in the world.

But with all the agency's size and success, Frank never permitted the personal touch to be lost. He still knew every client intimately. He had dinner with them regularly, preferably in their homes or his. He agonized over their children's diseases, he prevented disastrous divorces, he covered up indiscretions, he advised them on every facet of their lives, both business and personal. He was available to them, day or night. Invariably, since it was one of the diseases of the industry, many of his clients, tasting success too soon, too fast, had a tendency to live beyond their means. Frank tried to advise against it, but if he failed, he never hesitated in offering loans, at acceptable interest rates, to bail them out. He was friend, mentor, confessor, teacher, guardian and God Almighty to them.

And what of Frank's personal life during that time? Any newspaper's morgue would disclose the fact that he had married early, to a small-town southern belle named Eileen Cooper—a lovely girl whose ambition was limited to being the best wife, housekeeper, and mother the world had ever known. She was not competitive with her husband as their fortunes grew, she was not jealous, she was not demanding, she was not bitchy. She merely adored him with every once of her one-hundred-and-twenty-pound body.

Of this union, three children were born. The first, a girl, was christened Marilyn. The second, miracle of miracles, was a boy who arrived almost four years later, and was named David. The last child was another girl, Sarah. Shortly after Sarah's birth, a hysterectomy had been necessary and Eileen Savage's childbearing days were over. The tissue removed during the operation had been malignant, and for years Frank had lived with the sensation of having the cold tip of death's dagger at his spine. Had they gotten the cancer—all of it—he often wondered as he gazed at his beloved wife? The possibility that a malignancy might still be growing within her caused a damp glaze of sweat to form over his body. As the years passed, and his wife continued to flourish, every day Frank Savage blessed her gynecologist in particular, and the medical community in general.

Tragedy struck when Marilyn, their oldest, was sixteen and just blooming into womanhood. She was a good-humored, lovely blond girl, the image of her mother. One day she was playing tennis, the next day she was hospitalized. The dreaded diagnosis of leukemia was confirmed, and the Savage family agonized as the medical profession exerted every effort, every ploy known, to save her. It was all in vain and Frank watched as his darling slowly faded, and finally died.

Instead of being embittered, Frank recognized the almost superhuman endeavors which had been expended to save his daughter. Even though they failed, he was grateful. Whether it was from the experience of not losing his wife, or whether it was his recognition of the herculean efforts made to save his daughter, Frank looked upon doctors as gods. When they opened their mouths, he expected to hear the Mormon Tabernacle Choir singing behind their words of wisdom. It soon became known that the first door to knock on if you were soliciting for a charitable medical cause was Frank Savage's. Polio . . . cancer . . . arthritis . . . muscular dystrophy . . . he gave with extreme generosity, quietly, unobtrusively, with no thought to possible favorable publicity. He was soon asked to head charitable committees and found himself respected by his moneyed co-members. Before long, their friendship led to positions on the advisory boards of banks, industrial corporations, and hospitals.

His daughter Sarah was much like her mother, no

special talent or ambition, except that she would make some lucky man a marvelous wife. Her family carefully and deliberately instilled in her a high regard for home and family. Frank would make sure that the right young lad came along, and that his fortune would be assured merely by showing the good taste of choosing Frank's lovely daughter.

David was a handsome child and had known nothing but love and adoration from his family all his life. Frank had listened indulgently while his son had gone through the normal phases of expressing a desire to be a sea captain, a fireman, and a deputy sheriff. He had smiled and listened—and bought his boy books. Fact or fiction, they had one thing in common: they were about doctors or medicine. On Halloween, when the neighborhood sprites went trick-or-treating as devils or pirates, little Davy went door to door in a white doctor's outfit, sewn up in a size eight by Frank's personal tailor, augmented by an authentic stethoscope and a small black bag. On his birthday, the child received a microscope; at Christmas, a chemistry set. Frank fell into the habit of clipping newspaper articles about scientific breakthroughs and tributes to men of medicine. Among the family's close friends were several physicians, and the young boy was quick to notice the subtle change that came over his father when he was with them. Then he was like a peon amid royalty. He did not interrupt. He did not contradict. He hung on every word with reverence. About him was an aura of respect, deference, homage, almost idolization. Timidly, David sought an explanation.

"God sits on a doctor's shoulder, David," his father had said. "Never forget it. In his hands is the power of life and death."

When David was about twelve, at breakfast, he had casually said the magic words between spoonfuls of cornflakes: "I think I'll be a surgeon."

The young boy's life changed from that moment. That morning Frank's eyes took on a feverish zeal that increased each year until he saw his son registered in medical school. The fact that the boy would be a physician was endlessly discussed over the dinner table. His father now introduced him, "This is my son, David. He's going to be a doctor." Just the stated intention made the youngster feel that he was already a prince. His family now treated him like one. Once he had become a surgeon, he would be king. That year his father began his annual sizable donations to a famous medical school in northern California, thereby assuring his son's eventual acceptance and entry. It would be some years before David Savage would realize he had not really been given a choice. But he hadn't minded. He was someone special. *Doctor* David Savage! To the boy it sounded nice; to Frank it was a dream come true.

But if he had ambition for his only male offspring, Frank had a vision of his own. More than anything else, he wanted to head a motion picture studio. He knew his goal was not an easy one. If you wanted a studio, you just didn't go out and buy one. But he knew of several in shaky financial condition. They were blithely going ahead with production, full-steam, the executives assuring each other over lunch in the commissary that there was no need for belt-tightening, no necessity for investigating more frugal operational procedures. The trend of falling attendance at the box office was sure to change. The competition from television was a flash in the pan. So the red ink was flowing, and the stockholders were making restless noises. Screw them! You had to spend money to make money, didn't you? Frank saw opportunity in their foolishness and he bided his time.

Personally, Frank Savage was a completely moral man. He went to church, he tolerated no profanity, he met his obligations on time, his handshake was as good as any written word. He had never cheated on his wife—the thought of infidelity was repugnant to him. He spent time with his children, he was benevolent with his employees and paid them well. Had he been asked, he would have been against wars, plagues and corruption in government. But the motion picture industry was dog-eat-dog—cut your friend's jugular vein before he cut yours. And Frank Savage found himself a personally moral man in a thoroughly immoral business. There were times that compromise was mandatory.

One of the majors, Sutter Studios, was preparing a biblical epic, budgeted at two million dollars. As a talent agent, Frank was given a script. Reading it, he realized that five of the top stars under contract to his agency were perfect for the roles and he could make them available. The next morning he had an appointment with the head of the studio and offered him the five actors at a figure which the movie mogul knew for a fact was less than half their going price. It was a package deal he couldn't turn down. The box office insurance that these five stars assured was hard to come by, and his mouth watered at the thought. The contracts were signed within a few days.

It was no great mystery how Frank got his protégés to work for less than half their usual salaries. The thought of questioning his deals or his wisdom was beyond them. What else Frank told them would never be divulged.

It was a fact, however, that once shooting began, it was as if the production company were accursed, as if a great ominous black cloud hung over wherever they were working. Suddenly the top stars could not remember their lines. Equipment broke down. There were fights between producer and director—director and star—star and cameraman. It was if the weather itself were bewitched. If the scheduled scenes were exterior, it rained. If they moved the company indoors, the sun came out. The director was replaced. The lab ruined two reels in developing that had to be reshot. Script changes were demanded by the stars that had the writers rushing revised pages to the set each morning for that day's shooting, with the inevitable shut-down of production while the actors memorized their new lines. Few of the unfortunate incidents were covered by insurance. The projected budget climbed from two million to five, then to twelve million. The eight weeks' shooting schedule grew to four months, eight months.

Frank was well aware of the panic in the financial suite of Sutter Studios. Executives negotiated bank loans at high interest rates, and all other production was halted in order to funnel every dime into completing the disastrous endeavor. Their only hope was to get it finished, into the theaters, and resume a cash flow. Clerical help was cut to the bone; a parking charge was instituted for the remaining employees. Morale nose-dived. The feeble attempts at salvage, of course, were ludicrous. By the time ten million dollars had been borrowed, Frank knew that the interest payments alone were eating the studio alive. There was no way they could recuperate; there was no way they could survive.

He quietly requested another meeting with the head of the studio. The choice he offered—buying controlling interest for a fraction of its actual worth, or engaging in a proxy fight—was elemental. There was no money left to woo the stockholders. Attorneys got their heads together, and before long Frank sat behind the door of Sutter Studios that was marked "President."

Once he was entrenched, the biblical epic was magically completed. It was one of the biggest-grossing films in the industry's history. Fresh money poured in from unknown sources, bank loans were paid off, and a policy of complete efficiency was instituted. Instead of competing with television, Frank made it his ally. Deals were made with networks to supply programming. Every single dollar was used to its best advantage. The studio took on the appearance of a factory churning out products—not especially good from a creative standpoint, but highly profitable.

Frank had always envisioned himself as a great pioneer in his field, and he had sensed that a movie lot, properly run, was a potential source of great wealth. And under his guiding hand and as a result of his astute—if sometimes questionable—business practices, his dream materialized. Unlike most of the other studios in Hollywood, the town of tinsel that everyone now agreed was slightly tarnished, Sutter Studios showed a handsome and growing profit each quarter. Even his critics acknowledged that the success was due entirely to one man.

Frank Savage.

It was midmorning. Dr. Savage had called his father immediately after the meeting at the hospital. Now he waited impatiently at the entrance to the studio lot while the uniformed gate guard detained the car ahead of him and carefully directed the passenger to his destination.

That Dr. David Savage found the occurrences that morning inconceivable—unbelievable—was not entirely his fault. From the time he'd been twelve, he'd been conditioned—reminded constantly that doctors were gods. They were not like other people. They commanded and deserved special treatment. For instance, David had received innumerable speeding tickets, and each time an officer handed him one he was, besides being furious, slightly confused. Didn't they understand? Couldn't they comprehend? His time was at a premium, his work was all-important. He had a right to speed. Man-made laws applied to humans, not to him. Unable to find a space, he simply double-parked. You'd think the other drivers, the inconsiderate sons of bitches, mere mortals that they were, would realize the urgency, and leave a space for him—a doctor—wouldn't you?

After being treated with special deference for almost ten years at home, he entered medical school and immediately sensed a reverence that was not extended to his fellow students. That it was his father's tremendous donations, that a building on campus had already been named after the Savage family as evidence of the school's gratitude for the financial support, didn't dawn on him. The administrators and teachers could certainly see the aura of deification that engulfed him. When on occasion he had sex with a girl after classes, he glanced down, surprised that his prick wasn't royal purple. Inwardly, he sneered at the normality of his classmates. They laughed, they kidded, they made fun of themselves and each other, and occasionally even gibed at the profession they'd chosen. David came to a conclusion which satisfactorily explained their odd behavior and sustained him in his. They were not doctors; they would never be. They were simply mortal men who might some day practice medicine.

Once he had finished his training and opened the doors of the substantial practice Frank had bought him, his image of himself continued uninterrupted. Nurses waited on him hand and foot. Patients came in and whispered their questions and waited for his words of hope or his sentence of doom with reverential resignation. He was a superb surgeon, and he knew it. He saw it in his colleagues' eyes and in the grateful glances of his women patients. Sometimes the glances were more hungry than grateful. He knew they wanted him—not only because he was an extremely handsome man, but because he was a doctor.

As he continued to wait at the gate, Dave still fumed over the morning's meeting, his thoughts an incoherent jumble. Goddamn it, he raged. I'm a *doctor*. And those other guys are *doctors,* too. Why should they attack me? he wondered. *Doctors* should stick together. That's what's wrong with medicine. He had a sobering, comforting thought. Even Jesus Christ had had the rabble tearing at him. Are these doctors harassing me because I perform feats of medicine they know are beyond them? he speculated. Are they jealous? Jealous like the adorers at the feet of a holy man? Are they persecuting me because I'm perfect and they are not? His fury began to build again. Still, as *doctors,* they should understand my problems. They know the strains and stresses. They know the dedication. How dare they side with other people against me, a *doctor*? I didn't spend all those years going to school . . . studying medicine . . . interning . . . doing my residency, for nothing. I did it so I could be a *doctor*. So I'd be respected, admired, appreciated. I never needed the money. Those things they said—even if they were true—so what? Crazy patients . . . incompetent nurses . . . that cock-happy

Susan Thomas . . . and that sonofabitch Merrick. Compared to Dr. David Savage, they were nothing. Why didn't they understand he should not be touched by problems that confronted lesser beings? Why?

He suddenly recalled Merrick's comment about his not being needed and fought down a rising panic. I don't need Marin Medical Center, he assured himself. I'm on the staff of half a dozen other hospitals. When this is all straightened out, I may never go back there anyway. Who needs them? But they're not going to push me out—not Dr. David Savage. But if they do, what will I tell my friends?

He was still seething as he proffered his name to the guard who checked a list, handed him a pass, and tucked under his windshield wiper a small cardboard square that attested his right of access to the VIP parking lot.

He walked up the imposingly broad marble steps to the Executive Building and was stopped by another guard behind the desk. The man was dressed in maroon slacks and a gold military jacket, the studio's official colors. As he carefully examined the pass, Dave bit back a sarcastic remark, at least the motion picture industry protected its own, which was more than you could say about the medical profession.

He headed for the end of a long corridor and two huge bronze doors, obviously the realization of an art director's concept of what the entrance to a president's office should be. The knobs were gilt replicas of eagle's heads, and although the carved doors stretched from the floor to the ceiling, they swung open with surprising ease. Dave was confronted by Mildred Fraley, his father's secretary, who sat at a desk directly opposite the doors.

She glanced up and smiled pleasantly. "Good morning, Doctor Savage." Her eyes flicked to the complicated telephone console, resting for a moment on an illuminated button. "Your father just took a call from Rome. As soon as he's off, I'll tell him you're here."

Her smile hid a certain resentment she felt at the

sight of her employer's son. Not that she didn't like him—she really didn't know him that well. But his unexpected call demanding an immediate appointment with Mr. S. had necessitated the canceling of a screening of the trailer for Sutter's newest feature release. The change in schedule had meant notifying all department heads—eleven calls in all. As if the morning hadn't been hectic enough. First, their top western star, sarcastically known as "Mr. Clean," had been arrested the night before in a motel—with their child star, who was actually sixteen years old. The director of their newest epic had told the composer where he could stick his music and had walked off the set. An undetected hair in the camera had ruined some of yesterday's science-fiction flick footage. And Bessie, Sutter's famous canine star, had picked up laryngitis. Those were just the highlights, she thought grimly, just the hit tunes from the show, as she attacked the mail. Dave perched on the corner of her desk, watching as she stapled intra-studio routing slips on some letters and tossed them into her out-box. The others she stacked in various piles, according to thir importance and urgency.

"So what's new in the glamorous world of show business?" he asked inanely.

She gazed at him and hesitated only a moment. Discretion was her middle name. "Not much," she replied smoothly. "It's been very quiet. We start shooting *Once Is Only Yesterday* next Monday." She looked pointedly at the papers his hip was crunching. "You'd probably be more comfortable on the couch, Doctor Savage. Can I get you some coffee?"

He laughed shortly and moved to a chair. He didn't care for Mildred. She was in her early fifties, expensively dressed in a perfectly tailored light green suit, her gray hair softly and fashionably cut. She had been his father's secretary for over twenty years. As he had moved up the ladder, he had taken Mildred with him. She was efficient—and prudish.

"Where are all these beautiful, sexy, racy gals I hear about in the film industry?" he remarked snidely.

"Probably in front of the cameras; certainly not behind them." She picked up the phone. "Your son is here, Mr. Savage." She hung up. "Would you like to go in, now?"

Frank Savage beamed genially at his son as he watched him cross the forty-five feet from the door to the desk. He did not get up.

"Hi, Dad. How's Mom?"

"Fine. Maybe if you'd call her once in a while, she'd give you a firsthand report."

Dave shrugged and sat down in the seat near his father's desk. "How're Sarah—the kids—and Paul?" It was a prescribed ritual, and he might as well have it over and done with. Sarah, his sister, had married the head of accounting at Sutter Studios about two weeks before he was suddenly appointed treasurer of the company.

"Good, good," Frank said enthusiastically. "Paul's in Japan this week. Sent him over to see if he could make a deal to get some of our blocked money out. He's doing all right. Paul's a good man."

Sure, thought Dave. Sarah and Paul. The perfect match. They each called their respective mothers four times a week, had dinner with them every other Sunday, and had presented Frank with two grandsons.

"Mildred tells me that you start *One Is Only Yesterday* next week. With Inga Svenborg, isn't it? I read in the columns that there's some pretty sexy nude scenes." He winked lasciviously. "For that I'd rearrange my schedule and come out and take a look."

"She's a tramp—and it's a closed set," his father said shortly. "Dave, I've never interfered. Your life's your own. But why don't you find some nice girl, get married, and settle down? Like your mother says, it would be nice if we could dance at your wedding while we're still young enough to do it without having a heart attack."

Dave sighed. The question needed no answer. They'd been through it many, many times before.

"So how are things with you at the hospital?" his father asked.

"Well," Dave said slowly, "I don't know. It's been four years since you talked me into working down there—and I've worked hard. I've done a lot of surgery, and done it well. I've kept up my charts, worked in the clinic, attended all their meetings, helped teach the house staff. I've tried to be a credit to you—make you proud of me. I've broken my ass . . ."

He stopped as his father's hand slammed down hard on the desk. "Gutter talk," Frank hissed. "You were raised in a fine home. You've had the best education. But still—gutter talk!"

"Your're right. I'm sorry, Dad."

His father smiled his forgiveness. "Now, you were saying about the hospital?"

"Wouldn't you think that after all this time I'd get some recognition? As much work as I've done down there? By now I should have been appointed to the Executive Medical Board—and I'm not even on the Surgical Committee. Just recognition is all I ask—not gratitude. Why, I'm not even a member of the Senior Staff," he complained bitterly.

"Do you have any idea—any inkling—why that is?" his father asked softly.

Dave shook his head sadly. "I don't know."

Frank's voice hardened. "If they're giving you trouble, you've asked for it, David."

"But Dad, I *have* worked hard— I *have* produced," he whined defensively. "They ignore that. They take little, picky things, and exaggerate. Well, you wouldn't believe what I went through this morning."

"I believe it," his father said quietly. "I know about the meeting."

Dave stared at him in surprise.

"Don phoned me. Doctor Bruckheimer. He wanted to make sure that I understood that he wasn't a party to the whole thing, that he had no choice. He also remembered that stock tip I gave him when those two eastern film labs merged. He returned the favor. We're even. But you think I don't know what goes on at the hospital? That I need telephone calls from friends? That I sit with my head in the sand? I would have found out anyway. You think I don't know about that blond with the pushed-in face? You think I don't know about all the fights in the hospital? You've got trouble, David, big trouble—and you've got nobody to blame but yourself. Nobody! Just remember—you shouldn't fight unless it counts! You don't fight unless you're sure you'll win!"

Dave dropped his eyes. "Does that mean you won't help me?"

"Who said anything about not helping?" the older man said casually. "Where should a son go for help unless it's to his father?" He watched his son through narrowed eyes. "Now, about that girl—"

"That's a god . . . that's an absolute lie."

"Now, about that girl," Frank repeated, ignoring the interruption. "Were there any witnesses?"

"We were alone," David admitted sullenly.

"Good, good. Then she'll be no problem. We'll offer her some bucks and she'll snap at them. If she doesn't, I have a floor full of fancy lawyers who'll convince her that if she goes to court, she'll be painted as the biggest hussy that ever lived."

Hussy! Jesus, thought Dave, a word as mid-Victorian as the old man. How in the hell did someone like this manage to accumulate the wealth, the power, the respect—?

"So much for the girl. Now," Frank said sharply, "we get to the important part—the meeting. Palmer, Merrick, Welker, and Bruckheimer."

"It's Merrick who's out to get me," Dave proclaimed bitterly. "The others, they just went along. It's Merrick, all right," he repeated. "The others—they like me—they respect me."

"You're sure?"

Dave nodded. "I'm sure. I know I'm right."

"You're wrong," his father said coldly. "At the end of the meeting—after you left—they voted. Their recommendation to the Executive Medical Board when it meets Friday is that you be expelled from the surgical staff as an incorrigible troublemaker!"

Dave stared at the man seated at the desk. Stunned, disbelieving, he barely heard the words as Frank went on. "They all went on record in favor of rescinding your surgical privileges, except Bruckheimer, of course. The best he could do was try to talk them into settling for a year's probation. But it didn't work. He failed."

Aware of his father's intent eyes upon him, Dave made what was probably the most gigantic effort of his life. He squelched the boiling anger and the torrent of profanity that threatened to erupt within him. The most important thing now, he realized, even through his rage, was to enlist and assure his father's help. Experience had taught him the surest way.

"Why? Why would they do this to me?" He deliberately kept his voice low, almost humble. "Can we handle it, Dad? What do we do?"

"I can handle it," Frank said slowly. His thoughts were racing. It wouldn't be easy, but a lot could happen before Friday. "I'll tell you what *you're* going to do," he said decisively. "You're going to go back to that hospital and apologize—to Palmer, Welker, and Bruckheimer. Stay away from Merrick. Tell them you're sorry, that you've seen the error of your ways, that you'll try to do better."

"But—" Dave protested.

"And I want you to go to the nurses. Talk to them, smile at them—"

"But—"

"Then go to the pharmacy and the lab. Chitchat . . . tell a few stories—"

"But—"

"No buts," his father said firmly. "I want you back in that hospital this afternoon. And I want you there— *smiling!*"

Their eyes locked in silent battle for a long moment. Finally Dave nodded his agreement.

Mildred showed littler interest or surprise when Dr.

David Savage stormed out of the office without so much as a nod or a good-bye. She shrugged. She was used to people leaving a meeting with Mr. S. unhappier than when they went in. Her buzzer sounded.

"Mildred," Frank asked, "would you get Arthur Fleischer for me? And you'd better get him on the private line."

She dialed the number of Fleischer, Fleischer and Orman, the renowned firm of attorneys which Sutter Studios retained as outside legal counsel for corporate matters. The use of the private line did not pique her interest. Mr. S. had a deep distrust of the studio's switchboard operators, convinced that their main hobby in life was listening in and monitoring interesting conversations. Well, she thought, could be. Once connected with the firm, she asked for Arthur Fleischer and chatted with him for a few moments before she buzzed twice into the inner office, signaling Frank that his party was on the line.

"Arthur?"

"Frank, how are you? How's it going? I was going to call this afternoon. We were able to get an option on the Mueller novel, and I wanted to know—"

"Later, Arthur, later," Frank snapped. Neither man said anything for a moment. "Look, Art," Frank continued, "there's a problem at Marin Medical Center I want you to handle."

"Okay," Fleischer agreed. The attorney, besides being retained by the studio, was also house counsel for the hospital, an arrangement that was just one more trump card in Frank's carefully stacked deck. Fleischer and Savage had been involved over the years in many types of manipulations and business transactions. They understood each other. There was neither sham nor need of pretense between them.

"They're getting heavy with my boy, and I want it stopped." Quickly, completely, and with utter frankness, Frank outlined the events of the morning. Before he finished, Fleischer, who had listened carefully with-

170

out interrupting, had every shred of information, including the Susan Thomas incident. "He's my son, Art, and if he's out of line, *I'll* handle him. They've got him by the short hairs, and I don't like it."

"Well, there're several ways to approach your problem," Fleischer said slowly.

"It's not my problem, it's your problem—and I want it solved!"

"Right," Fleischer replied. "Now what we could do—"

"Not we, Arthur," Frank said shortly, "—you! And I don't care how. Just do it." The president of Sutter Studios returned the phone to its cradle, abruptly terminating the conversation.

Arthur Fleischer leaned back in his leather swivel chair and gazed out the window at the spectacular vista of Century City which his twenty-third floor office afforded. Oddly enough, he did not resent the conversation with Frank Savage nor the problem pushed upon him. He found it a challenge. Besides, nothing came cheap, and his relationship with Sutter Studios was extremely lucrative, for his firm and subsequently for himself. The Marin Medical Center account was just a dab of icing on the cake—the annual billing to the institution was almost inconsequential in ratio to the total business Fleischer, Fleischer and Orman handled each year. But because of the affiliation with Frank Savage, Fleischer handled the hospital account personally rather than, as would be normal, delegating it to a junior member of the firm. He liked the head of Sutter Studios, he admitted. He was in the minority, but he liked him. They were two of a kind. Ruthless, successful, astute in the game of keeping business dealings just within the boundaries of legal jurisprudence. When Frank Savage spoke, Arthur Fleischer jumped, and he was enough of a realist not to resent it. He suddenly turned to the desk and spoke into the phone.

"Mrs. Rievner, would you mind delaying your lunch a little while today? I have a lot of phone calls to make.

Oh, and has Mr. Regent returned from lunch?" Kenneth Regent was one of the many young attorneys the firm employed—the sharpest of the lot. "When he gets back, would you ask him to come in? I have a little errand he can do, and it should be done right away." He started to hang up. "Mrs. Rievner, are you still there? Good. Will you bring me the file on Marin Medical's Board of Directors, the one which lists their annual charitable donations?"

He edged his chair closer to the desk, withdrew a yellow pad from a drawer, and quickly started to make notes. It was time to get to work and earn his money.

"So . . . your patient is afraid that he has cancer," Dr. Merrick said, taking a sip of water.

"Hell, no, he's not afraid he has cancer. He *wants* to have cancer!"

The words were spoken by Dr. Eugene Kelly, the internist. He was of medium height, with blond, slightly wavy hair which was beginning to recede from his forehead. He wore a fashionable brown pin-stripe suit, tan shirt and conservative dark brown tie. The two men sat in Marin Medical Center's Doctors' Dinning Room, awaiting the lunch they had ordered a few minutes before.

"It's true. He wants to have cancer! And he's driving me right up the wall! Let me fill you in on the background of Mr. Brian Murdoch." Kelly tossed the bread he had been buttering back on his plate and forgot it as he launched into the personal and medical history of the patient he had asked Merrick to see. He took a deep breath.

"First of all, Murdoch is forty-four years old, married—second wife—has two kids, a seventeen-year-old boy by his previous marriage, and a four-year-old girl by his present one. His father owns the Murdoch Building Supplies Company, and sonny is employed by papa as sales manager at a pretty good salary—I'd judge maybe forty, forty-five thousand per. But even so, it seems like dear old dad, once or twice a year, has to

172

come up with a few thou to bail Brian out. Our boy's an alcoholic, and he's been married to wife number two for five years. The first Mrs. Murdoch died of ovarian cancer just a month or two before Brian remarried. They were very devoted to each other and she was the strong one—made most of the decisions. When she died, Brian remarried in a hurry, mainly because he couldn't bear facing the world alone. Donna, his present wife, was only about twenty-three when they married and, where her husband's concerned, is not the mothering type. Shortly after the wedding Brian started the heavy drinking. Donna finds it repulsive, and nags and rejects him. And when Donna rejects him, Brian drinks."

Merrick had not tried to hide his increasing amazement as the monologue went on and on, Kelly was oblivious. Though his patience was wearing thin, the chief of surgery could no longer contain his curiosity.

"Jesus, Gene," he interjected, "what kind of medical records do you keep? How do you know all this?"

Kelly shrugged, a little annoyed at the interruption. "Hell, I've taken care of the whole family for years. They've fed me this story chapter by chapter. That's the trouble with you surgeons, you don't take the time to really know your patients."

Thank God, Merrick offered silently, and willed himself to listen.

"Now every time Brian goes on a drinking binge," Kelly continued smoothly, "she retaliates by going on a shopping spree, and the bills pile up. She has expensive tastes. When the invoices come in, Brian panics and takes refuge in a bottle."

Merrick nodded. "A terrible problem, but not one that needs a surgeon," he said, hoping to bring Kelly to the point.

"I'm getting to that part," said Kelly. "Anyway, Brian can't control his wife, and he compensates by fancying himself a sharp disciplinarian with the kids. Wants them to toe the line. Which isn't easy nowadays, even if you know what you're doing. Brian ordered his son to cut his hair and get a summer job. And the kid . . .

173

well . . . he told his old man to go to hell. In just those words. So Brian punishes him by withholding spending money; Mama slips him bucks on a regular basis when he needs them. The little girl is all screwed up from the dissension in the house—still wets the bed."

Kelly had called him to consult, and Merrick reminded himself that courtesy was mandatory, but he pointedly looked at his watch. "Gene," he said warningly.

"It's important you know why the patient wants to have cancer," Kelly said, half defensively.

Merrick couldn't help himself. "Because the kid pisses in bed?"

Kelly waved away the sarcasm and went blandly on. "Still wets the bed, and she also flunked out of nursery school because she couldn't adjust. And Donna makes no bones about accusing Brian of being a pretty poor excuse for a father."

The waitress brought their lunch, a seafood salad for Kelly and a club sandwich for Merrick. The chief of surgery started to eat his sandwich slowly, but Kelly ignored his food as he continued. The internist's penchant for excessive and nonstop chatter and gossip was a joke around Marin, Merrick knew.

"About a month ago," Kelly said, "Murdoch came to me with a duodenal ulcer. He can't cope—he's never been able to—and he felt all the ground suddenly slipping out from under him. I put him on a bland diet, the usual medication, ordered him to cut out the smoking and drinking and to take a leave of absence from the job. He was hurting pretty bad, I guess. Anyway, he followed the program and the ulcer apparently healed. While he was away from work, someone subbed for him and it then became evident that sonny-boy hadn't been able to cope with his job, either. All that work he'd been shoving under the blotter came to light. The unsigned contracts, billings that hadn't gone out, correspondence that had been ignored, estimates that he'd miscalculated. After all those years, it was evident to everyone that Brian had expended all his efforts in making people think he was doing a hell of a job instead of actually doing it. From various phone calls and a little subdued chiding from Murdock, Senior, Brian realized that the fraud he'd been perpetrating had been discovered. I wasn't really aware of how serious his personal problems were when, about a week or so ago, I told him what I thought was good news—he was doing well enough to go back to work. A few days later I got this call from him: 'Doc, you gotta help me . . . I got cancer!' I assured him that I had examined him pretty thoroughly when he first came in and that it wasn't likely."

Merrick could stand it no longer. "Eat your lunch, Gene," he instructed. If the game plan was going to be "amateur psychiatrist," Merrick would show Kelly that he could play, too. "Let me see if I can do a little educated guessing. Stop me if I'm wrong." Kelly started to pick half-heartedly at the crab and lobster chunks on the top of the greens. "When our boy was sick with the ulcer," Merrick deduced, "a lot of his problems were temporarily solved, right? His wife became solicitious. After all, nobody's unkind to an invalid."

Kelly could not stand having his thunder stolen. He nodded and quickly took up the story. "And his son felt guilty. An ulcer! His father had an ulcer, and his bugging the old man had probably caused it, so he straightened up and mended his ways a bit. And even the mess at the office was excusable. It wasn't his fault, he'd been sick. But now the ulcer, which had made his life so unexpectedly pleasant, is no more. And soon he'd have to face up to all the troubles at the office. But if he had cancer! If he had cancer, then everybody would feel sorry for him. Even the lousy job he'd been doing at work would be glossed over. Like the psychiatry books would say, it's a classic example of secondary gain."

"So," asked Merrick, "what do you want from me? I'm happy to consult. But from all indications, what he needs is a shrink—not a surgeon."

Kelly laid down his fork and pushed the half-eaten salad away from him. "Well, would you like the paradox for dessert?" he queried, regaining his enthusiasm. "Brian was absolutely sure he had cancer. He complained that he'd lost his appetite, that he was having steady pain in his upper abdomen and chest. Oh, I figured he was crying wolf, but I didn't want to take any chances. So, to get him off my back and to stop the midnight phone calls, I admitted him here for tests. I ordered the usual: barium enema, IVP, gallbladder, and, of course, another upper GI series. I wanted to check on his ulcer anyway. There was a lot of pyloric scarring, but the ulcer itself had apparently healed. The ringer was that the radiologists thought there might be a pancreatic tumor, so we did a pancreatic scan and a hypotonic duodenography. The scan showed decreased uptake, but then, so what? Pancreatic scans are notoriously equivocal. But the duodenography! Some of the pictures look like a tumor of the Ampulla of Vater, and others look as normal as the day is long. And to make matters worse, the orderly had placed Murdoch's wheelchair just outside the door when I was going over the films with Reichner. He heard the word 'tumor' mentioned, so now any doubt he had is removed. He has cancer. As far as he's concerned, he's sure of it. Well, maybe he does. But one way or another, he's going to need surgery—either for the tumor, or to prove that it isn't there. The radiologists are on the fence. We repeated the study and they're still hedging. But one thing is for sure: for his psychological well-being, I'm going to have to be absolute." Kelly slapped his napkin down beside the plate with disgust. "And all I can absolutely tell him now is that if this keeps up, if he doesn't need a psychiatrist, I will!"

"Well," Merrick chuckled, reaching into his pocket for a tip, "we don't want Marin's most revered internist to end up on the funny farm. Let's go see your Brian Murdoch. Seriously, I'd like Keith Johnson, our resident surgeon, to be in on this. Do you mind if he comes along?" Kelly shook his head. "It's a good teaching situation," Merrick commented, "and if surgery should be necessary, I'd like Keith to be acquainted with the case."

A quick call to Keith from the phone in the dining room resulted in the resident surgeon meeting them in X-ray, where they studied the films of Mr. Murdoch. Next, all three meticulously scanned the patient's chart before heading for his room.

Brian Murdoch lay in bed, puffing furiously on a cigarette. He was a big man, with an ex-athlete's body, heavily muscled. As the doctors entered, Kelly leading the way, Murdoch lit a new cigarette from the butt of one he had just finished. The ashtray was overflowing with the residue of his chain-smoking, possibly twenty or twenty-five remnants which had been smoked down to the bitter end. Keith Johnson stayed unobtrusively in the background as Kelly made the introductions.

"Mr. Murdoch, this is Doctor Joseph Merrick, chief of surgery here at Marin." He knew the patient would be impressed by the title, and he was. Brian's eyes lit up with anticipation. "And this is Doctor Keith Johnson, our resident surgeon." Murdoch nodded acknowledgment, but his eyes were glued on Merrick.

"Did Doctor Kelly tell you I have cancer?" he asked quickly.

"He told me that some of the tests were inconclusive, Mr. Murdoch. Tell me, are you having any pain now?"

"No, not really," Brian admitted.

"Any nausea?" Merrick asked.

"Nausea? No . . . but I have no desire for food at all."

The questioning stopped as Merrick threw the sheet away and started examining the patient. He felt his neck, listened to his heart and lungs and probed the duodenal area where Murdoch complained of pain. There was some tenderness, he noted, but it was nominal and not surprising in light of the recently healed ulcer. He paused as he noticed the scar of an old incision which he guessed, from its location, had resulted from the patient's gall bladder, and glanced at Kelly.

177

"Cholecystectomy—about five years ago," Kelly confirmed.

Merrick finished with a rectal examination. Most of this routine was a sham and a hoax—and all three doctors in the room knew it. Kelly had examined the man previously, and there was nothing to be determined by another physical examination that the earlier one or the results of the tests had not indicated. Besides, in someone as well-muscled as Murdoch, it was ludicrous to believe that a tiny mass buried deep in the duodenum could be discerned by touch. But a patient expected the observance of this ritual and was disappointed and suspected incompetence, negligence, or disinterest unless it was done. Then, too, if Murdoch didn't feel he'd gotten his money's worth, he might not pay the bill.

"Well, Doc," Murdoch said eagerly, "I guess there's no choice except exploratory surgery, huh? When do you plan to do it?"

Merrick skillfully hid his annoyance. I've never seen anyone so anxious to be cut, he thought. Exploratory surgery—the medical equivalent of looking for a needle in a haystack—was seldom done anymore. Nowadays, sophisticated tests were usually able to zero in on a definite problem, and surgery was performed only after the diagnosis was made.

"Don't spare me, Doc," Murdoch pressed, miscalculating the reason for Merrick's delay in replying. "Give it to me straight. The only choice is an exploratory, right?"

"No," Merrick said smoothly. "There are a few additional tests to be made. First, I'd like to repeat the X-rays. Then we'll do a fiberoptic duodenoscopy."

"That sounds like pretty complicated surgery," Murdoch said gratefully.

Kelly shook his head and entered the conversation. He had to justify his billing, too. "A fiberoptic duodenoscopy is a test, Mr. Murdoch. They spray your throat with an anesthetic to deaden it, and give you some sedatives to relax. You'll swallow a small tube which will be run through your esophagus, into the stomach, through the pylorus and into the duodenum. They'll actually be able to look down there. And if there's any malignant growth, they'll be able to see it. We'll know for sure."

Murdoch's disappointment was clearly evident as he lit another cigarette and disconsolately tossed the pack on the bedside table. "When are you going to do it?"

"It takes a specialist," Merrick explained, reclaiming the floor from Kelly. "A gastroenterologist. I probably won't be able to reach him until tonight, and today's Tuesday. I'd guess maybe sometime tomorrow or Thursday. I'll let you know."

"Wednesday or Thursday, huh?" Murdoch mused. "I bet it won't prove anything, but okay. That means the exploratory surgery will probably have to be put off until the first of next week."

Merrick didn't reply as the three doctors exited the room. Outside, they looked at each other for a moment, then Merrick shrugged.

"He's a weird one, all right. We've got to bend over backwards to avoid operating on him. He doesn't want to have cancer. I doubt that he's given any thought to what it means. What he really wants is an operation. Any operation. An excuse to be sick. If we drop the knife on him, you can bet your last buck he'll have post-op pain that'll never go away. He'll be on your back for years."

"*My* back?" Kelly yelped.

"You know him so well, Gene. I'm sure he'd prefer to call you with his problems." Merrick let that sink in. "At any rate, I'll be in touch."

The internist nodded and, still shaking his head, went toward the elevator.

"I'll take care of the chart," Keith volunteered. The older doctor nodded. He was still marveling at Muroch when he heard his name called.

"Hey, Joe, wait up a minute. I was just going to phone you." Dr. Whitney Palmer had just emerged from a room a short distance away. "About the meeting this morning—and Doctor Savage."

"Nasty business," Merrick said. "But we made the

179

right decision. Has the recommendation to the Executive Medical Board been typed yet? I'd like to read it."

"Well, no . . . that's what I was going to call you about," Palmer said hesitantly, struggling to hide the embarrassment he felt. "Joe, a little while ago, Doctor Savage came up to me and apologized. He assured me we'd never have trouble with him again. He just hadn't realized . . . and, thinking back, things did get a little out of hand this morning . . . most of the problems weren't all that important. Anyway," he hurried on, anxious to unburden his conscience, "I've talked to Welker and he feels pretty much the same way. I . . . well . . . I wanted you to know that both Doctor Welker and I have changed our minds. I'm going to submit a recommendation for a year's probation." He stopped for a moment. "It's a far wiser course, Joe, it really is. It's a committee decision, and I'm glad I ran into you. I've also told Bruckheimer, and he's delighted."

"Jesus, Whit," Merrick said, astounded, "after all you heard this morning? And what about that girl? What about Susan? You can't be serious! It was settled. It was all settled this morning."

Palmer shook his head slowly. "A little time and discretion can't hurt anything. Believe me, it's the only sensible way to go. Doctor Savage deserves another chance. If you don't agree, well . . . we've made up our minds. Like I said, not five minutes ago Doctor Savage said he was sorry . . . and I believe him!"

The chief of staff had the grace to face the amazement in Merrick's eyes for a few moments before he lowered his own. What Merrick didn't know was that *fifteen* minutes ago, Palmer had gotten a very disquieting call from Arthur Fleischer. The attorney had not bothered to be especially subtle when he imparted the information that Mr. Frank Savage thought the decision made that morning was a great mistake. A mistake that Frank had every intention of rectifying. Also, it hadn't soothed Palmer's frazzled nerves when Fleischer had been thoughtful enough to ask how the Century Linen Service was doing. It wasn't general knowledge that Dr. Whitney Palmer owned the company that was Marin's chief source of linen service, and that the company's contract would soon be up for renewal. Fleischer hoped that the Board of Trustees, who had the final approval in such matters, would see the advantages of extending that contract.

"Got to go," Palmer mumbled apologetically. "I have this meeting—" He turned and hastened off, acutely aware of the almost physical force of Merrick's fury, which followed him down the corridor.

Merrick watched through slitted eyes as the chief of staff retreated. Damn it, Palmer had been with him this morning, all the way. As the facts about David Savage had been disclosed, Palmer had been thoroughly outraged, and his voice had been the loudest, the most definite, during the voting for expulsion. Something had occurred to change his mind. What could have happened? wondered Merrick. What? That Palmer had easily influenced Welker, there was no doubt. The mild-mannered hand surgeon had been a bit unsure, slightly indecisive before he had finally agreed that Savage's rights should be rescinded. Merrick's determination to get Dr. David Savage was unshaken. He had hoped for the support of the Executive Medical Board, had been sure he had it, but now with the defection of Palmer and Welker, it was very much in doubt. The fact that Savage was proving a bit elusive made Merrick that much more resolute a predator. He had to exercise the power to which his appointment as chief of surgery entitled him. Savage was out! He had decided it! That's the way it would be!

Someone had gotten to Palmer, and it was mandatory to Merrick that he discover who it had been. In his mind, he ran back over the morning's meeting as one might rerun a documentary film, searching for a clue.

Taylor. Louis Taylor. The administrator had not been entitled to vote, but he had plainly favored expulsion. He might know something. Merrick hurried for a phone and dialed the extension. He was told that Taylor was on another line. Would he wait? He would.

"Lou?" Merrick asked, after holding a considerable time before Taylor came on. "Joe Merrick. Lou, have you talked to Whit Palmer about the meeting this morning?"

"No," lied Taylor. He had just hung up. "Why?"

"He's changed his mind about Savage, decided to go for the probation bit. And he's talked Welker into going along, too. I personally think that route would be a disaster—for the patients, for the hospital, for all of us. If he calls you about it, try to make him see how wrong it is. The decision was made—"

"Doctor Merrick," Taylor interrupted, "it's odd that this should come up." He stammered for a moment. "I've been thinking about the matter all day, and well, I'm afraid I tend to agree with Doctor Palmer that the committee was hasty. It's possible that an error in judgment was being made that we all might regret. Actually, if it hadn't come up, I wouldn't have made an issue of it. But since Doctor Palmer and Doctor Welker now feel the way they do, I'd concur with that decision. In fact, I'm considerably relieved."

Louis Taylor felt no qualms about the lies. His job and main concern was the fiscal responsibility of Marin Medical Center—and Arthur Fleischer had been careful to remind him of that fact during a phone call just a short time ago. Taylor had been brooding about the conversation ever since.

First, the attorney had announced his intentions of attending Friday's meeting of the Executive Medical Board. As house counsel, he had that right. He had also casually mentioned that he'd been talking to Frank that morning. Times were tough in the movie industry. The annual fifty thousand dollars that Mr. Savage always donated to the hospital's building fund? Well, he wasn't sure he could swing it this year. Time would tell. As he had listened, Taylor's mind had been clicking away at computer speed. Fifty thousand dollars. Fifty thousand

182

less for the building fund . . . well, it wasn't happy news, but it wasn't disaster, either. But Fleischer had gone on. He'd also been talking to Jerry Davidson, who was president of Consolidated California Insurance. Would Taylor believe that he faced the same tight money problem and was also wavering about his annual donation to Marin? Fleischer had laughed indulgently. So many of Frank's friends had a tendency to overextend themselves, and squeal when they felt the pinch. And charitable donations were the first to go. He hoped Taylor understood. Taylor did, completely.

"I have a long-distance call on another line, Doctor Merrick," Taylor excused himself. "Can I call you back?"

"Do that, Lou," Merrick said.

Taylor *and* Palmer—they had both been gotten to, but good, Merrick realized. His last chance was Welker. If he could bring Welker back to his side, the vote would be split, and it would be heavy ammunition to use at the upcoming Executive Medical Board meeting. He dialed again.

Welker came on the line. "Hello, Joe."

Merrick sensed that the hand surgeon suspected the nature of his call. Why pussyfoot around? "Howard, I'm calling about the Savage decision. May I ask what made you change your mind?"

"Oh, I don't know, Joe. Whit called, and he seemed so upset . . . so sure that it was a mistake. I really didn't feel too strongly, one way or the other. And then Whit pointed out that Savage hadn't even been given a warning." Merrick felt for the first time that, at least, he was getting an honest answer. "I don't know why Whit was so anxious to change the recommendation, but he put it to me, well, almost on the basis of a personal favor. After all, it doesn't give Savage eternal rights. If he doesn't behave during the probation, he's out. Anyway, I wouldn't do anything to hurt Whit."

"I see, Howard. Okay, I was just curious." Merrick hung up. You couldn't argue with that logic, he realized.

He had a pretty good idea who was exerting all the pressure, and the certainty was growing in his mind. There was only one man who had the necessary weight to throw around—Frank Savage. Merrick searched for an avenue that would confirm his suspicions. Susan—she was the only other person directly involved. It was a slim chance, at best, but he hurried to her room.

She was in bed, raised to a semisitting position, avidly engrossed in a fashion magazine. She glanced up.

"Hi. Twice in one day? Why all the attention, doctor?" she asked anxiously. Merrick had been in that morning, on his regular rounds, as he had been each day since she was admitted, and Susan wasn't sure whether this extra attention boded good news or bad. The plastic surgeon had done his work expertly and extremely well, and the only evidence of the operation was two small wires protruding from her cheek. The swelling was down and the bruises had begun to fade. But Merrick forced himself to hide the shudder he experienced each time he saw her. The facial paralysis had not improved. On one side, her features were still lovely, smooth and waxen. On the other—the right side—it was as if that wax had been exposed to a flame which had melted it like a cheap candle. The eye drooped grotesquely, the side of the mouth was pulled down. Every muscle had lost its tone, allowing the flesh to sag. It was, thought Merrick, as if some amateur sculptor, using too-wet clay, had abandoned his task.

"I just happened to be on the floor, Susan, and had a few minutes, so I thought I'd look in on you." He sat down in the chair nearby and lit a cigarette.

"I guess this is my day for visitors," Susan remarked. "First you, then Mary, then Mr. Regent—and you again. I like it. It gets kind of lonesome up here."

"Mr. Regent?"

"Yeah. He's with—" she turned on her side and fished in the drawer of the table, extracting a business card—"Fleischer, Fleischer and Orman. Attorneys. Ever heard of them?"

"Yes," said Merrick cautiously. "I've heard of Arthur Fleischer."

She replaced the card in the drawer. "He came about my face." She paused for a moment. "You know, I was looking in the mirror this morning, and I think it's better, I really do." She looked hopefully at him for confirmation.

Merrick kept his face blank in deference to her self-delusion. Maybe the bruises were fading, but the paralysis was unchanged. "Susan, have you decided to file assault-and-battery charges against Doctor Savage? Is that why Mr. Regent was here?"

"No, he represents the Savage family. He's one of their lawyers. We did talk about it. He feels it wouldn't be very smart. After all, there weren't any witnesses, and I did go to Dave's apartment of my own free will. And Doctor Savage has a good reputation—it's really his word against mine." Merrick realized Susan was aping the attorney's words. "Mr. Regent thinks I'd be awfully embarrassed on the witness stand if some smart attorney decided to hinge his case on the fact that I might have asked for exactly what I got. He said that's what he'd do if he was against me instead of trying to help me. It isn't true," she said resignedly, "but I wouldn't want to go through that."

"Why did Mr. Regent come, Susan?" Merrick asked patiently.

"He said Mr. Savage wants to give me five thousand dollars for all I've been through. That Dave's father heard about me and felt very bad about the whole thing, and wanted to make it up. Not that he had to, mind you, he just wanted to be nice. Mr. Regent said he might even get Mr. Savage to pay any medical bills that aren't covered by insurance. He wasn't certain of that, but he said he might be able to swing it. Do you think if I held out, I could get more?"

"Did he ask you to sign anything, Susan?" Merrick asked grimly.

"No. Oh, he said if I accepted the money, I'd have to

185

sign a release. I have to let him know by tomorrow. I'm not sure what I'm going to do."

"If I were you, I'd wait."

Dr. Joseph Merrick was suddenly torn between ethical, humanitarian, and personal considerations. Susan was not aware of the seriousness of the facial paralysis. Her electromyogram, a test that would indicate the extent of seventh nerve damage, could not be scheduled for several weeks, when the necessary time would have elapsed to indicate the extent to which the muscle had been denervated. Not until the test was done could he be sure that the nerve injury was serious and permanent. But years of clinical experience made him strongly suspect that this was the case. There should have been some improvement, if only the slightest bit, when the swelling had begun to disappear. And even though Susan was a nurse, and probably a good one, he thought, her training and her work as an admitting nurse could in no way give her the same insight as his. She was certainly aware of her sagging face, but Merrick knew that Susan had convinced herself that it was a temporary condition that would clear up, just as the swelling had done. Merrick and Palmer had not told her this, but neither had they told her she was wrong. They were pessimistic, but you just didn't tell a patient bad news until you were absolutely sure. There was no harm in this practice . . . normally. Now Merrick realized that Susan was about to make a decision that could affect her whole life—a decision which, because of withheld information, she was in no position to make. How much should he tell her? He would have to feel his way.

"Don't make any decision now, Susan," he advised.

"But Mr. Regent said I had to let him know tomorrow. He's going to call me in the morning."

She must not sign a release, Merrick decided. For her own good. The fact that the existence of such a paper would lessen David Savage's jeopardy was beside the point, he righteously assured himself.

"Susan, you've seen your face. You know there's seventh nerve dysfunction, and until the tests are made we have no hard prognosis of how much recovery there's going to be."

"How much recovery? *How much!*" Susan shrieked. "You told me there wouldn't be any problem. That I'd get well. That—" She stopped, her voice dropping to a whisper as she remembered. "No, you didn't tell me that, did you? *I* told me that!"

"Quit kidding yourself." He had no choice, he told himself, but to emphasize the point. "You've looked in the mirror. Your face should have shown some improvement by now. It hasn't. You know it and I know it. The paralysis may be permanent. If it is, how will you get a job? Where will you work? What will you do? How will you live? Until you know, don't make any deals with Doctor Savage!"

"Oh, God!" wailed Susan, running her fingertips lightly over the damaged side of her face. "Oh, God . . . Oh, God . . . Oh, God . . . Oh, God!" Her voice rose in a crescendo of anguish. Merrick left, shutting the heavy wood door behind him. He could still faintly hear her screams outside. He felt sorry for her, but he was too set on nailing David Savage to console her. He went to the nurses' desk.

May I have Miss Thomas' chart, Mrs. Rosen?" he asked. "And would you call my office and ask my girl to get in touch with Doctor Hauptmann? He's a gastroenterologist. Tell her to have him call me here."

As she handed him the chart, he spied the five-pound box of chocolates prominent on the desk. "From a patient . . . an admirer . . . or both?" he asked lightly.

"You're never going to believe this, Doctor Merrick," Mrs. Rosen responded. "We still don't." She handed him the card that was attached to the candy.

"To all the nurses on four-north," he read, "with my affection, respect, and gratitude." It was signed, "David Savage."

"Would you like a piece?" the nurse asked brightly, starting to remove the lid.

"No," Merrick said shortly. "And Miss Thomas is going to need another 10 mg of Valium. Right away." She nodded.

Joseph Merrick's hand shook slightly as he wrote the covering order. He didn't have a battle plan yet, and the enemy was gathering strength—but he had not exhausted his stratagems. If it meant taking on the whole Savage tribe to destroy David, so be it.

Chapter V

... wednesday

"How are we doing?"

"Fine, doctor. Pulse eighty-two, blood pressure one twenty over eighty," the anesthesiologist reported.

Keith glanced at Mike curiously, then checked the clock on the wall in Operating Room Number Two. It was 7:22 on Wednesday morning and Mike had started the hysterectomy on Mrs. Mendosa some ten minutes before. They were already almost half through and everything was going smoothly—couldn't be better, in fact—but this was the third time Carrington had checked with Dr. Durham. There was something special about this girl, Keith decided, thinking back. Everything indicated it.

Roger Durham was admittedly the best anesthesiologist available, and Mike had gone to considerable pains to secure him for this operation which, from all indications, was a routine, uncomplicated procedure. Carrington had scrubbed early and had made it a point to be in the operating suite when the patient was wheeled in. He had joked with her, reassured her, and hovered like a mother hen during every step of the anesthetic. And just the fact that Mike was doing Mrs. Mendosa as his first surgical case of the day, Keith reminded himself, gave credence to his opinion. Carrington had five operations scheduled, and a couple were tough ones. There was a varicose-vein ligation which was a tedious, tiring, time-consuming procedure; the biopsy of a breast that would probably result in a mastectomy; a hiatus-hernia repair; and a cholecystectomy, the removal of a gall bladder. Yet Mike was operating on Mrs. Mendosa first, veering from his normal routine of doing the lengthiest, most difficult procedures early, while he was still fresh, and delaying the easy, routine ones until later in the day.

It was true. Mike had deliberately scheduled Jeannie for 7 A.M. Knowing the anguish that the anticipated hysterectomy was causing her, he could at least spare her the additional torture of waiting.

He's quite a man, Keith thought. He enjoyed assisting Carrington. No, he thought, he could go a step further: he'd rather work with him than with any other surgeon on Marin's staff.

Keith remembered the surge of admiration that had swept over him a short time ago when, after Durham had given the go-ahead, he had watched Mike deliberately walk around and take his place to the left side of Mrs. Mendosa, rather than step to whichever side of the patient was closer to him, as most surgeons would. He had been surprised for a moment, then with sudden insight, it had occurred to Keith that Mike, through careful analysis, realized a fact that few other surgeons had considered. When an operation involved deep suturing in the pelvis, if the surgeon was right-handed, the pubic bone in the lower end of the surgical field was an obstruction if he stood on the right. But if he stood on the left, manipulation of the curved surgical needle was much easier and more graceful. Keith made a mental note of it. He was here to learn. And Carrington was an extraordinary teacher.

Keith straightened up and simply watched Mike for a few moments. His surgical technique was a pleasure to observe. Carrington operated with a smoothness and natural rhythm, without a single superfluous movement. Every motion was made to count. There was no sense of hurry, yet he worked extremely swiftly. He was relaxed, easygoing, pleasant; he hoarded his energy. There was none of the frantic, spastic, wasted activity and bustle that so many of the other surgeons displayed. Carrington was easy on himself, and easy on his surgical team. His operations were completed in minimal time, saving the agonizing, boring, unnecessary hours that a slow, disorganized, tense surgeon inflicted on his assistants. As Keith continued to watch, a basic truth suddenly dawned on him: each surgeon operated exactly according to his own basic personality. They were what they were, and stepping into a surgical suite did not change them.

"How's it going?" Mike asked Durham for the fourth time.

"No problems. Couldn't be better," the anesthesiologist confirmed. Over Mike's head, Durham grinned at Keith. He too, was aware of Carrington's special concern for this patient, and cheerfully respected it.

In deference to Mike's concentration, Keith delayed the usual small talk until the uterus had been removed and the two men had begun the task of closing the incision.

"I didn't see you in the Record Room this morning," Keith observed.

Mike glanced up. "Yeah. What about that? I couldn't get in."

"Didn't they tell you? They lock it every night now. Two typewriters were stolen. Just disappeared. So that whole area is locked until nine in the morning."

"Then how'd you get in?"

"Oh," Keith explained, "they have a key in Admitting, but you have to get them to let you in and out."

"That's going to be a pain in the ass," Carrington grunted. "It's really that bad, huh?"

Keith chuckled. "That's nothing. You know the old black-and-white TV set in the Residents' Lounge? Well, it was stolen about three weeks ago. In broad daylight. Two guys in white uniforms appeared and asked where the television set was. And Housekeeping obligingly showed them. They took the back off, shook their heads, and then said they'd have to take it into the

191

shop. No one questioned them, and no one ever saw them or the set again."

Mike made a disapproving sound with his tongue, but he couldn't conceal the twinkle of laughter in his eyes. He glanced at Durham once again. The anesthesiologist anticipated the question.

"Everything's fine, doctor."

The sewing, tying, and cutting procedure of closing was almost finished as Keith continued.

"But that's not the end of the story. Two days ago, the residents took up a collection and bought a brand-new color console set. Boy, it was a beauty. And sometime, right in the middle of last night, it disappeared. No one can figure how in the hell they got the set out. The elevator to the ground floor from the lounge is shut off at night. They had to carry it down three flights of stairs. It weighed a ton!"

"So what now?" Mike pressed.

"You know Doctor Bolker?" Keith asked. "Well, he's up in the lounge right now drilling holes in the floor and baseboards, anchoring ring bolts in cement. They've got a new set coming this afternoon. And when it comes, it's gonna be chained so tight to the wall that it'll take an army to get it loose."

"Chained to the wall, huh?" Mike muttered, without looking up. "My God, tomorrow the whole third floor will be gone!"

He breathed a sigh of relief as, the surgery finished, they exited the O.R. Jeannie would be fine. The pre-operative X-rays had demonstrated no evidence of spread, and after his careful and meticulous examination of Jeannie's entire abdominal cavity during the surgery, there was nothing even to suggest that the malignancy had not been confined to the uterus. They'd gotten it! Mike was as sure as he could possibly be.

Keith could contain his curiosity no longer. "Is Mrs. Mendosa somebody special?"

"She is to me," Mike grinned. "A school pal from way back." He thought for a moment. "You know, she's probably one of the first friends I ever had. Hey, if you have a few minutes now and then, and happen to be on the floor, stop in and see her. I think you two would like each other."

Mike paused as usual to check if there were any telephone messages taped to the door. At this early hour, there was only one: "Call Mrs. Edith Frankel," and the number. He crumpled the note and was about to discard it, then suddenly had second, and more charitable, thoughts. Taking a moment, he smoothed the wrinkles from it, folded the paper, and slipped it into his tunic pocket. As much as he disliked Aaron Metz' daughter, she probably *was* concerned about her father—it was only natural. He owed her the courtesy of returning the call. In due time, Mrs. Frankel, he thought—in due time. He was not sure he could stomach the woman at this early hour.

After dictating the required operative note, he wrote the covering orders on Jeannie's chart and went to check on her in the Recovery Room. She was coming along just great. He touched her face, gently awakening her.

"It's all over, Jeannie, and you're fine—just fine!"

"Hmmmmm?" she said sleepily. "Neat—now go away." And she was back under the effect of the anesthesia. He grinned to himself. Reaction normal. But she would remember his assurance when she finally awoke, and that was important.

Arriving early, Johnny Mendosa had been able to spend a few minutes with his wife before they had taken her upstairs, and Mike knew he was still waiting in the room. He realized that although Johnny was concerned that the operation itself had gone well, his real worry was whether the cancer had been caught in time, so he hurried down with the good news. Her husband's tremendous elation and relief were evident as the two men shook hands warmly. He'd be back later, Johnny promised.

There was usually about forty-five minutes between surgical cases while the operating room was cleaned and sterilized in preparation for the next procedure. Mike mentally ran over the details of his second case: the breast biopsy. The woman was almost seventy and her age, plus the physical characteristics of the tumor, made malignancy almost a certainty. The advanced years of the patient did not overly concern him. Experience had proven that elderly people could withstand the planned, gentle physical trauma, and once the malignancy was removed, Mrs. Fogarty had an average chance of living eight or ten more years. She'd be able to enjoy her grandchildren, tend her garden, and play bingo at her church for a considerable while longer. It was worth it.

Mike headed for the doctors' lounge to kill the necessary waiting period, having a cup of coffee and a cigarette. He had just left the lounge to begin scrubbing when he heard the page.

"Doctor Carrington. Doctor Michael Carrington."

After Mike had identified himself, a brisk, masculine voice came on the line.

"Doctor Carrington?"

"Yes."

"This is Francis Emmert of the law firm of Grosbeck, Emmert and Meyers. Our client, Mrs. Edith Frankel, has been appointed by the court as conservator of her father's person. We are sending you a letter to that effect today by registered mail. It is also ordered that you cease and desist all treatment of Mr. Aaron Metz until he is seen by a consultant who is to be designated by our client."

Well, Mike thought, as he hung up, Edith certainly hadn't wasted any time making good her threat. He fished in his pocket and glanced at his watch. He still had a few minutes to spare before they'd be ready for him in surgery. As he replaced the watch, his fingers contacted the message from Edith Frankel. He stared at it for a moment, then crumpled it, squeezing it into a tight little wad, and basket-balled it into a nearby trash container. So much for common decency. He wondered if Patrick Schuster, his attorney, was in his office yet. It wouldn't hurt to try. He dialed the number and was delighted when Schuster answered.

"Pat, I've only got a moment, but do you remember the incident I talked to you about a few days ago? Aaron Metz and his daughter, Edith Frankel?"

"Yep," said Schuster. "What now?"

"I've just been notified by baby-doll's attorneys that she's got a court order appointing her conservator of Aaron's person. Also, that I'm to stop all treatment until a consultant is designated by her. Pat, we're just starting the X-ray and chemotherapy on Mr. Metz. I'd hate to interrupt it at this point. What do you think?"

The attorney pondered for a moment. "Mike, is there anything that's being done which might result in a difference of opinion among doctors? Anything that a legitimate consultant could point an accusing finger at?"

"Hell, no," Mike snorted. "What's being done is the accepted therapy. I've already had Doctor MacPherson in, and he's the top chemotherapist in the Los Angeles area. He worked out the treatment schedule, not me. And our radiologists here concur."

"Then don't sweat it," Schuster advised. "Just take care of your patient. Besides, you know, there has to be a formal hearing to prove that her father's incompetent if she persists in this. And that could take weeks—months, even. Of course, that's probably what she's counting on. Do you remember the name of the attorney?"

"Mr. Emmert," Mike recalled, "of Grosbeck, Emmert and Meyers."

"Emmert? Francis Emmert?" Schuster asked. "I think I met him at a Bar Association meeting a few months ago. Let me give him a call. He's pretty sharp, and has a good reputation, too. I have a feeling that Metz' daughter has misrepresented some of the facts to him. Once Emmert is aware of the actual situation, I think he'll see the light and advise his client not to press for a formal hearing. In the meantime, Mike, like I told you, continue to do whatever is medically proper."

"Thanks, Pat," Mike said. "Sorry to bother you with these crappy problems. Why don't they just let me practice medicine?"

Schuster laughed. "Crappy problems? You think you've got crappy problems? Give a thought to poor old Francis Emmert. He's got Edith Frankel. Call me any time," he assured Mike, before cutting the connection.

Over an hour ago, Mike had completed the mastectomy on the elderly woman, and he and Keith were now involved in their third surgical procedure of the day: the hiatus-hernia. Mike had just made the incision—from sternum to belly button—when the circulating nurse spoke from the door.

"Doctor Carrington," she called. "The surgical desk has four-north on the line. You have an Aaron Metz? His daughter is down there insisting on seeing him. Mrs. Rosen wants to be sure that the 'no visitors' order is still in effect."

Mike was concentrating on placing the wound-spreader and didn't look up. "The order stands. Be sure they enforce it."

"Right, doctor," the girl said. "I'll tell them."

The two men were working their way deep into the abdomen toward the diaphragm, and for want of something to talk about, Mike filled Keith in on some of the most interesting facets of Aaron Metz and his experience with Edith Frankel. As he finished the brief saga, he grinned.

"That daughter's a bitch on wheels, let me tell you. For Mrs. Rosen to call me in surgery to confirm a written order, somebody must be giving her a hard time. I wonder what's going on down there?"

It was probably just as well he didn't know.

Edith Frankel, accompanied by her husband Ed, had sailed through Marin Medical Center's lobby some minutes before. They had not stopped at Admitting, but had made their way directly to the elevators and on to the fourth floor. As they moved along the corridor, Mrs. Rosen, the head nurse, watched intently. She recognized Mrs. Frankel, and the scene with the ambulance attendants was still fresh in her mind. Her eyes followed them as they swept past her, deeply engrossed

196

in conversation, their low tones practically inaudible. When they had almost reached Aaron's room, Mrs. Rosen moved quickly to intercept them.

"I'm sorry, Mrs. Frankel," the nurse said firmly, indicating the prominent yellow-and-black card hung on the door: "No visitors. Doctor's orders."

"Now look here, young lady," Edith said sharply. "This is my husband. And we're sick and tired of the high-handed methods of this hospital—and your Doctor Carrington. You have no legal right to prevent me from seeing how my father is, and I've every intention of going in there to check on him."

"I am sorry, but we're just following orders," Mrs. Rosen explained crisply, still blocking the door. There was a strong smell of alcohol about the couple, she noted. Not that they were drunk, but they had probably had several stiff ones to bolster their courage, she surmised.

"I've gotten a court order," Edith blustered, "and in an hour or two, this hospital will be put on notice. So unless you want lots of trouble, just get out of my way."

Mrs. Rosen shook her head. "I don't know anything about court orders, Mrs. Frankel, but if you'd like to see someone in Administration, the offices are on the first floor and—"

Ed Frankel entered the argument. "This is the most ridiculous thing I've ever heard. We're family. Edith is his daughter—his next of kin. She's responsible for him. We intend to find out what's going on in there"—he indicated Aaron's room—"and we intend to find out right now! I want to talk to someone with a little weight around here. Suppose you get the head nurse."

"I am the head nurse, Mr. Frankel. No one can see Mr. Metz without Doctor Carrington's personal approval."

"Well . . . I've never heard of such a thing," Edith fumed. "Suppose you get Carrington here, then. And get him here right now!"

Mrs. Rosen sighed. She could tell it just wasn't going to be her day. "I'm sorry, but Doctor Carrington is in surgery. If you like, I'll try to reach him by phone. Would you mind stepping over to the desk with me?" It was actually a ruse to move the conversation farther from Aaron's door. She was afraid the words might filter into the room, and she had become very fond of the old man.

Mrs. Rosen made the call to the surgical suite, and was forced to hold on for some minutes. As Edith and Ed Frankel waited, they spoke in low, guarded, conspiratorial tones.

"What did Mr. Emmert tell you again, Edith?"

"How many times do I have to tell you," his wife said crossly. "He said Carrington's attorney had advised the doctor to ignore the order and continue medical treatment."

"Then what the hell good is a court order? What's Emmert going to do?"

"I don't know," Edith admitted, "but he said it might take months to enforce the order if Carrington doesn't cooperate. He suggested another meeting with me to go over the facts again."

"Edith, did you pay Emmert?" her husband demanded.

"Wh—why, yes. I gave him a check," Edith stuttered.

"We'll stop payment," Ed decided. "He hasn't earned it."

Edith stared at her husband, but finally nodded in agreement. "But right now," Ed continued, "let's remember that there's over sixty thousand dollars at stake here. And every day that passes decreases that figure by a couple of hundred dollars. Think of it, Edith. A couple of hundred dollars a day—at least! Our only chance is to talk your father into leaving here of his own free will. Once we get him home—"

He stopped, noticing Mrs. Rosen hanging up the phone. The nurse shook her head. "I'm sorry."

Suddenly Ed Frankel darted for Aaron's door. "Come on, Edith," he called. Mrs. Rosen watched, a trifle stunned, as the two disappeared into Mr. Metz' room. She spoke to the other nurse behind the desk who, up to now, had been an innocent but interested observer.

"Peggy, will you call the Nursing Office? Tell them what's happened. And ask them to get somebody up here on the double." She then hurried to Aaron's room.

Edith had flung herself across the bed to embrace her father, obvious of the running IV. Aaron looked up in surprise, clicked off the television set which was his constant companion, and then winced as Edith's purse caught on the tubing, painfully jiggling the needle.

"Edith? Ed? How are you?"

"How are *we*?" gushed his daughter. "How are *you*? You'll never know how worried we've been, how concerned. Why, Ed even took the day off from work so—"

"I'm feeling better—much better," Aaron said quietly. Before he could go on, Mrs. Rosen was in the room.

"Please, Mr. and Mrs. Frankel, I'm asking you once more. Please leave." The nurse turned to Aaron. "Doctor Carrington left orders that you were to have no visitors without his approval, but your daughter—"

Edith ignored Mrs. Rosen. "Papa! Papa—please," Edith cried, "please come home with us. All you have to do is say you want to, and they can't keep you here. You've got to come home with us, we've gone to so much trouble."

Beatrice Lamont, Marin's nursing supervisor, strode into the room. She was middle-aged, a tiny woman, not quite five feet, but the air of authority about her brought the conversation in the room to a standstill. Louis Taylor was right behind her. A quick, hurried consultation in the corner of the room permitted Mrs. Rosen to bring Mrs. Lamont up to date. Louis Taylor, however, had been generally apprised of the situation over the phone, and he wasted no time in taking over.

"Mr. and Mrs. Frankel, I'm Louis Taylor, administrator for Marin Medical Center," he said briskly.

"Well," said Ed bluntly, "it's about time someone with a little authority took some interest in this whole can of

199

worms. It's a deplorable situation, believe me, when a daughter is prevented from seeing her own father. I think it's time that this whole matter was straightened out."

Pointedly ignoring Mr. Frankel's tirade, Taylor turned to Aaron Metz. "Mr. Metz, Doctor Carrington has left specific orders that you are to have no visitors without his prior approval. Mrs. Rosen has just checked with him, and he does not want you upset. Now, do you want your daughter and son-in-law to stay—or leave Basically, you're the one who has the right to decide."

Everyone stared at Aaron expectantly.

"Well—" the old man hesitated. He realized that Taylor had unwittingly made him the heavy. "So, now you are all looking at me—and Solomon I'm not. If Doctor Carrington says no visitors—"

"Papa," Edith interrupted, "you heard him. It's up to you."

Aaron pondered for a moment. "What can I say? All I know is that I maybe felt a little better before you came in than I do now."

"Papa, please," pleaded Edith, envisioning her last chance disappearing. "Tell them you want to go home. We've gone to so much trouble. I even went to court and had myself appointed your conservator. But it's going to take time, and well, Papa, the attorney fees Ed and I have paid for you—you wouldn't believe it. We've done everything we can. Don't make it all for nothing."

"Conservator?" Aaron repeated, picking up on that single word.

"Papa, *somebody* has to look out for your interests— your welfare!"

"You went to court for it?" There was little doubt that Aaron correctly recognized the implications of his daughter's newest gambit.

"Papa, what's the difference?" Edith tried to mend her fences.

"Just come home. Do you think any of these people care about you?"

"Yes," the old man said softly, "yes, I do." He

turned on his side. "I'm tired, Edith. I thank you and Ed for coming. I thank you from the bottom of my heart. But please—go home now—and check with Doctor Carrington before you come again." He deliberately closed his eyes.

It was all the answer Louis Taylor needed. He started to herd the Frankels out the door. Suddenly, Ed stopped, planting his feet firmly.

"Just a minute—just a goddamned minute. Now, my wife's got a court order for Carrington to cease and desist all medication until we get a consultant in on this case. So what's that stuff running into the old man's arm? We've got a right to know."

Taylor shrugged and looked at Mrs. Rosen questioningly.

"It's a cancer chemotherapeutic agent," she whispered. The word "cancer" was a no-no in medical circles when the patient was within earshot. "Malignancy," "carcinoma," "tumor"—all were used instead of the dreaded word which was so firmly linked with sure death in the public's mind. "It's 5-Fluoro-Uracil," she explained.

"And just how much does a bottle of that junk cost?" Ed Frankel asked, his voice loud and aggressively harsh.

"I'm not really sure, Mr. Frankel," Taylor said. He didn't like the way this was going. "If you and Mrs. Frankel would like to come to my office, I'll be happy to check with accounting." The immediate strategy, he knew, must be to get them out of the room.

"The hell with you," the man suddenly rasped. "We paid good money for that court order. And it said all medication was to be stopped—and by God, that's the way it's going to be. No one's going to make fools out of us!"

Unexpectedly, he ducked behind Taylor and rushed to the side of the bed. Grasping the IV bottle, he wrenched it from the hook and smashed it to the floor. The violent action literally tore the needle from Aaron's thin arm. He gave a shriek of pain. Mrs. Rosen ran to him, and Edith was right on her heels.

"Papa, Papa," Edith moaned. "Ed didn't mean it. I'm sorry. I'm sorry," Mrs. Rosen brushed her aside and began repairing the damage.

"Mrs. Lamont," Taylor ordered, "call the police—call them right now!"

"Police!" hissed Ed Frankel. "Police! For what? For wanting to take care of my father-in-law? We're good people. We've got this court order. The law's on our side!" He grasped his wife's elbow and propelled her from the room. "Come on, Edith, let's get out of here."

When Mike finished the hiatus-hernia surgery he checked in with Mrs. Rosen. As she related the details concerning the recent Frankel incident, Mike shook his head. He studied the chart. From all indications, the patient had suffered no lasting ill effects.

"I'll look in on Mr. Metz now, while I still have a few minutes," he told Mrs. Rosen. "If they call for me from the O.R., let me know."

She nodded. "I think he's okay, Doctor Carrington. The needle ripped his arm pretty bad. It was painful, but I don't think serious. We patched it up and gave him a light sedative."

"Has anyone heard anything more from the Frankels? Something is going to have to be done about them. They're real menaces."

"Well, Mr. Taylor has notified Admitting and everyone here on the floor that if they come again, we're to call Security immediately. They'll escort them off the hospital premises. And if that doesn't work, he said he'll talk to you about getting our legal department to sue for a restraining order."

Mike shook his head. "The Frankels are the type who make the members of the legal profession very happy and wealthy men."

Carrington entered Aaron's room. The television set was on, but the old man was lightly dozing. He opened his eyes as the doctor approached the bed.

"Well, Mr. Metz—I heard you had a bit of excitement down here today. How do you feel?" As Mike spoke, he gently removed the compress from Aaron's arm. Like Mrs. Rosen had reported, it was painful, but no serious damage had been done.

"How do I feel? Okay. A little tired, maybe."

"Any nausea?" Mike asked.

"No."

"Well, look, Mr. Metz, sometimes these treatments make you a little sick to your stomach, but you don't have to be. There are pills that will cope with that. I've left orders for them, so if you have any nausea, you tell the nurses right away. Okay?"

"Okay, doctor," Aaron agreed.

"Got two more operations to do, Mr. Metz, so I have to get back. I'll see you later tonight. Now don't forget about those nausea pills." Mike turned and was just about to leave the room, but stopped as he heard Aaron chuckle. He looked back, questioningly.

"Those pills, doctor? Will they work when the nausea is caused by relatives?"

Mike grinned. "I don't know, Mr. Metz. But if they do, maybe we could patent them, and both make a million dollars."

"A million I don't need," Aaron said drily. "Look at the trouble a few thousand is causing." The old man's laughter followed Carrington out the door.

Dr. Joseph Merrick was unaware of the skirmish that had been waged on the fourth floor. He was busy preparing for his own war—the one that he expected to erupt in open, no-holds-barred fighting come Friday morning at the Executive Medical Board meeting.

He had spent the past few hours phoning the various members of that board, using one pretext or another. And while it wasn't exactly ethical to discuss such business outside the hallowed walls of the Board Room, he was able to justify it satisfactorily. By God, he thought, the opposition wasn't concerned with the rules. Not by a damn sight. He knew that the recommendation for a year's probation by the joint meeting of the chiefs of staff would be tremendously influential. In fact, in all his years, he couldn't remember a single instance when the Executive Medical Board had not followed the recommendation of one of its ad hoc committees. A year's probation, he thought angrily. A light tap on the wrist for Dr. David Savage. Bullshit! Savage didn't deserve breathing space in the same hospital with Joseph Merrick. The facts concerning the situation were unique. And he made this clear as he managed, one by one, to contact each of the twenty members that constituted the Executive Medical Board.

He had hit upon a strategy for these conversations that worked extremely well. As chief of surgery, Dr. Merrick was privy to certain highly confidential information, and a few days before he had learned that Marin Medical Center was currently in negotiations with one of the city's largest trade unions—a union with a membership of almost ten thousand individuals. During a recent election, the labor organization had promised its members a unique type of medical and hospitalization coverage, and it intended to keep that campaign promise. The plan would make it possible for any member to check into Marin Medical Center, and get his problem diagnosed; once that had been accomplished, a specialist would be assigned as the case necessitated—a gynecologist, a general surgeon, an internist, whatever. It was a step toward socialized medicine—a looming and constant terror to the medical profession—but it would be tremendously lucrative for Marin and its staff of professionals. Negotiations were still in the embryonic stages, Merrick knew, and none of the administrative details had yet been touched upon. But that did not deter him.

He reached for the phone again and placed a call to Dr. Randolph Maughm, a gynecologist member of the Executive Medical Board. Merrick's strategy hadn't failed yet. He'd see if he could bat 100 percent.

"Randy? Joe Merrick. I was just reading your Op-Note on that Fallopian pregnancy. Beautiful job." First step accomplished. The ego had been inflated and buttered, his target was receptively mellow. "The reason I'm calling, Randy . . . have you heard about this new contract Marin is about to sign?" Naturally, Maughm had not, and as Merrick casually explained the proposed union tie-up, Dr. Maughm became all ears. You could practically hear him panting on the other end of the line. "Anyway, Randy, I'm not sure how the doctors will be assigned, but I certainly would want to see someone who is as fine a gynecologist as you get his share. There are a couple of thousand women in that membership, and most of them will need a good GYN man sooner or later. I just wanted to make sure you were interested . . . that it was okay to include you on the list I'm preparing."

It wasn't an out and out lie; nothing Merrick had said was an utter falsehood. There was a vast difference, the chief of surgery assured himself, between lying and implying. He had not stated, really, that the list he was preparing had anything to do with the union contract, nor had he actually said that he would have the authority of assigning doctors once the deal was made. Merrick was counting on the inbred reticence of every doctor, and their intrinsic desire for both work and financial gain, to prevent repercussions from his premature disclosure of the potential union contract. Each doctor, Merrick was sure, would carefully abstain from discussing his call with any colleagues. The doctor in question would, number one, feel that he was among a chosen few and, number two, would be extremely reluctant to divulge the possibility and source of such a windfall of business to his competitors.

As soon as Merrick was sure that he had Dr. Maughm properly impressed, he effortlessly swung into the crux of the call.

"Well," he said as though about to hang up, "I'll see you at the Executive Medical Board meeting Friday morning, Randy." He paused briefly. Experience from the previous calls had indicated that a count of four was exactly long enough. "It'll be an interesting meeting.

From what I hear, something weird is going on. Anyway, I'll see you then." He waited. Doctors were naturally extraordinarily curious. It was a requisite of a good diagnostician. The reply was always the same.

"Wait a minute, Joe. What do you mean, weird? What's happening?"

"I probably shouldn't tell you this, Randy," he countered, willing the properly embarrassed, perplexed tone into his voice. "But I guess I have to talk to someone—" Merrick then went into the details of the chiefs of staff's meeting, the original vote, Palmer's inexplicable turnabout, his own feelings that outside forces were at work, insidiously undermining the good of the patients, the doctors, the Medical Center. He ended up with a heartrending account of the Susan Thomas case, so dramatic it would have shamed Lionel Barrymore, imparting the information that even she was being bought off for a pittance.

"God," Merrick concluded, "I can't believe that I'm the only member of the Executive Medical Board who still has integrity. But there's no doubt that David Savage's surgical rights should be rescinded, and I can't imagine any intelligent, honorable man voting otherwise."

The response was, of course, absolutely predictable. Merrick could certainly count on another vote for expulsion.

"You won't mention this conversation to anyone, will you, Randy?"

"Not a soul, Joe," Maughm sincerely assured him. "It's just between us. You have my word on it. And I appreciate your calling."

And that's the way it had gone, all the way down the list. The phone calls were almost photostatic in their alikeness. Even Dr. Fulton, who had been Dr. Savage's champion at the original meeting, had expressed a gratifying degree of dismay and outrage. "Jesus, Joe, if what you say is true—" he had said.

"It's true," Merrick had assured him, before trium-

206

phantly hanging up. The Fulton call was the acid test, he knew. If it swayed Fulton—

Double-checking, he found that he had called every member, and even allowing for a certain percentage of defection at the last moment, he was confident that by next week, Dr. David Savage would be barred from practicing medicine at Marin Medical Center. Dr. Joseph Merrick would have won!

He glanced at his watch; he was running late. He had reached Dr. Hauptmann, the gastroenterologist, the previous afternoon and explained the Brian Murdoch problem. Luckily, Hauptmann was available on such short notice because of a foul-up in scheduling at another hospital. He had promised to be at Marin by four thirty to do the fiberoptic duodenoscopy, and it was past that time now. Merrick wanted to be present when it was done, so he left his office immediately.

Up on the eighth floor, Mike and Keith had just begun Carrington's final surgical procedure of the day: the varicose-vein ligation. Both men were busy clamping off veins and tying them when the circulating nurse poked her head through the door.

"Doctor Carrington, I hate to bother you again, but your office is on the phone. They've had a call from the District Attorney's office, wanting to know if they can see George Selkins at ten thirty tomorrow morning."

Mike considered for a moment. "Tell my office to check with Mrs. Selkins and an attorney by the name of Robert Bradley—see if they're available then. If Bradley can't make it, have my receptionist tell the DA they just haven't been able to get in touch with me."

Mike had been measuredly tapering off the alcohol IV Selkins had been receiving for the past few days, and knew that his patient was in as good a shape to face the confrontation with the law as he'd ever be. But Mike had made a promise that he intended to keep.

A short time later he was advised, "Your office called. Ten thirty tomorrow morning it is. Everybody's been notified."

As Dr. Joseph Merrick traveled the distance between his office and Marin Medical Center, he was in high spirits, bolstered and encouraged by how well his strategy was working against David Savage. He entered the hospital still humming. The only tiny cloud on his personal horizon was that he half regretted calling Dr. Adolph Hauptmann to do the fiberoptic duodenoscopy on Brian Murdoch.

The practice of patient referral between doctors was unbelievably complicated, with as many varied and subtle facets as a high-styled ballet. The giant and rapid strides being made in medicine made specialization mandatory. No doctor—no human being—can possibly hope to keep abreast of the new discoveries, procedures, and techniques in every field. So many referrals were made on that basis alone. The patient's doctor, realizing he didn't have the scope of knowledge demanded by a particular problem, and having the best interest of his patient at heart, referred him to the best specialist in the area. That, of course, was the ideal referral.

Unfortunately more mundane and selfish considerations also cast their shadows. If a doctor was a specialist, it was necessary for him to preserve that status and image in the eyes of his colleagues. It was necessary for survival. For instance, a surgeon, having had the same basic medical training as an internist, would be perfectly capable of treating and prescribing for mild diabetes. But if word were to get out that he was doing so and not referring his diabetic patients to a diabetic specialist, it would be a cold day in hell before any of the diabetic specialists sent that particular surgeon patients who required amputations, one of the many hazards of the disease. So the surgeon played the referral game or suffered the consequences.

It was true that some satisfied patients recommended their surgeon to relatives and friends. But the vast majority of business came from referrals by other doctors. After all, nobody decided they needed surgery and then looked in the Yellow Pages under "S." So it was only natural that often instead of choosing the best, most capable specialist, a patient was referred to a doctor who was sure to return the favor, and whose practice was large enough to make the volume of reciprocating referrals monetarily rewarding.

In the past year, Merrick had got into the habit of using three gastroenterologists, rotating the calls as he needed them. Two of them had reciprocated—as expected—by referring patients to him or bringing him in on a consulting basis. But his relationship with Hauptmann had been unexpectedly one-sided, for some unaccountable reason. Merrick had never received any referrals from him—and he was bitter about it. Then, three months ago, that bitterness changed to deep resentment. It had been early on a Monday morning when his service had called, just as Merrick was leaving his home, with the information that a Dr. Adolph Hauptmann was on the line.

"Joe," Hauptmann had said genially, "I didn't call too early, did I?" Merrick reassured him that he hadn't. "The reason I wanted to catch you—there's a guy at Marin, a patient of mine, John Lohman, that I'd like you to take a look at if you can."

Merrick was pleasantly surprised and gratified. Maybe Hauptmann was going to pay off after all. "I'd be happy to. What's the problem?"

"Possible intestinal obstruction, Joe. Ordinarily I wouldn't bother you with this; I think it'll work out by itself. But I just want to avoid a situation where he might really get in trouble. He's about forty, slightly overweight, and a mild diabetic. As I said, he'll probably get well without an operation, but if he doesn't, I'd like you to be familiar with the case so that if surgery is necessary, you can do it."

"I'm on my way to the hospital now, Dolph," Merrick said warmly, "and I'll see him this morning. Then I'll give you a call. And thanks for thinking of me. I appreciate it."

"Don't mention it," Hauptmann said and hung up.

So, Merrick had seen Mr. Lohman. And had roundly cursed Hauptmann. The patient was not slightly overweight—he was grossly obese, a huge man. His diabetes was not borderline, as the gastroenterologist had indicated, but severe. As Merrick examined him, he noted that sometime in the past, Mr. Lohman had undergone an abdominal operation, developed a ventral hernia, and now much of his intestine was protruding through the abdominal wall, just under the skin. Checking the chart, he was relieved to discover that the patient was doing better: the white count was going down, the X-rays showed improvement, and the distension was slowly going away.

Gazing at the chart, Merrick felt his fury mounting. The one patient Hauptmann had sent him—the one and only patient in almost a year—had been the world's lousiest surgical risk. Hauptmann hadn't done him a favor. He hadn't been repaying past obligations. He was unloading, dumping a patient on Merrick that no one else would want. To the uninitiated, one might think that being referred a difficult patient, one almost certain to have dire complications, was a compliment, an ego builder—a testimonial to that surgeon's ability. But that wasn't the way it was! The fee was exactly the same for a difficult or an easy procedure. Doctors are human. They don't want grief. They don't want calls in the middle of the night. They don't want their infection rate statistics to soar, they don't want their surgical fatality percentage to jump. They don't want to have to justify a death at the weekly hospital mortality committee meeting. They don't want the personal trauma which, no matter how hard they try to insure themselves against it, they feel at losing a patient who by close involvement has now become more than a patient—a human being, a friend.

Undoubtedly, someone had to take the obese, the frail, the ones with weak hearts, those who had waited too long. They couldn't just be left to die. And there were no complaints from a surgeon when a referring doctor, in the course of sending numerous patients, occasionally and naturally included a few bad surgical risks. It evened itself out. But when a doctor sent a surgeon just one patient over many months' time, and that patient was a John Lohman—that was no favor. The referring doctor was no friend.

Merrick's voice had been tight with annoyance when he finally called Hauptmann with his report and diagnosis. "About your Mr. Lohman. I saw him a little while ago. He's doing better—this time! But you know this guy is almost certainly going to need an operation sooner or later. And he's a lousy surgical risk!"

"I don't think there's any doubt about that." Hauptmann concurred.

"Could I ask you just one thing, Dolph? Why throw this one my way? Why me?"

"Joe, the ulcers, the hernias, the gall bladders—these I can send to younger guys. On this one, I wanted someone with mature surgical judgment. Someone who wouldn't be halfway to the operating room before he saw the patient. Besides, I figured I owed you a favor."

Some favor, Merrick thought. There had been no further contact between them since the episode.

Reaching the fourth floor, Merrick found himself examining his motives for calling Hauptmann. Was it because of the three gastroenterologists, Hauptmann really was the best? Or was it that Merrick instinctively sensed that Brian Murdoch was a problem, and was evening the score?

"Has Doctor Hauptmann started the endoscopy on Mr. Murdoch yet?" Dr. Merrick asked the nurse as he entered the Special Procedures wing.

"Oh, yes," she acknowledged, "he should probably be just about finished now. Why don't you go right into the examining room, doctor?"

Merrick entered the door she had indicated. It was a square room, about sixteen by sixteen feet, with glass cabinets stocked with supplies lining one wall. The only furniture consisted of two tables: one for pelvic examinations; the other, an automatic table designed in movable sections enabling a patient to be raised, lowered, bent, and tilted at any angle, any degree. Brian Murdoch lay on the automatic table, and as Merrick joined them, Dr. Hauptmann was just removing the long, flexible tube which had been passed through the patient's throat and esophagus into his stomach. Hauptmann was short and heavy, almost rotund, and his sparse hair jutted at odd angles from his balding head. He glanced up as Merrick came in.

"Glad you're here, Joe," the gastroenterologist greeted him. "I was just about to call you. Let me just get out of this—" He turned slightly, enabling the assisting nurse to undo the ties, and slipped out of the gown. Merrick followed him to the door and both doctors stepped into the corridor, out of Murdoch's earshot.

"Well," Merrick asked, "what did you see?"

"I'm afraid the examination wasn't entirely satisfactory," Hauptmann said thoughtfully. "He had a little reddening and thickening in the distal stomach, but the pylorus is so scarred and contracted that even though I pushed the instrument against it several times, it just wouldn't go through. I was afraid that might be the case when I looked at his X-rays." They moved a few steps farther down the hall, each man engrossed in his own thoughts. "He must have had an ulcer a lot longer than his history indicates," Hauptmann continued. "But the real problem is that I couldn't get the scope into the duodenum, and that's what we were interested in. I'm afraid we're just going to have to depend on the X-rays."

Merrick shook his head. "As you know, he's had special examinations of his duodenum twice now, and both times there's been evidence strongly suggestive of an ampullary tumor." He thought for several moments. "I guess this means he's going to need an exploratory surgical procedure after all." Merrick sighed inwardly, remembering his words to Kelly. No matter how inconvenienced the internist would be by a chronic complainer who refused to get well, it would be he, Merrick, who would bear the brunt, at least for the first few weeks. But as a surgeon, he had no choice. The indications were there.

Hauptmann shrugged. "It's either that or re-X-raying him in four to six weeks."

"No way," Merrick disagreed. "This man's emotional makeup is such that if we made him wait six weeks, he'd have his ulcer back just thinking about it."

"You're probably right," Hauptmann hesitated, "but I'd feel a lot better if we were just a little more sure of the diagnosis."

Their conversation was interrupted as the door to the room opened and the attending nurse and an orderly carefully wheeled out a gurney bearing Mr. Murdock. Merrick stopped the group as they were about to go past.

"Mr. Murdock, you're too groggy to discuss it now, but I'm going to schedule your operation for tomorrow morning. I'll be up to talk to you about it a little later."

Even though Murdoch was heavily sedated to facilitate the procedure he had just experienced, Merrick was slightly annoyed as his words caused what he knew was a triumphant smile to spread across the patient's face.

Immediately after Mike had checked on his surgical cases of the day and assured himself there were no complications, he started his evening rounds. He had looked in on Jeannie and she was still heavily sedated and sound asleep. Johnny sat in the nearby chair, reading a magazine, determined that he would be there when his wife awakened. Mike whispered his assurance that the patient was doing fine.

From there, he went to see Mr. Selkins and was relieved that he already knew about the scheduled visit of the detectives in the morning. Both Mrs. Selkins and Bradley had phoned, assuring him they'd be on hand. His patient was nervously contemplating the coming ordeal, and Carrington prescribed a sedative to alleviate his anxiety.

George watched as the needle in the nurse's hand punctured his flesh and the liquid was squeezed into him. He was grateful for it. God, yes, he was grateful. Anything to cut the need he was feeling—the strange sense of foreboding, the cold, shivery sweating, the ache in every bone. He knew he couldn't have stood it much longer, and he knew what it was. He had felt it so many times before. He was grateful for the shot—it would help. But what he really needed was a bottle.

Even when he'd felt the alcohol streaming into him from the IV, it had not been quite the same. There was something about the ritual of lifting the glass or, he thought, more recently, the bottle, to his lips that was part of the pleasure and oblivion of drinking. He was not stupid; he had recognized for years that he was drinking too much, and, like any intelligent man, he had made attempts at abstinence. Short-lived attempts— usually just one day—before the need became overpowering.

He had started drinking early, in high school, the usual kidstuff: a now-and-then beer, a swig of wine, a flask at the football games. Nothing unusual about that. Then, when he was just starting the Academy, there were so many problems. Loans, scrounging for students, constant interviewing to get good teachers. In a snooty school like his, you didn't recruit kids, you recruited parents. The name of the game was selling them on the merits of laying out the substantial tuition fee, convincing them that four years at Greenglen was better than the public and many private schools open to them. It took a lot of wooing, and these sales sessions usually took place over martinis at lunch, the cocktail hour, dinner with drinks before, wine with, and brandy after. He would come home night after night dead tired, discouraged, wound up tight as a steel coil. A few more drinks in the security of his home where he could drop the mask made him feel human again.

And at one point, he had stopped, hadn't he? For a long while. Until five or six years ago. Marion and he had gone to a doctor because the children at the Academy weren't enough—other people's kids. They wanted one of their own. George frowned to himself. He still found it hard to accept the fact that *his* sperm count was low, that *he* was the problem. Feeling guilty and inadequate each time he looked at Marion started him off again. Fuck all those who righteously advised you couldn't find solace or solutions to problems in a bottle. It sure as hell helped! He began to drink more and more. Dead drunk every night before bedtime; a hangover every morning. He used to console himself. The drinker was lucky: he knew his headache, his nausea, and his hurt would be gone by noon. The other guy who woke up sick would stay that way all day. But jokes didn't help. His wife jumped into the battle with the usual placebos: vacations, hobbies, even suggested they adopt a kid. George went on the trips, played the games, nixed the idea of an adoption, and went right on drinking through it all.

He had assured Marion he didn't drink at work. It was a lie, he sipped all day. He hated it, but he couldn't help himself. Many mornings he made the notation on his desk calendar—"N.D.T."—a code meaning "no drink today." But he felt so lousy, and the solution was so obvious. It was clear, it was white, it was so close in the bottom drawer of his desk. It was labeled vodka. One drink and the cure was instantaneous. He couldn't resist. He'd get it if he had to crawl to it. He found himself hating his addiction, but he assured himself that no one knew he was drinking, and enjoyed the knowledge that he was fooling the world! Still, wondering if his breath was really clear, he found himself backing off a foot or two when engaged in conversation with others.

A doctor had told him his alcoholism was a physical thing. No amount of searching for a cause, or trying to divert himself, would help. He was carrying some alcohol in his blood all the time. When the level fell, he hurt physically. Like any addict, the doctor pointed out, he needed professional help. Balls, he'd remembered thinking. I can stop. I can stop anytime I want. He went once to an Alcoholics Anonymous meeting at Marion's insistence. He had chosen a chapter near the foothills where he was sure he wouldn't run into anyone he knew. He had gotten up and made the suggested announcement: "My name is George and I am an alcoholic." It had been easy. He hadn't believed it.

He felt the sedative begin to take effect. His thoughts were becoming jumbled. That poor little boy. Billy Harris, in the other car. He had injured him, maybe killed him. And how many others? A tear slid down George's cheek for the child, his mother, his father, and for the wife the little boy would never have, the children he would never sire. For months, George had been conscious of brief memory lapses. It didn't surprise him that he remembered very little of the accident. The evening had started off innocently enough. Bridge at a private club, sipping the entire time. Rubber after rubber, until the foursome had discovered it was near dawn. They'd been playing for almost nine straight hours. How much had he drunk? He wasn't sure. He remembered the stop sign. He thought he had stopped, or at least paused for a moment. Again he couldn't be sure. Then the crash. And oblivion. He just couldn't remember anything else. He didn't want to.

As the injection took its final effect, and George drifted off to sleep his last thought was, God, I wish I had a bottle!

It was a little before seven when Mike popped in on Aaron Metz. As he entered the room, Mike had the vague feeling that something was missing—something as physical as a chair or dresser—and it was a few moments before he realized that the incessant TV chatter was, for the first time, stilled. His patient was awake, but lying almost flat in bed, the dinner tray still on the table. The food had the appearance of having been moved about on the plate, but little had been eaten.

Although Aaron's chart showed no deterioration in any of the important vital signs, there was a decided change in his usually cheerful disposition. Depression in any patient was a problem to be watched and dealt with. In a case such as Aaron's, it was especially undesirable.

Mike suddenly realized how tired he was. He had

been on his feet almost without respite since five that morning. The chair and matching ottoman near the bed seemed unusually inviting, Mike decided, and it was imperative that he pinpoint, if he could, exactly what had effected the change in Mr. Metz. Aaron nodded to him and watched as Mike crossed the room and slumped in the chair.

"You shouldn't work so hard, Doctor Carrington. Take it from an old man—it's not worth it."

Mike simply nodded his agreement, found a cigarette, lit it, propped his feet up, and silently enjoyed his first few puffs. His lack of response was not entirely unstudied. A line from George Eliot ran through his mind. He was too tired to remember it exactly. How did it go? ". . . a scheme to shed some broken light upon the depth of the unspoken." The long minute of silence was a ploy to see if Aaron might volunteer what was bothering him.

"Do you have a family, doctor?" Aaron suddenly inquired.

Mike shook his head. His silence accomplished the first step. It forced Aaron to turn to face him.

"Maybe you're lucky," Aaron theorized.

Still Mike was mute.

"You take Edith, she's my only child," Aaron observed. "And Ed, her husband? I've always looked on him as a son."

Mike made no response.

"And they tried to kill me today," Aaron said softly.

The baldness of the words shocked Mike, and it was a moment before he opened his mouth to protest, but Aaron raised his hand. Mike's intended words trailed off to nothingness.

"Yes, they tried to kill me. They threatened my life just as sure as if they had put a gun to my head, a knife to my chest. They want me dead!"

Even though he recognized the basic truth, the underlying logic, in Aaron's words, Mike struggled desperately for phrases that might refute it, that might ameliorate the torture that the admission was costing Aaron.

But before he could speak, the door opened and Miss Kellogg entered.

She was one of the nurses on the three to eleven shift, a young girl, but extremely plain. Her straight, mousy brown hair was parted in the middle and combed back behind her ears; the unfortunate shape of her glasses served only to highlight the unattractive, angular features of her face. As Mike watched her, he was surprised to note that her warm smile caused much of the homeliness to vanish. Spying Dr. Carrington, she hesitated, and Mike realized that her timidity was caused by the unconscious frown which had creased his face at her untimely interruption. He was about to suggest that she come back later, when he noticed Aaron's obvious pleasure.

"Miss Kellogg!" Aaron greeted her, and then turned to Carrington. "Doctor, this young lady is my favorite nurse." He chuckled. "At least on this shift." He motioned to the girl, bringing her closer. "And don't go blabbing what I said to Mrs. Rosen," he said confidentially, his eyes twinkling, "or she'll be suing you for alienation of affection. What is it this time? My temperature or my pulse?"

Miss Kellogg glanced at Dr. Carrington. He nodded his approval for her to go ahead.

"Pulse, Mr. Metz. Can I have your wrist, please?"

As he extended his hand, Aaron glanced at Mike. "See what I mean, doctor? The rest of them, they just come in and take my arm like they own it. Not this one. She always asks. It's nice to feel like I've got a choice."

The girl grinned. "How are you tonight, Mr. Metz?"

"Fine, fine," Aaron said. He glanced up at her mischievously. "One of these days, they'll be kicking you out of the nurses' union, young lady. Don't you know you're suppose to say, 'How are *we* feeling tonight?' like that old biddy does on the night shift?"

Miss Kellogg shrugged, feigning seriousness. "Sorry. I know how *I* feel. My feet hurt, and my girdle is cutting me in half." Aaron laughed, as the nurse continued. "You didn't eat your dinner, Mr. Metz." He shook his head. "Well," she said philosophically, picking up the tray, "I hear the lamb chops were nothing to brag about. Maybe some graham crackers and milk later. Okay?" Aaron nodded, and his affectionate smile followed her from the room.

"She's a nice girl," Aaron reflected after she'd left. He suddenly reached toward the side of his bed, feeling for the lever that would raise him to a sitting position. Mike moved to do it for him, but stopped as Aaron waved him away.

"Sit down, Doctor Carrington, I can do it—and you're tired." Mike relaxed, gratified to see that a certain animation had finally replaced Aaron's lethargy.

"So, where was I? Edith and Ed. I've been lying here all day thinking about them. I'm sorry about the trouble they made, upsetting all these nice people here." He looked directly at Mike. "Do you know why they tried to kill me, doctor?" Mike still winced inwardly at the words. "For my money." Aaron nodded solemnly. "That's right—for sixty thousand dollars." He paused for a moment. "It's a lot of money, but they're not going to get it. Not a penny! It's been a big week for Aaron Metz. First he decided to retire and enjoy life a little, and then he decided not to leave his money to his daughter and son-in-law." He raised his bed a little higher. "I'm through being a doormat. Don't try to talk me out of it. I've made up my mind."

Mike fought to conceal the satisfaction he felt. His emotions surprised him. He hadn't realized until this moment how thoroughly he detested Edith Frankel.

"I wouldn't try to stop you, Mr. Metz. It's your money, and you've worked hard for it. You should do whatever you want with it."

"You're right," the old man agreed. "Whatever I want. And do you know what I want? I want to spend it—to have a good time. And I'm going to do it. But whatever is left—*if* there's anything left—I don't want Edith to have it!"

Mike felt a sudden surge of regret. Why had Aaron

waited so long? Sixty thousand dollars. At best, he estimated that his patient had no more than six months to
live, maybe less. Of course, Aaron didn't realize it, but
then, who did? Almost everybody basically felt that he
was indestructible. Death happened to other people.
Subconsciously, almost every person believed that he
would be the one to beat the system. Sixty thousand
dollars! Ten thousand a months. Aaron would have to
go to a lot of baseball games, see a lot of plays, buy a lot
of hamburgers in the little time he had left.

"Doctor, will you do me a favor? A lawyer I don't
have. Maybe you know a good one?"

Mike thought for a moment. "Well, I don't know,
Mr. Metz." He was not anxious to become involved in
this, but Aaron had no one else to turn to. "Let me give
my attorney a call. His name is Patrick Schuster. I'm
not sure how busy he is, but if he can't handle it, maybe
he can recommend someone."

"I'd appreciate that. You won't forget, will you?"

Mike shook his head as he arose from the chair. "I'll
try to get in touch with him tonight."

When Mike went to chart Aaron's progress, the nursing station was temporarily deserted. Pulling a phone
toward him, he dialed Patrick Schuster's home number.

"Pat? Mike Carrington. I need a favor."

"Okay," Pat agreed.

"You do remember Aaron Metz, don't you? And his
daughter, Edith?"

"How could I forget them," the attorney sighed.

Mike laughed. "Well, there was another installment
this afternoon." He briefly ran over the unfortunate
scene that had occurred earlier.

"Jesus, this Edith Frankel and her husband are real
charmers, aren't they?"

"They're going to be two very frustrated, sore-as-hell
charmers, I'm afraid. Listen, Pat, Mr. Metz has decided that he doesn't want his money to go to Edith.
There isn't a whole lot at stake, maybe sixty thousand.

But he doesn't have an attorney, and he needs a will drawn up right away."

"Don't tell me—and you cheerfully volunteered my services, right?" Schuster guessed.

"Well, not exactly, but the thought kind of crossed my mind. Pat, he just doesn't have anyone else to turn to, and he doesn't have much time. He's really determined. He's not going to have any peace of mind until it's done. What do you think?"

"I have to be downtown tomorrow morning anyway, Mike, so I'll drop in on him. I'll handle it."

"I'd appreciate it. Oh, and Pat—there's one other problem."

"Naturally," Pat said good-naturedly. "I'd be a little disappointed if there wasn't."

"Aaron's worked hard for that sixty thousand, and, well, he thinks it's all the money in the world. And I guess to him, it is. Every quarter of that sixty thousand represents a tray full of dishes carried from the kitchen to a table—every buck required a 'yes, sir,' 'no, sir,' 'thank you, sir.' Fifty years of listening to complaints that the steaks weren't rare enough. Anyway, the old man is probably going to resent every penny he has to spend on this. Every dollar is part of his security blanket. To avoid upsetting him, I'm afraid you're going to have to keep any immediate costs pretty low. Whatever you make on this one is going to have to come from the eventual probate and executor fees." Mike paused, suddenly embarrassed. "I've got a hell of a nerve to ask you this, haven't I?"

"Forget it, Mike. I understand. You know, Aaron reminds me a little of my own father. He's a good man but tight with a buck. It can be worked out. I'll see him in the morning."

"Right. If there are any problems, let me know, will you?"

"Okay. Talk to you soon."

Mike hung up and started to leave, then suddenly turned back.

He smiled as the thought struck him. About all Pat needed was a confrontation with a militant Mrs. Rosen and the "no visitors" edict. He penned a note giving approval for Schuster's visit and clipped it prominently to Aaron's chart.

Chapter VI

... thursday

Dr. Joseph Merrick strode briskly into the doctors' dressing room and extracted a ring of keys from his pocket. Selecting one, he opened a locker and began to undress. Even though he operated only two or three times a week at most, he maintained a permanent locker, keeping the key, disdainful of the problems and inconvenience that the locked compartment—empty most of the time—caused the other staff surgeons. It was only right, he felt, that he enjoy the special privileges and comforts which balanced the responsibility and status that his title of chief of surgery entailed. *Noblesse oblige.*

As Merrick walked to the surgical board to determine the operating room assigned him, he checked the fine Accutron timepiece strapped to his wrist. 6:55 A.M. He pushed his way into Operating Room Number One. It was empty except for the two already gowned nurses sitting . . . chatting . . . waiting.

"Where is everybody?" Merrick snapped.

"The patient isn't up yet, sir," one of them volunteered.

"Where is the anesthesiologist?" he demanded.

"Haven't seen Doctor Durham yet, either," the other nurse advised him.

Merrick glared, then stalked through the door and searched out Kate Grady, the surgical supervisor. "Page

Doctor Durham," he ordered sharply, "and tell him to get up here so we can get started." Kate reached obediently for the phone. "And where is my patient, Mr. Murdoch?"

"We sent for him fifteen minutes ago, doctor," Kate replied.

"He snatched the receiver from the other phone on the desk and asked the operator for six-south, then curtly demanded the head nurse. "This is Doctor Merrick. Would you like to let me in on what's going on down there?" he asked sarcastically. "Where is Mr. Murdoch? We're ready to go up here—and no patient!"

"I'm sorry, doctor. We've been trying to get the Levine tube down, but we can't get him to swallow it," she explained. "He keeps gagging and—"

"Well, forget it!" Merrick raged. "Just send the patient up right now, this minute, do you understand? And send the tube with him. We'll put it down up here." As he slammed down the phone, Dr. Durham appeared.

"Morning, doctor. The traffic this morning—"

"You're going to have to pass the Levine tube," the surgeon rudely interrupted. "They weren't able to do it downstairs."

Durham nodded, ignoring Merrick's annoyance. Leave it to Joe, thought Durham, to palm off the happy-happy jobs on someone else. Keith ambled up, joining the two men.

"We're going to be late," Merrick informed him, not bothering to hide his anger. If the truth were known, this was Merrick's only commitment of the day, and he was under no pressure. It was simply that, in his mind, schedules were made to be adhered to meticulously.

"Fine," Keith said amiably. "Gives me a chance to get that cup of coffee I haven't had this morning." The assistant surgeon's casualness only served to infuriate Merrick to a greater degree, and he watched icily as Keith headed back to the doctors' dressing room, poured a cup of steaming coffee, sat down, and opened the paper to the sports section.

Merrick remained at the supervisor's desk, alternately pacing and stopping to stare at the elevators until finally Brian Murdoch arrived and was wheeled into the operating room. Once inside, Durham and the nurses helped the patient to a sitting position, expertly inserted the Levine tube through his nose and had him swallow it with little difficulty. Gently urging the patient back to a prone position, Durham kept up a casual, running conversation with Murdoch, easing his anxiety. Strapping the patient's arm to the arm board, he started the IV and attached a blood-pressure cuff on the opposite arm and took a reading. Without seeming to hurry, he administered some Pentothal to the patient, inserted the endotracheal tube and connected it to the anesthesia machine. Dr. Durham was ready.

Outside, Dr. Merrick's fury had not yet subsided as he started his ten-minute scrub, and his disposition was not helped by the fact that there was no sign of Keith.

"Would it be too much trouble," he asked the nurse, "to find Doctor Johnson and impart the information that it is time for him to scrub?"

The girl nodded and scurried off. It was four or five minutes before Keith appeared. Wordlessly, he started to scrub at an adjoining basin.

"You'd think, by this time, that the nurses would have learned how to pass a Levine tube, wouldn't you, doctor?" Merrick muttered.

Keith, sensitive to the chief of surgery's foul mood, simply nodded. It was the wrong response, Keith realized immediately.

"Did you see Mr. Murdoch last night, Doctor Johnson?"

"Yes," Keith said quietly. "I went through his whole chart."

"Did you write a note on the chart?"

"When I know I'm going to scrub on a case, I always write a note on the chart, Doctor Merrick."

"Then the nurses must have known you were going

to scrub." Merrick snatched hungrily at this telling bit of information. "Did they call you when they couldn't get the Levine tube down?"

"If they did, I didn't hear the page . . . sir."

"Well, the tube wouldn't go down and we've been delayed thirty minutes," the chief of surgery ranted. "There's no excuse for that. If I can get up and get down here on time, I don't see why everybody else can't. You know, doctor, it's your responsibility to go down and check on patients before they're brought up here and make sure everything is squared away. If you did, we wouldn't have these kinds of delays."

Keith made no reply. Merrick shot several glances at the young doctor, begging for a reply, yearning for additional fuel to stoke his burning anger. Dr. Johnson held his tongue and watched as Merrick finally stopped scrubbing, meticulously rinsed, fingertips to elbows, and started for the surgical suite. Keith immediately rinsed in the same manner and, anxious not to contribute to any further delay, started to follow the other man into the operating room. At the door, Merrick whirled to confront him, his face livid.

"Doctor Johnson! I have scrubbed ten minutes, but you are four minutes short!"

"Yes, sir." With an inward sigh, Keith returned to the basin, took a new brush and resumed scrubbing. He knew it was useless to explain that he had been involved, and consequently had scrubbed, on three surgical procedures during the preceding night. He counted off the minutes as he religiously scraped the bristles against the sink, willing himself to keep his cool. He had scrubbed with Dr. Merrick many times before, and he knew remaining calm was his best chance for survival.

Merrick entered the operating room and ran a critical eye over the scene. There was nothing to censure: the patient was draped and anesthetized, the nurses and Dr. Durham were waiting. He went through the gowning procedure and gestured impatiently when the nurse extended a glove in a manner not to his liking. He stood

226

fretfully for a few minutes until Keith entered and watched closely as the assistant surgeon got into his gown and gloves.

"You know," Merrick commented to his audience at large, "when I was a resident, I was always in the operating room first—before the surgeon." He turned to Keith pointedly. "It's just good manners!"

Merrick straightened his shoulders and dramatically moved up and took his place on the patient's right. You compulsive son of a bitch, Keith thought, as he moved to the opposite side. If I hadn't scrubbed those four unnecessary minutes, I would have been here. He braced himself for a tense, tedious few hours. From experience, he knew that Merrick would insist on doing everything himself. Keith's assistance would be minimal, and there was no music or small talk when you scrubbed with the chief of surgery.

Keith watched as Merrick was handed a scalpel, and winced as the surgeon made the vertical incision in the upper abdomen, just penetrating the skin. He stopped, using the electrocautery to buzz six or seven minor subcutaneous bleeders. With another scalpel, he cut slightly deeper, perhaps three-eights of an inch, and again halted to seal seven or eight capillaries. Finally, on his third attempt, Merrick reached the fascia.

Keith couldn't help but compare Merrick's techniques with Carrington's. Mike, he knew, would have gone to the fascia with one confident slash of the knife, and only then stopped any significant hemorrhaging, knowing the minor bleeders would stop by themselves. Merrick's proclivity for nit-picking and his preoccupation—it might almost be called a fetish—for dealing with each minor bleeder was widespread knowledge in the hospital. Keith recalled an incident of a few weeks before. He and a nurse had just exited from the operating room following a surgical procedure by Merrick. As they passed the supervisor, Kate Grady had glanced at them.

"Finished?" she had asked.

"Finally," the scrub nurse had nodded.

"That was a long one," Kate had observed. "Everything okay?"

"I don't know," the girl had shrugged wearily. "I have a feeling Doctor Merrick may have pinched the patient to death."

Merrick had already spent five minutes screwing around, Keith noted, glancing at the clock. Time was a relative thing, he ruminated. Five minutes to catch a plane was a desperately short time, but five minutes of anesthesia time—wasted—while the patient was in hazard, was something to be reckoned with. A slow, over-finicky surgeon such as Merrick also put an additional and unnecessary financial burden on his patient. Both the anesthesiologist's fee and the Operating Room charges were calculated by the minute, Keith knew. Many, many bucks were involved. The assistant surgeon's idle thoughts were disrupted as Merrick suddenly glanced to the head of the table where the anesthesiologist stood, and broke the tense, leaden silence of the room.

"Doctor Durham, you'd better check the patient's airway—the blood is much too dark down here."

"It looks red to me," Durham replied smoothly, "but let me check."

Keith watched as Durham, well aware that the surgeon was riding him, pretended to make adjustments. "Is that better, Doctor Merrick?" the anesthesiologist asked innocently.

"Much!" the chief of surgery snapped. He incised the peritoneum and sighed in annoyance. "The patient is too tight, Doctor Durham."

Keith glanced at the incision Merrick had just made. If the patient had not been properly relaxed, the guts would have pushed through the peritoneal wound. There was no such problem, and Keith was grateful for the mask that hid the grin that popped unbidden across his face as Durham once again made a great ado, feigning a number of adjustments which, in actuality, he did not make.

"How's that, Doctor Merrick?"

The surgeon simply grunted and requested a self-retaining retractor, placed it, and inserted his hand into the patient's abdomen, meticulously feeling for a suspicious mass. Nothing. He shook his head. Then, taking wet laparotomy pads—foot square thicknesses of gauze—he packed the guts away and carefully felt the duodenum. In looking at the X-ray films prior to the surgery, Merrick had felt in his own mind that a tumor was present, and he doggedly searched the area, determined to prove the infallibility of his judgment. The duodenal wall felt slightly thick, but he finally was forced to admit to himself that there was no evidence of a tumor. Still dissatisfied, Merrick made an incision in the duodenum over the ampulla, to permit direct visual examination. It was swollen and prominent, but in no way tumorous. He fought his disappointment. There was something there—there had to be! It was mandatory to find the source of the problem. Taking a small piece of plastic tubing with a sharp end, he threaded it through the wall of the common duct.

"I'll want a cholangiogram," Merrick barked at the circulating nurse. The girl hurried to the phone as the scrub nurse placed a sterile towel over the patient's open wound, anticipating the necessary delay. Keith was well aware that the cholangiogram involved injecting a dye into the common duct and X-raying to pinpoint the source of any problem. He remembered the area under the patient and inwardly groaned. No X-ray cassette holder had been inserted before the patient had been placed on the table. The holder was a wooden frame, covered by several sheets for comfort, which replaced a section of the normal padding of the table. Should X-rays be necessary during the surgery, the cassette could easily be slid into the frame without moving or disturbing the patient. Keith debated calling Merrick's attention to the omission and diplomatically decided to wait until Merrick discovered the problem himself. It didn't take long.

"Miss Gibbs!" Merrick's outrage was obvious. "How long have you been scrubbing?"

"Nine years, sir."

"Then it would seem to me that you would know enough to anticipate the need for an X-ray cassette holder. Do you realize that we are going to have to lift this patient for every film? Do you know what Mr. Murdoch weighs? Do you realize the problems you've caused me?"

There was absolute silence in the room. Everyone present knew that while a cassette holder was standard for a gall bladder procedure, Merrick had listed this case as an exploration of the duodenum, and there was no reason on earth for the nurse to anticipate the need. Besides, thought Keith, it's the surgeon's responsibility to request the equipment he needs, and to double check that it's available. Merrick paced. The others stood, wordlessly uncomfortable.

"Where is X-ray?" Merrick ranted. "How long has it been since we called?"

"About eight minutes, sir," the nurse answered sullenly.

Finally the technician and portable equipment arrived, and between Merrick's accusing glances at Miss Gibbs, the laborious and awkward procedure of lifting the patient for each film was accomplished. As they waited the report, Merrick again paced and fumed. Eventually, the phone rang—and the circulator repeated the message.

"There's a small stone impacted in the ampulla. They're bringing the film up so you can take a look, Doctor Merrick."

"A stone?" repeated Merrick peevishly. "There can't be. There was no evidence of a stone! The patient wasn't jaundiced . . . he had no real pain . . . the blood chemistry didn't indicate it . . . he had absolutely no symptoms." It was not that Merrick was questioning the X-rays. The stone was there. He knew it was true. It was just that the chief of surgery didn't handle surprises too well.

When the technician returned with the film for verification, Merrick viewed it angrily and ascertained the stone's position. Then, clearly showing his irritation at this unforeseen complication, he opened the common duct and began his search for the stone with a variety of instruments. He snapped a series of requests.

"Scoop." It didn't work, and he slammed the used instrument into a waiting basin. "Common duct forceps." He fished intently for the stone as though it were a culprit deliberately evading him, but to no avail. Again he slammed down the instrument. He unsuccessfully utilized a catheter, flushing the common duct with saline, hoping to dislodge the stone. His agitation was apparent by the increasing spasticity of his efforts and the beads of perspiration which had formed on his forehead and temples. He paused as the nurse wiped the moisture away. His mind was racing. He had no choice, he told himself, but to incise the ampulla and remove the stone.

"Well, Doctor Johnson," Merrick said, "what would you do at this point?"

Merrick was not interested in the assistant surgeon's opinion—the query was a teaching question. Keith recognized the fact, and hesitated. "A Fogerty catheter might work, sir," he volunteered quietly.

"Right!" Merrick agreed. A Fogerty catheter—he hadn't thought of it! Keith watched as Merrick carefully inserted the catheter, slid it past the stone, then blew up the end to form a small balloon which, hopefully, would provide the bulk and pressure needed to dislodge the source of trouble. Big morning, thought Keith. So far I've held the retractors and made a suggestion. Merrick sneered at the idea of surgery being a team effort and never utilized an assistant surgeon to his full ability. The Fogerty chatheter didn't work. Tight-lipped, shooting an accusing glance at Keith, Merrick discarded it.

"Well, I guess I don't have any choice. I'll have to open the ampulla." Inserting a probe through the ampulla into the common duct, Merrick incised to it. There was considerable relief as the stone was quickly delivered.

"Now, Doctor Johnson, I suggest you observe carefully. Perhaps you'll learn something," Merrick advised patronizingly. "By placing several stitches here, the opening of the ampulla will be permanently wider, and should there be any additional stones, they will dislodge themselves and fall through."

Keith nodded as he watched Merrick sew the common duct to the duodenal mucosa with 4-0 catgut. Once that was completed, the surgeon closed the duodenum with two layers of suture and before repairing the common duct inserted a T-tube into it and brought the tube and drain out a stab wound. The correct sponge count was verified and Merrick requested 2-0 black silk thread to begin the closing procedure.

"I will sew and tie, Doctor Johnson," he announced pontifically. "You will cut."

Keith sneaked another glance at the clock. They had been involved just short of three hours—a long time for this procedure. Once again the thought crossed his mind that Mike could have done this in half the time. Now, Merrick's penchant for insisting on doing everything himself would add extra minutes. The closing could be accomplished much more rapidly if Merrick sewed, and Keith tied and cut. The assistant surgeon shrugged. Why fight it? The first two or three stitches were made before the suture suddenly broke.

"Miss Gibbs," Merrick snapped indignantly. "I asked for 2-0 silk!"

"That is 2-0, doctor."

"It can't be. It feels too light for 2-0. If it were 2-0, why would it break? Are you sure it isn't 3-0?"

"I'm sure, doctor. It's 2-0."

Merrick stared at her. "Let me see the package."

Miss Gibbs bit back her annoyance. Her exasperation was evidenced only by the fact that she held the packet some four inches from Merrick's eyes. Partially vindicated, she watched as he involuntarily stepped back to focus his eyes. He examined it suspiciously, but could not argue with the labeling.

"I still don't understand why it would break," he

muttered accusingly, but resumed sewing and tying. Keith cut, meticulously leaving the pescribed one-eighth of an inch ends.

"Doctor Johnson," Merrick suddenly snarled, "you are cutting too short. Do you want my stitches to pull out?"

Keith assessed the ends. He would have been willing to bet that they were within a millimeter of the correct length. "Sorry," he apologized. They continued for a few more minutes.

"You are cutting too long, Doctor Johnson," Merrick suddenly observed sarcastically. "The ends will irritate my patient."

Keith did not trust himself to reply, but rectified his already perfect work by snipping an invisible portion from the ends Merrick had just criticized. Unable to resist the impulse, he paused before cutting the next stitch.

"Pardon me, sir," he blandly asked Merrick. "Would you like this one cut too short . . . or too long?" The two doctors' eyes did silent battle over the supine patient for a long moment before the closing continued.

"Good morning, I'm Patrick Schuster. I'd like to see Mr. Aaron Metz, please," the attorney notified Mrs. Rosen. He was about forty, with light brown hair, a little long in the back, but with the front and sides carefully styled. He was casually dressed in dark gray slacks and a lighter gray and white striped sport jacket with black leather elbow patches. It was a little after ten o'clock.

Mrs. Rosen nodded. "You timed it just right, Mr. Schuster." She indicated the elderly man in a wheelchair who had just left the elevator and was being pushed down the hall by an orderly. "There's Mr. Metz now. He's just come back from X-ray. Room 409."

As Aaron approached the nursing station, he gaily waved at the head nurse. She beamed at him.

"How goes it, Mr. Metz?"

"Fine, fine . . . couldn't be better," he called cheerfully.

"There's a Mr. Schuster here to see you," Mrs. Rosen informed him.

"Come in, come in," the old man invited him happily.

Pat deliberately waited a few moments to give the orderly an opportunity to get the patient settled, then walked into the room. Aaron was sitting almost straight up in bed, his eyes sparkling with anticipation. He extended his arm and shook hands.

"I'm happy to meet you, Mr. Schuster. Doctor Carrington is a fine man—and since he recommended you, I'm sure you are, too." He scrutinized Pat approvingly. "You're young—that's good. It takes a youngster to keep up with the world today. Sit down, sit down. You're a busy man, I bet, so we should get right down to business."

Pat grinned. He instinctively liked this man. He opened his briefcase and took out a note pad.

"Now, about my will," Aaron said eagerly. "Did Doctor Carrington tell you about it?"

Pat nodded. "Have you ever made a will before, Mr. Metz?"

Aaron shook his head, "All my life, I've never worried about it. A worrier I'm not. Edith's my only living relative. Up to now, I wanted everything should go to her."

Pat refrained from explaining the necessity and justification for a will in any event. There was really no point, and he was anxious not to tire Mr. Metz.

"Now, about this will . . ." Aaron repeated.

"We'll get to that in a minute, Mr. Metz. But there are a few things I think we should talk about first. Doctor Carrington told me your daughter had obtained a temporary order appointing her conservator of your person."

"Temporary?" Aaron asked. "It's only temporary?"

"Yes. There would have to be a formal hearing before it could be finalized," Schuster explained. "But the

234

mere fact that this conservatorship exists casts doubt on your status and ability to make decisions. While we could probably cope with this, nevertheless, in my opinion, the best way to handle a legal battle is to avoid it. Once your will is made, we don't want anyone in a position to contest it. So, I think the first thing we have to do is get that temporary conservatorship set aside."

Aaron nodded in full agreement and understanding. "You are a bright young fellow."

"And since you're here, Mr. Metz, and are unable to appear in court, that means you'll have to give a deposition. I'll make arrangements for a judge and a court reporter—"

"Such important people. They'd come here?" Aaron's eyes widened with a sudden thought. "Mr. Schuster, tell me—how much will this cost?"

Pat had been anticipating the question and, having been tipped off by Carrington, was glad it had been asked early. He had deliberately steered the conversation in that direction. "Maybe as much as two thousand dollars, Mr. Metz," he replied honestly. "There are briefs and petitions to file, court fees, the judge, the stenographer, a lot of necessary, incidental expenses."

"Two thousand dollars," Aaron repeated in a hurt whisper. He wanted to punish his daughter, but he hadn't realized how expensive a vendetta could be. Schuster went on.

"You understand, of course, that most of the expense is because of this temporary conservatorship. If it was just drawing up a will . . . oh, probably a couple of hundred dollars would cover it. But there's no sense drawing up a will unless it's uncontestable. And to be sure of that . . . well, we've got to get that conservatorship out of the way."

Aaron weighed the attorney's words carefully. His daughter's rash actions had cost him two thousand dollars. He couldn't help but mentally calculate the number of work days that sum represented. It served to fortify Aaron's determination.

"All right," he said decisively. "It's worth it."

"Okay," Pat said. "I just don't want you to have any surprises. I want to be certain that you're fully aware of everything that's involved." Aaron nodded, recognizing and feeling gratitude for the respect and integrity this young man was demonstrating.

"Second, I understand that Doctor Carrington had a psychiatrist in to see you when you were first admitted. I'm sure he explained the reason for that. When your daughter originally threatened to go to court, he wanted to make sure that there was no question of your ability to make decisions."

Aaron nodded. "Doctor Carrington is also a very smart fellow."

Pat smiled. "He is, indeed. Now, Mr. Metz, I'm going to ask him to get another psychiatric report on you the day the will is signed. It'll be made part of the official records, and if the question should ever arise regarding your competence and ability to make that will, it will be good insurance. Okay?"

"Okay, I guess. If you think it should be done, okay. And speaking of insurance, I don't think these psychiatrist fellows are covered by my medical policy. Do you have any idea what they charge?"

"I don't know, but you could ask Doctor Carrington," Pat replied. "He could check for you. And you're probably correct, psychiatric services aren't usually included. But you're lucky to have hospitalization coverage—at least you won't have to worry about the major portion of the bills here."

"You're right. I am lucky—I have a fine policy. You know, I'm a member of the waiters' union," Aaron said proudly, "and the girl there called me just the other day to find out where to send the forms."

"Good," acknowledged Pat. "Now about the will. About how much money would you say is involved?"

"$66,051.10," Aaron answered instantly. He took Pat's look of surprise for doubt, and hurried on. "That's right. I have $9,615.42 in the Pacific Savings and Loan . . . $8,973.14 in Venice Home Savings . . . $9,002.00 in United Federal Savings . . . $10,004.93

236

in my Bank of America Savings Account . . . $7,851.85 in Homeowner's Federated Loan Company . . . $9,248.36 in the Fernando Savings and Loan . . . and $6,555.40 in my checking account. And, of course, the $4,800 I had with me when I came here—which they're holding for me in the safe downstairs. Yes—it's $66,051.10!"

Pat had been spellbound as Aaron rattled off each figure, to the penny, without hesitation, as if he were reading from a financial statement.

"Mr. Metz," he gulped, "why on earth were you carrying $4,800 on you?"

"Why? You're asking why? What else could I do? I couldn't leave it home, could I? It wouldn't be safe."

"But . . . but why didn't you just put it in the bank with your other money?" Pat asked.

Aaron shook his head. "Look, when I worked—you know how you get into a routine? Every night I got the cashier to change my tips into the largest bills possible. Then, when I got enough, I exchanged those for a fifty-dollar bill. And I just kept pinning those fifty-dollar bills on me until I had a hundred of them." He noticed Schuster's absolute bewilderment. "I wouldn't open an account at a new Savings and Loan until I had five thousand dollars, could I? That's the minimum amount you can deposit and still get a bonus—right? The last time I got a portable radio . . . and the time before that, an electric alarm clock. This time I thought I'd get an electric coffee percolator. If you open your deposit with less than five thousand, you don't get anything."

"All right, Mr. Metz," Schuster said hurriedly, anxious to change the subject while he still had his sanity, "let's get back to the will, now. This $66,051.10—who do you want to leave it to?"

The old man suddenly dropped his eyes. "I . . . I don't know," he confessed. "It's a problem. I just know I don't want to leave it to Edith—and I don't have anyone else."

"I understand, Mr. Metz," Schuster said sympathetically. "It's still a pretty new idea to you. Let's think about it for a while. Perhaps you'd like to remember someone who's been especially kind to you?"

Aaron's eyes lit up. "Yes. Yes, that's a good idea—that's what I'll do!" Pat turned to a fresh page of his notebook and poised his pencil, waiting to write down the specific bequests.

"There's Mrs. Frankheim," Aaron mused, savoring every moment of this tremendously important and crucial drama. "She owns the apartment building where I live. When I had the bad back she brought me chicken soup. Oh, it wasn't home made. It was canned—Heinz', I think. Can you imagine a nice Jewish woman not knowing how to make chicken soup? But she was concerned about me." Aaron pointed decisively to the note pad. "One thousand dollars—I'll leave a thousand dollars to Mrs. Frankheim. Maybe she can get the plumbing fixed." Schuster nodded, wrote it down, and looked up expectantly. Aaron thought for a long time.

"Then there's Billy—William Donovan. He's a busboy at the restaurant. He's a good kid, always kept my tables cleared. Put him down for . . . for five hundred."

Schuster made another note.

"And Mrs. Rosen . . . and Miss Kellogg," Aaron blurted excitedly. "They've been awfully nice to me. They're both nurses here. Can you find out their first names?" Pat nodded. "Let me see, now—five hundred each. Boy, will they be surprised!"

There was a longer pause. "Who else, Mr. Metz?" Pat prompted. "You still have over sixty-three thousand to go."

Aaron stared at his blanket. Oh, God, thought Schuster. The pathetic old man! He can't think of anyone who's been kind to him. In his more than sixty years, he can't think of one other individual who's been kind! He watched a grin suddenly light up Aaron's face.

"Doctor Carrington—I want him to have whatever's left."

Schuster doodled curlicues on the pad for a few moments, hiding his dismay, mentally inventorying the problems Aaron had unknowingly thrust upon him. He finally looked up.

"Are you sure, Mr. Metz? It's a lot of money. Take your time."

"I'm sure. Besides, it's a lot of money, *now*. But I've just retired. I won't have anything coming in—and I'm going to live it up. I'm going to spend that money, Mr. Schuster. When the time comes, there isn't going to be so much left for Doctor Carrington to get. Enough for a new suit, maybe—something to remember old Aaron by." He pointed to the notebook. "Put him down— write down Doctor Carrington." Schuster reluctantly obeyed.

"What about your daughter, Mr. Metz? You have to leave her something. Five hundred, maybe?"

Aaron shook his head.

"A hundred," Pat suggested.

"Nothing," Aaron said softly. "Not a red cent."

"Look, Mr. Metz, to prevent legal complications, it's wise to mention Mrs. Frankel," Schuster explained. "Otherwise, as your only blood relative, she could contest the will. If she's completely omitted, if she's not mentioned at all, she can use the excuse that you just inadvertently overlooked her. There's legal precedence, believe me. How about one dollar?"

Aaron shook his head stubbornly. "Not a penny. I promised myself."

"Mr. Metz—" Schuster patiently pleaded.

"I know," Aaron interrupted. "My '61 Studebaker. I'll leave Edith that. It's going to need a new transmission anyway. Put her down for the Studebaker. Does that make it legal?"

Schuster nodded, suppressing a laugh. "That makes it legal, Mr. Metz," he said as he made a hurried notation. "Now, there's one other point," he continued. "We have to make provisions for the residual estate if Doctor Carrington should predecease you." He noticed the old man's puzzled look. "Let me explain. If Mrs. Frankheim, Mr. Donovan, Mrs. Rosen, or Miss Kellogg

239

should die before you, Doctor Carrington would get their share. But if Doctor Carrington should die—"

Aaron looked at him with surprise. "You're expecting a national disaster, maybe? God is going to strike them all down?"

"It's just a technicality, Mr. Metz," Pat hurriedly assured him. "To make it binding, so there can be no question, we have to make such a provision. Most people name an institution, a place which is sure to be in existence for many years to come—you know, like the Cancer Society, or a university, or the Red Cross."

Aaron thought for a long, long minute. "How about the Society for the Prevention of Cruelty to Animals?" He rolled the thought around in his mind, savoring Edith's outrage. "Yes," he decided. "She hates animals. Put it down—the ASPCA." Pat obediently made the notation and rose to his feet.

"I guess that just about covers it for now, Mr. Metz. I'll wrap up all your bequests in proper legal language. I'll start working on things right away, especially that temporary conservator problem. It'll probably be a few days before you hear from me."

"Fine, fine," the old man said contentedly.

Pat paused at the door. "Just one thing. Are you sure about the bequest to Doctor Carrington?"

"I'm sure. I've made up my mind."

Schuster nodded and walked out, careful to hide the concern he was feeling. As he passed Mrs. Rosen on the way to the elevators, she nodded pleasantly. Just a little past her, he stopped and turned back.

"Would you know if Doctor Carrington is in the hospital?" he asked.

She shook her head. "I'm afraid not. I just talked to him at his office."

"Could I use your phone?" he requested. She inched it toward him. He dialed Mike's number and waited until Celeste got him on the line.

"Mike? Pat. Can you spare five minutes?"

"Sure. What's on your mind?"

"I think it would be better if I came to the office. I'll be right over." He hung up, smiling his thanks at Mrs. Rosen, and headed once more for the elevators.

Upon entering Mike's office, he carefully shut the door, edged the large leather chair a bit closer to the desk and sat down with a sigh.

"Well?" Mike asked curiously.

"A problem," Pat said shortly. "I take it Mr. Metz didn't discuss any of the details of his will with you—any of the specific bequests?"

"No," admitted Mike. "Just that he wanted his daughter out."

"Interesting," Pat said quietly. "I've got news for you—you're in."

Mike stared at him. "I'm not quite sure I follow you."

"He's leaving his money to you—almost all of it. Oh, he left a couple of thousand to assorted landladies, bus-boys, and nurses. But what's left goes to you."

Mike scrutinized the attorney's face, searching for some clue that his friend might be ribbing him. But it was obvious. Pat was dead serious.

"Jesus! Why me?"

"Well, he decided to remember everyone who had ever been kind to him. And it took him a long, long time just to come up with five names. Five fucking names, Mike! Just five people he could think of who had ever shown him consideration. He thought and thought—and I sat there, cursing the whole human race. But actually, it goes much deeper than that. He wants to get even with his daughter. She's his only kin—his own flesh and blood—but I guess when blood goes bad . . . anyway, he's well aware of how antagonistic she is toward you, and he knows it's the best way of slipping her the shiv, but good." He shot a dead-pan look at Mike. "And if that hasn't deflated that considerable ego of yours enough, I think you should know that if you die first, the money goes to the ASPCA. Edith hates animals almost as much as she hates you. But

241

cheer up. At least, you've got first dibs—to the tune of about sixty-three thousand dollars!"

"Sixty-three thousand dollars!" Mike breathed. "God, Pat, he can't do that! I can just see Edith when she finds out. She'll spend the first few hours filing her teeth to points, and then she'll get in touch with her lawyer, the medical board, the hospital, and everybody else she can think of. And when you get right down to it, she can make a pretty damning case. Take Aaron: a casual acquaintance . . . my patient for less than a week . . . it's a matter of record that I've blocked his daughter from seeing him . . . he's terminal . . . and my own attorney draws up the will. Jesus! You just can't let him do it!"

"Look," Pat logically pointed out, "it's Mr. Metz' prerogative to leave his money to whomever he chooses."

"I know that. But I can just see Mrs. Frankel now—"

"No matter whom he leaves that money to," Pat interrupted, "his daughter is going to blow her top. The most important thing is to protect you—to make sure it doesn't look like any undue influence or pressure has been exerted on Aaron."

"And just how do you plan to do that?" Mike groaned. "God, the trouble she could cause."

"Mike," the attorney said pointedly, "are you saying you don't want the money?"

"Hell, no, I'm not saying that." Mike got up and stared out the window behind the desk. "Everybody always says they don't know a poor doctor. And it's probably true. But the reason we're not poor is that we work our asses off." He turned to face Pat. "Why do you suppose the average mortality age of surgeons is about fifty-three? How would you like to sweat four or five hours over someone, knowing full well that after taxes, operating expenses, the office, insurance, and what have you, you might get to keep about twenty cents of each dollar you bill? Hell, do you realize that nowadays, when a patient is in the hospital—let's say two weeks—and gets hit with a whopping five or six thousand dollars in medical bills, only about five or six hundred dollars goes to the surgeon? And, if that surgeon is lucky, he just might get to keep about a hundred and twenty dollars? Sure, I'd like the money. I could use it. But not if it's going to invalidate Aaron's will. If it comes down to me getting nothing or Edith Frankel getting nothing, I'll choose the latter. Because that's the way Aaron wants it."

"Come on, Mike," Pat chided him. "Save the speeches for an AMA convention. I can write an incontestable will, and you know it. That's not the problem. What we have to decide is, if Mrs. Frankel did complain to the medical board and the hospital, exactly how much grief could it cause you?"

Mike sat down and considered for some time. "Not much, really. What could hurt me is if she contests the will, and it gets in the papers. Even if she has no basis, even if she didn't have a prayer, the publicity could still do damage. The press would headline her lurid implications, and bury my side of the story on page twelve. Ethically, I probably couldn't even defend myself."

The two men mulled over the problem in silence for several minutes. Mike was the first to speak. "As much as I could use the money—and as much as I appreciate Aaron's gesture—I have a feeling it would be better if you explain to him the jeopardy he's causing me and suggest that he get another attorney."

"Where?" Pat asked sarcastically.

"How in the hell do I know? The Yellow Pages, maybe. Anywhere, as long as the attorney can't be connected with me."

"Mike, be sensible. You know most attorneys would take months to get that conservatorship set aside and to draw up a will. At least this way, if the document is drawn up now, six months or so before his demise, there won't be any question of Aaron's wishes being carried out. How hard do you think it would be for Edith to break a deathbed will, let's say one that's signed maybe forty-eight hours before her father died? Aaron doesn't have time to go the Yellow Pages route, and you know it better than anybody."

Mike nodded and again the two men pondered the problem in silence. Suddenly Pat sat up straight and slapped the flat of his hand against his temple. "Jesus, Mike! We're sitting here like two dumb asses when the solution is right in front of us. How stupid can we be?" Mike stared at him with interest as Schuster went on. "Tell me, why does Edith dislike you?"

"Why?" Mike shrugged. "Because I insisted on trying to prolong her father's life, that's why."

"And why didn't she want her father's life prolonged?"

"Because she's a bitch!"

"Come on, Mike. Why? What's her real reason? Think!"

"Well, according to Aaron, she wants his money. That's what he said."

"You're damned right. She's greedy, but she doesn't especially want her father to die," Pat deduced. "She just doesn't want money spent keeping him alive. Money that she looks on as already hers. She doesn't especially care *when* she gets the loot. She just wants to be sure it isn't spent *before* she gets it!"

Mike nodded. "So?"

"So . . . is it possible that Mrs. Frankel doesn't realize that her father has hospitalization insurance? Is it? He indicated to me that he has an insurance policy that just about covers all his medical expenses. Sure, he'll have to pay some small percentage himself, but certainly not enough for her to get conniptions about!"

"You know, you're probably right," Mike admitted slowly. "I hadn't thought of it."

"Well, think about it now," Pat commanded excitedly. "If the daughter knew that Aaron's treatments are not costing him—and eventually, her—very much, what would she do? She's got to be bright enough to realize that she's alienated and antagonized her father—and that's risky."

"She'd probably try to get back in his good graces,"

Mike said, entering the guessing game. "She sure wouldn't want to gamble that he might do anything rash, like disinheriting her."

"Right! Mike, when do you think Mr. Metz will be well enough to go home?"

"Oh, he could leave the hospital any time—the first of the week, probably. How soon a patient is released in a case like this depends, oddly enough, on whether he has transportation so that he can get back for daily treatments. And also how reliable he is. In other words, can he be depended on to keep his appointments. In Aaron's case, we certainly don't have to worry about that."

"Okay," said Pat. "This is beginning to sound better and better. Now, if we could let it slip to the daughter that papa has good insurance coverage . . . that very little money has been spent . . . that he can go home soon . . . and that, in the meantime, you've removed all the restrictions against her seeing him, she's going to come running. She's going to want to protect her future windfall. I'll bet we could even get her voluntarily to withdraw the temporary conservatorship immediately, and that would save a hell of a lot of time, trouble, and money. Then we could get the will drawn up and have Mr. Metz sign it right away. Of course, everything hinges on Edith's not finding out about the new will. But I can warn Mr. Metz about that. Once it's signed, he could be released. And I'd be willing to bet sixty-three thousand dollars that Edith will be the most devoted daughter that God ever created."

"It might work," Mike said slowly. "It probably will work. But all this intrigue and conniving . . . well, it just grates on me."

"You want things to go Aaron's way, don't you? You've gone to one hell of a lot of trouble so far on his behalf. So you go a little further. Besides, who's to say he won't change his mind about the bequests, and reinstate Edith? She'll have her chance. Who knows what might happen. She certainly wouldn't be able to accuse you of preventing her from seeing her father." Pat stood up and pushed the phone to Mike. "Go ahead, call her right now."

Mike stared at the phone and shook his head. "I can't. I'm sorry. I can't talk to her. I'm just not that much of a hypocrite. I agree that your plan is one hell of a solution—and it's to Aaron's advantage. But it's to my advantage, too. And I guess that's what's bothering me. I just can't call her."

Pat gazed at him, then shrugged. "Okay. To each his own. It's a good thing you're a doctor and not a lawyer—you'd starve to death. I'll give her attorney a call. That's probably better, anyway. I'll just break the news to Emmert about the hospitalization insurance in a nice, subtle way. Then I'll tell him Aaron will be going home soon and pass the word that if, in the meantime, Edith behaves herself, all restrictions on her visiting papa are lifted. Somehow the suggestion will be made that a beautiful way for Mrs. Frankel to clear the air would be to withdraw the conservatorship. I think Emmert will be quick to see that once Mr. Metz is home—and out of your clutches—there's really no longer any need for it."

Schuster rose. "In the meantime, I have work to do." He hurriedly gathered his papers and briefcase. "I have a will to write."

The head nurse on the seventh floor glanced up as the two men paused by her station.

"I'm Detective Fornetti, and this is Detective Ben Stoller. We'd like to see Mr. George Selkins. They told us downstairs that he's in 723. We have Doctor Carrington's permission."

Vince Fornetti was fortyish, of medium height, sallow-complexioned, obviously Sicilian, with a dark shadow of beard already marring his early morning's shave. His partner was approximately the same age, with a fringe of dark hair surrounding the prominent cap of baldness on the top of his head.

The nurse nodded. "Mr. Selkins' attorney went in a short while ago, and left a message for you. He'd like a few minutes alone with his client. He asked if you'd mind waiting. It won't be long."

Fornetti politely moved from the nursing area, out of the way, leaned against the wall and carefully unpeeled a stick of chewing gum. His eyes searched for a receptacle in which to dispose of the wrappings and finding none, he compromised by stuffing the strips of paper into his jacket pocket. Stoller walked idly down the hall, gazing at the various signs on the closed doors—"no visitors" . . . "contagious, do not enter" . . . "no smoking, oxygen in use"—until he reached the drinking fountain, where he took a prolonged gulp of water.

About five minutes before, Marion Selkins had preceded Robert Bradley into the room, and had gone directly to the bed, and kissed her husband. It was not a duty kiss; she was genuinely warm and concerned.

"Hi, darling. How do you feel today?" she asked.

"Okay, I guess." He grinned sheepishly. "A little nervous. I feel like a school kid about to be chastised." As Bradley shook hands, Selkins voiced his immediate concern to him. "Bob, just exactly what's going to happen? What am I in for when those detectives arrive?"

"It's a formality, really. You've already been charged in absentia with felonious drunk driving. Now that you're medically able to accept it, they'll serve you with a summons to appear to be booked. There's nothing to worry about," Bradley assured him as he sat down next to Marion.

Nothing to worry about! Selkins squirmed in bed for a few minutes, then reached for the water carafe, poured a glassful and took a long drink. His mouth was suddenly dry.

"I know you're upset, honey," his wife consoled him. "It's only natural. But we've got some good news. Tell him, Bob," she urged.

"Well, one of my assistants came up with something which I think will enable us to get the felony drunk driving charge against you dismissed," Bradley said. "A couple of days ago he happened to be in Traffic Court on behalf of another client of ours who was involved in

247

a freeway pile-up. The preceding case involved a driving-under-the-influence charge, and a hotshot young attorney hinged his defense on the fact that the blood sample taken from his client for an alcohol content test had not been treated with a preservative as specified by the Administrative Code. It's really an obsolete technicality. With improved testing methods, the preservative doesn't change the results, but it's on the books, and it's been there for years. Since it doesn't make any difference, it's been ignored for a long time. In fact, I doubt if too many people are even aware it exists. But this attorney happened to ferret it out, and based his defense on it."

"So—?" Selkins pressed.

"We did a little nosing about in the Emergency Room here and at the Police Chemistry Lab," Bradley went on. "The blood sample taken from you was in a violet-capped tube. Everyone concerned will have to admit that under oath."

"And a violet-capped tube means no preservative?" Selkins surmised. Bradley nodded.

"Isn't that wonderful, darling?" Marion exclaimed enthusiastically.

"Well, maybe not wonderful," Selkins admitted, "but at least encouraging." He looked at Bradley. "Does that mean the charges against me will be dropped?"

"No," Bradley replied ruefully. "Once they're aware of what we're doing, they'll reduce the charge to reckless driving." Bradley smiled encouragingly and Selkins closed his eyes for a moment. Big deal! He wondered if either his wife or his attorney had any conception of the magnitude of the problems facing him—and if they had any solutions. Before he made any big decisions, he resolved, he'd better find out.

"Have you heard how the little Harris boy is doing?" Selkins asked. Marion lowered her head. Bradley knew he had to answer.

"Not good, George. Billy's still alive . . . but he's in a coma. It's touch and go. The parents haven't filed yet. I guess they're waiting to see what happens."

"And if he dies?" Selkins speculated. He found the words catching in his throat, wrenching themselves out in a voice that was not his own. He had spent his life among children—he had an affinity, a love for them. The greatest disappointment in his existence was his inability to produce children of his own. The mental picture of the little boy he had injured, swathed in bandages, constantly haunted him. Bradley had shrugged in response to his question, preferring not to answer. Selkins willed the image away and forced a hardness into his voice, determined to pursue the issue. "What's the penalty for manslaughter, Bob?"

"Five years."

"But he might get well, George," Marion said optimistically. "He might recover."

"But his brain's no good, right?" George asked, deliberately blunt. He would not let them know the agony it caused him to verbalize those words. The silence was his affirmative answer. "So, if he lives, besides a settlement and the medical bills, they'll get a judgment against us that'll mean our supporting the kid for the rest of his life. I don't have that kind of insurance. Nobody does. And if he dies, there's still the settlement— and I get five years." There was a long silence; no one could refute the facts. He might as well have all of it, thought George. "How's the Academy doing, Marion?"

His wife averted her eyes. "Once the publicity dies down and you get back to running things—" she stammered.

"Bullshit!" George exploded. "The school's had it. I can hear the cocktail hour and dinner conversations in Beverly Hills and Bel Air now. They wouldn't trust the education and welfare of their neurotic pet poodles to me after this—much less their precocious little darlings. Let's face it. As a source of income, the Greenglen Academy went down the drain when I hit the Harrises—and it's the only source we have!" He looked thoughtfully at Marion and Bradley. "Well . . . does anybody have a solution?"

"Things will work out somehow," Bradley said inanely, pointedly glancing at his watch. "I guess I'd better go see if the detectives have arrived yet." He got up. "Don't let them upset you. Just listen, don't say anything. That's why I'm here." He headed for the hall. "I'll be right back." As soon as Bradley was out of the room, Selkins turned to his wife.

"Marion," he whispered, "did you drive down with Bradley?"

"Yes."

"Well, when it's time for him to leave, make some excuse. I want to talk to you alone."

"Oh? How will I get home?" Marion hesitated, bewildered. "Couldn't I just ask him to wait for me downstairs?"

"Just do what I tell you," Selkins hissed, aware of the approaching footsteps outside. "It's important." His wife simply nodded, as Bradley escorted the two detectives into the room.

"Good morning," Ben Stoller said cordially. He stared at the patient. "Mr. George Selkins?" George nodded. "I have a summons for you." He extended the document to Selkins, who continued to lay motionless.

"Accept it, George," Bradley advised. Nodding again, Selkins took the paper and immediately handed it to his attorney.

"Your client has been officially served, Mr. Bradley," Vince Fornetti said formally. "Bail has been set at fifteen thousand dollars. If bail is not posted within twenty-four hours, arrangements will be made to transfer your client to the prison ward of County General Hospital."

Bradley silenced the inadvertent gasp from Marion with a gesture. "Thank you, gentlemen. I'll make bail arrangements immediately." The two detectives nodded pleasantly and left the room.

The attorney proceeded to pick up his briefcase, opened it, and tucked the summons inside. "Well, that's that. I'll go back to the office and arrange for someone to get down here with a withdrawal form on your account, George, so we can get a cashier's check for the fifteen thousand. If we hurry, we can make it before the courts close. If you're ready, Marion—"

"Why not use a bail bondsman, Bob?" Selkins asked. Bradley turned to his client, surprised.

"A bail bondsman? Well, I guess we could, but the fee would be over fifteen hundred dollars. And as long as you have the money just sitting in your account, I think it would be better—"

"Marion may need the money, Bob, and I don't want her to run short. She may have all sorts of expenses. I think it's better if you use a bail bondsman. Now, my stomach's starting to hurt and I'm tired. I don't want to argue about it—just do it my way."

Bradley was tempted to debate the matter, but Selkins had shut his eyes, feigning a grimace of intense pain that discouraged any further discussion.

"Well, in that case—" On the graduating scale of attorneys, Bradley would have been rated closer to weak than strong. But in all charity, his forte was corporate, not criminal, law. "Marion, I'd better go directly from here to Acme Bail Bonds. Do you want to come with me, or shall I drop back and pick you up when I'm finished?"

"I—I have an appointment in town at noon, Bob, so I think I'll just stay with George for a little while until it's time to leave. I don't want to put you out. I'll have the desk call me a cab."

George hastened his attorney's departure with a deep, shuddering groan.

"All right, Marion," Bradley agreed. "And I'm sorry you had to go through this, George, but it couldn't be helped." He started to leave, but turned back. "Shall I ask the nurse to come in? Maybe a sedative or something would help."

Selkins shook his head. "I think I'll be all right. If the pain gets any worse, I'll have them give me something." Bradley nodded and went out. As soon as the lawyer had gone, Selkins sat straight up in bed, propping the pillows behind him.

"Bradley and his little colored tubes can go fuck

themselves! Marion, we're getting out!" She stared at him, uncomprehending. "There's a hell of a lot to do, and you've just got the rest of today and tomorrow to do it."

"Do what, George? What do you want me to do?"

"Marion—what do we own?"

The incongruity of the question completely baffled her. "I don't think I understand." She thought a moment. "You mean, like the Academy?"

George shook his head. "Things, Marion. What *things* do we own?"

"Well, we own the Academy, don't we?"

"The Academy is a *service*. We run a school. Parents pay us for our services in providing an education for their children. But the ground, the buildings, the equipment, even the furniture, are leased—leased on a yearly basis. We don't *own* anything there. Do you see what I mean?"

She nodded, only half sure. "There's the house. I know we lease that, too, but the furniture is ours."

"Okay," he agreed, "the furniture. What do you think the furniture is worth?"

"I don't know. I've never thought about it. Do you mean if we had to replace it. Or if we were to sell it?"

He gestured impatiently. "What's the difference? Twenty-five . . . maybe thirty thousand dollars?"

She shrugged. "I guess."

"What else?"

"Well, the cars are leased—both of them. George, I don't see what you're getting at. What—"

"What else?" he insisted.

She sighed, deciding to humor him. "Our clothes." He nodded. "Money, my jewelry—"

"Forget about the money and jewelry," he snapped. "They're portable."

"Portable?"

"Like I said—we're getting out. We're going to run." He watched her closely, assessing her reaction.

"George, I don't know what—"

"Marion, did you hear what Bradley said? Did it sink

252

in? I've been giving it a lot of thought since I've been here. Because of four or five martinis and a split second's inattention to a stop light, the future holds just two things for us. No choice. Only two things. Losing every penny we have, and every dollar we ever make again for the rest of our lives—that's for sure! And five years in jail—that's a maybe!"

Their conversation was interrupted as a nurse entered the room, extended a small paper cup holding a pill, and watched while Selkins gulped it down. There was silence until she left, then George continued as though there had been no pause.

"If I go to jail," he asked Marion intensely, "how will you live? Do you think you could survive in one room, maybe work as a beauty parlor receptionist, or sell hosiery in a department store? What else could you do? And what about me? If I don't go to jail, do you suppose any member of the exalted Academic Society would ever again give me a tumble? Do you have any alternatives? Well, do you?"

Marion's eyes had widened as each basic fact hit her—utter truths which, up to now, she had ignored, unable to face. George took advantage of her panicky reaction.

"We're lucky, Marion. Most people just couldn't afford to run. The only thing we have to lose is the furniture—and they're welcome to that. Twenty-five thousand dollars worth of junk—against five years in a cell. Everything else of value, we can take with us. Now listen. You have to do exactly what I say. Do you remember Nate Boyle?" She nodded. "Nate has a couple of private planes, and I happen to know he needs money. Call him. Tell him I've been sick and want to go to San Jose, Costa Rica. Tell him there's a specialist I have to see there. It doesn't make sense and he won't believe you, but it doesn't matter, just stick to the story. Offer Nate twenty-five thousand in cash to get us there and make all the arrangements—and that's to include everything. Be sure to stress that."

"Arrangements? What arrangements?" Marion said,

almost tearful in her efforts to keep up with her husband's scheming.

"Look, Nate probably has contacts in Costa Rica. I know he's been there. And if he doesn't, the twenty-five thousand will urge him to get some. Have him find out the best hospital in San Jose. Probably be a flea trap, but it'll have to do. Get them to recommend a staff doctor, and ask the hospital to have an ambulance or something at the airport to meet us. He can grease a few palms when we get there. The promise of a couple of bucks will work miracles. And have him make reservations for you at a hotel near the hospital. Thank God, our passports are in order."

"George," Marion interrupted, appalled. "You can't leave here yet. You're not well enought to travel. Why can't we wait?"

"Knock it off, Marion. We're leaving late tomorrow night. Every day we wait just lessens our chances. Everything hinges on the element of surprise. A doctor who speaks Spanish will be just as capable of removing the drains and stitches as Carrington. Now, tell Boyle he'll get five thousand when that planes takes off, and the other twenty when I'm in a hospital bed in San Jose. We'll leave from a private airport after dark—Van Nuys, maybe, or Santa Monica—that's up to him. I've been to those small fields. You step from a car into a private plane and take off. No questions asked."

"Why Costa Rica, George?"

He was delighted that her words indicated that she had already accepted his plan. "There's no extradition agreement with the United States, baby, and that makes it nice."

"We'll never make it."

"We'll make it. What's to stop us?"

She stared at the carpeting. She couldn't live without her husband. "What else do you want me to do?"

"Once you've made the arrangements with Nate, you make the rounds of every bank, every savings and loan, where we have accounts. Withdraw every dollar. Thank God, I got out of the stock market. There's about thirty thousand in the safety deposit box, so be sure to get that, too. The way I figure it, we can get our hands on just under a quarter of a million in cash. It's not a fortune, but it represents a lot of living in the land of the sugar cane. Get most of it in big bills, but get some small ones for incidental expenses—like bribes. Believe me, we'll need it. Wait until tomorrow afternoon—the banks are open until six—and do it quick."

"What about your medical expenses?" Marion suddenly interjected.

"What about them? I have hospitalization."

"It won't cover everything. Maybe we could just pay whatever the difference is before you check out—the hospital and Doctor Carrington."

George stared at her, unbelieving. "Are you out of your mind? Can you think of anything more suspicious than someone *volunteering* to pay medical bills?"

"But Doctor Carrington saved your life."

"Well, like they say, he'll just have to get his reward in heaven, I guess. And the hospital, too."

"And the bail bondsman." Marion looked at him with sudden understanding. "He'll have to forfeit the money, won't he? And Bob——"

"All I can say," George chuckled sardonically, "is that the paymaster's window up there by the pearly gates is going to be mighty crowded." He suddenly became serious. "The little boy won't suffer, Marion. The insurance will pay off regardless, and my being in jail won't make him normal again. If it would——" He rubbed his hand over his eyes, and then became intense. "This is important, honey. You know, technically I'm under arrest. Don't arouse any suspicions. Don't fire the maid . . . don't stop the paper deliveries . . . leave the dog at the vet's for a bath." He saw the hurt rebellion in her eyes. "We can't take him with us. They'll find him a good home when we don't show to pick him up. Don't have the water or electricity turned off . . . say nothing to the gardener . . . leave some lights burning when you leave. It's got to look like you've just gone out for a few hours. Pack us each a couple of bags and a

255

small one for the money and jewels. Put them in the trunk of the car after dark. You can meet me at the airport, and we'll leave the car nearby."

"How will you get to the airport?" Marion asked her husband.

"By ambulance. When Carrington comes in tomorrow night, I'll spring the news on him that I intend to go home. Oh, he'll squeal like a stuck pig, but I'll insist. I can carry it off. Once I get in the ambulance, I'll tell them where to take me. Just leave everything to me." He suddenly reached out and took his wife's hand. "Marion, for God's sake, be discreet, be careful. Do you think you can do it? I hate to put all this on you, but we can't trust anybody." He noticed her hesitation. "Look, it's them or me. You see that, don't you?"

She nodded slowly.

"You'll do it, won't you?"

She nodded again. "I love you," she explained simply.

Dr. Joseph Merrick approached his home in the Los Feliz area of Los Angeles, noting, as he turned in, that the tree roses lining the spectacular circular driveway were beginning to bloom. The architecture in this section was varied, but Merrick realized with satisfaction that his English Tudor home was, by far, the most prosperous-looking one on the street. Los Feliz was an older, wealthy and conservative residential area. Almost all the homes had been built between twenty and thirty years ago, and their age enhanced the beauty of the neighborhood. Huge, broad oak and elm trees were the rule here, rather than flashy, artificial-looking palms. The ground coverings were rich Augustine grass or dichondra, not the ivy or vining geraniums which the nouveau riche in other affluent sections favored. The Merrick house itself was permeated with a feeling of solidarity and understated elegance.

He left the long, dark blue Eldorado in the driveway, rather than garaging it, a habit unbroken from earlier years when he could expect emergency calls which inevitably he had to answer. As his wealth, status, and independence grew, the unexpected demands on his time lessened, but he still maintained the habit of keeping the car in readiness.

It was just a few minutes past three. He felt a righteous satisfaction in the knowledge that he had kept his promise to Elizabeth, his wife, to try to get home early. It was the fifth wedding anniversary of his son and daughter-in-law, and they would be coming for cocktails at five. The intimate dinner, just the four of them, would begin promptly at six—an unsophisticated dining hour, but a habit formed way back when early rising, dictated by his medical career, had been mandatory.

Entering the house and making his way up the broad staircase to the second floor, he surveyed the interior. Everything was in perfect order, bright and colorful. The surfaces of the furniture were polished and shining; cut flowers were artistically arranged on the coffee table, on the dining room sideboard, in the entry hall. From the kitchen came the discreetly muted rattle of dishes. Maggie, their housekeeper, he was sure, had the coming dinner well in hand. As he reached the top of the steps, Elizabeth emerged from the master bedroom, a welcoming smile on her face.

"Hi," he said easily. "I thought I'd take a shower and change. Then I'll start on the cocktails." His wife was not a beautiful woman, but she was attractive in the way that money invested in good beauty salons like Elizabeth Arden's and fine dress shops like Amelia Gray's could assure. She was short, and the high puff of dark hair, threaded with gray, gave an illusion of additional and needed inches of height. Almost thirty years of marriage had added an unbecoming stockiness to her figure that good living and contentment sometimes produce. Her slightly stubby fingers were busy fastening the tiny buttons which lined the front of her long, apricot hostess gown.

"Plenty of time," she said comfortably. "In fact, if you wanted to, you could probably nap for an hour."

257

He smiled at her, and remembered an observation he had recently heard: "You marry the person who is available when you are most vulnerable." It was true—and he had never regretted it. He had met Elizabeth shortly before he had completed his residency and was drawn by her warmth and good nature, and the fact that her father was an elderly surgeon who had a lucrative and desirable practice in Los Angeles. His wedding present was a full partnership, and Merrick had been grateful to his wife for being the means of eliminating the uncertain and financially hazardous period most young doctors faced in establishing a practice. There had been times, he remembered, in the seven years before her father had died of a cerebral hemorrhage, when he deeply resented Dr. Bannister. As the old surgeon's competence and earning ability had decreased, Merrick had occasionally and briefly cursed the partnership arrangement that assured Elizabeth's father of half the income while the ambitious, young surgeon did 90 percent of the work. But that was the established medical hierarchy: the older doctor literally and financially supported the younger, less-experienced doctor until that imperceptible moment when the syndrome reversed itself, gradually forcing the younger doctor to bear the bulk of the responsibility. It might not be a bad idea, Merrick thought idly, to start looking around for a successor to his own considerable practice. It was the medical profession's answer to old-age insurance. He was slightly startled as his wife's words brought him back to the present.

"Everything go okay today?"

He nodded. "Did the duodenal exploratory this morning. I checked before I left. His temperature was a bit high, but I told Doctor Johnson to keep an eye on him and to call me here if there were any problems."

"Oh, I hope not," she said absently. "We've all been looking forward to tonight. Well, if he calls, I hope it won't be until after dinner."

He grinned. "We'll keep our fingers crossed. You know, maybe I will try to nap. Will you wake me in time?" She nodded and went downstairs, heading for the kitchen.

It was almost four thirty before she shook him awake. He hurriedly showered, ran the electric razor quickly over his face, and started to don dark slacks and a sport shirt. Then, remembering his wife's attire, he quickly replaced the multi-colored shirt with an off-white one and slipped a boxy, dark lounging jacket over it. Downstairs, he was gratified that someone had already placed ice in the bucket and laid glasses out. Elizabeth was thumbing through *Time* magazine, and the *Wall Street Journal* was in the rack by the fireplace. He opened it, and both spent the remaining minutes reading until the doorbell rang.

"I'll get it, Maggie," Elizabeth called.

As his wife ushered Gregory and Caroline in, Merrick regarded his daughter-in-law with approval. She had a fresh-scrubbed look, and her slim body was covered by a beige sheath, augmented with pearls in honor of the occasion. Her light blond hair contrasted nicely with his son's dark attractiveness. For a while, he had thought Gregory might show some interest in the medical field, but he soon realized he was wrong. From grade school on, his only offspring had been a mediocre scholar, and after a liberal arts course at the University of Chicago, had gone into the produce brokerage business. He was moderately successful, and seemed happy in his profession of outwitting the weather and labor unions in guessing what the future prices of lettuce, tomatoes, and avocadoes might be.

They had their cocktails and had just settled themselves at the table and started on Elizabeth's specialty—cold melon soup—when Merrick heard the phone ring. He remained seated until Maggie came in.

"It's for you, doctor. Your exchange."

He nodded and rose. "I'll take it in the den, Maggie. Thank you."

Keith Johnson came on the line. "Sorry to bother you, Doctor Merrick, but we've got problems with Brian Murdoch. His temperature's up—one hundred and three degrees, now. Pulse, one forty. Blood pressure down, eighty over sixty. His abdomen is tender, tense and distended, and he's complaining of severe pain in his back."

Even as Keith was speaking, Merrick was mentally reliving that morning's operation. Every surgeon knew that if a problem arose soon after surgery, a step-by-step review of the entire procedure would almost always facilitate pin-pointing what could have gone wrong. Acute pancreatitis! Merrick was practically certain of it. The symptoms Keith had just recited were classic and he knew it was the outstanding hazard and complication of the procedure he had performed that morning. There were two possibilities. First, there was a chance—just a bare chance—that one of his stitches was around the pancreatic duct. But it wasn't likely. He had used extreme care not to go too deep during the anastomosis. But if it were true! He shrank at the thought of doing corrective surgery in Murdoch's present condition. It was far more probable, he assured himself, that one of the sutures had caused either bleeding or swelling, and temporarily occluded the pancreatic duct. But regardless of the cause, the mortality rate from acute pancreatitis was extremely high. There was a good chance that Brian Murdoch might die.

His voice, however, was calm and contained as he gave the necessary orders to Keith. "Monitor urine output hourly . . . insert a central venous catheter . . . get stat blood work . . . amylase . . . CBC . . . calcium . . . give plasmanate as needed. And I'll be right down, Doctor Johnson. See you there." Once he had hung up, he sat for another moment, his mind still riveted on the problems confronting him and his patient. As he started to leave the room, the phone rang again. He picked it up quickly.

"Doctor Merrick?" his exchange queried. "We have a Pamela Gibson on the line. She says it's an emergency."

"All right," Merrick said shortly. He spoke as soon

260

as he heard a click, indicating that his party was connected. "Pam, are you at home?"

"Yes."

"I'll call you right back." He hung up, walked to the open den door and closed it gently—then, from memory, he dialed her number. On confidential conversations, he preferred never to use the exchange hook-up, since absolute privacy was not guaranteed. The phone rang only once.

"Pam? What's the matter?"

"Joe, when am I going to see you?" The voice was soft and pleasant, but the words were slightly slurred.

"You know I told you tonight was my son's anniversary, Pam. Calling like this—when you know I'm home—that isn't like you at all. Is there anything wrong?"

"I have to see you, Joe. Right now!"

"That's impossible," he told her quietly. "I'm on my way to the hospital. I have an emergency. So tonight is out. And I'll be tied up tomorrow morning in an Executive Medical Board meeting, but I'll try to drop by or call in the afternoon."

"Not good enough, Joe." The girl's voice, while still soft, had taken on an underlying tone of harshness. "Tonight! Right now!"

"I told you I'm on my way to the hospital."

"Well, it can damn well wait for a half hour. Right now, Joe—if you want to see me alive. Otherwise, I guess there's no hurry!" The echoing deadness at the other end of the line indicated she had hung up.

Merrick had schooled himself to analyze a problem rationally and unemotionally. He had to get to the hospital—that he knew—but it was true, a half hour would make little difference. At the moment, there was nothing he could do for Brian Murdoch that was not already being done. And Pam was very dear to him. Besides, while she didn't have his home number, he shuddered at the thought of her trying to reach him, in her present mood and condition, at the hospital. He'd stop by her apartment on the way to Marin Medical Center. He walked slowly back to the dining room. Elizabeth looked up inquiringly.

"I guess we didn't cross our fingers right. I have to go to the hospital. I'm sorry."

His wife shrugged matter-of-factly. She had lived with doctors her whole life and was used to emergencies and interrupted parties. "I'll tell Maggie to keep something warm for you." She sighed. "I don't think I've ever tried to reheat Beef Wellington."

Merrick laid his hand gently on his daughter-in-law's shoulder, and glanced at his son. "If you're gone before I get back, happy anniversary! I only hope that your lives will be as happy and uncomplicated as your mother's and mine have been. My only advice is—always be honest. Never keep secrets from each other."

As Dr. Joseph Merrick guided his car along the surface streets and eventually on to the Hollywood Freeway, his thoughts were a jumble of recollections.

He had met Pamela Gibson about two years before in Chicago. He had gone there for a four-day AMA convention, checking into the Drake, which was the site of most of the meetings. Dr. Byron Oppenheim, a casual acquaintance from college days and now a leading psychiatrist in the area, had invited him to a cocktail party at his home on the final night, and since he was booked on the 11 P.M. flight to Los Angeles he had checked out of the hotel, taking his luggage with him to the party so that he could leave directly from there for the airport.

Among the mob of people to whom Merrick was introduced was Pamela, a longtime friend of Oppenheim's wife. She was a beautiful woman, not young, perhaps thirty-seven, with an air of grace and smoothness that was distinctive. Once he was exposed to the perfect enunciation, the timbre of her voice, it came as no great surprise when she informed him that she was a musical comedy star. At the moment, she had the lead in one of the touring companies of a Tony Award-winning play. Her name had never been on a Broadway marquee, she hastened to warn him, although she had, from time to time, understudied some of the most famous names in show business. She did manage, however, to earn a good living from her profession. And she exuded the animation, the sense of drama, the lithe movements, and the humor that was coincidental with the roles she played. Against her, every other woman in the room looked dowdy. She was tall, almost five feet seven, with auburn hair and luminous dark hazel eyes. The theater had taught her the subtle art of proper makeup and costuming to a fine degree. Merrick could not take his eyes off her.

Along with her considerable physical attributes, she was intelligent, and they spent much of the evening together talking. Merrick had never enjoyed himself so thoroughly. As he was making his apologies to his host and hostess for his necessarily early departure, Pam had appeared and offered to take him to the airport. It was on her way. He accepted after the usual few minutes of polite and half-hearted proclamations of reluctance about inconveniencing her.

It was December and a few flakes of snow spotted the windshield as they headed for O'Hare Airport. The traffic was heavy, the going was slow, and it was almost 10:50 before she pulled up in front of the terminal entrance.

"What time does your flight leave?" she asked.

"Eleven," he replied, glancing at his watch. "They should be boarding now. Pam, I've enjoyed meeting you, and I can't thank you enough for bringing me all the way out here. If you're ever in Los Angeles, be sure to let me know."

She nodded and watched as the porter piled his luggage on the hand truck and preceded him inside.

Approaching the check-in counter, he glanced at the departure board and knew he was in trouble. Flight sign 881 was listed—and opposite it was the word "cancelled." He groaned as the girl behind the counter apologized. They had tried to reach him at the Drake to advise him of the delay, but had been told he'd checked out. Indianapolis was experiencing a blizzard, and the flight was snowbound. There would not be another until

9 in the morning, and the same held true with the competitive airlines. Would he like her to make reservations for him at the Airport Motel—as the airline's guest, of course? He nodded. She proceeded to validate his ticket for the morning flight. He glanced as his watch again and shrugged. Even with the time difference, Elizabeth would be happier if he awakened her and explained the delay. Stepping into a phone booth, he placed a collect call to his home and assured his wife of his arrival in the late afternoon of the next day.

Rescuing his luggage, the porter accompanied him to the entrance, where Merrick stood for a moment, searching for a taxi. It was then he noticed the white Pontiac in front. Pam slid across the seat, opened the window, waved madly, and hailed him.

"What's the trouble? Are you grounded?"

He crossed to the car. "What in the world are you doing here? How come you waited?"

She laughed. "When you travel as much as I do, doctor, you develop an ingrained suspicion of airlines. The Pamela Gibson Airport Service always waits until it's sure that the client is safely aboard and actually airborne before departing." She chuckled again at his surprise. "Seriously, I noticed a lot of people milling around in there, looking kind of confused—and with the weather—well, I figured it wouldn't hurt me to wait ten minutes. What do you do now?"

He explained about the reservation at the nearby Airport Motel.

"Get in," she suggested.

"Pam, look—you can't imagine how much I appreciate it, but I really can't put you to any more trouble. I'll just grab a cab and—"

"Get in."

He grinned. "Okay. On one condition. When we get there, will you let me buy you a drink?"

"Sure, why not?" she giggled. "It's better than waiting out front in the cold for ten more minutes to be sure they haven't fouled up your room reservation."

They reached the modern, glossy motel in a few moments. She dropped him at the entrance and went to park the car, after agreeing to meet him in the lounge. He joined her a few minutes later.

"No problem. The room was waiting and I had my bags sent up. Now, what would you like to drink?"

It was almost an hour later when he requested the check from the waiter serving them.

"I'll see you to the car," he suggested, as they crossed the lounge. Upon reaching the entrance, she gave a slight gasp of dismay. The earlier scattered snowflakes had burgeoned into a driving storm, and already the parking lot and the street beyond were covered with white.

"Well," she said, disgustedly. "That's Chicago for you. Anyway, Joe, you know how much I enjoyed the evening. If the show gets to L.A., I'll see that you and your wife get house seats." She extracted a scarf from her coat pocket and tied it, peasant-fashion, around her hair, and turned up her collar. As she went through the door, a blast of wind hit her and she braced herself, ducking her head against the onslaught.

"Pamela, wait," Merrick suddenly called after her. She turned and he hurried to catch up, shutting the door and pulling her back a few steps into the lobby.

"Are you sure you can make it?"

She nodded. "I think so."

"I wish you didn't have to go out in this."

She turned slowly and faced him. "Are you inviting me to spend the night here, Joe? With you? Because if you are, I'd be delighted."

He was stunned for a moment, trying to sort out the emotions he felt. In his twenty-seven years of marriage, he had never been unfaithful to Elizabeth. Not once. He was not a lustful man, he admitted, and whatever sex drive he had, Elizabeth had managed to service. On the other hand, he was tremendously flattered that this unusual, desirable woman found him attractive. And he was curious. God, he was curious. It had been so long since he had sampled the unfamiliar, the forbidden. A slight smile of amusement indicated that Pam understood the turmoil within him.

"Look, Joe, it's just for one night. No strings. I'm cold, and I'd rather be warm. My apartment is lonely, and I'd rather be with someone. I like you and you like me. In the morning, you get on the big bird, and I go back to practicing my vocalizing. It's no big deal—but it's up to you."

A sudden blast of wind rattled the glass door and blew powder puffs of snow across the parking lot. On such insignificant omens were decisions made. He took her arm, fighting not to display the sudden eagerness and possessiveness that warmed him. Arm in arm, they headed for the elevators. . . .

It had been about six months later—in May—he recalled. It was midafternoon, and he had been in his office, when the call had come from Las Vegas.

"Doctor Merrick? Joe? This is Pamela Gibson. Remember me?"

He was surprised at the electric shock he felt in his loins at the mere mention of her name, the sound of her low, musical voice. "Of course, Pam," he said carefully. "How are you?"

"Not very good, I'm afraid. Joe, you know the show I was with? A mini-verson is playing one of the hotels here. We were rehearsing this morning—a simple little dance skit—and somehow I slipped and fell. I cracked something and just had X-rays. The doctor wants to hospitalize me."

He sensed the tight concern and anxiety in her voice. "Did the doctor there tell you what the problem is?"

She hesitated. "Let's see if I can remember . . . No. Well, I wrote it down someplace. Hold on a minute." He heard the slight rustle of papers. "A broken sacrum . . . and a herniated disc. Does that sound right?"

"Yes," he agreed. "You must have gone down pretty hard. The only treatment is bed rest, Pam. And you should be in a hospital for a week or so."

"Well, not in Las Vegas. I don't want to stay here. I hate this town."

He considered—but only for a moment. "Do you think you can stand the plane trip here? Did the doctor give you any pain pills?"

"Yes."

"Well, give me his name and I'll call him. If he thinks you can travel, I'll arrange a bed in my hospital. Meanwhile, check on available flights. I'll call you back."

He had driven to the airport to pick her up personally, arriving early enough to make certain arrangements. Even as he watched her gingerly manipulate the long flight of steps from the plane to the ground and settle herself in the wheelchair he had ordered, he felt a surge of great pleasure. But his voice was cold and professional as he indentified himself to the steward pushing the chair as they entered the waiting area.

"I'm Doctor Merrick. This is my patient, Pamela Gibson. I'll bring my car around to the main entrance and meet you there. Please wait with Miss Gibson until I arrive." The steward nodded.

As Merrick helped her into the car, inwardly wincing as she winced from the pain accentuated by her twisting effort to get seated, he felt an unaccustomed protectiveness, coupled with sheer delight in seeing her again. Even though the dark circles under her eyes indicated the pain she was experiencing, she looked beautiful.

On the trip from the airport to Marin Medical Center, their conversation was limited to a discussion of her physical well-being. How much pain she was experiencing . . . what pills she was taking . . . how many. He volunteered that he had enlisted the services of Dr. Ullbrecht, a fine orthopedic specialist, who would meet them in the room Merrick had already arranged for her.

During her week's stay at the hospital, Merrick deliberately maintained his cold and professional demeanor, limiting his visits to once a day, smothering his desire to pop in each time he was in the vicinity. Her attitude was nothing more than patient to doctor. He was relieved—and utterly frustrated! Not once had she even mentioned that night in Chicago. Did it mean so little to her? The remembrance of that affair was now an erotic and constant vision in his mind.

It wasn't until a few days before she was scheduled to be released that he had broached the subject. He had broached it—not she. There had been some casual discussion between them regarding where she would stay, once she left the hospital. The thought of a hotel room, he knew, was odious to her. On his way home the night before, he had noticed a sign indicating a vacant apartment in a comfortable building on the fringes of Bunker Hill, a luxurious urban redevelopment project, not far from the medical center. Impulsively, he had investigated it. The building was not new, but it had been completely redecorated, and while its five stories did not afford the view that the surrounding high rises promised, the apartment available on the fourth floor was cheerful, suitable, and relatively inexpensive. The following morning, he had mentioned, with some embarrassment, that he had taken the liberty of holding it for her with a small deposit. She was delighted and reached for her checkbook instantly, insisting on reimbursing him for the small amount. As he tucked the check into his pocket and turned to leave, some compulsion made him pause.

"Pam . . . about that night in Chicago—" he began hesitantly, not sure where he wanted the conversation to go. She solved the problem.

"You were good," she said softly—and turned on her side as if to sleep.

On the day Pam went home, Merrick promised himself he would not see her again. The self-imposed Spartan edict lasted almost a week before he compromised. He would not see her, but, he reminded himself, it was unkind not to call. After all, she knew no one in Los Angeles, she was a bit depressed, and a broken sacrum and herniated disc were not to be taken lightly. It was the nature of the affliction to flare up at unaccountable times, and Dr. Ullbrecht was often difficult to reach. Thus justifying his motivations, Joe fell into the habit of calling Pam once a week—religiously at 3 P.M. each

Wednesday. In his ordered, almost geodetic way, he scheduled those moments which were becoming the most important in his life, almost as he would an office appointment. If she felt that the impersonal, carefully regulated calls were almost duty-like in their regularity, Pam never mentioned it.

For a while, the calls consisted of small talk—how the apartment decorating was coming along, or funny anecdotes about her neighbors. But one day he called her and she sounded ecstatic—happier than she'd sounded since the accident.

"Joe, guess what? I have an agent. He's not with one of the big talent groups, but he thinks he can do something for me—maybe an occasional commercial or a bit part. I kind of like this town, so I think maybe I'll try my luck here for a while."

Listening, Merrick had coldly and scientifically tried to dissect the reason for his keen pleasure and relief at her words. It was considerably later before he admitted to himself that he had been dreading the possible announcement that she had decided to go back East.

His elation matched hers when they next talked. "I have my first audition tomorrow, Joe. Wish me luck!"

Then the next week: "I had the audition. I think they liked me. But it was a real cattle call."

"Cattle call?"

She giggled. "Poor Joe. Don't let the show business jargon confuse you. A cattle call is when the producer or ad agency has one or two parts to cast, and calls maybe fifty or sixty people to audition. It's awful. You sit and wait—and wait—and everybody looks at each other suspiciously, trying to figure what their own chances are, knowing all the while that the odds for rejection are pretty big. And the casting people—they look at you like you're a piece of meat." Merrick unaccountably found himself loathing all producers and ad agencies.

But on the next Wednesday at 3 P.M., she was soaring. "I got a call-back, Joe. A call-back means I'm among the finalists—now there are just three or four of us in

269

the running." He cursed producers and ad men for their dumbness. How could they consider someone else when they could have Pam?

"I got it. I got the job!" she sang on his next regular call. "It's a commercial for a cosmetic company . . . and we shoot next week. Oh, it's only a day's work, a hundred and twenty-five dollars or so, but you've got to think of residuals. I do, anyway—the old bank account is getting a mite low." Money! He berated himself for not once giving her financial plight a thought. She hadn't worked in months. What if there were times she had gone hungry? Deprived herself of something she longed for? He remembered his own bank balance and couldn't bear the thought.

The next six or seven weeks were filled with discussion of the actual television shooting . . . of show business gossip . . . of auditions . . . of hopes . . . of disappointments.

He was just crossing through the living room from the kitchen to the den, as Elizabeth watched her favorite evening game show, when a station break occurred. Pam's image suddenly appeared on the screen. The camera accentuated her extraordinary, flawless beauty. Her long, supple fingers applied the sponsor's eye shadow and mascara, and she smiled the warm smile Merrick remembered so well. He stood mesmerized while the camera moved in slightly closer and she breathed the soft, provocative words of the sales pitch: "When you look at your lover, doesn't he deserve the most beautiful eyes in the world?" As she spoke, it was as if she were addressing herself directly to him—no one else in the world existed. Merrick glanced guiltily at Elizabeth, but his wife had been perusing the *TV Guide* and did not look up until the game show resumed. Merrick continued on to the den, carefully shut the door, and dialed Pam. She answered promptly.

"I just saw the commercial," he said. "You're wonderful."

"Thank you," she said simply. She waited for him to go on.

"Pam . . . what are you doing?"

"Just sitting here debating whether or not to make myself a drink. I know I'm too keyed up to sleep tonight and, well, it seems like some kind of celebration is in order. But drinking alone isn't much fun." She paused. "Joe . . . you wouldn't be free to come over?"

"I'm not sure," he lied. "I have to go to the hospital, but maybe I can stop by."

As he started upstairs for his jacket, Elizabeth glanced up. "Do you have to go downtown, dear?" He blessed her for preventing the need for lying, and nodded. "Well, drive carefully," she said, twirling the television dial to another channel.

Merrick avoided his usual liquor store, stopped at an obscure shop, and with all the excitement and awkwardness of an eighteen-year-old, bought a bottle of imported champagne. He started to prop it up on the seat alongside him, then changed his mind, discreetly placing it in the car's trunk, and proceeded to the hospital. He cursorily checked a few charts before leaving for Pam's. When she opened the door, he wordlessly handed her the champagne.

"We'll have it in the bedroom, okay?" she asked.

It was the beginning of a new and exciting phase in the life of Dr. Joseph Merrick. Abruptly, the 3 P.M. Wednesday phone calls were replaced by eager visits—interludes so wonderful that the euphoria from them sustained him until the following week. It was not hard for him to dilute any guilt feelings he had. It was not a question of being unfaithful to Elizabeth, he assured himself. How could it be? His life, except for those few hours, went on as before. He was depriving his wife of nothing.

Then, on one of his regular Wednesday visits, he let himself into Pam's apartment with his recently acquired key and found the door almost blocked by one of the dinette chairs. On it was a magnum of champagne, with a hand-drawn arrow propped against it, pointing to the bedroom. To dispel any possible confusion, another arrow had been Scotch-taped to the bedroom door, which

271

was slightly ajar. He smiled. One of Pam's fascinations was that he never knew what to expect. Her sense of the dramatic and humorous made complacency and boredom impossible.

She was propped up in bed, lying naked under the sheet, each hand grasping a hollow-stemmed goblet. He opened the champagne and filled the glasses.

"I take it we're celebrating," he said, starting to undress.

"You bet we are," she bubbled enthusiastically. "Oh, Joe, I signed a contract today for a featured bit in a movie. It's not a big role, but I've got a solo song and dance number in a campy new musical. The part's perfect for me. It starts in two weeks. If I'm any good—and I'll be good, Joe, I know I will—it'll open so many doors." He ran his hand slowly down her nakedness and she shivered, causing some of the champagne to slosh across her breasts. Hungrily, he licked the champagne from her, continuing long after it was gone. She had deposited the glasses on the bedside table.

"One of these days," she murmured as she turned to him, "you're going to be fucking a big-time, full-fledged star."

The trouble started two days after shooting had begun. Ironically, when the call came it was on Wednesday, around three o'clock. He had been sitting alone in his office, oblivious of several waiting patients, wanting her so badly that he didn't care.

"Joe?" Was she crying?

"Pam, what's the matter? Are you all right?"

"My back, Joe!" she gasped. "I don't think I can stand it. The pain is so bad, I'm not sure I can finish the day. Do you know what that means? I'm established! They've already got film in the can on me! If they have to replace me now, it'll mean reshooting. I'll never work again. But it hurts so bad, I'm afraid I'll black out. Joe! What am I going to do?"

"Can't the company's first aid man give you a pain pill?" From being with her, he had already picked up an easiness with motion picture terminology.

"I've *got* pain pills. I had some left over that Doctor Ullbrecht gave me when I left the hospital. I've already taken two. They're not doing any good. Joe, please, you've got to help me!"

Demerol—by injection. Merrick knew it was the solution for Pam's pain. But she would need a shot about every four hours to enable her to cope with the demanding performance to which she was committed. "Pam, calm down," he urged her quietly. "What about your calling the studio doctor and having him write a prescription for pain shots? The studio nurse could give them to you."

"Joe, my God!" she sobbed. "You've got to come up with something better than that! I lied—I didn't mention my back problem to anyone here. If I had, I'd never have passed the cast insurance examination. It can't be public knowledge. If it leaked out, do you know what the columnists would do with that? Nobody would hire me the rest of my life!"

The thought of news hounds digging into Pam's past—and possibly linking her to him—was chilling. The solution, he decided, was to give her the Demerol so she could give herself the shots in the privacy of her dressing room. But he was hesitant about putting Pam's name on a triplicate narcotic prescription. It would not only make it a matter of record that she was using Demerol while working, but it would be proof of their association. A thought occurred to him—and he toyed with it.

One of his patients, Willard Hayes, with far-advanced cancer and tremendous pain, had recently died. And his family, not wanting the drug in the house and yet reluctant to waste it, had brought an unused 30cc bottle of Demerol to Merrick's office and left it. He realized it would provide the solution to their problem.

"I'll come by with something tonight that will do the trick, Pam," he promised. "But what about the rest of today? Do you think you can make it?"

"I'll try," she gulped before hanging up.

So that night, as he left his office, his attaché case held the 30cc bottle of Demerol prescribed to one Willard Hayes—enough for thirty injections—and about two dozen disposable syringes. It was contrary to the Federal Narcotics Act and the penalty if discovered would be great. But her career meant so much to her . . . and she meant so much to him.

The picture was finally finished, and Pam's exhilaration was only slightly dampened by the fact that she was forced to attend the wrap-up party—that ritual at the end of every film where the cast and crew celebrate their joy at having survived another celluloid epic—alone. As much as he wanted to share her triumph, he couldn't risk their being seen together. The brief argument about the limitations which their clandestine affair imposed was quickly resolved, their ardor later only heightened by the previous harsh words.

Merrick insisted that Pam take it easy for several weeks, prescribing lots of rest and relaxation to relieve the tremendous physical strain she had been under. It was during that period that he allowed himself the luxury and pleasure of seeing her more than once a week, dropping in often, whenever his schedule permitted. He was secure in the fact that their trysts were unlikely to be discovered. His wife was complacently secure; his schedule was normally erratic enough to prevent suspicion; his answering service discreet in finding him.

It would be six or seven months before the picture would be scored, edited, and released to theaters, but Pam was impatient to begin once again the rounds of auditions and interviews. There was no doubt in her mind that the news of her role in the highly publicized musical would lead to golden opportunities. Such was not the case. Although her agent secured numerous appointments for her, she encountered a dry spell—notorious in the motion picture industry—and job offers were nonexistent.

It was rainy and blowing outside as Joe let himself into Pam's apartment. She was sitting in the corner of the couch, sipping the drink she held tightly in her hand. On the table in front was an almost full bottle, some soda, and a bowl of ice. She watched as he crossed to the kitchen to deposit his drippy umbrella on the drain board, and raised her face apathetically for his kiss. She waved toward the table.

"Drink?"

He poured just a trace of vodka into a tall glass and filled it with ice and soda. He hid his curiosity. Pam was a light drinker, her alcohol intake usually being a glass of wine during dinner, an occasional brandy or cordial in the late evening.

"How did the audition go?" he asked, knowing she had received a call for a motor scooter commercial interview.

She shook her head, and he watched as she deposited two additional ice cubes in her glass and added straight vodka. "There must have been twenty girls there, Joe, and I don't think one was over nineteen. They were so fresh and lovely and . . . young!" She took a long drink from her glass. "Do you know what I overheard the director say to his assistant as I was leaving?"

He waited for her to go on, sensing that her inability to do so was telling evidence of a tremendous hurt. He had to know. "What did he say?"

"He said," she gulped, closing her eyes at the remembrance, "he said: 'Will somebody tell me why the agencies send out these old broads? They ought to be considerate enough not to waste our time.'" Joe took the glass gently from her fingers and enveloped her in his arms.

"Honey, what does it matter? It was just one interview."

She buried her face against him. "I've got to work, Joe."

Before he left, he wrote a sizable check and gave it to her. "Joe, you mustn't," she protested with widening eyes. "I don't want it!"

"It'll cover the rent and your immediate expenses."

"It makes me feel like a whore!"

He gathered her into his arms once again. "I hope it

makes you feel like the most loved, the most beautiful, the most adored woman that ever lived," he said softly.

He started calling her early the next morning, but it was late afternoon before she answered.

"Joe, I'm sorry about last night. Being maudlin isn't my style. But anyway, there's good news. I've got a job."

"Commercial or feature film?"

She hesitated. "Neither. I start in Saks' Cosmetics Department tomorrow, demonstrating makeup." He started to protest vehemently, but she stopped him. "Like I told you, I have to work. I appreciated the check, Joe, but it hurt. The job at Saks is just until something breaks for me, but at least I'll be able to pay you back."

Pam was able to keep the job for almost a week. Then the uninterrupted standing from nine until six took its toll. When he saw her, her face was white and drawn with pain. It was then that he supplied her with the second 30cc bottle of Demerol, this time ordering it for office use and falsifying the records. He insisted that she quit her job. Once the pain eased up, she made a few half-hearted attempts to find employment. Exactly when she stopped searching, Joe didn't know, but she accepted his generous and regular checks without protest.

As Merrick turned his Cadillac into the parking lot located a discreet half-block from Pam's building, he recalled that over the past few months the checks had been larger and more frequent. He didn't care. He couldn't imagine what his life had been without Pam. Yes, he *could* remember—it had been dull, sterile, pointless.

Slipping the key into the lock, he entered the apartment. She was becomingly dressed in a striped, long-sleeved silk blouse and dark green slacks. She had been pacing, and turned to meet him as he came in. He took her in his arms and kissed her. Sullenly, she stiffened—and he instinctively drew back. Then, as if remorseful of her mood, she flung herself upon him and kissed him

276

passionately. He guided her to the couch and sat beside her.

"Now, then," he said, hiding his impatience, "what was so important? Whatever it is, there's got to be a better time to talk about it. I really do have to get to the hospital. I've got this patient who's critical, and I'm not sure he's going to make it. He needs my attention—"

She jerked away from him. "Well, I need your attention, too. So let him die!"

His anger flared. His medical career was sacrosanct. He looked at her closely. Her eyes were bright, her movements were spastic, her pupils were contracted, her speech was slurred. She was evidently high on something.

"What do you want, Pam?" he asked quietly.

"Well, for beginners, I'm almost out of Demerol. When you come tomorrow, bring another bottle."

He shook his head. "No more, Pam. It's too dangerous. You're not in any pain. Why do you need it? You must still have some left. You couldn't have taken it all."

She got up and laughed shortly. "Look, Joe!" She slipped off her stylish, low-heeled shoes and turned up the cuffs of her slacks. On close examination, the area where the veins were prominent in her feet and ankles were covered with tiny needle marks. "You never noticed, have you? While I was in the picture, I got into the habit of giving it to myself where it wouldn't show. Do you think those two bottles of Demerol you gave me were a big deal? A drop in the bucket, Joe. I've been buying it on the street."

He stared at her. While he had been concerned about breaking the law, he had consoled himself with the small amount he had given her. Now the realization hit him: he had been supplying narcotics to an addict. It was the truth, and there was no justifying it.

"You've been mainlining it? Why, Pam?"

"Why? Because it makes me feel good. It makes me feel young and warm and wanted. And it's company when you're not here. It helps me pass the time when

I'm just sitting, wondering if you'll come. It makes those hours go faster. It helps blot out the picture of your having dinner with your wife. You know something, Joe? It's your rival! So you can just damn well bring me another bottle when you come tomorrow."

"You've got to stop, Pam. It's an ugly, dangerous habit, and you have to get rid of it. I'll help you."

She laughed shortly. "There's only one way you can help me. I'll get rid of your rival . . . when you get rid of mine!"

"Elizabeth?"

She nodded. "Marry me, Joe."

"You know I can't do that. I can't hurt Elizabeth. And my respectability is important to my career. Besides, what's so important about marriage? There's plenty of money. Have I ever denied you anything? You can have anything you want."

"Joe, I'm frightened. What's going to happen to me?" He suddenly realized the absolute terror she was experiencing. "What if you get tired of me?"

"I'll never get tired of you, Pam." He reached for her, but she twisted away.

"What if you die?" she asked bluntly. "Will you mention me in your will?" She mimicked the sonorous manner of a mythical attorney. ". . . 'And to my faithful and beloved whore and mistress, I hereby specify that she be supported for the rest of her life inasmuch as she's too old and too dumb to support herself.' Will I be listed in the paragraph with your other faithful retainers, Joe? Along with your housekeeper, your gardener, and maybe the boy who parks your car? Will you be willing to admit my existence after you've gone, when you can't hear the gossip and the snickers. Will it be okay to hurt Elizabeth then?"

He was just beginning to understand, it was impossible to argue with her logic. He dropped his eyes. "Pam—"

"Oh, Joe. I'm not a prostitute . . . not a whore . . . not a gold-digger. I don't care about money. I'm not afraid of poverty. I just want to be assured of companionship, of living a normal, legitimate life with someone I love—with you. Let Elizabeth have everything—the house, the money. You'll still have your career and me. And I'll have you—all of you—forever."

Merrick got up and began walking back and forth to the window. He was tempted. Pam was everything he wanted. Did he dare sacrifice all the things necessary to have her?

"I've got to think about it, Pam. I'll need time. I have to consider what's best for everyone concerned." He glanced at his watch. "I have to go to the hospital now." He opened the door.

"Think about it!" Her voice rose to a scream. "Consider it! What in the hell are you going to do? Review some medical reference books? Take a few X-rays? Call in a consultant? Try to prescribe what the correct treatment is?" Her voice was piercingly shrill as she came to the final question. He stood at the still-opened door.

"I've got to go. I'm sorry. I'll call you tomorrow."

"You're not leaving until it's settled! Do you hear me?"

He stepped out the door, gently closing it behind him and started to walk down long, carpeted corridor to the elevators. The door was suddenly flung open behind him.

"Joe! Come back here! I'm warning you! We're going to settle it tonight! Right now." He did not turn, just continued walking. "If you get on that elevator—if you leave now—you'll be sorry," she screamed. "I mean it! You'll never see me alive again. I promise. I'll kill myself!" He stepped on the elevator and as the heavy door slid shut, he heard her repeat the threat. "I'll kill myself!"

Across the hall, in apartment 4-B, Doris and Clint Whitmore were just about to leave for dinner when the argument erupted in the hall. They stood, indecisively, inside the door, loath to create the embarrassment their appearance would cause. They could scarcely help but overhear, as Pam screamed her threat. They looked at

279

each other with apprehension. "She said she was going to kill herself," Clint said worriedly. "Do you think she's serious? Maybe you should go over there."

"I can't," Doris protested. "I don't even know her."

After Dr. Merrick left, Pam stood for a few seconds waiting, sure that he would return. Finally convinced that, despite her words, he had actually departed, she went directly to the bathroom. She tore the paper covering from a disposable syringe. Opening the cabinet, she took the bottle of Demerol and inserted the needle through the protective rubber top, carefully withdrawing the plunger until the liquid reached the 2cc gradation. She paused and examined the contents remaining in the bottle. There was only a little left. Shrugging, she continued until every drop was in the syringe. She rolled up her pants leg and tried to inject the Demerol directly into the vein of her leg, but she was too unsteady. She tried again without success, and looked at her ripped ankle with dismay. A little frantic, she finally settled for plunging the needle deep into her hip and injecting the solution.

She hazily remembered giving herself a shot only about an hour and a half ago, right before she had reached Joe at home. But if ever she needed a lift, it was now—and what the hell!

She went back to the couch and filled the large glass with ice and straight vodka. As she attempted to replace the bottle on the table, she misjudged the distance—the liquor overturned and spilled on the floor. In a sudden fit of temper, she picked up the now empty bottle and hurled it against the opposite wall with a resounding crash.

The sound of splintering glass was all Helen and Clint Whitmore needed to move them to action. He walked resolutely to the phone and picked it up. The Whitmores were very efficient people, with a list of emergency phone numbers attached to the base of their phone. At the very top of that list was the number of the police department.

Pam sipped the vodka, waiting for the soothing effect

280

of the Demerol to wash over her. She continued drinking until the glass slipped out of her hand and she lost consciousness.

All thoughts of Pam were eradicated from his mind as soon as Dr. Merrick reached the hospital and quickly read the new notations on Brian Murdoch's chart. The amylase was back. Thirty-four hundred! Normal was one hundred and fifty. The count reflected the amount of enzymes released in the presence of pancreatitis, and it made his previous diagnosis—which had been presumptive—unequivocal. The patient, he noted with relief, had responded to the plasmanate. His hematocrit had fallen and his pulse and blood pressure were slightly better, although the fever was still dangerously high. Most important, the chart indicated 30cc of urine in the past hour.

He hurried to the patient's room, where Dr. Keith Johnson was checking the Levine tube to make sure it was functioning properly. The resident moved aside as Merrick picked up a stethoscope and carefully listened to Murdoch's chest and belly, then examined the surgical wound.

"Well, there's not much doubt about the diagnosis, is there?" Keith commented.

Merrick shook his head. "It's my opinion that one of the sutures is causing swelling and occluding the pancreatic duct. I'm sure there's no stitch around it. And even if there is, in my judgment it would be unwise to operate on the patient. We'll continue to try to support him as we've been doing. Just wait, and hope for the best. Additional surgery now would make his problem worse. One more thing we should do is put him on a cooling mattress to get his temperature down. You write the order for it and I'll try to get in touch with his family."

Keith nodded. Whenever a patient was critical—when he was in danger of dying—it was, of course, standard procedure to call the family. Contrary to popular belief, the motivation for this gesture was not entirely bathed in the milk of human kindness. There were other solid reasons for viewing this call as mandatory. Premise number one: if you were nice to the family, they seldom sued. Premise number two: it was good psychology to force them to live the crisis with you, thereby eliminating possible shock and surprises if things turned out badly. And premise number three: the bill would be more readily paid, regardless of whether the patient lived or died, if the family was aware of the effort and concern you were expending.

Merrick fingered through the chart until he found the phone number of Mrs. Murdoch and used the phone at the nurses' station.

"Mrs. Murdoch? This is Doctor Merrick. I'm down at the hospital now, seeing your husband. His temperature's up and he's having some blood pressure troubles. I'm afraid he's a pretty sick man tonight." Merrick's words were, of course, interrupted at intervals by questions and gasps from Mrs. Murdoch. "Well, yes, I think he's going to be all right, but he's sick enough what I felt I should call you." They talked for some time. Mrs. Murdoch, at first frightened, gradually gained some measure of confidence. Merrick was doing his best to be as gentle and reassuring as the facts permitted, and yet he was still concerned that he impart the seriousness of the situation. His concern was unnecessary. The mere fact that the surgeon had called her at such an hour left Mrs. Murdoch with an apprehension no amount of sympathy and reassurance could allay. And she asked the question Merrick expected.

"Should I come down?"

"Well, you can if you want to," Merrick replied cautiously. "He really wouldn't know you, and I don't think there's much purpose to be served by your coming. If things should get any worse, I'll let you know. I think it would be far better if you'd visit him tomorrow." His words were carefully calculated to indicate there would be a tomorrow for her husband, without actually stating it.

It was important to Merrick that she not come down,

but it must seem to be her own decision. He understood her anxiety, but his prime responsibility was to the patient. If she elected to come, she would be in the way, constantly under foot, asking questions, demanding assurances that could not be given. She would be a distraction that could consume time and effort that should be expended on her husband's care. Furthermore, should his condition require frequent visits by the nurses and the resident surgeon, she would be unnecessarily frightened. That would be unkind to her. Merrick was relieved that his strategy worked—it usually did—and after again eliciting his promise to call if there was a change, Mrs. Murdoch decided to stay home.

He hung up the phone, again consulted the chart, and dialed Dr. Eugene Kelly, Brian Murdoch's family physician. The tone of the conversation was far different and considerably less reassuring than his previous one. As one doctor to another, he would tell it like it was.

"Gene? Joe Merrick. I'm down here at Marin with Murdoch. He's got big, big trouble tonight. His amylase is thirty-four hundred and there's no doubt he has acute fulminant pancreatitis. We've done everything there is to do, but it's nip and tuck. I've just called his wife, so I thought you'd want to know."

"Is the family coming down?" Kelly asked. It was his only question.

"No, I don't think so," Merrick replied.

"Well, you've got the situation in hand, so there's really nothing I can do. If the family were coming, I'd haul my ass down there for appearances' sake. As it is, I'll give Mrs. Murdoch a call. What's her phone number?" Merrick gave it to him, hung up, and walked back to Murdoch's room.

"I'm going home, now, Doctor Johnson," he announced crisply. "There's one base we haven't touched. We need X-rays of his abdomen tonight. They'll be useful as a comparison if his distension increases. I'll call you later to see how he's doing."

As Merrick was about to pull out of the Doctor's Parking lot, he was forced to pause as a police ambulance roared down the street and turned into Marin's Emergency Entrance. Another poor son of a bitch with problems, he thought idly. It was only a little after nine. If he hurried, perhaps Greg and Caroline would still be at the house. He accelerated the car and headed for home.

* * *

The police ambulance attendant stuck his head through the sliding doors and spied Dr. Jeff Melburn. "Got a drug overdose for you, Doc," he announced cheerfully.

"Hi, Buck," Jeff greeted him genially, "Okay, bring him in."

"It's a her," the attendant called, as the doors slid shut behind him.

Seconds later, they wheeled Pam into the Emergency Room. She was conscious, but groggy and confused, squinting at the bright lights and at the swimming figures of Dr. Melburn and Betty as they hovered over her. While the nurse strapped on a blood-pressure cuff, Jeff extracted blood, handed the syringe to Betty, and took the patient's pulse.

"We'd better pump her stomach," he decided. The nurse nodded and quickly returned with the large tube needed for the procedure. As she tried to insert it, Pam pushed her hand away.

"What are you doing?" she demanded, still dazed. "I didn't swallow anything. I gave myself a shot."

A glance from Jeff was an order to Betty to delay the pumping for the time being. "A shot of what?" the doctor demanded.

"Big D," Pam murmured sleepily. "Demerol."

"How much?" Jeff noticed she was on the verge of losing consciousness again. "How much?" he insisted, shaking her.

"Oh . . . about 2cc's . . . more or less."

"What strength?" The more information he had, the more quickly and efficiently she could be treated. "Come on, what strength?"

284

"Leave me alone," Pam protested with irritation. "How do I know? Ask Doctor Merrick . . . he gave it to me."

The policeman was approaching, having finished his task of filling out the report. Jeff's eyes warned Betty of the need for discretion. "Stay with her," he told the nurse pointedly. "I'll make a few calls and see if I can find a staff G.P. to admit her."

Betty assessed the patient through slitted eyes. She was a beauty. What was her connection with Joseph Merrick? She wondered. The slacks were Jax originals, the blouse pure raw silk, the low-heeled shoes, ornamented with jeweled buckles, were expensive and unusual. She bent down to examine them more closely. It was then she noticed the unmistakable pattern of multiple needle marks.

"Okay," Jeff announced, as he returned. "I got Doctor Valdez, and he's making arrangements. We'll send her upstairs."

Betty grinned. "Looks like the fun and games are starting early tonight. Do you suppose you could spare a girl for five minutes so she can go to the powder room?"

"Better now than later. Go ahead."

Betty walked down the deserted corridor and entered the main lobby. Casually glancing about to make sure she was not observed, she slipped into the public phone booth, dug into her purse and finally found a small, slim, green book. It was true that, on the whole, Emergency Room nurses were smart, attractive, and ambitious. Betty, especially, appreciated nice things. And even with the extra pay the duty commanded, sometimes a girl was forced to moonlight to afford life's luxuries. She had information of value, and she was not above using it. She quickly turned the pages of the book—then found a dime and inserted it. It was after nine. He'd probably be home now.

She carefully dialed the number and waited impatiently until the connection was established. She took a final look around, and then spoke quietly.

"Mr. Frank Savage, please."

Around midnight, Keith Johnson made his way to the X-ray Department to check on Murdoch's films. He couldn't find them. They weren't there. He checked the registry of examinations done during the evening. No Brian Murdoch. Why they hadn't been taken, he didn't know. He sure as hell had ordered them. In addition to writing the order, he had personally called the department to relay Dr. Merrick's request. They had to be done.

Not only would Dr. Merrick chew his ass to ribbons because of the negligence, but the films could also provide information important to the care of a very sick patient. He had no choice. At his request, the telephone operator awakened Rita Jenkins, the night X-ray technician, with the message that those films must be taken immediately, despite the hour. And shortly thereafter, the portable X-ray machine rumbled down the hall to Murdoch's room. Later, Keith answered the page. The somewhat disgruntled technician's voice came through loud and clear——the films were ready, and since she'd been dragged out of bed to take them, he'd better haul his ass up there and look at them.

Keith grinned as he hung up. Rita Jenkins was efficient. She was all business. That girl got things done. She'd have the films on the view box, waiting. As he walked toward the X-ray Department, Keith thought about her. Divorced, foxy as they came, she knew what was happening. They had bantered before on several occasions——just friendly stuff——Keith remembered. But those big round tits . . . how she liked to show them off. And he had seen her smile——just a knowing little smirk——when she had caught him watching their bounce.

He stood behind her, looking over her shoulder at Murdoch's films on the view box. Her hair was arranged in a short Afro and teased high away from her collar. He leaned forward, touched her bare neck with his lips and nibbled lightly at her ear. She smiled over her shoulder at him.

"That was nice," she said with a tinge of sarcasm.

"Not half as nice as these," he whispered, his hands now around her, cupping both breasts. She made no attempt to pull away.

"Black boy, you could get yourself in a lot of trouble that way."

"What kind of trouble?"

She turned and faced him, her eyes twinkling, a jest on the tip of her tongue. But he pre-empted her. The thought struck him suddenly. Shit. This kind of game could go on forever. Why waste time? What the hell, all she can do is say no. And for some reason—maybe the look in her eyes, perhaps the unuttered jest—she just didn't figure to be a no-type girl.

"Screw the small talk," he said. "How about doing me a favor? Let me ruin your reputation."

"Be my guest."

The embrace was passionate—the pressure of their lips and the erratic motions of her tongue in his mouth increased. Keith felt himself getting an erection and pressed it hard against her. He wanted to stick it in her right there. He looked around the room—the department was deserted—but did he dare? Even in his condition, the thought of pulling her down and fucking her right there on the floor of the X-ray lab was ludicrous to him. His mind raced, grasping for possibilities, and the inspiration struck.

"Why don't you let me show you Reichner's office?" With his hands around her ass, moving himself up and down against her stomach, a grin on his face, he continued. "He's got one of the nicest carpets in this hospital. I guarantee you'll like it."

"Not so fast, lover boy. What about these X-rays?"

"Screw them." And you, too, he thought. "I'll look at them later."

Giving her no time to think about it, he reached into her pocket for the keys and led her to the chief radiologist's office. She followed him, laughing, and standing close behind him as he unlocked the door, she pressed her tits into his back and grasped his erect cock in her hand.

A rush of pleasure and anticipation shot through him, almost making him dizzy. He shut the door, locked it behind him and grabbed her hungrily—kissing her roughly, insistently, biting her lips and nibbling her neck. Her buttocks in his hands, like the conquering hero he felt himself to be, he pulled her up against his crotch. They pawed at each other and rubbed their bodies together. Then, pulling apart, they began to undress. At first he tried to help her, but the animal instinct he felt took over, and he tore off his coat, tunic and pants.

Keith was tall and lanky, and his passion for sports had defined each muscle in his frame. They glistened through the sweat on his deep black skin. The contrast to her light chocolate complexion was striking. God, she was really something—those big tits, especially the dusky pink of her erect nipples against the café-au-lait softness of the rest of her body. He ran his hand down his chest and shook himself into full erection. Smiling broadly, she pushed her breasts out to their fullest and walked to him.

Keith had no doubt about where he wanted to go. Pulling her down to the floor, between passionate kisses, persistent caresses and heavy breathing, he rolled his body half onto hers. Like young wrestlers they strained, striving for closer and more complete contact. Twisting himself, Keith maneuvered into a position for mutual oral sex. He nibbled and kissed the inside of her thighs as one of his hands wildly manipulated the object of his eager lips. Rita, self-confident in her own experience, hesitated not one moment in her part of the scene.

"Oh, baby!" Keith murmured. "I just knew you were going to be good."

But he knew how it could be better! Groping for his jacket, he fumbled in the pocket and withdrew a small box of poppers.

He'd been introduced to them by a girlfriend a few

nights before. He remembered that as he'd mounted her, entered her, she'd reached for a nasal inhaler and had taken several deep sniffs. His first thought had been that it was a hell of a time to worry about a stuffed up nose, but the peculiar odor escaping from the device had told him this wasn't a cold remedy. The fumes alone had made him a little giddy, but as he neared his climax, she had breathed deeply once again and then had stuffed the inhaler up his nose. For a second, as the drug sped through his system, dilating his arteries, giving him a feeling of heat about the face and neck, he'd thought he might be going crazy, but then the drug had really taken effect and he'd found himself lost in a world of complete sexual awareness. He thought he'd go on coming forever. Later he'd discovered that the original contents of the inhaler had been replaced by an ampule of amyl nitrite. It was a prescription drug—hard to get—but he had promised to replenish his girlfriend's dwindling supply. He'd written a prescription just that day, and the full box of the netted ampules had been secreted in his jacket.

Now with a popper between his forefinger and thumb, he looked down at their bodies. Rita's breasts were pressed against his stomach and her hips responded eagerly to the manipulations of his experienced hand.

"Sweetheart, you're going to love this," he whispered, and crushed the small vial, confident that the heavy netting would protect his fingers from the fragments of glass. Its pungent odor filled the room and within seconds it brought them to mutual orgasm.

Chapter VII

. . . friday

It was not quite 7 A.M. when Dr. Eugene Kelly strolled into Brian Murdoch's room. It was the first time he had seen his patient since being notified of the crisis the evening before. He had been concerned, but he had managed to get an uninterrupted good night's sleep, secure and comforted by the fact that if anything dire—like death—occurred, he'd be the first one notified. Doctors Joseph Merrick and Keith Johnson were already hovering over the patient, deep in animated discussion, and they paused long enough to allow Kelly to join them and to bring him up to date. Murdoch had improved during the night and was continuing to do so, and although the patient would need much supportive treatment, he was out of danger, barring unforeseen complications. Doctor Kelly nodded contentedly at the optimistic report. By God, he congratulated himself, he had pulled another patient through!

The three men walked out together and headed for the elevator. Merrick and Kelly were due at the Executive Board Meeting and Keith was on his way to emergency ward rounds. As they waited, Merrick casually noted the young black female X-ray technician approaching from the far end of the corridor. Rose . . . Rosa . . . no, Rita. Rita Jenkins! Merrick prided himself on his ability to remember names. He nodded politely as she sauntered toward them and then, out of the corner of his eye, he saw the young woman wink at Keith and go into a paroxysm of several convulsive deep sniffs before she passed by. Keith's shoulders shook with smothered laughter.

She's quite a girl, Keith thought. She was better, somehow different from the others he remembered. Sure, he played around with some of the single nurses. Hell, what intern or resident didn't? On-call time at the hospital was usually busy, but there were slack nights, too—and recreation was limited. How much television could you watch? How much pool could you shoot? And the gals were willing enough—it was better than trudging off to a singles bar in the middle of the night. And so, when the shift was over at 11 P.M., there was often a light tap on the door of the resident's room and before long, two young, healthy animals were no longer bored.

There were sexual liaisons in the hospital, but they were no more prevalent than in factories, business offices, government agencies—any place where men and women were thrown together. It started off casually enough, but Keith was aware that more than once the fun and games had led to true love and wedding bells.

Most of his friends were married now, Keith mused. Many of them had bought homes and had already started families. He longed for stability. Yes, Rita was quite a girl. Quick as a whip. Good-looking, passionate and an artist at making love. He'd give her a call, he decided suddenly. They'd have dinner together, and he'd find out what else they had in common.

Merrick had noticed the wordless play between Keith and Rita. Now what in the hell was that all about? he wondered as the three men stepped into the elevator. While the chief of surgery would never admit it, much went on in the hospital which he didn't know about.

In the Executive Board Room, it was a minute or so after seven thirty, and most of the members were already in attendance. Kelly opted for a seat near the end, while Merrick selected an unoccupied chair just one place removed from the head of the table. They were scarcely settled before Dr. Palmer, the administrator, Louis Taylor, and Arthur Fleischer made their entrance. As Palmer took his place, he waved Fleischer to the adjoining seat, next to Merrick. After a flurry of informal greetings, Palmer ran his eyes quickly over the group. Everyone was present, including the young male stenographer.

"Gentlemen," the chief of staff said, "the meeting will come to order. You all know Arthur Fleischer? Since we are here to discuss the disciplining of a staff member, the administrator deemed it advisable for our legal counsel to be present."

Merrick felt no surprise. He had expected that David's father would throw in the heavy artillery on this one. He nodded politely to Fleischer as Palmer went on.

"At the last meeting of the Board, you'll remember that you appointed a special committee which was to be composed of Doctor Welker, Doctor Bruckheimer, Doctor Merrick and myself to review with Doctor Savage his conduct at this hospital—and to make recommendations to you as to the course that the Executive Medical Board should take to alleviate the problem. That committee met last Tuesday morning at 8 A.M. in the administrator's office. Mr. Taylor was also present. We discussed with Doctor Savage, item by item, the problems that were presented at the last meeting of this group. Initially, there was some concern among the members of the committee as to what recommendation to bring you, because Doctor Savage seemed to be taken somewhat by surprise and was not too receptive to what we had to say." Merrick could not help a slight snort of derision, and Palmer carefully avoided eye contact with him.

"However," he continued, "after the meeting was over, and Doctor Savage had some time to think about our discussion, he personally contacted and assured me that he had seen the light, and that he would in no way be any further problem to the hospital, its ancillary personnel or any of the staff members. In view of that, I re-polled the committee, and it is now our recommenda-

292

tion to you that we place Doctor Savage on probation for a period of one year. It is understood that if, during that period of time, any complaints are received by the administration concerning Doctor Savage, they will be presented to this group at the first possible meeting for review of his probationary status."

Merrick could stand it no longer. "Mr. Chairman!" Palmer negated the interruption with an upraised hand and hurried on.

"I am aware that there are those of you who feel that more drastic measures should be taken, but it seems only right to me, and to the majority of the members of your committee, that Doctor Savage be given the benefit of the doubt and a second chance to prove himself. In view of the assurances he has given us, the committee would like to place a motion before the Board to the effect that Doctor Savage be placed on probation for a one-year period, with the understanding that any misconduct on his part during that time will be immediately reported to the Board for review."

Arthur Fleischer had been slouched low in his chair during most of Palmer's speech, his hooded eyes expertly weighing the reactions of the others in the room. When Palmer had ignored Merrick's interruption and continued, the attorney had shot him a warning glance. Unfortunately, the chief of staff, mesmerized by his own oratory, had missed it. Fleischer shifted slightly in his chair, the only visible evidence of the extreme annoyance he was experiencing. He admittedly had told Palmer to make the motion and get it passed as quickly as possible. He hadn't imagined the man would be so insensitive as to use such obvious, steamroller tactics. His methods, Fleischer knew, were liable to antagonize any undecided physician in the room. So he was not surprised as Merrick, face flushed, practically exploded as Palmer finally paused.

"Mr. Chairman," the chief of surgery said angrily, "I would like to make it a matter of record at this time that I was a member of your committee, and it was my recommendation at that meeting that Doctor Savage be permanently suspended." He turned to the other attending doctors. "I would add that, at the time the committee voted, the majority of the members—including the chairman himself—agreed with me. Frankly, I can't understand the desire of Doctor Palmer and other members of the committee for leniency, regardless of the new attitude Doctor Savage apparently now has. I, for one, cannot condone letting a few 'I'm sorrys' and promises to be a better boy cloud the magnitude of the reprehensible things that Doctor Savage has done. I'm sure you all remember the deliberately early laboratory tests . . . the virtual desertion of a patient here in this hospital . . . the ridiculous orders, which really amounted to punishment of patients, to satisfy a petty and personal grudge against one of our best nurses. Perhaps we can, as Doctor Palmer suggests, simply shake a finger at him for these actions. But there's more. Another serious charge was brought to light at the committee meeting—a charge which most of you know nothing about. There is a young girl in this hospital right now who, because of a severe beating by David Savage, suffers grievous, disfiguring, and possibly permanent injury. I just don't believe that this staff can afford to allow a man who has such a temper, and who is capable of such violence, to practice medicine at Marin. I, therefore, would like to amend the motion submitted by the committee to the effect that Doctor Savage's rights be permanently rescinded."

Palmer camouflaged his discomfort with a friendly but patronizing attitude. "Joe, I understand your sentiments, but parliamentary rules hold in this meeting. You can't amend a motion to change its whole intention. If the motion for probation should fail, you will have every chance to make your own motion then."

"Very well, Doctor Palmer," Merrick agreed, "if that's going to be the way we play the game today, I want to urge every member of this Board to vote against probation, so we can then vote for or against suspension."

During Merrick's words, Fleischer had sat upright in

his chair, placing his hands on the table in front of him. His innate sense for judging emotional climate, for which he was so famous in a court room, told him this was not going well. He spoke quietly, almost diffidently.

"Doctor Palmer? I feel we are dealing with a special and difficult situation here, and I'm sure that everybody would rather discuss the facts without the restrictions of parliamentary rules. Couldn't we just agree that there is no motion on the floor for the moment, and discuss the entire matter before any vote is taken?"

The attorney's words were a source of surprise for both Merrick and Palmer. The chief of surgery was astonished at the implied agreement that the vote was being pushed too fast, without adequate discussion, that the outcome was cut and dried. Palmer's surprise, on the other hand, bordered on confusion. He had thought he was doing so well.

"Why sure, Art," Palmer sputtered. "I . . . well . . . I have no objection. I . . . uh, if the Board agrees. Is there any objection?" He paused for a moment, and hearing none, went on. "Okay, then that's the way it is."

Fleischer leaned forward, subtly taking over the meeting. He spoke informally, confidently, keeping his voice deliberately low so that every man in the room would have to concentrate on what he was saying. "Before we go any further, let me explain one thing. My purpose in being here today is to guide you through any legal intricacies that might arise. Whatever decision you make is yours. But there is one thing I would like very much to point out to you. The incident which Doctor Merrick has described involving Doctor Savage and Miss Thomas—however disagreeable and unfortunate it was—did not take place in this hospital and had absolutely nothing to do with the practice of medicine. It was an altercation between two adults in a private environment. I am forced to point out that if this incident is in any way a basis for your ultimate decision, you are legally on very shaky ground."

"Mr. Fleischer," Merrick said pointedly, "surely a man's character, how he conducts himself, his morality, are important, especially when we are considering whether or not we should accept the apologies and assurances of that man concerning how he will conduct himself in the future."

"It seems to me it might make a difference," Dr. Valdez volunteered.

"I don't know—" Dr. Kelly put in hesitantly.

"Perhaps I had better clarify the point I'm making," Fleischer said quickly. "It comes down to a matter of jurisdiction. If action is desired against Doctor Savage for his personal behavior, unrelated to the practice of medicine, it would have to be taken before the State Board of Medical Examiners on the basis of moral turpitude. That's their bailiwick, and I must warn you that you have no legal right even to discuss it here." He deliberately smiled and adopted a more relaxed manner. "On the other hand, let's face it. This isn't a court of law, and a formal approach to the problem really clouds, rather than clarifies, the issues." He changed again to the intense, legal taskmaster. "I just want to warn you, to make it very plain, that nowhere in the record should it be reflected that the incident of which Doctor Merrick speaks was used as a basis for your final decision, whatever it may be."

Several of the doctors around the table looked at each other, baffled. A few whispered questions at each other. Several stared pointedly at the young stenographer who, suddenly aware of the unaccustomed spotlight cast upon him, paused in his frantic note-taking and raised his pencil. What was to be part of the records? What was to be omitted? His eyes desperately searched about the table for guidance, but there was none. Arthur Fleischer had successfully managed to play on the doctors' fears of legal jeopardy, infusing them with seeds of doubt and confusion. When the attorney resumed speaking, a number of the members looked to him almost as a messiah who could lead them from the darkness.

"As Doctor Merrick inferred, there are aspects of this situation which have about them an unsavory sound," Fleischer announced dramatically, "but frequently there is more than meets the eye. I have information that bears on this case, but it would be legally imprudent to discuss it here. If it's all right with you gentlemen, I would like to have a few words with Doctor Merrick in private."

One or two doctors nodded readily. If somebody was to periled by a possible lawsuit, let it be Merrick, not them.

The chief of surgery shook his head peevishly. "I have nothing to say to Mr. Fleischer," he snapped.

Unprovoked. Fleischer removed a slim file from his briefcase. "Doctor," he said sincerely, "I have information here that I'm positive will interest you. It will explain why I'm so concerned, and why I am sure this matter is really beyond our jurisdiction. It is truly pertinent, but far too dangerous a matter to discuss, as a matter of record, at this meeting." He leaned over and placed the closed file directly in front of Merrick. "If the vote is for expulsion," he continued quietly, "I should imagine Doctor Savage would appeal. Only then would I consider the legal advisability of making this information a matter of public record." He stood up and genially addressed himself to the members at large. "Gentlemen, would everyone welcome a brief recess as much as I would? Perhaps we could have some coffee sent in."

There was an immediate murmur of agreement and Palmer headed for the door to relay the request. The other doctors rose also, grateful to stretch their legs and relieve the tension.

Merrick remained seated at the table, staring at the folder in front of him. He would have had to be superhuman to resist the curiosity that the purple-stamped word, "Confidential," imposed. He opened the folder. It contained only three sheets of paper.

The first a simple and very brief memo to Frank Savage from a Robert Dickenson, dated that morning. Robert Dickenson—Merrick had never heard of him, but he correctly assumed he was one of the many assistants the head of the studio employed. He began to read. . . .

"At 9:06 on Thursday evening, May 3rd, an addict identified as Miss Pamela Gibson, occupation actress, known address 221 West Second Place, Los Angeles, was admitted by Dr. Valdez to Marin Medical Center, suffering from a drug overdose."

Merrick stopped reading abruptly as the words blurred and swam before his eyes. Oh, God! Pam had been serious in her threat. She had deliberately tried to destroy herself because of him. He was her lover, but when she had needed him, he had left her. He was entirely to blame! He started to rise, intending to flee the room. He had to know that Pam was all right. He had to comfort her. She was more important than anything! Or was she? What was he waiting for? Why did he hesitate? What did he care what the other members of the Board thought of him? Sickened, the realization hit him—he cared!

He knew his face was ashen, his hands were icy. He was going to be sick! Right here, in front of all of his contemporaries, he was going to be sick! He took three or four deep, raspy breaths, furtively glancing about the room. With relief, he noticed that no one was watching—except maybe Fleischer. His eyes searched out Dr. Ramon Valdez, a member of the Board, and found him sipping coffee, talking in a small group by the window. He cursed him, then remembered that Valdez would have no reason to inform him of the routine admission of an addict.

He swallowed the fluid that rose in his throat, willing himself not to retch. He started to reach for a cigarette, but his hands were shaking so badly that instead he clasped them, dropping them into his lap to hide them under the table. He forced himself to reread the first few sentences of the memo, and continued beyond them, hardly seeing the words.

"Unofficial investigation indicated the illegal supplier of the drug—indentified as Demerol—as a Dr. Joseph

Merrick. This information is not, as yet, a matter of public record."

Merrick had really not digested the words until he came to his own name. He gazed at it with disbelief—almost wonder. He reread the damning sentence that spelled his total ruin, and a second wave of emotion hit him, crashing against the terrible guilt he was experiencing. Fear—utter, absolute fear. He propped his head between his shaking hands and looked down, as if reading. He must, he knew, struggle to control himself. He would not be stripped naked before the other doctors in this room. Merrick closed his eyes. How could he have gotten into a position where somebody could hand him a piece of paper which condemned him, his career and his family to eternal purgatory—oblivion? Another wave of nausea swept over him. How long would it take Frank's paid eyes and ears to uncover the canceled checks drawn to Pam, the falsified narcotic records, the forbidden trysts? It would be child's play for them. He was ruined! He glanced once again around the room. Did he imagine it, or were several members watching—curious? He willed himself to display a semblance of normality and pretended to be engrossed in the second memo. He had intended it for a prop, a means to gain time, an instrument to allow himself to gather his wits as much as possible. But as his eyes rested on the words, he found himself compelled to read. It was also addressed to Frank Savage, dated that morning, from Sutter Studios' Casting Director.

"As you requested, last night we were able to obtain and review the rushes on the new musical featuring a sequence with one Pamela Gibson. As you indicated, Miss Gibson seems especially talented and should be considered for the uncast role of 'Cissie' in our forthcoming film based on the Mueller novel. Since it will be filmed in New York, I am forwarding a copy of this memo to our casting office there, with the suggestion that she be offered our standard, three-year-minimum player's contract. We have notified them to check with you personally before proceeding."

Burning hatred of Frank Savage began to push aside the guilt and fear that threatened to crush Merrick, but little by little, a fourth emotion stirred within him. Was it gratitude? Merrick reread the memo, gradually marveling at the man's genius. Frank had not only managed to inform him that Pam was okay, but offered a ready-made solution for removing her from his life. In addition, the memo eliminated any suspicions of continuing blackmail. Once Pam was under contract, Merrick knew, it would be imperative for Sutter Studios to quash any hint of the addiction problem. And they had the means to do it. Frank was offering him a gilt-edged certificate of immunity!

Merrick went on to the third and final sheet in the file, mentally wondering if Frank could manage to top himself. He not only could—he did. The heavy parchment paper, bearing the expensively engraved name and home address, was Frank Savage's personal stationery—the words on it were handwritten.

"Dear Dr. Merrick," it began. "Mrs. Savage and I have never had the pleasure of meeting your wife, Elizabeth, but have heard she is a fine, wonderful woman—and we are anxious to do so. Would you and Mrs. Merrick be free to join us for dinner early next week? If your schedule is such that you must refuse, we'll understand." It was signed, "Sincerely, Frank Savage."

The final, implied threat was not wasted on Merrick. Completely crushed, he gazed about the room. As far as Dr. David Savage was concerned, Merrick had lost—and he knew it. He was surprised that he felt only a twinge of regret over the outcome of a matter which, only a short time before, had been so vitally important to him. When the chips were down, for Joseph Merrick—as for everyone else—self preservation overrode all other drives. What stunned him now was the necessity of whipping together a logical reason for the words he knew he must say. How could he explain his turnabout? What phrases could he use to the curious doctors to justify his change of heart in now endorsing the disciplinary action to which he had gone on record as being so violently opposed? He sat, willing salvation from his brain which had been numbed by the recent ordeal.

He was only half conscious when Arthur Fleischer came up quietly behind him. The attorney reached into his inside jacket pocket, extracted an envelope and removed the sheet of paper from within. Unfolding it, he placed it in front of Merrick, removing the file as he did so. Fleischer casually returned to his place, dropped the file into his briefcase and snapped the lock, while Merrick tried to concentrate on the words before him.

"Doctor Merrick," he read, "may I suggest the following statement when we reconvene? . . . 'The file I was handed contained confidential and privileged information concerning Doctor David Savage, Miss Susan Thomas, and this hospital. In light of what I have just read, I wish to recommend to the Board that the probationary period for Doctor Savage is a reasonable action.' " There was a postscript at the bottom "Your making the motion would be more effective than another source, and I can assure you, your graciousness will not go without notice."

Fleischer's almost imperceptible nod to Palmer caused the chief of staff's booming voice to fill the room. "Well, gentlemen, shall we get back to business?" They were barely reseated around the table before Merrick spoke.

"Gentlemen, as many of you know, I have felt very strongly about what measures we should take concerning Doctor Savage, but"—his eyes glanced down to the paper and he read, without seeming to—"the file I was handed contained confidential and privileged information concerning Doctor David Savage, Miss Susan Thomas, and this hospital. In light of what I have just read, I wish to recommend to the Board that the probationary period for Doctor Savage is a reasonable action." Merrick paused only briefly, slipping the paper into his pocket as he went on. "Mr. Chairman, if I may, I would like to move to accept the recommendation for probation."

"Is there a second?" Palmer asked with relief.

"I second," Dr. Bruckheimer quickly volunteered.

"Is there any further discussion?" Palmer queried—then, almost in the same breath, "All of you in favor of the motion say 'aye.'" There was a half-hearted scattered respose of "ayes." Palmer frowned. "All opposed?"

There was not a sound in the room.

"Motion passed!" Palmer announced. He turned to the administrator. "Mr. Taylor? Will you see to it that the appropriate letter is prepared for the secretary of the staff's signature advising Doctor Savage of our decision?" Taylor nodded. "Well, gentlemen," Palmer continued heartily, "much to my surprise, we have dealt with this matter quickly. I had expected it to take a full morning's session, and consequently there is nothing else prepared for your consideration. If no one here has any new business to discuss, I propose that we adjourn."

There was still absolute silence in the room. Dr. Merrick was the first to stand, nod briefly, and hurry from the room. He could not get to a phone fast enough. He dialed Admitting. The line was busy. He waited a few moments and dialed again. Still busy. He glanced at the elevators and noticed both were moored on the top floor, indicating a considerable wait. Starting for the stairwell, he hesitated, came back and gave the phone one more chance. He could not get through. Thoroughly annoyed, he rushed down the steps and hurried to the Admitting Desk, making a controlled effort to pull himself together as he neared it.

"A Pamela Gibson was admitted last night. What is her room number, please?"

More moments passed as the nurse checked her records. "349, doctor." He nodded and walked across the lobby and stood, impatiently tracking the progress of the elevators by the lights, floor by floor. As he waited, a humiliating realization swept over him. Frank's forces had predicted the morning's events with satanical preciseness. They had known and judged in advance every thought—every action—every reaction. The file—the

302

statement—everything had been prepared, withheld, and used exactly on cue.

He finally reached the desired floor and strode rapidly down the corridor to room 349. His hand was reaching for the door as a familiar voice stopped him.

"Doctor Merrick?"

Arthur Fleischer was leaning indolently against the wall on the opposite side of the corridor, several rooms removed. The attorney made no move to join Merrick, and the chief of surgery was forced to walk to where Fleischer stood.

He stared at the lawyer wordlessly. Again his adversary had uncannily been able to predict his every move.

"I wouldn't go in there," Fleischer said in a low, pleasant voice. Merrick was tempted to retaliate with a sarcastic reply, but instead, simply turned and started back toward Pam's room. He would not dignify this confrontation by argument or discussion.

"Doctor Merrick," Fleischer said insistently. "Just a moment." This time the attorney covered the few steps between the two men. "I know you're concerned, but I can assure you that Miss Gibson is fine. There are no problems—no problems whatever. She doesn't remember much of last night. According to Doctor Valdez, she will be released this afternoon. When she gets home, she will receive a call from her agent, informing her of the contract with Sutter Studios. She has been booked on an early morning flight tomorrow, and the studio's publicity people will meet her in New York. Everything's been taken care of." He gazed directly into the eyes of Dr. Merrick. "If I were you, I wouldn't see or talk to her again, doctor. She doesn't need you anymore."

Merrick was torn by his desire to see Pam—at least one more time. But the implication was obvious. Savage was keeping his part of the bargain. He expected Merrick to keep his. Finally, the chief of surgery nodded. Utterly dejected, he turned and slowly made his way back to the elevators—not even allowing himself to glance at the closed door of Room 349.

George Selkins had been squirming impatiently in his bed for the past thirty or forty minutes, checking his watch so often that the hands seemed motionless. Damn that Dr. Carrington! Every day since he'd been in the hospital Carrington had made his evening rounds between five thirty and six. But it was already six thirty, and there was no sign of him. Wouldn't you know that today, of all days, the dumb son of a bitch would veer from his schedule? Fuck him, Selkins decided with unreasonable outrage. He'd give him ten more minutes. If he hadn't shown up by then, he'd simply call the desk and demand a release form. There wasn't much time. That afternoon, Selkins had made arrangements with the Golden State Ambulance Service to pick him up at the hospital at seven o'clock. Who needed Carrington?

He did, Selkins admitted reluctantly. He hurt, and he shuddered at the thought of that long plane trip to Costa Rica without the benefit of a pain pill or two. But if worse came to worse, he'd grit his teeth and get through it somehow. You could stand anything for a limited time, he reminded himself. He hoped Marion had the sense to tuck a bottle or two of Scotch into the hand luggage. He spent a few moments toying with the idea of calling his wife to make sure, but hesitated, glancing at the intercom box directly overhead. The damn nosy nurses—they had a built-in spy system. They could activate that switch any time and listen to every bit of conversation in the room. He was technically under arrest, and for all he knew, maybe his calls were being monitored.

He glanced at his watch again and bade himself not to panic—at least, not for another ten minutes. With extreme satisfaction, he ran over the conversation with his wife earlier in the day. Even then, he had let her do most of the talking, limiting his replies to monosyllables and grunts. If the nurses were listening in, they got damned little information to use against him. Naïvely and openly, Marion had started to give him the details of her activities and the results until he had obliquely warned her.

304

"Were you calling me, nurse?" he had said loudly. There was no reply. "I thought I heard the intercom click on," he said pointedly to Marion. There was a long, confused moment of silence from his wife. For years, he had known she was not the brightest woman in the world. And that was charitable. Some of her acquaintances condemned her as actually dim-witted. But he loved her. At any rate, she had gotten the message, sensed the danger, and risen to the occasion.

"I talked to Nate Boyle, darling. He wishes you well, and says to tell you he'll be seeing you soon." He breathed a sigh of relief. It was Marion's way of telling him the deal had been made.

"This is important, George," she continued. "Nate says that if you ever want to look him up, he's not at Santa Monica any longer. It just got too busy—too much air traffic for safety. He'll be at Whiteman Field, in the San Fernando Valley. That's near Anita's house. You take San Fernando Road—" He knew they didn't know any Anitas, but her continuing directions were carefully to the point. "He says it's a lovely field, not much activity, and not even a control tower. He's easy to find. His twin-engine Beech is always hangared at the east end of the field, and usually is the largest plane there."

"That sounds fine," Selkins said cautiously.

"I'm sorry I couldn't get in to see you this afternoon," she apologized. "I had such a busy day, dear, but I got everything accomplished." So, he thought, the money was in her hot little hands. "Got to run now," she continued. "I'll see you around seven thirty or quarter to eight." She couldn't resist, he realized, a final. "Be careful, darling. I love you."

Everything was laid out. Where in the hell was Carrington? He thought he heard the doctor's voice in the hall and he tensed as Mike came into the room.

"Evening, Mr. Selkins," Mike said pleasantly. He walked to the bed, withdrew the sheet and removed the bandage over his patient's incision.

"How am I doing, Doc?" George asked heartily.

305

"Okay. How are you feeling?"

"Fine," Selkins said convincingly. "I've never felt better. As a matter of fact, I want to go home."

"Sure you do," Mike said sympathetically. "Probably by next weekend, we can—"

"I want to go home now—tonight," Selkins interrupted.

"No way," Mike said absently, still probing and examining the incision. It was a moment or two before the urgency of his patient's stare caused the doctor to look up and meet his eyes.

"Like I said—tonight, Doc," Selkins repeated quietly.

Carrington replaced the bandage and straightened. "Look, Mr. Selkins, you may be feeling just fine—and as a matter of fact, you are doing very well—but with an injury of the magnitude that you had, and the surgery we had to do, we need to have you here, where we can watch you closely, for at least another week."

"Why?" It was a flat question, but tinged with anxiety.

"To begin with, your drain is still in. I plan to start working it out tomorrow, a little bit at a time."

"Take it out now," Selkins urged.

Carrington shook his head. "By taking it out slowly, a little each day, it will force the wound to heal from the inside. Otherwise, it could leave a pocket, which would be an invitation for an abscess to form. That we don't need."

"Come on, Doc," Selkins said smoothly. "I'm really fed up with these four walls. They're starting to get on my nerves. Couldn't you stop by the house every day and do whatever you have to do with the drain? I'd be glad to pay you extra for your trouble. I just want to get out of here."

Mike stared at Selkins. If he agreed, it would take over an hour each day to drive to the patient's home and perform the required service—a procedure which he could accomplish in the hospital in about two minutes. There might, he knew, be cases where he would be

306

willing to inconvenience himself, extend himself as a courtesy. But he didn't really like Selkins. He was just being childish, petulant, in his demands about going home. But like him or not, he wouldn't antagonize him.

"Ordinarily, I'd be glad to," he said cheerfully, "but there are additional X-rays and lab work which you're going to need."

"Like what?" Selkins demanded. There was no way—nothing that Carrington could say or do—that would change his plans. But he wondered about the competency of Costa Rican doctors. It wouldn't hurt to gather all the information he could as a double check on his continuing treatments in San Jose.

"I'll want X-rays to make sure your diaphragms are moving all right," Mike explained, "and that there's no collection of fluid underneath. Then tests should be done to determine your liver function."

"I can come back for those," Selkins explained, "after I'm home for a while."

Mike struggled to hide the annoyance he felt at the man's persistence. "Going home is out of the question, Mr. Selkins. Discussing it is a waste of time. Even though you feel pretty good now, when you try to get up and around, you're going to be surprised at how weak you'll be for a while. Everything's gone so well for you up to now. Just stay here with us for a few more days and all those problems will be behind you. Don't rock the boat."

"I don't want to rock the boat," Selkins snapped. "I just want a more inviting harbor!" He waved around the room. "Look at this dump!" Mike glanced about the room, willing himself to see it through a patient's eyes that were used to luxury and jaded with the boredom of lying in bed. Even so, the room was bright, cheerful, clean.

"As far as feeling weak or tired," Selkins continued, "I don't plan on running any foot races. I can rest just as well at home—a damned sight better, in fact—as I can here, with people running in and out all night, the page blasting."

The argument was beginning to irritate Mike. He decided to become a little tougher. "I don't think you realize how sick you've been. You know, it's only been a day or so since you got over the D.T.'s. There's no way you can go home at this point." He started to turn to leave the room.

"What you really mean is that the great doctor doesn't want to take the trouble to make house calls." Selkins' tone had turned raspy and slightly insulting.

"To be perfectly honest with you, Mr. Selkins, I simply don't have the time. You belong here in the hospital," Mike snapped.

"Well, I'm going home whether you like it or not. If you won't come out to see me, I'm sure Doctor Kentner is competent to remove my drain and do whatever else has to be done. If I wave a few bucks in his face, he'll come running."

Mike was suddenly weary of the entire discussion. "If you really have made up your mind to go home, you can sign out of the hospital against medical advice and go home in the morning. It's up to you." Carrington started to leave the room. He was confident that Selkins would back down. His patient's words stopped him cold.

"Tonight, doctor! Get me the forms. I'll sign anything you want." Mike nodded, somehow instinctively realizing that additional discussion would be futile. "Hey, Doc!" Selkins stopped him when he was almost to the door. Good, thought Mike. He's finally seen the light after all and changed his mind. "There is one thing you could do for me. Can you get me a couple of pain pills to take with me. And maybe a sleeping pill or two—to tide me over?"

Carrington was bristling with annoyance—both at his patient and at his own lack of expertise in convincing him of the foolhardiness of his decision. "If Kentner's going to be your doctor, get them from him," he snapped.

"Aw, come on," Selkins wheedled. "It's Friday night. If I know Kentner, he probably left hours ago for Palm

Springs. Have you ever tried to track anybody down at the Racquet Club? It'll be a hassle."

Mike hesitated. Selkins' refusal to follow his advice had bruised his considerable ego, and he really wanted to wash his hands of the whole business. But there was no reason to punish a patient because he was being foolish. "I'll give you just enough to last over the weekend," Mike agreed coldly. It was not until he had acquiesced that the thought occurred to him. "You fully realize, don't you, that once you sign those forms, I'm no longer your doctor? And with Kentner out of town, that means if you have any problems, you're going to be in big trouble?"

"I'll risk it," Selkins replied airily.

Mike struggled for insight to the man's illogical thinking. Why would anyone be so stubborn as to insist so doggedly on a course of action that was potentially detrimental? He tried to get into Selkins' head, put himself in the patient's place, but it still made absolutely no sense.

"By the way," he asked casually, "how are you planning to get home?"

"An ambulance is already on its way."

Mike was stunned at Selkins' words. For the first time he understood that this was not a spur-of-the-moment decision. The plans had been implemented hours before. The doctor stood for a moment, weighing what might be an effective course of action. No matter how much he disliked the man, he reminded himself, no matter how annoyed he was with him, he should still make another effort to keep the patient from harming himself. Should he question . . . should he warn . . . should he plead? Before he could decide, Selkins spoke.

"The forms, Doctor Carrington. And the pills. Get with it, okay? There isn't much time."

Biting back an angry reply, Mike left the room and walked slowly to the nurses' desk. He picked up Selkins' chart and started to make a notation. Then, with sudden resolution, he turned to the last sheet of paper in the chart which listed the admitting data. Finding Selkins' home number there, he picked up the phone and dialed. He waited patiently as the phone rang . . . and rang . . . and rang. Finally, as he was about to hang up, a voice that was undeniably Marion's answered. She was breathless.

"Mrs. Selkins?"

"Yes," she answered, gasping to catch her breath.

"This is Doctor Carrington. I've just been in talking to your husband, and he's gotten it into his head that he wants to go home. He wants to go home right now. And that just doesn't make any sense at all. In fact, it could be dangerous."

"I know," Marion stammered. "I . . . well . . . I tried to talk him out of it . . . but I think his mind is made up. George is a very stubborn man . . . and . . . I think we'd better just humor him . . . and . . . well, if he wants to come home—"

Carrington interrupted sharply. "I'd appreciate it, Mrs. Selkins, if you could call him now—in his room— and tell him you've talked to me and that he really is taking a chance with his recovery in doing this. And it's such an unnecessary risk. I'm sure you can find some way to convince him."

"Call him? Call him now?" Why, wondered Carrington, did she sound on the brink of tears? "I'm sorry," she continued. "I . . . I . . . well, I just don't have time. I have to go. I have an appointment. I can't explain. I . . . I just don't have time." The words tumbled from her in almost incoherent haste.

"Mrs. Selkins! Your husband has already called an ambulance to come to get him. They'll probably be here any minute. It's important you call him now."

"I'm sorry, doctor," she quavered. "I . . . I just have to go." He heard the phone go dead in his ear as she hung up.

Jesus, thought Mike with disbelief. They're both lunatics. They deserve each other. He stared for a moment at the phone, then glanced up, aware that the nurse was watching him curiously.

"Get the release forms and have Mr. Selkins sign

310

them—right away. Be sure they're witnessed. He's leaving." As he gave the instructions, he quickly wrote prescriptions for ten codeine pills for pain and for five sleeping pills, signed and handed them to her. "And get these filled for him."

The nurse examined the prescriptions. "How soon is he leaving, doctor? It will take the hospital pharmacy a little while—"

"I don't know," Carrington snapped. "He called an ambulance himself. Never mind. Let me have them." He took back the prescriptions and headed for Selkins' room.

"The nurse will be down in a few moments with the 'against medical advice' forms, and I've written you a couple of prescriptions for the pain and sleeping pills. There's no time to get them filled here, so you'll have to get your wife to take them to a drug store."

Mike did not notice the look of guarded apprehension and disappointment that crossed his patient's face, so quickly did it disappear. "Hell, can't you just *give* me three or four pills?" Selkins asked. "What's the big deal? I'll pay for them. It's getting late, and Marion isn't going to—" His voice trailed off.

"Sorry," Carrington snapped. "It's the best I can do." He stared at Selkins for a moment. "Speaking of your wife, I just talked to her, and she was going out. I take it she'll be home when you get there? You shouldn't be alone." Damn it, he thought, why in the hell do I feel so responsible? God knows I've done all I can to forestall this insane action.

"Oh, I'm sure she's just gone on an errand. In and out—in and out of the house all the time—that's Marion," Selkins said unconcernedly, stifling a small, smug grin.

That Carrington caught. Puzzles were a challenge to him. He liked games that stressed skill and mental agility. But Selkins was an enigma that was frustrating the hell out of him. He didn't give up easily. He had the glimmer of what might be an additional clue. He'd try it.

311

"By the way, Mr. Selkins," he said quietly, handing him the prescriptions, "you know, you're not fooling me one bit."

Startled, the patient glanced at him with a surge of guilt and foreboding. For the first time, his composure and self-assurance seemed ruffled. "What do you mean?"

"The reason you want to go home so damned bad is so you can drink! And let me tell you, in your physical condition, there's nothing you could do that would be any more dangerous."

Selkins visibly relaxed and placed the prescriptions on the table alongside him. "I've sworn off, Doc," he said affably. "Believe me."

"Then why do you want to go home?" Carrington practically shouted.

"What's the difference?" Selkins shrugged. "I'm going."

Fed up to the teeth, Carrington slammed from the room. He returned to the nursing desk to make the final notations on his ex-patient's chart, and while he was still writing, the nurse returned with the signed, witnessed forms, which were made part of the record. Mike had barely finished when the elevator door opened and two attendants, wheeling a stretcher, made their way down the hall to where he was standing. They greeted the nurse on duty.

"Hi. Golden State Ambulance. We have orders to pick up a Mr. George Selkins."

The nurse indicated they should follow her and headed for Selkins' room. Deliberately hurrying, Carrington completed his notes and went to the floor below to continue his evening rounds. He did not want to see George Selkins as he left. In fact, it was his earnest wish that he never again lay eyes on the man.

At their luxurious house on Roxbury Drive in Beverly Hills, Marion took a final look around her. Leased though it was, it had been her home for the past eight years, and in leaving it she felt as if she were abandoning an old and trusted friend. Up until late afternoon,

312

she had been too busy—dashing from banks to savings and loan companies—even to think about anything but the task George had assigned her. Each time she stepped to the teller's window, she had cringed, sure that embarrassing questions would be put to her, expecting any moment that a uniformed arm would reach out to detain and interrogate her concerning her suspicious withdrawals. But without exception, everyone had been polite and accommodating, handling the transactions in the routine manner that individuals in repetitious and boring jobs affected. At the bank, the guard had even held the door for her, touching his cap politely, wishing her a pleasant day. With the cash accumulating as she made stop after stop, she began to view each passerby, each shopper, even the florist delivery man in the adjoining stall of a parking lot, as a potential armed thug, threatening to steal her and her husband's future. Every eye was on her, she sensed—every footstep behind her fraught with danger. The afternoon had passed without incident, but she had arrived home in a state close to physical and mental collapse.

The maid was just leaving as she returned—thank God! Ellie came in five days a week, and had been with them over six years. "Anything I can help you bring in from the car, Mrs. Selkins?" Ellie had sung out in her usual accommodating effort to be helpful.

"No . . . Ellie. Thank you . . . nothing. I . . . don't think so. I . . . well, I didn't buy anything today."

"Okay," the girl said cheerfully. "See you Monday. Have a nice weekend."

The temptation was great to save Ellie the long, unnecessary trip to the house which would be locked and empty upon her arrival. Marion stopped herself just in time. As the girl waved and drove off in her battered compact car, Marion tried to visualize what would happen. Once, several years ago, she and George had gone to Palm Springs for a party at some friends' on Sunday. George had really laid one on, becoming increasingly intoxicated as the evening progressed, and they had finally been talked into staying the night, starting the hundred mile drive back late Monday morning. Faithful Ellie had still been waiting on the front steps when they arrived, a little surly and sullen, but understanding. Poor Ellie! Marion wondered how long she would wait this time. Perhaps she should call, or leave a note. George's warning rang in her ears, and she shook her head resolutely.

Entering the house, she wandered about aimlessly. Decisions were hard for her. She had packed the night before, agonizing over articles of clothing which she knew she dared not take. The fur stole that George had given her as a tenth-anniversary present. She stroked it lovingly for a few moments. Stoles were out, she knew, but the nostalgic pain of leaving it, draped in a garment bag for strangers to find later, brought tears to her eyes. All the furs were too bulky—they would have to stay. And the long dinner dresses. They also took up far too much room in the four large bags—two for her, two for George—which she had chosen from their cache of assorted luggage. They were already in the car trunk, stashed there the night before with much difficulty due to their weight. She was sure no one had seen her. Beverly Hills was an area where landscape architects grew rich from their commissions for placement of high hedges and leafy trees to insure the psychotic need for privacy the wary residents demanded. After eight years, Marion didn't even know her neighbors, having bowed to the unwritten law that normal friendliness was a trait to be viewed with suspicion. An overnight case, once empty except for her jewels, also nestled in the car's trunk, and it was now heavy with the cash she had collected that day.

She glanced about the kitchen. There were smudges on the canisters that Ellie had missed, and she hurried for a soapy sponge to expunge them. She had no idea who would be the first to enter the abandoned house once they were missed, but whoever it was, it was important that they find no fault with her housekeeping!

Going into the library, she gasped. The plants! Dashing back to the kitchen, she returned immediately with an ornamental watering can and soaked each one thoroughly. Even if she would never see them again, she couldn't let them die!

Marion stared at the wine rack over the bar. So many wonderful bottles, some of special vintage. She shrugged—and suddenly turned back. From the cabinet underneath, she removed an unopened bottle of Scotch and scrutinized it speculatively. Should she take it? It might make the forthcoming journey more bearable. And she once again hurried to the kitchen for a paper bag, put the Scotch into it, and laid it alongside her purse. As a final thought struck her, she opened a drawer of the sideboard and removed the remaining packs from a carton of cigarettes. American cigarettes were probably hard to get in Costa Rica. She sighed. They were going to be there a long time—the rest of their lives. What did it matter when the supply ran out?

She glanced at her watch and was panicked to see how the time had flown. She should have left almost five minutes ago. Throwing her all-weather coat over her shoulders and balancing her purse and the bag containing the liquor and cigarettes, she started to leave, automatically performing the ritual of extinguishing the lights. She had almost completed the task, when she remembered George's admonition about the lights. She hurriedly retraced her steps, leaving at least one light burning in each room. She was just opening the door when the phone rang. She hesitated—debating.

She had to leave. George was always railing at her, faulting her chronic tardiness. Should she let it ring? She waited, hoping it would stop. But what if it were her husband? What if something had gone amiss? With a strangled gasp, she sped to the phone and answered it. And was immediately sorry. She knew she was responding to Carrington's remarks in idiot fashion. She couldn't help it. Her brain, unused to the arduous exercise which had been demanded of it throughout this day—probably the worst in her life—refused to answer the challenge. She hardly listened to the doctor's words. Her only thought was to end the conversation—cut short

315

the dialogue which was threatening to abort the meticulously planned strategy of their escape. At her wit's end, unable to devise a better solution, she had simply hung up and hurried out the door.

Marion got into the car, and for a frightening moment had trouble starting it. Finally, the engine responded and she breathed a sigh of relief. She had spent considerable time studying a map, tracing the labyrinth of streets which she must follow to get to Whiteman Field. She said a silent prayer as she pulled out of the long driveway. She had no sense of direction—she admitted it freely. Once she had gotten lost going to Schwab's Drug Store. Let me make it, she pleaded to the deity who watched over women who loved their husbands. And let me make it in time!

In the hospital room, George Selkins watched the emissaries from Golden State Ambulance and the nurse enter, rehearsing the scene he was destined to play. Silently, he cooperated as much as possible as the two young men efficiently transferred him from the bed to the stretcher. The nurse hovered solicitously.

"Mr. Selkins—are you all right?" she asked.

"I'm fine." His manner was deliberately brusque and rude. "Why don't you just get out of the way?"

Offended, she retreated from the room. Now alone with the ambulance attendants, George went into his act. "Christ, you're late. What time is it?"

"Just a few minutes after seven," the taller attendant volunteered. "I don't understand. Late? Our orders specify a seven o'clock pick up—"

"Seven!" Selkins ranted. "What kind of operation are you running? I told them *six!* Jesus, what in the hell's the matter with you people—you got shit in your ears or something? I told them six. Six o'clock. I stressed how important it was. I said six on the nose." Flustered, the two attendants glanced helplessly at each other. "Well, Jesus, just don't stand there. Get going," Selkins commanded. "Let's not waste any more time."

On the defensive, they hurriedly wheeled the stretcher bearing the patient from the room. For the entire length of the corridor, Selkins invented disparaging remarks about the supposed hour delay, the inefficiency of the company, and the state of a world where nobody gave a damn. Finally, in the elevator, as both men squirmed with mounting discomfort, he made the announcement.

"Well, there just isn't going to be time now—thanks to you. I wanted to go home first—and then my wife was going to drive me to the airport. Damn it, if I miss that plane, I'll sue." His tone softened slightly. "Look, I know it's not your fault, not personally, I mean. But I want you to write down the name of the manager or owner of Golden State Ambulance. I'm not going to let this go by. I want to make a formal complaint." The attendants were growing more uncomfortable by the minute. "There's just one solution, I guess," Selkins finally sighed. "I sure as hell don't have time to go home now. You'll just have to take me to the airport. Whiteman Field in the San Fernando Valley. And even at that, you're going to have to hurry like hell to make it."

The attendants nodded, intimidated. They would have agreed to almost anything to placate this customer who had been fouled up and was even threatening legal action. Quickly and efficiently getting him into the ambulance, they started off. Within a few minutes, one attendant activated the car radio and contacted his company's dispatcher. Selkins caught only snatches of the conversation, but what he heard made him relax with smug satisfaction.

"I don't *know* how it happened, Dick," he heard the attendant say. "He ordered for six, so it's some mistake down there. How the hell do I know who he talked to? Look up the order. Well, I don't care what it says. Somebody goofed. Look, we'll straighten it out later. Just change the destination record, will you? Instead of Beverly Hills, we're on our way to Whiteman Field. Sure we'll collect the difference, just relax. Okay. We'll be in touch."

Dr. Carrington had returned to the seventh floor and was in the middle of writing preoperative orders for a

317

thyroidectomy case which was soon to be admitted. He was only half aware when the floor nurse came from the room Selkins had recently occupied and stood at the desk beside him, attempting to iron the wrinkles from two small wadded balls of paper with her hands. She continued the task until she caught his attention, and he finally glanced up.

"This is strange, doctor," she said, her puzzlement evident in her voice.

"What?" he asked absently.

"These two prescriptions. Signed by you. I found them on the table when I went in to check the room."

He examined the two sheets curiously, recognizing them as the prescriptions for codeine and sleeping pills he had given Selkins earlier. The thought crossed his mind that Selkins, in the flurry of leaving, had forgotten them. But there was no doubt that they had been crumpled and deliberately discarded. He shrugged his perplexity at the nurse and tore the small sheets in quarters, disposing of them in a nearby trash receptacle. It was unwise to leave prescriptions for narcotics lying around. He had just resumed his chart work when the phone rang beside him. The young nurse on duty behind the desk picked it up.

"Seven-north," she said brightly. "Oh, he's checked out. I'm sorry. No, I'm afraid I don't know." She listened for a few moments. "He's right here." She extended the phone to Carrington. "It's for you." Mike identified himself.

"Doctor Carrington? This is Robert Bradley, Mr. Selkins' attorney. I tried to ring George's room, and didn't get an answer. Now the nurse tells me he's checked out. That's impossible, isn't it? What in the hell's going on?"

"He did check out, Mr. Bradley—about a half hour ago—against medical advice. I tried to talk him out of it, but it was no use. All I know is an ambulance picked him up. He said he was going home."

"Well, I tried to call Marion a few minutes ago, but there's no answer there, either," Bradley informed him.

"I'm a bit concerned. The little Harris boy died this evening. It was just on the news. I didn't know if the Selkinses heard it or not, but I wanted to call and assure them I'd do everything I could." There was a lull as each man became engrossed in his own speculations.

"You know," Carrington remarked, "I talked to Mrs. Selkins earlier. I was upset when I came in and found her husband so absolutely determined to leave. He had even made arrangements for the ambulance without consulting me. Anyway, when I talked to his wife, she seemed very distraught. She said she had to go out, was in a hurry, couldn't talk and hung up. She wasn't much help. Maybe they heard about the Harris boy from some other source."

"It isn't likely," Bradley said thoughtfully. "It was just announced."

"Another strange thing," Carrington said, and proceeded to fill him in on the details of the discarded prescriptions. "And he was so adamant, so anxious about his need for them," Mike finished. There was another pause.

"I hope nothing's happened to George, doctor," Bradley finally resumed. "I wonder, do you know which ambulance he used? Would it be possible to check with them and see if there's been an accident or if they were delayed for any reason?"

Mike hesitated. Was he destined never to rid himself of the specter of George Selkins? "Why don't you hang on, Mr. Bradley?" he finally agreed. "I'll see what I can find out." Putting the attorney on "hold," Mike glanced at the nurse. "Will you look up the phone number of Golden State Ambulance Service?" She nodded, reached for a directory, and in a few moments relayed the requested information. He dialed immediately.

"This is Doctor Michael Carrington at Marin Medical Center," he announced when his call was answered. "You picked up a patient of mine, Mr. George Selkins, about a half hour ago. Can you tell me, please, where he was taken?" He waited while the records were checked. "Thank you."

He switched to the other line. "Mr. Bradley? I just spoke to the ambulance dispatcher. Mr. Selkins changed his destination enroute. They were instructed to take him to Whiteman Field, a private airstrip in the San Fernando Valley." Mike's mind was racing. George Selkins, he suspected, was running.

"He's running," Bradley said with disbelief, as the obvious answer simultaneously dawned on him. "I didn't think he was that stupid, but it really looks like he's running." There was another brief silence.

"I wouldn't be surprised," Carrington agreed slowly. "Damn. You know, I'm no longer his doctor. Legally, ethically, morally, I have no more right to interfere than a stranger."

"Don't worry about it," Bradley finally said. "I'm still his attorney. I'll take care of it. Thank you, doctor, thank you for your help," and he hung up.

In the den of his Westwood home, Robert Bradley did some soul-searching, but not for long. He cursed silently. Damn George Selkins. As an attorney, Bradley reminded himself, he was an officer of the court, and George's obvious flight to avoid prosecution nullified the normal ethics of a lawyer-client relationship. His legal responsibility was fortified by the unhappy thought that he had personally signed the bond for the fifteen thousand bail and could be held accountable for it. Bradley had done it out of kindness, as a token of friendship for his client who lay helpless in a hospital bed. He did not intend to sustain the financial loss if he could prevent it. Consulting the fine leather phone index on his desk, he dialed the number listed for Acme Bail Bonds. He knew that, within moments, the police would be notified and alerted.

Nate Boyle leisurely completed his visual preflight check and patted the fuselage of his twin-engined Beech Eighteen affectionately. All fueled, warmed up, and ready to go. She wasn't the newest thing in the skies, but she was dependable—and he'd hate to lose her.

There was a chance that he might. At thirty, Nate

was a perennial bachelor, and from the time he had been graduated from college—the final period in his life which had been subsidized by his now-deceased parents—he had overextended himself. He had borrowed the money to buy the Beech, optimistically certain that he would make a killing with it by providing a jump service at Elsinore, the major mecca for the sky-diving cult in Southern California.

So enthused, so positive was he of the great financial rewards in store for him which would accrue from his service that he bought a house he couldn't afford, a sports car well beyond his means, and even a small, secondhand plane, a Bonanza, for his private pleasure and convenience. Nate's penchant for high living was undeniable. Good-looking, tall, blond, muscular, he had attached himself to a group of friends to whom money was no problem. He liked girls—he liked liquor—he liked gambling.

It had not occurred to him that sky diving was primarily a weekend sport, nor that there would be fierce competition from other flying services. He could accommodate only eight people, plus their parachutes, and he soon discovered that the care and feeding of the Beech's two big Pratt and Whitney engines required a great deal more money than a solid weekend of flying could produce. He picked up some supplementary work—an occasional charter, a cargo contract now and then—but little by little, the plane was eating him alive. He didn't have the financial strength to own the Beech unless it could earn its keep. But he couldn't bear to give her up. The thought of getting a steady job had occurred to him, but only momentarily. He had an aversion to the limitations and the degradation that a salaried position would impose upon him.

Boyle's solution had been to refinance his car to make house payments, take a second mortgage on his home to maintain his planes, and borrow on his life insurance to make car payments. It was a vicious circle which, if broken, threatened total disaster.

The twenty-five thousand offered by the Selkinses

wouldn't completely bail him out—but it sure as hell would help. Nate had no illusions about the charter to Costa Rica. George and Marion Selkins were in serious trouble, and he knew it. After all, for less than a thousand, they could enjoy a luxury of first-class accommodations on a regularly scheduled airline to San Jose. He could read. He knew about Selkins' accident. But that was their problem. For twenty-five thousand, you didn't ask questions. Boyle knew he was placing himself in a certain amount of jeopardy, but was egotistical enough to be sure that when the time came, when the chips were down, he could cover himself. Hell, whatever happened, he couldn't be any worse off than he was.

He climbed into the plane and inspected the interior. It was commodious, originally designed with space for a pilot, a co-pilot, and six passengers. But in deference to his sky-diving clients, and to facilitate his freight contracts, he had stripped it to the hull, leaving only the cargo strap rings and a couple of removable metal bucket seats which were anchored along one side of the passenger compartment. He had rented a folding cot and equipped it with a blanket and pillow, lashing the makshift bed to the cargo rings on the floor of the plane for stability. It was little enough concession for twenty-five big ones, he thought.

He exited the plane and surveyed Whiteman Field with satisfaction. Traffic was light, even for a Friday night, and the strip was virtually deserted. The doctors, the lawyers, the executives who would be frantically taking off for various recreation spots and long weekends preferred the status and facilities offered at the more popular and convenient airfields located in Van Nuys or Santa Monica or Brackett Field near Pomona.

It was nearly dark now, and except for the small, evenly spaced lights bordering the runway, the strip was almost ghostly in its quietness. The silhouettes of the small planes tied down in lines on the perimeters resembled grotesque, shadowy sentries. He became alert as he spotted the headlights of a car slowly making its way down the long driveway to the field and watched as it paused uncertainly at the chain-link gate posted with a sign, "No Admittance, Authorized Personnel Only." He walked the few steps from the plane to the gate and cracked it open.

"Mrs. Selkins?"

Marion breathed a hugh sigh of relief. She had lost her way twice before arriving at the field and, frightened at the thought of making herself conspicuous by asking directions, had circled until she got her bearings. The car radio had been on, and she had heard the news broadcast concerning Billy Harris. The brimming tears in her eyes had almost caused her to rear end a car halted by a stop light, and she had swerved just in time. How she made it, she'd never know.

Nate approached the Mercedes. "Your husband hasn't arrived yet, but I'll start getting the luggage stowed. Drive it right up to the plane." He swung the gate wide for her and followed as she drove through. "Where's your trunk key?" he asked as he courteously opened her door.

Marion started to hand it to him and had second thoughts. "I'll open it," she said quickly. Once it was unlatched, she took possession of the blue vinyl overnight case, gripping it with an intensity that turned her knuckles white. One by one, Boyle removed the four bags and carried them into the plane. The door was already ajar and a small stool stood on the ground, allowing easy access to the passenger compartment. Completing his task, he returned to where she stood. He indicated a sparse line of automobiles in the parking lot on the other side of the gate through which she had just entered.

"It would probably be smart to dump the car over there where it won't be so conspicuous," he advised. "Do you want to do it," he asked, "or shall I?" She thought for a moment, not fully realizing that her recent ordeal had conditioned her to question the simplest decision. Finally, she handed him the keys.

Walking back from parking the car, he intercepted the ambulance which had just entered the area and directed it through the open gate and to the plane. As they lifted her husband out, tears of relief sprang to Marion's eyes. He had made it. She wasn't alone anymore.

Deftly, being careful to jar the patient as little as possible, the attendants maneuvered the stretcher into the plane, and Marion entered just as the transfer from stretcher to cot was being made. Tenderly she tucked the blankets around George and paused to daub at his face with a tissue, removing the wetness caused by weakness and exertion. She was aware of one of the attendants waiting hesitantly, holding a bill, and she quickly removed the wallet from her purse. Glancing at the total, she paid the amount, voiced her thanks and watched with relief as the attendant left the plane and joined his partner who was standing near the ambulance, engaged in idle conversation with Nate.

"George," she whispered urgently, "the little Harris boy. He died! I heard it on the radio."

George closed his eyes as the stab of pain and guilt hit him. He had taken a life! He was a murderer! He forced himself to be practical. Nothing would bring back the child. Now it was more important than ever to get away. Costa Rica was so close. A little luck was all they needed. "Tough," her husband replied, forcing the coldness into his voice. "Where's Nate? Let's get going." Before she could reply, Boyle stashed the stool in the baggage compartment by reaching behind the door, and vaulted into the plane. He slammed the door shut and latched it.

"All set?" he asked. George nodded. Nate simply stood, pointedly, expectantly.

"Give him the money, Marion," George ordered. Wordlessly, she removed an envelope from her purse and extended it. Boyle quickly riffled through the fifty hundred dollar bills—the five thousand that he had been promised at take off. He grinned as he tucked the money into an inner pocket of the scruffed World War II leather flight jacket he wore. It was his pride and joy. Notwithstanding the fact that he had picked it up at an army surplus store, in his eyes the jacket put him in the league with "the big kids."

"You'd better sit down, Mrs. Selkins," he advised, "and fasten the safety belt." Nate went to the rear of the plane and returned almost immediately with a long strap which he proceeded to pass under the cot and around George, buckling it snugly.

"Watch it!" George protested. "The incision—it's still tender. Anyway, I don't need that."

"Cool it, man," Boyle said decisively. "It's just till we get in the air. You can stand it till then. If anything should happen, I don't want you bouncing all over the plane. You might scratch the wallpaper," he laughed. Marion had obediently taken the bucket seat Nate had indicated, and as he passed her he double checked that the belt was securely fastened.

"Good girl," he called back over his shoulder as he stepped through the bulkhead. It suddenly occurred to Marion that those were the first kind or appreciative words that had been directed toward her, but she pushed the uncharitable, disloyal thought from her mind.

Seated in the cockpit, Nate quickly fastened his own safety belt and adjusted the two throttles on the control quadrant, then glanced at the complicated design of switches, instruments and dials in front of him, making sure that all was in order. He flipped the magneto switch for the starboard engine and engaged the starter button. The starter motor whined as the blades of the propeller slowly started to turn, and then, with a sudden muffled explosion, the powerful engine shuddered, belched a cloud of blue smoke, and caught. With Nate carefully nursing the throttle, it settled down to a steady, well-tuned drone. Glancing at the instruments once more to assure himself that all was well, Nate repeated the procedure with the port engine and grinned as the smoke from it wafted over the two ambulance attendants who, not immune to the universal fascination of watching a takeoff, still stood on the field intending to track the progress of the plane. As Boyle eased the throttles to get the plane moving and then braked to turn it, the prop wash blasted dirt and debris over the attendants. Through the window, Marion watched as they turned slightly, shielding their faces with their forearms. Impulsively, she waved at them as the plane started to lumber forward, and was rewarded by a smile from the taller of the two.

After taxiing to the far end of the runway, Nate wasted what seemed to be an eternity with his before takeoff check. Finally swinging out, he lined up on the runway and revved the powerful engines. The plane vibrated in response, gathering power for takeoff. It was then that Nate saw them.

At the opposite end of the field was a flurry of activity. Two—no, three—cars were converging there. In addition to the headlights, he caught a flash of blinking red and yellow lights. He shrugged. The engines were roaring now, and he locked the tail wheel. The plane moved—slowly at first, then faster.

When the police cars had screeched through the gate, they had first encountered the ambulance attendants. Hurried questioning and frantic pointing made them aware of the Beech Eighteen, a dim form at the far end of the runway, almost half a mile away. The senior officer turned to one of the patrol cars, manned by two rookies.

"Stop that plane," he ordered.

Startled into action, the driver careened down the center of the runway, lights flashing, siren screaming.

The Beech was approaching takeoff speed before Nate was fully aware of the car hurtling toward him. The powerful machine he was controlling was fully committed now. He could not abort the takeoff even if he wanted to. The rookies saw the running lights of the plane approaching head on, and it was a moment before it dawned on them that the aircraft had no intention of stopping or altering its course. They were totally unaware that the pilot had no choice. Halfway down the field, self-preservation overcame the call of duty, and the officer who was driving applied the brakes hard, sending the patrol car into a skidding J-turn. In the cockpit, Nate cursed and pulled back on the control column with all his might, literally hauling the plane into the air. At the same time, he hit his gear switch, raising the wheels. Even with the maneuver, the Beech pratically skimmed the top of the police car as it staggered into the air.

"Jesus Christ!" breathed the sergeant at the end of the field as he watched the near disaster. His partner glanced at him.

"What did you tell them to do," he asked drily, "Head him off at the pass?" The sergeant glared for a moment, watching as the Beech gained speed and altitude. He turned to another officer nearby.

"Quick. Get on the radio to the Watch Commander. Tell him what happened. Give him a description of the plane." He paused uncomfortably. "Uh . . . two motors . . . a double tail . . . silver."

His partner, more familiar with aircraft, interrupted, grinning in amusement at the floundering of his superior. "It was a Beech Eighteen, sir, Number N–9723B."

The sergeant glanced at him with surprise. "Okay. Maybe they can verify registry." He pointed at the two ambulance attendants who were enjoying themselves immensely, vying with each other in giving vivid details of their participation. "And pass along any information those clowns are able to come up with."

The young patrolman nodded and hurried for the car. Halfway there he hesitated and turned back. "If the Watch Commander asks, sir, what do you want him to do?"

"Tell him to order the goddamned plane down—or something!" the sergeant shouted, still smarting with the frustration of losing his quarry by a hair.

As he broke ground and zoomed off, just missing the patrol car, Nate expelled the breath he had been holding. It had been close—damned close! He wondered if there was black and white paint on the underside of the plane. He smiled mockingly as he remembered the sight of the flailing arms and gestures of the policemen at the end of the field.

"We just missed a pretty official-looking bon voyage party down there," he called back to his passenger. "All the guests were dressed in blue." Marion twisted in her seat, shading her eyes to see the activity in the field.

"George," she said, horrified. "The police!"

"Fuck 'em," her husband replied philosophically. "There's nothing they can do now."

Nate, however, wasn't too sure. There was a chance that Burbank Departure Contol could have them on radar. It all hinged on whether the cops had been sharp enough to alert the F.A.A. *before* his takeoff from Whiteman. With the field known, they could have easily zeroed in on their target, since his was the only plane taking off from there. Once they isolated him . . . spotted him . . . marked him . . . they could follow the little blip on their screen, handing him off from one radar control to another as he progressed. It would certainly blow his plan for sneaking across the border. On the other hand, if they had not been notified until he was in the air, the plane would be hopelessly lost amid the heavy air traffic, and the small smear that represented his Beech would be just one of many identical smudges criss-crossing their radar scope.

Actually, the law enforcement request had been received by Burbank too late. By the time the Watch Commander was contacted . . . who in turn had to get the F.A.A. Duty Officer on the line . . . plus the minutes spent by the Duty Officer getting in touch with Burbank Departure Control—sufficient time had elapsed to make the target impossible to identify.

Nate had no way of knowing. He couldn't be sure. But he was wily enough to map out a procedure which could tilt the odds in his favor. Boyle waited until the gleaming red light atop the power plant stacks southeast of Whiteman Field passed under him. Then he veered slightly and headed for the Angeles Crest, a mile-high mountain range which separated the Greater Los Angeles basin from the San Gabriel and Cucamonga wilderness area. He hugged the sides of those mountains, flying just below their jutting tips, secure in his knowledge that the distortion and ground return fed back to radar due to the terrain would be confusing. He cut his air speed drastically. If all else failed, they would be likely to identify that slow-moving dot on the screen as his Beech, and would assume it was a smaller plane, incapable of greater speed.

He continued the ploy, noting the Rose Bowl on his right, then the twinkling red lights on the cluster of radio and television antennas on Mt. Wilson on his left, until he reached a small canyon north of Azusa. Ducking into the canyon, Nate made a steep, climbing turn to the left and picked up a regular airway which led directly over Pomona. Once he emerged from the obscurity of the canyon and joined the flow of heavy air traffic, the other planes, he knew, would serve as excellent cover.

Nate finally leaned back comfortably and relaxed behind the controls. The appearance of the police hadn't bothered him at all. It had just gotten the old adrenaline going, and it was a pleasurable sensation. Instead of dismaying him, it had simply whetted his curiosity. He was caught up in a great adventure, and was impractical enough to enjoy every minute of it. It strengthened the secret image he had always held of himself—the derring-do pilot—a combination of the Red Baron, Charles Lindbergh and Smilin' Jack.

To him, it was almost gratifying that the trouble had started so soon. Nate had anticipated a boring and monotonous flight. Marion and George Selkins certainly weren't the most stimulating or titillating companions. The fun, the drama—and the real test of his ingenuity and superintelligence—would begin, he had thought, when he tried to get back. He had a scornful disregard for authority. He'd match wits with the law any day.

He tuned his radio to the Los Angeles Center frequency but only half listened to the unending crackle of communication transmitted—the garbled, constant jargon between planes and the controllers, almost a foreign language to the uneducated ear. Soon the lights of Pomona should be sparkling beneath them. It was a beautifully clear night—an almost full moon—perfect flying weather. He became suddenly alert.

"Twin Beech November niner seven two three Bravo—this is Los Angeles Center. Do you receive? Over!"

Nate called over his shoulder to the passengers behind him. "Seems like we're pretty popular, folks." He turned the radio volume higher and waited until the message was repeated. "That's me they're calling!" He watched with sadistic satisfaction as Marion and George showed their agitation and anxiety. He let them squirm for a few minutes, and suddenly clicked the radio off, half turning to face them.

"You know," he said, almost lazily, "I'm as game for a caper as anybody. But I have certain ground rules. And the first one is—I like to know what in the hell is going on!"

Marion shot an anguished glance at her husband. George shut his eyes, feigning disinterest. "What's the difference? We made a deal. You get twenty-five thousand—and we get to Costa Rica."

"True," Nate grinned. He deliberately turned the radio back on, increasing the volume until it was almost unbearable. The message endeavoring to contact them was repeated with monotonous, almost maddening regularity. Nate listened wordlessly for several long minutes, correctly judging the devastating psychological effect on his passengers, then turned the radio low.

"Let's get one thing straight. My ass is in this, too. As long as I ignore that message, they can't be sure they've reached me. Once I acknowledge, I'm committed. If they order me down—then down we go. Now, quit playing games, and let's have the details."

"George—!" Marion gasped.

"All right," her husband said shortly. "I take it you know about the accident. Well, the kid I hit died tonight. I'm not about to serve five years in jail." He shot an accusing glance at his wife. "How they discovered our plans, I don't know. So, what are you going to do?"

"No problem," Nate announced genially, once again clicking the radio off. "I have no objections to aiding and abetting a fugitive. I was just curious, that's all." He turned his attention back to the piloting chores, scanning the various instruments on the panel in front of him, and peering through the semidarkness around them.

Marion sat uncomfortably for a moment, tortuously reliving her day. Despite George's implication, she was almost positive that she had done nothing stupid—nothing to tip off the authorities. But she couldn't be sure. She glanced at her husband and was alarmed at the gray tightness of his face. She spoke timidly, anxious to make amends.

"George, I . . . I brought some Scotch and—"

"Well, Jesus," he shot back, "let me have it!" Withdrawing it from the paper bag, she removed the top and handed him the bottle. He took a tentative taste, sighed with relish, and followed it with a prolonged gulp.

In the pilot's compartment, Nate settled down to some serious planning. With Pomona behind him, he would soon be in the Elsinore district—an area he knew like the palm of his hand. He would zigzag, dipping in and out between the familiar hills and valleys, he decided, as final insurance to throw off the hounds. Once he reached Rancho California, he would fly low, following the road that led to Warner Springs and Julian. Out of Julian, he would plot a direct course through the desolate area, over Coyote Wells to the Mexican border, and cross about twenty-five miles east of Calexico, using the sand dunes of the isolated area as his cover.

He mentally rechecked the calculations he had made the day before. San Jose was exactly twenty-seven hundred and fifty miles from Los Angeles, and Nate had selected Manzanillo, Mexico, as his refueling stop. It was thirteen hundred miles, about halfway. With the Beech's four wing tanks and the auxiliary tank in the nose, it had a fuel capacity of exactly two hundred and eighty-three gallons. The power settings he had chosen would result in a true air speed of a hundred and fifty-two miles an hour, the two engines, he knew, would use thirty-three and three-quarter gallons per hour. It would be close—terribly close. He would be almost out of fuel when he arrived in Manzanillo, almost nine hours after takeoff, but Nate was sure he could make if. Of course, he had not figured on the extra time and fuel consumed in the maneuvering he had been forced to employ to eascape detection. But he could still make it, Boyle assured himself optimistically. It would be by a hair—but he'd make it!

The flight had turned uneventful, even monotonous, the drone of the powerful engines almost hypnotizing in their steady hum. Marion dozed fitfully, waking occasionally and glancing at her husband, who passed the time alternating between smoking and sipping Scotch. Nate came alert as he passed over Coyote Wells, knowing that he was perhaps ten miles from the international border. In front of him he spied the sand dunes, undulating, almost irridescent in the bright moonlight. There was nothing—nothing except the huge mounds of powdery sand. It was as if a small corner of the Sahara had been picked up and magically transported to this spot. Swooping low, Nate flew within twenty feet of the ground, the Beech resembling a huge snow owl lazily reaching for prey as it floated in and out between the silent dunes.

At a Military Defense Radar Station in the ADIZ—the Air Defense Identification Zone—an operator had been diligently scanning his scope, using his video equipment to survey the line separating the United States and Mexico. His senses suddenly tightened. Had he seen a momentary blip? Or was it his imagination? He concentrated on the area that had caught his attention, and was rewarded by a fragmentary smear of less than a second's duration. He watched for a few more moments and the dot again appeared, and just as suddenly disappeared. There was something there! And it was hopscotching, moving in a strangely suspicious, erratic pattern. He knew that no flight plan had been filed by the unidentified craft and, hesitating no longer, he sounded the alarm. Moments later, two F-4 Marine Air Corps fighters were scrambled out of Yuma, Arizona.

Twisting, turning, zigzagging, keeping close to the ground Nate dodged through the dunes, always heading south. Finally, he allowed himself a triumphant chuckle. He had busted the ADIZ. They had made it. They were in Mexico. They were safe! He climbed, intending to regain cruising altitude.

Something outside caught his attention, and his eyes became riveted on two moving specks, barely visible in the bright moonlight. As he squinted at them—as they neared—they became planes, traveling at tremendous speed—on an exact intersecting course with him. He had no choice but to hold his altitude and direction. At the speed they were approaching, evasive action was impossible. The F-4s were on him in a few moments, buzzing around the Beech like two vengeful and angry hornets. The roar from their engines as they made pass after pass was shattering to both ears and nerves. Nate was able to identify the Marine Corps insignia prominent on the sides of each fighter, and was surprised. How dare they chase him into Mexico? He didn't know that an international agreement existed between the United States and Mexico permitting such action.

"We've got company," Nate sang out. His announcement was unnecessary, of course. Glancing back at Marion and George, he saw them peering wide-eyed and unbelieving through the windows as the fighters swooped about, seemingly close enough to touch. Marion's hands were pressed over her ears to muffle the deafening sound of each pass. Curious, Boyle flicked on his radio, turning it to the Emergency Frequency. The message came through loud and clear.

"Twin Beech November niner seven two three Bravo, southbound, one-three-niner degrees. What are your intentions? Acknowledge—Emergency Frequency one-two-one-point-five." The F-4s, because of their design for speed, were unable to pace him without stalling. Instead, they buzzed about ominously, waiting for him to reply.

"What are you doing to do?" George shouted over the din.

"Well, this is a bit more than I bargained for," Nate admitted cheerfully. He was psychotic enough not to be unduly worried at the situation in which he found himself. He liked being the star of the show. But he was fully aware of George's and Marion's absolute terror. The trouble with some people, Boyle thought idly, is that they have no sense of adventure, they value their lives too much. *They value their lives too much!* The thought intrigued him, and he turned it over and over in his mind. It generated an idea—a capital idea, he thought—and inwardly became hysterical at the play on words.

"Can you get rid of them?" George asked anxiously.

"Maybe," Nate said easily. "But not for twenty-five thousand."

"God damn it," Selkins exploded. "We made a deal!"

The fighter pilots, impatient at being ignored, swooped down even closer and repeated the message. "Twin Beech November niner seven two three Bravo, southbound, one three niner degrees. Repeat—*what are your intentions?*" The tone was more threatening now. "Acknowledge—Emergency Frequency one two one point five!"

"Sure we made a deal," Nate remarked innocently, "but, George, you have to admit, conditions have changed."

"All right!" George said, struggling to keep the panic from his voice. "All right, I'll up the ante by ten. Thirty-five thousand."

"When do I get it?"

"As soon as we're in Costa Rica," George said, almost strangling on the words. He glanced out the window just as one of the fighters buzzed them again, veering off just in time, it seemed, to avoid a collision. *"What are you, a lunatic!"* George shouted mindlessly in its direction.

"I don't take checks," Nate said conversationally, as if the fighters didn't exist, enjoying the growing suspense. The second fighter whizzed past, so close that the wings of the two craft seemed to touch.

"No check!" George screamed, now utterly panicked. "Cash! For Christ's sake, Nate. Thirty-five thousand in cash!"

"It's a deal," Nate said laughingly. He casually picked up the microphone and keyed the transmitter.

"Mayday, Mayday!" he forced fright into his voice. "This is Twin Beech November niner seven two three Bravo. I am being hijacked. Repeat—*I am being hijacked!* Destination unknown. Repeat—destination unknown!" He paused dramatically. "Screw off! Do you want to get me killed? Jesus, call off your dogs!!" He deliberately clicked the radio off, calmly maintaining his speed and direction. Perhaps two minutes elapsed before he saw the two fighter planes roll away from him and disappear.

Nate was extremely satisfied with himself. The hijacking ruse had been a stroke of sheer genius. The aviation community was close-knit and protective of one another. They would rather see a dozen fugitives escape than risk the life or well-being of one of their own. He knew the F-4s would now drop far back, out of sight. They would track him on airborne radar, wait and watch, keeping their fingers crossed for his safety.

But if they were out of his sight, he was not out of theirs, Nate realized. The time had come to lose them entirely. Almost directly ahead was Laguna Salada, Mexico's huge dry lake, extending for almost forty miles. Heading down until he reached an altitude of less than twenty feet, he maintained it, skimming the dry, briny surface, as he followed the lake for its entire length. It was below sea level, and he knew the fighter's airborne radar could not pick him up. He would have been gratified to hear the message radioed by the Marine Corps planes to Command Headquarters some minutes later.

"Target lost. Repeat—target lost. Unable to reestablish contact. Returning to base. Repeat-returning to base."

Reaching the end of the dry lake, Nate continued his southeasterly course until he spied the Gulf of California directly ahead. His flight plan called for him to follow the coast, just off shore maintaining his low altitude of twenty to twenty-five feet. The bright moonlight provided sufficient light and he anticipated no trouble. His path would lead them directly to Manzanillo, situated on the coast, just twenty-five feet above sea level.

"How about that?" he called back to his passengers. "The old master has done it again. We've lost them," he announced jubilantly. Marion and George sat wordlessly, still drained by their harrowing experience.

Boyle's enthusiasm camouflaged the concern he was beginning to feel regarding his fuel situation. Carefully he recomputed, comparing the number of miles against the remaining fuel. He would have to go far out of his way to find an airport closer than Manzanillo, and he had no way of knowing if the tiny strips had fuel on hand. Many did not, and the risk of waiting many hours, or even until morning, when a fuel truck could be dispatched, was a risk which did not appeal to him. The larger fields would be alerted, the authorities might be waiting. Manzanillo had no tower and he knew and trusted the operator. Manzanillo it would have to be. It would be close. In fact, if he made it, it would be a minor miracle. Nate was sweating, but he gave no indication of his anxiety to his passengers.

"Mrs. Selkins," he said cheerfully, "there are sandwiches and coffee in back. Help yourself."

"Thank you." Marion got up and made for the rear of the plane. Mounted on a wall rack were four stainless steel thermos bottles, the spigots at the bottom, especially designed for aircraft. Directly below was a small cardboard box with an assortment of sandwiches. She examined them carefully. "George," she called, "we've got ham and egg . . . roast beef and cheese . . . turkey . . . and egg salad."

"I'm not hungry," George replied sullenly, taking another sip of Scotch. The bottle was now almost three-quarters empty. Marion made her selection and returned with the sandwich and coffee. She started to sit down, and then went instead to the bulkhead.

"Mr. Boyle," she asked, "are you hungry? Can I bring you something?"

Nate grinned his appreciation. "You bet. Coffee would be great—and a sandwich, too. Whatever kind's on top. Surprise me." She handed him the coffee and sandwich she had chosen for herself and went back a second time, then returned to her seat. She ate with relish, slowly drank the coffee, and then closed her eyes. They still had a long way to go, and if she slept, the time would pass more quickly.

Nate had been sitting for the past few hours, whistling tunelessly through his teeth, his relaxed manner belying the fact that he had one very worried eye on the fuel gauges. He had watched them drop, slowly and steadily, and he had been employing every trick in the book—nursing the throttles, reducing airspeed—to get the most mileage out of the few gallons that remained. The gauges had been registering "empty" for some minutes. Each second seemed like an eternity. He hurriedly checked his chart to see if there might be an airport—any airport—closer than Manzanillo. There wasn't. He cursed silently and continuously to himself. He felt perspiration running down the back of his neck, and the shirt under the leather flight jacket was damp and clammy.

If they crashed off the coast, their chances of survival would be almost zero. He could see no sign of life below him, and once down in the water, the Beech would float only for a short time. Perhaps he could swim to safety—but what about George? He couldn't even walk, much less swim. And Marion—what help would she be? Could he simply abandon them? He shuddered at the thought of the sharks that must infest the warm waters below. Looking down, Nate breathed a sigh of relief as he recognized the few houses that made up the tiny town of Tenacatita. It wouldn't be long now. Maybe they would make it. He found himself holding his breath. He *should* have set down sooner. The hell with the risk! Why had he gambled on being a statistic? He remembered shaking his head at the foolishness of other pilots he had known who, running out of fuel, had crashed. He had never been able to fathom their stupidity. As they passed over Cihuatlan, the portside engine missed a beat . . . and then another.

From the cot, George whispered, "What was that?" Cautiously, he half sat up. He didn't want to wake his wife. "Nate, what's happening?" he hissed.

Boyle forced a calmness in his voice that he certainly didn't feel. "Don't worry about it." He patted the side of the plane. "It's just our friend's way of telling us she's thirsty. I'm going to take her down at a little airport I know just ahead." As George started to ask anxiously about the authorities Nate cut him off. "Don't worry—they mind their own business in Manzanillo." George relaxed, lulled by Nate's easy manner. "Come on, baby," Boyle murmured softly to the Beech, "Don't disappoint daddy now."

Rounding a small promontory, he saw Manzanillo. He had never been so grateful for the sight of anything or anybody in his entire life. He glided the Beech in for the landing. As the tail wheel touched down, the portside engine sputtered to a stop, completely out of fuel; and as he progressed down the field and off the runway, the starboard engine quit. He rolled up to the fuel pit—dead stick.

"How's that for planning," he crowed, as he walked through the passenger compartment and unlatched the door. He hoped Marion and George would not notice the beads of perspiration which covered his face. He spied the operator on the field as he vaulted from the plane to oversee the refueling operation.

"Señor Perez," he called, waving, "buenos días." Inside, Marion got up and walked to the door and stood looking out.

"Where are you going?" George asked petulantly.

"Oh, I thought maybe I'd just stretch my legs," she said hesitantly.

"Well," her husband instructed, rolling on his side with difficulty, his back toward her, "try not to do anything dumb."

Marion stood for a moment, deeply hurt. Then she crossed back to the seat and picked up the blue vinyl case and walked once again to the door. She must not let the money out of her sight. She stood, judging the distance to the ground. Nate noticed her predicament and hurried toward her, took the stool, placed it, and steadied her descent. He glanced at the vinyl case with interest but made no comment. Yet he could not help noticing that as she wandered aimlessly about, she clasped it with dogged determination.

Nate turned his attention to the refueling in progress, willing himself to be patient with the leisurely operation. There was no way to hurry it, he knew. Perez had his own pace. Although Nate was certain he was no longer being followed, he would feel better, he admitted, once they were back in the air. The Beech, like any creature designed for flying, was most vulnerable when on the ground. He paced, and suddenly was amused by his edginess. What did he expect—the Third Cavalry to come rushing at him from behind a hill?

Finally, with the refueling completed, he assisted Mrs. Selkins back into the plane, secured the aircraft, took off, and began climbing. Even though the last leg of their journey was fourteen hundred and fifty miles—some one hundred and fifty miles longer than the first lap—and even though he had exactly the same amount of fuel, he was unconcerned. At altitude his true air-speed would be much better and his fuel consumption lower. And he was also aware of a low-pressure area off the Yucatan Peninsula which would provide him with a brisk tail wind almost all the way. The agony he had experienced before would not be repeated.

The sky had been showing a faint tinge of light when they had landed at Manzanillo, and taking into account the two-hour time-zone change differential, it was now almost seven in the morning. The rising sun cast pink, yellow, and apricot tints on the lush country below. Nate continued southeast, climbing to nine thousand feet, and then sat back, relaxed. Their course would take them down the coast most of the way, and then over practically uninhabited wilderness. They should be in San Jose by dinnertime. The plane would practically fly itself, and except for an occasional scan of their instruments and the sky around him, Nate had nothing to do. He resigned himself to hour after hour of sheer monotony.

He glanced back at his passengers, noting the now almost empty bottle of Scotch. George had finally fallen into a sleep bordering stupor. Marion also slept, the blue vinyl case resting on her lap. Nate stared at it. It intrigued him.

There was little doubt, from Marion's protectiveness, that it contained all of the Selkinses' valuables and cash. To relieve the boredom, Nate amused himself by speculating exactly what it might hold. The case, he estimated, was possibly fifteen inches long by eight inches wide by nine inches deep. A hundred-dollar bill was—he tried to remember—maybe six by two and half inches. A pack of one hundred bills would be . . . what? Three quarters of an inch thick? Nate tried to calculate the cubic capacity of the blue case and the number of packets it could contain. It boggled his mind and he gave up. He had never been very good at mathematics. He tried to think of something else . . . but couldn't. What if, instead of hundred-dollar bills, they were *thousand*-dollar bills? There could be almost a million dollars. Nate remembered the earlier incident when he had forced George to up the ante. Thirty-five thousand, his passenger had promised—without batting an eye. In cash! As soon as they got to Costa Rica! He knew the Selkinses lived well. The Mercedes Marion had been driving didn't come cheap, and they had abandoned it without a qualm. He had no way of knowing it was leased. The two diamond rings she wore were at least several carats each. The Selkinses had probably converted everything they owned into cash—and they had it all with them—in that little blue case! Jesus, maybe it was even *two* million! Boy, oh, boy, he thought—what I couldn't do with two million dollars!

He shook off his fantasizing with difficulty and refolded the flight chart to pinpoint his location. There were mountains and plateaus ahead which the map indicated as over ten thousand feet in elevation. He read the additional note on the chart—"Caution: vertical errors in excess of two thousand feet have been reported in the Mexican area of this chart." To be on the safe side, Nate decided, he'd take her up to about seventeen thousand.

He reached for the three portable oxygen units beside him and turned to instruct his passengers in their use. He wouldn't want anything to happen to them. He paused. *Why* wouldn't he want anything to happen to them? He glanced behind him and discovered they were still sleeping. He strapped on his own oxygen unit, and debated for a moment. They were in no danger . . . yet. There was time. Why wake them? They looked so peaceful. When the time came—*if* he decided to do it— he could give the units to them. He watched the altimeter climb—ten thousand feet, eleven thousand, twelve. He kept glancing behind him. Had George or Marion moved, stirred, startled him in any way, he would have been forced to make an immediate decision—and it would probably have been in their favor. It was so easy to do nothing. His altimeter now registered a shade under seventeen thousand feet. He glanced back again. How long, he wondered did it take, at this altitude, without oxygen, to die of hypoxia? What the hell, Nate suddenly decided, pushing the two oxygen units out of sight. They had a lot of money. And he wanted it. He might not have another opportunity like this again!

The Beech encountered some slight turbulence and dipped sharply, then returned to level flight. It was

341

enough to rouse Marion. She glanced at her husband. Thank goodness, the jolt hadn't awakened him. He was breathing deeply, rapidly. She sat for a moment, wondering at the marvelous sense of well-being she was experiencing. She felt a little dizzy, but it was a nice kind of dizziness, like the time or two when she had drunk too much champagne. She thought over the events of the past twenty-four hours. How silly she had been to worry. Everything was perfect now.

Marion had no way of knowing that she was experiencing the euphoria that preceded death by hypoxia, that she was actually dying from lack of oxygen. She glanced down at her hands, still resting lightly on the vinyl case. My fingernails, she thought—they look blue. She glanced around. It must be the light. George seemed to look a little blue, also. She shrugged happily. Anyway, it was a nice shade of blue. She watched her husband for a moment, vaguely conscious of his deep and rapid respiration. She was unaware that his body, starved for life-sustaining oxygen, was increasing the rate and depth of his breathing, compounding his physical problems by eliminating carbon dioxide at an excessive rate. Hyperventilating, George was much closer to death than his wife. His heavy drinking and smoking had deprived him of the ability to utilize what little oxygen his brain and bloodstream were receiving. Gradually his breathing slowed, and then stopped altogether.

Marion stared out the window at the beautiful cloud formations and the occasional glimpse of the lush countryside below. She smiled. She was feeling better and better. She glanced once again at her husband, not noticing his unnatural stillness. Darling George—he hadn't really meant the unkind things he had said to her. She continued to gaze at him fondly, then tilted her head back. Her eyelids were growing heavy, and as they closed—for the final time—the last thing Marion saw was her husband's beloved face.

For over an hour, Nate sat in the cockpit staring straight ahead, breathing his oxygen, keeping the Beech at seventeen thousand and on course, not daring to look back. In spite of his attempts to keep his mind completely blank, the tension grew, and finally he could stand it no longer. Putting the plane on automatic pilot, taking the oxygen with him, he stepped slowly through the bulkhead, filled with an odd mixture of curiosity and dread. He closed his eyes for a moment. He had never killed anyone before. He forced them open. It was not as bad as he thought. Except for the slight bluish tinge and an unnatural rigidity, George and Marion could be sleeping. But they weren't he knew, as he looked at them closely—they were dead.

Nate slipped the vinyl case from beneath Marion's hands, laid it on the floor, crouched beside it, and with his excitement mounting—opened it. He bit back a curse. On top was a fluffy pink nylon nightgown carefully folded. He removed it. Underneath was a matching negligee. He laid it aside. And there was the money— all in neat stacks. He grinned, and sat cross-legged on the floor as he began to count it. As he came to the last few stacks, his agitation was obvious.

"Shit," he breathed with disappointment, as he finally finished. Just a little over two hundred thousand? He turned and glared at George's body with unreasonable rage. You goddamned phony bastard, he thought. Where did you get off, living and acting like you had all the money in the world? You cheated me, you son of a bitch! Where's the other million? He caught himself. Come off it. What the hell. He had two hundred thousand dollars. Only yesterday, he'd been drooling at the thought of twenty-five. And then there was the jewelry, he reminded himself. One by one, he examined the pieces, each carefully wrapped in tissue, in the bottom of the case. He was no expert, but they looked like pretty good stuff. What was the market for hot jewels in Costa Rica? he wondered.

Two hundred thousand dollars. How long would it last—the way he liked to live? Ten, maybe fifteen years? He became practical. If he and the Beech could work, there were a lot of bananas and coffee that needed hauling down there. But if he couldn't work, if there was red tape and maybe government labor permits involved, what then? By the time he was forty or forty-five, the money would be gone. He shrugged philosophically as his good humor returned. At least, in the meantime, he wouldn't be dodging bill collectors, and he'd have one hell of a good time while it lasted.

Nate stood up. There was work to do. He transferred the money and jewels from the case to the paperbag that had previously held the Scotch. Then he methodically went through the four pieces of luggage, hoping they might contain something of special value, but found only clothes. He walked to the door of the plane. It had been modified to open inward, hinges forward, to facilitate parachute jumping. As he unlatched it, the prop wash held the door slightly ajar. One by one, he tossed out the bags, the vinyl case, and even the empty Scotch bottle. He examined the contents of Marion's purse, pocketed the forty-nine dollars and some change he found, and the purse followed the luggage. Now for the bodies. George first. Nate half dragged, half carried the corpse to the door and was about to push it through when he suddenly stopped.

A thought occurred to him. His mind raced. There was a chance—just a chance—that he could hedge his bet, up the eventual odds in his favor. When . . . if . . . he ran out of money, he might want to return to the good old U.S.A. Was it possible? He walked over to the cot and sat down on the edge. As far as the authorities knew, he had committed no crime—unless they could pin a murder rap on him. Nate concentrated for a long time.

Abruptly, decisively, he got up and carried Marion's body to the door, laying it alongside her husband's. Going to the baggage compartment, he returned with two parachutes and, with some difficulty, managed to strap one on each corpse. The macabre situation no longer bothered him. He was caught up in the drama he was playing. He was writing the script; he could be the hero. Carefully he hooked the static lines attached to the plane above the door to the proper parachute rings

344

on each of the bodies. He stared down at them for a moment, and suddenly stooped to wrench the two diamond rings from Marion's fingers. He walked back to the cot, dropping the rings into the paper sack as he passed, and sat down again. There was a lot at stake. Once more he would go over the details—rehearse the story he would tell the authorities if it became necessary.

"He had been hijacked by a known fugitive—that much was established. Recognizing that he was in great personal danger, he had gone along with the Selkinses' demands, biding his time, keeping his cool, waiting for the right opportunity. When they reached the Honduras–El Salvador border, he had deliberately feathered a prop and simulated malfunctioning of the aircraft. It hadn't been easy, but he'd played his part well, finally convincing them of a serious mechanical failure and panicking them into believing a crash was imminent. Their only chance, he had urged them, was to bail out. He had counted on their ignorance—that they wouldn't know that jumping at seventeen thousand feet was sure death. They had tossed their baggage out and jumped. And their money? What money? He knew of no money. Whatever they had, they had taken with them.

Boyle repeated the story over and over to himself, embellishing it here and there, establishing himself as the conscientious and clever pilot who had matched wits with a criminal and won. The outcome—the death of Selkins and his wife—was unfortunate. But it had been his only hope for survival. Nate admitted that an astute questioner would perceive giant holes in his story. But who could refute it? There were no witnesses. And in ten or fifteen years, who would care?

Under the circumstances, it was the best insurance he could buy. Hesitating no longer, he shoved the bodies out, knowing that as the static lines became taut and pulled the rings, the parachutes would automatically open. He leaned forward and watched as the bodies gently wafted toward the ground far below. They were over an isolated jungle wilderness. It was highly un-

345

likely that the parachutes would be seen, but if some adobe farmer should, by chance, spy them—if George and Marion Selkins should be found—their frost-bitten bodies, their death by suffocation, would merely lend credence to his story of an ill-advised, high altitude bail out. If they were not seen, the animals, the scavengers, the huge red ants of the jungle below, would soon destroy the remains.

Jubilant with his reasoning, satisfied with his day's work, Nate returned to the cockpit, happy with the thought that he would soon be in San Jose.

He had been cleared to land without difficulty, and Nate hummed softly as he waited at San Jose's Passport Control. His documents were in order and once they had been stamped, he proceeded to customs.

There were three people ahead of him—two women and a man—and he watched the procedure with avid interest. Unlike United States customs, many foreign countries took a relaxed and lenient attitude toward visitors. They were little concerned with what might be brought in. Nate noticed that in each case the luggage was passed through automatically, unopened, by the bored customs officials. It was his turn next, and he placed on the counter the small flight bag containing his razor, toothbrush, and the clothes he had anticipated would be necessary for an overnight stay. He held the paper bag in his arms.

The inspector nodded a greeting and marked his meager luggage without examining the contents. He pointed to the paper bag.

"What is in there, señor?" he asked routinely.

"A present," Nate said. "A going-away present from a couple of my clients." He tentatively extended the bag, fighting down panic. The customs agent nodded absently, only half aware of the reply, and waved him through.

"Welcome to Costa Rica," he recited. "Enjoy your stay with us."

"I'll try," Nate replied. "I'll certainly try."

He crossed the lobby, keeping his pace slow and casual. I made it, he congratulated himself. I've pulled it off. He was almost to the door, when he felt an authoritative tap on his shoulder.

"Señor? Señor Boyle?"

He whirled, terrified, ready to run, and was confronted by a lanky young Costa Rican in a white jacket.

"The ambulance you ordered," the man volunteered in broken English. "For Señor Selkins? It is over there." He pointed to another exit. Nate stared at the attendant for a moment, gathering his wits, regaining his composure.

"I'm sorry," he said softly, removing from his pocket two of the ten-dollar bills which had previously been in Marion's purse. "I won't be needing it, after all. Will this pay you for your trouble?" The attendant nodded, a little confused, but happily pocketed the money. "Mr. Selkins isn't coming," Nate continued. "He had a relapse. He had trouble breathing."

Chapter VIII

. . . saturday

Dr. Michael Carrington overslept on Saturday morning. Knowing that he had nothing in the offing except rounds and writing up orders for the weekend, he indulged himself by not hurrying and arrived at Marin Medical Center about 9:30 A.M. He went directly to the fourth floor.

Everything had worked out exactly as Pat Schuster, the attorney, had predicted. Once Edith Frankel had been made aware of her father's hospitalization insurance and his imminent home-coming, she quickly had withdrawn the conservatorship petition. Aaron had signed his will late Friday afternoon, and it had been witnessed. Then he had expressed a desire to go home and Mike had agreed. Edith was picking him up at ten this morning. As Mike arrived at the nurses' desk, Mrs. Rosen greeted him.

"Morning, doctor, I'm glad you're here." She grimaced, indicating the room. "Mrs. Frankel is already with her father." He nodded and wrote the discharge order. He was not anxious to see Edith again, but he had to be certain that everyone concerned understood the importance of the routine of Aaron's continuing treatments. Squaring his shoulders, he went resolutely into the room.

Edith was once again gathering her father's clothes and belongings, this time with a satisfied smile on her face. She greeted Mike graciously. "Doctor Carrington, isn't it wonderful about Papa going home? He looks so much better. He really does, doesn't he?"

Mike nodded shortly. "I just wrote the discharge order, and you can leave any time. I wanted to make sure, though, that there wouldn't be any problems." He grinned his good morning at Aaron. They had gone over this the night before. He turned to Edith. "You realize your father has a standing appointment here every day at two P.M. for his therapy treatments. That's Monday through Friday. It's important." It was standard procedure in such therapy to give five treatments and then skip two days, and Mike had arranged it so Aaron's weekends would be free.

"Oh, certainly, doctor, I understand," Edith gushed. "Papa insists on going back to his own apartment, but I'll be picking him up and bringing him in every day. You can count on it. I don't think he should drive—I'd worry about him, and his car isn't that dependable. We're just so happy to have him home."

"I'm going to pay Edith for her trouble, Doctor Carrington, " Aaron said softly from his bed. "Fifteen cents a mile. That's fair, isn't it?"

Edith paused in her bustling about. Fifteen cents a mile. She thought of all the luncheon dates that would have to be broken, all the bridge games missed, all the hair appointments canceled, all the gardening that would have to be delayed. She lingered on the monotonous drive from her house to the beach, to the hospital, back to the beach, and then home. Every day. Almost fifty miles. Three precious hours, at least, right out of the middle of every day, preventing her from planning anything either in the morning or the afternoon. Fifteen cents a mile—seven dollars and fifty cents—for over three hours. God, she paid her cleaning girl more than that. She shrugged. To keep her sanity over the coming months, she had to look on it as an investment—an investment that would pay big dividends in the long run.

"Papa, Papa," she forced herself to say, "I don't want the fifteen cents."

Carrington nodded his good-bye and started to leave the room as Edith continued. "Ed and I love you. We don't want the money."

Mike stopped directly outside the door. He was sure of it—he hadn't imagined it! Aaron had winked at him.

Jeannie scooted gingerly down in the hospital bed to avoid the side rails and sat on the edge of the mattress for a moment, feeling with her foot for the soft slipper that should be there on the floor—someplace. It was her fourth day after surgery, and the incision was still tender, but she was permitted to go back and forth to the bathroom now, and she was allowed to sit up in the chair while her bed was remade.

She found a shoe, hooked it with her right toe and struggled to get it on without stooping. Bending over was still agony-time. She wiggled her leg for several moments until she realized her trouble: the left shoe on the right foot won't go. She grunted with frustration as she shifted the shoe to her other foot and slipped it on easily. Now the other—where was it?

"Darn it," she muttered. Jeannie had turned her call-button light on about fifteen minutes ago, and it was still unanswered. Not that there was really any urgency in her request, but lying in bed somehow made every minute that passed seem like an eternity.

Maybe Mrs. Kowalsky was finally getting even by ignoring her light, she speculated. She'd gotten off on the wrong foot with the Polish joke—that was for sure—and the relationship between her and the head nurse had seemed to go downhill from there. She remembered the incident which had occurred the morning after her surgery. Mrs. Kowalsky had marched into the room a little after seven, carrying a deep basin, and had awakened her from the heavenly blackness of a deeply sedated sleep.

"Good morning, Mrs. Mendosa," the nurse had boomed. "It's time for our bed bath."

Jeannie had been lying absolutely flat, one arm anchored with tape to facilitate a running IV. The other arm was stiff and sore from numerous blood samplings taken before surgery. She was still a little dazed from her sound slumber, and as she tried to focus her eyes, a wave of nausea swept over her. Mrs. Kowalsky raised the covers from her feet and placed the basin, now filled with warm soapy water, directly on the bed.

"Put your feet in the basin, Mrs. Mendosa," the nurse instructed. Jeannie fought the nausea. She was positive that the slightest movement would result in her throwing up.

"Mrs. Kowalsky, just leave me alone," she finally gasped. "I just don't feel up to a bath now. Maybe later, okay?"

Mrs. Kowalsky stared at her irately. Jeannie was committing the terrible sin of threatening to disrupt the meticulously planned floor schedule which was so vital for the nurses' convenience and well-being. "Now, Mrs. Mendosa," the woman snapped, "don't take advantage of your friendship with Doctor Carrington by being difficult. Please place your feet in the basin."

"Get the hell out of my room," Jeannie said softly.

"I beg your pardon?"

"I said get the hell out of my room," Jeannie repeated tiredly, "and take your dumb basin with you." Mrs. Kowalsky beat a surly but hasty retreat, and when Mike came by about an hour later on his rounds, he was grinning widely.

"All right, ding-a-ling. What's happened now?"

"What do you mean?" Jeannie asked with genuine surprise.

"Mrs. Kowalsky has a big note on your chart— 'patient uncooperative.' What's that all about?"

"The witch," Jeannie muttered and then proceeded to give him a blow-by-blow account of the bath episode, admitting how she got the nurse to leave her alone. Mike roared with laughter.

"Honest to God, Jeannie, how come things happen to you that don't happen to anyone else?" She was still in a black mood.

"Just lucky, I guess," she retorted.

It was the following day, Jeannie recalled, that the jackhammers started. Yes, jackhammers! She rang for the nurse, and Mrs. Kowalsky appeared and stood looking down at her, as the room vibrated and the bed jumped in cadence to the jarring noise.

"What is it, Mrs. Mendosa?"

"Those jackhammers," Jeannie shouted, hoping to be heard over the ear-splitting din. "What are they doing?"

"Oh, we had some earthquake damage during the last big one, and they're just getting around to fixing it. I believe they're working right outside your window on the corner of the building." She moved to the window and peered out. "Yes, that's what they're doing," she confirmed.

Jeannie gritted her teeth. Her nerves were raw from her recent psychological and physical ordeal. "Well, I don't think I can stand it. Do you suppose they can move me?"

"That's up to your doctor, Mrs. Mendosa," Mrs. Kowalsky informed her before leaving the room. Jeannie picked up the phone and gave the operator Mike's office number. Celeste, his nurse, answered on the seventh ring.

"This is Mrs. Mendosa. Is Doctor Carrington there?"

"Oh, I'm sorry. He's at a medical seminar. I believe he'll be tied up most of the day," Celeste replied. "Can I help you?"

Jeannie explained the predicament, shouting to be heard over the jarring noise of the workmen. Celeste was properly sympathetic. "Let me call Admitting and see if there's another room available, Mrs. Mendosa. I'll get right back to you."

While she was waiting for the return call, Jeannie was startled by an erupting blast from the intercom box directly above her head. It was a step-saving device for the nurses and it was actually a pretty good system. When a patient turned on his call light, instead of a nurse being forced to come to the room, someone at the desk simply flicked a switch and asked what the patient wanted. It cut the daily mileage of the nurses at least by half. The intercom itself could only be activated at the nursing station, not by the patient. Jeannie cringed. The sudden blast of sound added to the cacophony of the jackhammers was almost like a physical blow.

"What do you want, Mrs. Warren," a voice blared from the box. "I want a pain shot," another voice whined. "You can't have a pain shot, Mrs. Warren, you just had one an hour ago." Then, almost immediately, another voice shrilled, "Have you finished with the bedpan, Miss Morgan?" "I don't think so." "Well, call us when you're through." And overlapping that conversation, "Can I help you, Mr. Roth?" A booming masculine voice answered, "Would you tell them I'd like iced instead of hot coffee for dinner?" "We'll call the diet kitchen." The intercom box was malfunctioning—it was picking up all the constant dialogue between the nurses' station *with every patient on the floor*. Desperately Jeannie rang for Mrs. Kowalsky, who returned to the room with a put-upon sigh.

"What is it now, Mrs. Mendosa?"

"The box," Jeannie shouted over the noise of the jackhammers and the intercom. "There's something wrong with it. I think it's gone ape!"

Mrs. Kowalsky listened judiciously for a moment, and nodded gravely. "I'll report it. But the engineers probably won't be able to get to it today."

Jeannie lay exhausted. She hurt, she really did. And the noise from the jackhammers outside and the continual jabbering from the intercom box immediately over her head were like a physical attack. She couldn't bear it. The phone rang. It was Celeste.

"Mrs. Mendosa?" She paused as the ungodly noise filtered through the phone. "My Lord, what's going on there?"

"Would you believe," Jeannie said through clenched teeth, "that along with the jackhammers, my intercom is picking up every conversation on the entire floor? And

353

they tell me it probably can't be fixed today. Were you able to get my room changed?"

"I'm sorry. There just isn't another one available. That's what they told me. When I hear from Doctor Carrington, I'll be sure to tell him about the problem. In the meantime, I'll call Adminstration. I'm sure they can get somebody up there about the intercom."

It was late when Mike came in. The jackhammers had ceased at four when the workers' shift ended. The engineer had finally shown up and found a short in the intercom box. But the hours of bedlam had taken their toll. Mike commiserated with her. There really wasn't another room available, but luckily, he reported, the repair work had been finished on that end of the building and there should be peace and quiet the following day. He said all the expected sympathetic and indignant phrases, but as he gazed at her, she was aware of the wonderment reflected in his face—out of several hundred patients in the hospital, why did everything happen to her? She sensed the hilarity that was struggling inside him. If he laughed, she knew she'd kill him.

Then about nine that night, Jeannie awoke from a light, restless sleep. She was still on a liquid diet, but the gas pains were gone. She had a sudden, overwhelming desire for a dish of chocolate ice cream. It was odd, because she really didn't like sweets, and she could count on one hand the number of times she had eaten ice cream during the past few years. But the more she thought of it—dark and cold and creamy—the more delicious it loomed. She put on her light. Luckily, a new shift had come on, and instead of Mrs. Kowalsky, a young Puerto Rican nurse appeared.

"Could you get me a dish of chocolate ice cream?" Jeannie queried.

"I'm sorry, you're on a liquid diet."

"Well, when the ice cream melts inside me, it'll be liquid, won't it?"

"We don't have orders covering choclate ice cream for you," the young girl countered before leaving.

Exasperated, Jeannie reached for the phone. Mike

had previously given his home phone number and she requested the hospital operator to dial it. No answer. The desire for the ice cream was overpowering now. She realized it was petty—at the same time, it seemed the most important thing in her life that she have some. She could think of nothing else. She called Mike's service.

"Is it an emergency?" the detached voice asked.

"It is to me," she said emphatically.

"Just a moment, I'll try to reach him. Who's calling?" A few minutes passed, and Mike came on the line.

"Jeannie?" The note of alarm was evident in Mike's voice. "Are you all right?"

"I want a dish of chocolate ice cream," she said shortly.

There was a brief silence. When Mike finally spoke, he was obviously relieved, but a little annoyed as well. "Why don't you tell the nurse, Jeannie?" he asked, forcing patience.

"I did, Mike, but they won't give it to me."

"I'll hold on. Ring for the nurse, and ask her to come in. Let me talk to her."

Jeannie rang, gave the message via the intercom and noted with satisfaction the alacrity with which the girl appeared. It was just as well she couldn't hear Mike's side of the conversation.

"This is Doctor Carrington. Look, I know Mrs. Mendosa is being unreasonable and that you're busy. But please, as a personal favor to me, would you get her some ice cream?"

"Yes, doctor. Right away, doctor."

After the nurse left, Jeannie waited. Fifteen minutes, twenty minutes, twenty-five minutes. She rang again and the nurse appeared.

"What about my ice cream?"

"You'll have to be a little patient, Mrs. Mendosa," the girl said crossly. "We're very busy." She disappeared. Jeannie waited for over an hour, counting the minutes, her fury mounting out of all proportion. She felt silly, but she wanted that ice cream. Once more, she

355

dialed Mike's exchange. She went through the same routine with the operator, and Mike was again on the line.

"Can you give me one good reason why I can't have some chocolate ice cream?" she snapped at him. Mike sighed.

"Get the nurse, Jeannie. I'll wait." The nurse reappeared.

"This is Doctor Carrington again. Who is this?"

"Mrs. Torres, doctor,"

"Well, Mrs. Torres," Mike said, his words deceptively soft and evenly spaced, "I am playing bridge. I have just bid four spades. There are three gentlemen waiting for me to play. But I am going to stay on the line until Mrs. Mendosa has her ice cream." His voice rose considerably. "And if she doesn't have it in five minutes, I'll leave this damned bridge game and come down there and get it for her myself!"

The nurse scurried out and within moments, the ice cream was there.

"Thank you, doctor," Jeannie said triumphantly into the phone, and hung up. She took a huge spoonful of the ice cream. It was blah, but she forced herself to swallow it. God, she didn't dare not eat it!

The following morning Mike came in, accompanied by Dr. Keith Johnson. The three of them howled over the episodes of the previous day. Jeannie apologized for the trouble she had caused.

"No need, Jeannie," Mike said, still laughing. "You weren't out of line. The jackhammers, the intercom—it was inexcusable. Even the ice cream. What I can't understand is—why you?" He had left, still shaking his head. Keith lingered. He and Jeannie had become good friends and he visited her throughout the day when he had the time.

"Don't feel bad, Sunshine. Somehow the night shift doesn't seem to draw the most concerned, ardent nurses. And they're badly understaffed to boot."

"I don't know what's come over me, Keith," she sighed ruefully. "I'm not usually like that. I guess it's because I've never been sick before. And I feel so darned helpless—"

"You've just learned a fact of life, Jeannie. When you're in the hospital, you give up all your independence and become completely at the mercy of your doctor and the nurses. But don't worry," he told her, "you have the one ingredient that insures a quick recovery. You want to get out of here." Keith sauntered out the door. That had been two days before.

Jeannie finally located the other slipper and put it on, then reached for the robe at the foot of her bed. She walked slowly to the door, stood a moment, and peered out, calculating the distance from her room to the nurses' station. She could make it.

She made her way slowly down the hall, staying close to the wall, sliding her fingers along for balance. She saw Keith at the desk, reading a chart, and she came up behind him. He turned.

"Hi, Sunshine. I'm glad to see you up and about. Fill me in on the latest episodes of the 'Perils of Jeannie.' "

She grinned, a little embarrassed. "No big problems, yet. But the day's still young. It's just that I've had my light on so long, and nobody answered. And I figured if the mountain won't come to Mohammed—" The nurse behind the desk glanced up. It was not Mrs. Kowalsky. Her eyes dropped to the call indicator.

"Gee, Mrs. Mendosa. I'm sorry. If your light's on, it doesn't show on the board." She tapped a fingernail against the unlit button without effect. Maybe the bulb's out. I'll have it checked. What can I get you?"

"When you have time, could I have a ginger ale? For some reason, I'm parched. A ginger ale—with lots of ice?"

"Sure thing," said the nurse, rising. "Right away."

"Oh," said Jeannie, "and I want to apologize for being such a problem—I guess pain-in-the-neck would be more like it. I don't know what got into me. But I'm sorry—and will you tell Mrs. Kowalsky, too?"

The nurse laughed. "You're no problem. Compared

to some of the others on the floor, you're a model patient." She turned and went off.

Keith studied Jeannie for a moment. "You're looking fine. Need any help getting back to your room?"

She shook her head. "The knees are a little weak, but I think they're getting stronger every minute. It feels good to be out of bed for a change." As she started back in the direction of her room, there was a minor commotion around the corner of the corridor at the far end of the hall.

"Giddap," screamed a childish voice. "Hiya, hiya, giddap there." A wheelchair careened around the corner. The smaller boy who occupied it had a hand on each wheel, spinning them for all he was worth. He came whizzing down the hall. Some distance behind, two nurses gave chase at a dead run.

"Ricky, you come back here," one commanded, her wide grin belying the sternness she forced into her voice. Keith stepped into the center of the hall and with a deft maneuver caught the wheelchair as it passed him, spinning the boy around and around.

"Whoa there, pardner, whoa. What you got there, a runaway team?"

The little boy nodded, his eyes sparkling. The nurses had caught up.

"Ricky, you know you have to stay in the pediatrics wing," the first breathlessly admonished him. The second ruffled his hair affectionately.

"You little imp." she turned to Keith. "It takes all we can do to keep track of this one."

"Never mind, girls," Dr. Johnson grinned. "I'll bring him back." They nodded, and hurried back down the corridor. Jeannie had been watching, giggling at the child's antics. Suddenly her knees sagged slightly. Keith was quick to notice.

"Look, pardner," he said to the child, "think you could loan us that mangy cayuse of yours for a couple of miles?"

Ricky nodded, delighted at the extension of the game. Keith swept him up in one arm and braced him

358

against a shoulder, maneuvering the wheel chair with his other hand until it was directly behind Jeannie. He indicated that she should sit down. She complied gratefully. Keith swung Ricky around several times and finally set the boy on his feet. Slowly he began to wheel Jeannie toward her room. Ricky took his place directly in front of the chair, barely keeping out of its path, half walking, half skipping, moving backward all the way, staring at Jeannie.

"Ricky, this is Mrs. Mendosa," Keith said. "Can you say hello?"

The child looked at her silently, his eyes gleaming with mischief. Solemnly he shook his head.

"I'll bet I've got something in my room that'll make this varmint talk," Jeannie said fiercely, entering into the spirit of the game. She turned to look up at Keith. "Can he have a piece of candy?"

"Well," Keith said slowly, "every cowpoke I know lives on beef jerky and beans." Ricky tilted his head, watching him with gleeful anticipation. "But since we don't have any . . . I guess a piece of candy would be okay."

When they reached the room, Jeannie sat on the bed and ceremoniously took an ornate, two-pound box of candy from the table. She removed the lid and extended the box to Ricky. His eyes gleamed as they roved over the assortment—chocolate-covered nuts, maple fudge, caramels, and pastel fondues. As he pondered, Jeannie gazed down at the child. He was a beautiful little boy, even-featured, probably Mexican, she decided. His dark, warm, liquid eyes, so large they seemed to mitigate the ugly purple and yellow bruises on his face, glanced up at her several times before returning to the visual delights of the candy. One portion of the heavy shock of dark hair had been shaved away, a gauze compress taped over a hidden laceration. The wiry arms extending from the hospital gown were also covered with scratches, welts and bruises, in varying conditions of healing.

Jeannie watched as the youngster deliberated carefully before selecting a large tan and white swirled caramel pinwheel and then popped it into his mouth. He watched longingly as she started to replace the top.

"Can he have a couple of pieces for later?" she asked Keith.

The doctor shrugged. "Can't see why not."

Jeannie extracted several tissues from a box and held them in her hand. "Take three more, Ricky, and we'll wrap them up for you to take with you." Delighted, the boy carefully chose the additional pieces—delaying the selection to prolong the pleasure—and laid them on the paper. Twisting the top to form a makeshift bag, Jeannie handed them to him.

"Come on, pardner, it's back to the ranch for you," Keith ordered, and hand-in-hand, the two left the room.

Jeannie had gotten settled in bed when Keith returned and plopped into the chair. She was delighted that the resident had fallen into the habit of dropping into the room as frequently as his time and schedule allowed. She found his presence pleasant and comforting.

"Do you have any candy left for a very tired, older-type wrangler who spent most of the night in the Emergency Clinic?" Keith asked. Jeannie grinned and handed him the box.

"Keith—?"

"Yeah?" he responded, almost as absorbed as Ricky had been in the vital decision of selecting exactly the right confection.

"About Ricky. What's the matter with him?"

"Nothing serious. He's okay."

"But all those bruises and bumps and scratches—was he in an accident?"

Keith handed the candy box back to her. "The only accident that happened to Ricky was being born." He noticed her bewilderment. "He's a child-abuse case."

"You mean someone inflicted all that damage, all that hurt . . . deliberately?" she asked, horrified.

"Happens all the time," Keith said shortly. "You know, some pediatricians believe that child abuse kills more kids than any other cause. I read somewhere that there are more than a hundred thousand cases investigated every year—and I guess that's just the tip of the iceberg. Most of the cases aren't reported or are listed as accidents, or death from unknown causes."

"But his mother—where was she?" Jeannie asked.

"That's a good question. She's disappeared. The police are still looking for her."

"And his father?"

"Who do you think worked the kid over?"

Jeannie listened with mounting disbelief as Keith filled her in—the nature of the injuries, the recurring pattern of abuse, all the details he knew.

"How could anyone help loving Ricky?" Jeannie commented, shaking her head.

"Well, I don't know," Keith said slowly. "According to psychologists, love has nothing to do with it. Some of the parents are mentally ill, but most are just plain, normal people who, for some reason, have a low tolerance for stress. Maybe the kid cries too much, or sasses them, or won't conform to their ideas of a behavior pattern, and the abusive parent just can't control an impulse to solve the problem by violence."

Keith paused for a moment. "Of course, sometimes one of the parents just hates the kid. I ought to know." Jeannie looked at him curiously, and noticing her interest, he went on. "When my father died, my mother remarried. I was about fourteen at the time. The old man hated me—got his jollies by pummeling the hell out of me. And then one day, I decided I just wouldn't take it any longer and slammed one of those heavy, black iron frying pans over his head. Knocked him out. God, I could have killed him. But he left me alone after that. But the little kids—" He shook his head.

Jeannie noticed the tightness that remembering had brought to Keith's face. "I'm sorry," she said quietly. He waved away her sympathy.

"Actually, Ricky is one of the lucky ones," he assured her. "His bruises are all on the outside, and

361

they'll heal. He doesn't seem to have any mental hang-ups from what he's been through."

"What's going to happen to him?" Jeannie asked.

"We'll keep him here for a few more days. Then, I guess, he'll be taken to McLaren Hall, and the people there will run through the adoption possibilities." He shrugged. "I'd say the chances are pretty slim. Most families considering adoption visualize a beautiful pink, golden-haired infant. Minority families have too many kids of their own. No one's going to want a seven-year old little Mexican boy."

"And if he isn't adopted? What becomes of him?" Jeannie demanded.

"Then they'll try for a foster home, probably. You know, the state pays families to board kids like these, so instead of an institution, they'll be raised in a home environment. But a lot of the families are elderly—people who need extra cash—and the government isn't exactly generous. They don't subsidize many luxuries. Usually the family situation changes after a year or two, and the kids are shuttled from one home to another. It doesn't give them much security. Don't get me wrong, on the whole, these foster parents are good people, but when you come right down to it, they're doing it for money." Keith shrugged. "But at least he'll be safe. Our social worker here told me that child abuse is increasing by almost twenty percent every year, and in the next five years, over a million and a half kids will be battered and neglected—and fifty thousand of them will die."

"Poor Ricky," Jeannie said softly. "He's such a beautiful child."

"Yep—as kids go, he's kind of exceptional." Before Keith could go on, the page summoned him and he rose with a sigh. "Humanity calls. See you later, Jeannie."

It wasn't too long before Johnny appeared, his arms filled with yellow roses. He kissed his wife emphatically. "How do you feel, honey?"

"Just great," she grinned. "Big accomplishment today. Walked to the nurses' desk. Didn't seem like more than five or six miles." The several hours each afternoon which Johnny spent with his wife always flew—filled with chit-chat, small talk, gossip about neighbors, Johnny's work. As he was about to leave, Jeannie stopped him.

"Johnny, when you come back tonight will you do me a favor?"

"Sure thing."

"Would you stop at a toy store and buy a gun and holster set—you know, the western type—something suitable for a little boy about seven years old?" Surprised, he waited for more details. "There's a little boy in pediatrics, honey, I met him this morning. He'd get such a kick out of them. Will you do it . . . please?"

"Okay," he agreed. "Sure. See you around seven."

Once Aaron Metz had gone, Mike continued his rounds and left the hospital shortly after noon. Arriving at his apartment in the marina, he made a few telephone calls, tried to read for a half hour or so, but finally slammed the historical novel shut with disgust when he realized that he had read, and reread, perhaps a dozen pages without a single word really registering. Deciding to take a nap, he lay on the bed, willing his eyes to close. Instead, he found himself staring at the ceiling with an intensity that hurt his eyeballs. Restlessly he turned on his side, and realized he was facing the part of the bed where Nedra should be. He was beginning to hate the apartment. He still saw her everywhere.

It was time, he decided abruptly, to try to exorcise the image which continued to haunt him. Wanting her—mourning her—would not bring Nedra back. He had not been near his boat for over two weeks, not since the last outing with Nedra. Remembering was too painful. Leaving the apartment, Mike walked the short distance to where the *Non Nocere* was moored.

He stepped onto the boat and ran his eyes over her affectionately. All appeared to be in good order, despite his neglect. He headed for the galley, took a ring of keys from his pocket, opened the liquor cabinet and poured himself some Scotch. Taking it on deck, he stood for a moment, surveying the harbor and its activity. The sight never failed to thrill him. Finally sitting down, he took a drink—then closed his eyes, enjoying the comforting warmth of the brilliant sun and the good smell of the sea air. It seemed only a minute later when a finger touched his shoulder. He started, looking up in surprise.

On the walkway next to the boat stood a girl—no, a woman, really—perhaps thirty years old. Her medium brown hair was short and sun-streaked, and her multicolored sleeveless overblouse picked up the bright red of the slacks she wore and made her eyes seem greener than they possibly could be.

"I'm sorry," she said, referring to Mike's startled surprise. He had been so engrossed in his thoughts that he had not heard her approach. "Would you happen to know where I can find Jerry Lafferty's boat? The *Delphi Dolphin?*"

"Four slips down," Mike answered politely, but barely turning. He reclosed his eyes. "You can't miss it." There was a brief moment of silence.

"I can't?"

He opened his eyes again and glanced up at her— then down to where he knew the Lafferty boat should be. There was a prominent gap where the *Delphi Dolphin* was usually moored.

"Sorry," he said shortly. "I guess Jerry's taken her out. Was he expecting you?"

She nodded. "He said between four and four-thirty. I'm a little early." She turned, about to leave. "Thanks anyway."

Mike watched for a few moments as she retraced her steps. He really wanted to be alone—and the proximity of another female—her nearness to the boat which Mike had unconsciously gotten into the habit of thinking of as his and Nedra's—caused an uncomfortable ache. An aching guilt as though he were being physically unfaithful. Yet something within him caused him to prolong the conversation. "What are you going to do?"

She paused, looking back over her shoulder. "I'll just wait in the car."

Mike hesitated. He wanted to be rid of her. He wanted to resume his silent contemplation. Still, there was a closeness enjoyed by the boat owners who shared the marina—a clannishness that dictated that they watch out for each other—an unwritten law which made them take on each other's problems.

"Would you like to wait here?" Mike asked begrudgingly.

She considered and came back. "Okay." He extended his hand to steady her as she stepped into the boat. As long as he had gone that far, he held up his glass.

"Would you like a drink?"

"Okay."

As he went into the galley, she followed him, watching as he once again unlocked the cabinet. He crouched to see the supply better and removed bottles of Scotch, bourbon and vodka.

"Scotch—" He noticed that there were only a few drops of bourbon and vodka remaining. "—Or Scotch," he finished ruefully. "Sorry," he apologized.

"Scotch is fine," the girl said sociably. "I'm Paula Lafferty. Jerry's my uncle."

"Mike Carrington," he introduced himself. While he was pouring the drink, Paula's eyes wandered about the galley, resting on a sheet of heavy paper, perhaps twelve by ten inches in size, taped on a bulkhead to prevent it from curling. It was a water color of the *Non Nocere* which Nedra had started. The faint lines of her original charcoal sketching were still evident, but here and there delicate paint had been applied, giving a promise of the finished work.

"Nice," Paula said appreciatively. "Lovely, in fact." She stared at it for another long moment. "Hey, that's your boat, isn't it? Did you have it commissioned special?"

Mike stopped and stared longingly at the painting. "Nedra was doing it—this girl I knew . . ." he said softly, and turned away.

"Is she going to finish it?" Paula pressed.

"She's dead," Mike said shortly.

"Oh."

Paula sat on the edge of the couchlike starboard bunk, watching Mike as he put the bottle away. He glanced up and quickly went toward her. "Pardon me," he said. Paula had not noticed the soft, feminine blue cashmere sweater next to her on the bunk. Her purse rested lightly on top of the neat folds. She watched with interest as Mike gently took the sweater, held it tenderly for a moment and carefully hung it in the small, adjacent locker.

He handed her the drink and, they both went outside and sat, silently sipping, until a movement in the harbor caught Mike's eye. "Here comes the *Delphi Dolphin* in," he said, pointing. Paula sensed the relief in his voice, quickly drained her drink and stood up.

"Thanks for the hospitality," she said, handing him the glass and gathering up her purse. She stood for a moment, watching the *Delphi Dolphin* edge into its mooring. Damn, she thought to herself, surveying Carrington from the corner of her eye. Damn! He's attractive and he's a bachelor. And he's carrying a torch big enough to melt the stars. A torch for a dead girl. There was no way to compete with that! He steadied her to the walkway and then resumed his seat, watching her through half-closed eyes as she headed for her uncle's boat. Mike noticed that the wind had chilled and the *Non Nocere* seemed strangely forlorn and empty now that she'd gone. He stood suddenly, of half a mind to call to her—but she had disappeared.

When Keith returned to Jeannie's room about six thirty, her dinner tray was still on the table, and as he headed for the chair, he surveyed it with interest.

"Aren't you going to eat the banana?" he queried.

"Yeeck," Jeannie answered with distaste.

He took it, peeling it as he sat down, and promptly finished it in five huge bites. He glanced at the tray again. "Anything wrong with the chicken?"

She looked at her plate. It was untouched. Jeannie shook her head. "I'm just not hungry."

Keith raised up from the chair just far enough to reach the tray and began to munch on the chicken leg with relish. No matter what his daily intake, which was considerable, he was always hungry.

The door opened and Johnny came in, carrying a green and white striped box. He grinned at Keith who was still eating. "Caught you—right in the act."

Keith laughed as he finished stripping the remaining slivers of meat from the bone. "I hope you're not hungry, man. If you are, you'll just have to manage to get here earlier."

"I got them," Johnny announced triumphantly, looking at Jeannie. "Hope they're okay." He removed the lid from the box and held up a child's holster set for her inspection. The wide, studded leather belt had a huge buckle, and nickel-plated toy guns rested snugly in the holsters. "The Lone Ranger Deluxe Model," he laughed. "Are they what you wanted?"

"I guess so," she replied laconically, barely looking at his prize.

Johnny hid his hurt at her unexplained lack of enthusiasm and turned to the resident. "Keith, these are for the little boy in pediatrics who was in here today. Will you see that he gets them?"

"For Ricky?" Surprised, the doctor rose immediately, removing a napkin from Jeannie's tray to cleanse his hands. "Sure will. Right now, in fact." He took the holster set from Johnny, then paused at the door and looked back. "You know, that was an awfully nice thing to do."

Once Keith had left, Johnny slid his arm around Jeannie. She pulled away. "I think I'll sit up in the chair for a while," she said in a monotone. "Will you hand me my robe?" Johnny helped get her settled, pushed the ottoman under her feet and sat on the side of the bed. Before long, a porter came in for the dinner tray, and Keith was right behind him.

"Did he like them?" Johnny asked eagerly.

Keith stared at them for a moment and looked away. "I wish you could have been there. No—I'm glad you weren't!" They waited for him to go on. "I showed them to him, and laid them on the bed." Keith began to pace, overwhelmed by emotion. "Oh, God." His voice was strained as he continued. "At first, Ricky didn't realize they were for him. When I told him, he just stared at them for a good two or three minutes. It was like . . . well, like if he tried to touch them, he knew they'd disappear. I couldn't stand it. I finally picked them up and laid them in his lap. He just kept looking at them and finally, with one finger, he touched them. Then he started to stroke the belt. First the belt—then one gun—and then the other." He turned to face them. "Ricky had never—never in his whole life—received a present before! He was still stroking them when I left."

Keith watched Jeannie's eyes filling with tears. It was all right for a patient to cry, but not the resident surgeon. With a hasty wave, he hurried out.

Johnny watched as the tears rolled down his wife's face. "Okay, honey," he said tenderly, "tell me about Ricky."

The words were cold, dispassionate, belying the tears streaming down her face. "Child-abuse case. They can't find his parents. Probably up for adoption, or at least a foster home."

Johnny watched his wife through narrowed eyes. There was something definitely wrong. Her tears were not those of genuine emotion, they were like a fountain over which she had no control. Her face was melancholy, her body sagged as though it couldn't stand the weight of her depression. As he stared, the door to the room cracked open, revealing a dark shock of hair and dancing eyes.

"Hi, there," Johnny called. "Come on in. I'll bet you're Ricky."

The boy slipped into the room quickly, dramatically glancing behind him as he gently shut the door. "Got to be careful," he whispered, "the posse's after me." He was wearing the holster set.

Johnny chuckled at a mental image of the posse—a horde of very harassed and annoyed nurses. "I'm Mr. Mendosa," he said "Jeannie's husband." As an acknowledgment of the introduction, Ricky fumbled an imitation of a fast draw, pointing both pistols at Johnny.

"Pow . . . pow."

Johnny, still seated on the side of the bed, went limp and sprawled backward. "You got me!" he groaned cooperatively.

Ricky giggled and came closer to inspect the corpse. Johnny slowly sat up and as he stared, there was utter fascination in his gaze. The steadiness of his look embarrassed the boy, who dropped his eyes. "Got to go," he announced suddenly and trotted from the room, closing the door behind him. Almost immediately, the door reopened and Ricky scurried to where Jeannie was sitting. He stood close, gazing at her intently, and then without warning, kissed her on the cheek. Before anyone could speak, he darted from the room.

Jeannie's tears and sobs increased to the point of hysteria. Feeling uncomfortably inept, Johnny handed her some Kleenex and waited for the tide to abate.

"Jeannie? What's the matter?"

"Nothing."

He tried to make conversation, but she buried her head in her hands and kept sobbing. Johnny shook his head in disbelief. This was a side of Jeannie he had never seen. Something was wrong. Terribly wrong.

"I think I'll go see if I can find a cigarette machine," he stammered. "Be back in a minute." There was no response.

Once outside, he hurried to the nurses' station and expressed his concern. The nurse nodded. "Sometimes this happens after a hysterectomy. Don't worry about it, Mr. Mendosa. It usually doesn't last very long. I just tried reaching Doctor Carrington through his service, and the message is that he's on his way here. I'll make a note on Mrs. Mendosa's chart and leave word for the doctor to look in on her when he gets here."

Slightly relieved, Johnny returned to the room. Jeannie was back in bed, a little more composed, but definitely in a blue funk.

"So tell me more about Ricky," he encouraged her, searching for a subject of conversation.

"What's to tell?" she snapped. "Some people can have children and don't want them; others want them and can't have them."

He grasped her hand. She did not jerk away, but the fingers were listless and unresponding. "I told you, it doesn't matter," he said softly. "Nothing matters except that you're alive and okay." He saw the tears start again.

"It matters to me," she said, hoarse from crying.

"Look, honey, if it's kids that's bugging you, we'll adopt one. A baby. As soon as you're better, we'll talk about it, and I'll contact one of the agencies."

"Everybody wants to adopt babies," she sniffed, "and I've heard there's a policy of giving preference to very young couples. It could take years—forever, even. I just couldn't stand the waiting. I'd go out of my mind." The tears were really flowing now.

"Well, how about an older kid? How about someone like Ricky?"

He saw her eyes brighten for a moment, and then resume their former lackluster appearance. "No." It was a flat statement, brooking no argument, but he didn't notice.

"Jeannie," he said excitedly, "did you notice how Ricky resembles my family? It's just uncanny. When he first came in, it struck me. He looks so much like Joe did at that age, I couldn't believe my eyes." Johnny dug into his pocket and extracted his wallet. He hastily leafed through the plastic pockets. "Here it is." He withdrew a dog-eared snapshot and peered at the faded image of two boys, taken some twenty-five years ago. His excitement was mounting. The older boy, who was most assuredly Johnny at about eleven years old, held the hand of his brother, Jose. The figures were small, but there was indeed a marked resemblance to Ricky.

Johnny extended the snapshot to Jeannie. "Take a look."

She ignored the extended photograph and his words. "If you say so," she said shortly.

"But what's wrong with adoption?" Johnny insisted. "We both want kids."

"Maybe nothing," Jeannie said slowly. "I've just never thought about it. I've never had to. And forget about Ricky. It just wouldn't work out. He's a cute kid, but by the time a child is six or seven, his personality is formed. We don't know much about Ricky's background, and what we do know is bad. He isn't exactly the product of a model home, you know."

"Aw, come on, Jeannie. You make him sound like Jack the Ripper. He's a little boy—and he needs somebody desperately. At least think about it."

"Forget it," she said irritably. "Let's talk about something else."

But they didn't talk. They sat silently. And they would continue to do so, unable to meet each other's eyes, for a long time.

Mike had hardly moved during the past two hours. Still sitting on the boat with his original, half-finished drink on the fantail nearby, he was completely relaxed, enjoying one of the most spectacularly beautiful sunsets he had ever seen. As the huge orange ball dipped below the water's edge, turning the entire marina to dull gold, he watched the sky change from bright orange to persimmon, and the perimeters of this splash of color shade from blue to lilac.

He actually jumped as the beeper in his pocket sounded. The device allowed his service to summon him even when he was without access to a phone. Rueful of the interruption, he flicked the switch on the little box, stilling its strident clamor, quickly rinsed and dried the glasses, and made sure the boat was secure. Then he hurried back to the apartment and dialed his exchange.

"We have a message for you to call a Doctor Joseph

Merrick at home," the voice relayed, and gave him the number. Mike obediently dialed a second time.

"Joe? Mike Carrington here. I just got your message."

"Right," Merrick replied. "Would you do me a favor?"

"Sure."

There was a long pause. What Merrick had to say apparently was not coming easy. "I haven't been to the hospital since yesterday morning. I . . . I haven't felt well and . . . anyway, even if I'm okay tomorrow, I thought maybe my wife and I might spend a couple of days in Santa Barbara. It's been a long time since Elizabeth and I've done anything together and—" His voice trailed off. "I've only got two patients in Marin now—a Susan Thomas and a Brian Murdoch. I'm sure there won't be any problems, but would you look in on them and explain?"

Merrick's words were slurry and some of the phrases had run together. Was he drinking, Mike wondered? He shrugged. What did it matter? He was being asked a favor and he was willing to oblige.

"Happy to, Joe. I have to go in tonight anyway. Got a couple of admissions I have to check on who are scheduled for surgery first thing Monday." He wrote down the two names Merrick had mentioned. "I'll see them. Oh—and Joe, hope you feel better."

"Thanks." There was a brief pause. "I'm glad I could locate you. It isn't easy to find someone on Saturday night."

After he'd hung up, Mike smiled ruefully. Merrick's last sentence had expelled any doubts he might have had that he had been Merrick's first choice to cover for him. He idly wondered how many calls the chief of surgery had been forced to make before he found one of Marin's staff surgeons available.

Whistling softly, Carrington headed for the bathroom, showered, shaved and changed into a business suit. It was a little past seven, and his patients should be admitted by now. He'd buzz down to the hospital, make the necessary arrangements, write the orders, and look in on Merrick's patients. Maybe he'd even get back in time to watch the nine o'clock movie on television—a horror classic which he had seen as a kid and fondly remembered. He was anxious to see it again.

As Mike entered the lobby of the hospital, he noticed the Sunday papers had been delivered, and paused to drop in the coins and remove one from the rack. The Sunday crossword puzzle was his favorite. While he stood there, he was aware of a heated argument at the Admitting Desk. He glanced up. Dr. David Savage was screaming insults at the admitting nurse, and he had prodded her past the point of civility. The sound of their heated argument carried throughout the lobby and the scattering of people waiting there watched and listened with interest. Mike unconsciously shook his head as he went toward the elevators. He had heard rumors via the white underground of a startling change for the better in the disposition and deportment of Dr. Savage. Mike hadn't believed it, and his doubts were justified as he studied the other doctor's increasingly angry gestures and shouts of frustration. It was true, of course. Once the immediate threat to his well-being was removed, the smiling, genial Dr. Savage had disappeared.

Mike had seen Merrick's patients, and was checking on and writing orders for his new admissions when he received the message about Jeannie. As he entered her room, a nurse was on his heels and gave her an injection.

"Hi," Jeannie said tonelessly. "What was that for?"

"A great big dose of estrogen to chase the blues away," Mike grinned. He spied Johnny, slouched in the chair, his expression a mixture of gloom and perplexity. He directed his words to Johnny, attempting to lighten the situation. "Well, that will take care of her, but it won't do you much good. What's the problem?"

Johnny glanced at Jeannie, who obviously was determined to maintain her icy silence, and with a sigh began

373

to fill Mike in on his idea of adopting Ricky and Jeannie's objections. Mike listened, and as the story unfolded, a number of things became apparent.

That Jeannie was experiencing a post-hysterectomy melancholia due in part to estrogen deprivation was obvious. The injection would replace the hormone. But part of her problem—the feeling of inadequacy—was mental. Some women suffered from it, some didn't. Usually the symptoms manifested themselves in direct proportion to the psychic trauma involved. In an older, stable woman, whose family was complete, where the hysterectomy meant only welcome relief from a medical problem, the depression seldom occurred. But in a younger woman, when medical findings had dictated the necessity and the hysterectomy had been unwanted, the melancholia could be devastating. Mike looked at Jeannie sympathetically. While they wouldn't last long, he knew at this moment her suffering and self-doubts were very real. He could almost read the thoughts tumbling through her mind. She was only half a woman . . . her world had crumbled . . . her marriage was at an end. She suspected the love her husband was exhibiting was forced—it was all a sham. The world was conspiring against her to snatch away everything she wanted.

From her reaction when Ricky's name was mentioned, Mike realized that Jeannie wanted the little boy desperately, but wouldn't admit it. She was going through a period in which she was convinced that anything she wanted was impossible, that the moment she expressed a desire, the object would be whisked away.

Johnny, on the other hand, out of his tremendous love for his wife and his ignorance of her mental state, was pressing too hard. He had accurately gauged his wife's overwhelming desire for children. Being an instinctive, decisive man, Johnny realized at once that adoption was the answer. And the sooner, the better. And coincidence of coincidences, here was a little boy—one that almost looked like him—enough like him to be his own flesh and blood—a very special little boy with a need for them far greater than theirs for him.

And Johnny had sensed that Jeannie had yearned for Ricky at first sight. So he had pushed, but Jeannie, depressed and fearful, had resisted. Deadlock, Mike realized, as he continued to listen until all the words died away and Jeannie and Johnny looked at him expectantly.

"You know," Mike suggested, "there's a social worker here at Marin. Why don't I have her drop in on you Monday, and you can discuss the whole problem with her. She can tell you all about Ricky—whether he's available or not. You could maybe take the kid on a foster-home basis and see how it's going to work out. She'll tell you all the pros and cons. Don't be impulsive. Be sure. You've got to be fair to Ricky, too."

Jeannie twisted her fingers and stared at them reflectively. She was calm now, and the estrogen coursing through her body was doing its work. "Tell me something, Mike, and be absolutely honest. Do you think adopting Ricky is a good idea?"

"What I think isn't really important. How do you feel about it?"

She lowered her eyes. "I wanted him the minute I saw him, but it seemed so impossible. I guess it was kind of like Ricky's guns. If I let on I wanted it too badly, it might be taken away."

The last sentence made no sense at all to Mike, but he let it pass. "Everybody needs something, Jeannie," he said quietly. "And it seems to me that you and Johnny need a child. Ricky might be just the answer." He saw the longing in her eyes.

"Well," she said philosophically, carefully hiding the eagerness she felt, "it can't do any harm to ask questions, that's for sure. Let's see this social worker and find out what the facts really are. If she thinks our adopting Ricky is possible—"

"Well, whatever happens," Mike cautioned, "take it slow. Just remember, it's going to be about six weeks before you're ready to chase after anyone—especially a seven-year-old. It'll take at least that long for you to recuperate from the surgery."

"Six weeks!" Jeannie wailed. "By then, somebody else might adopt him. What if his parents show up? What if he's beaten again?" Mike hid a grin. Already Jeannie was making sounds like a protective mother. Personally he felt it was the best therapy in the world. And what a break for Ricky!

"Six weeks!" she repeated.

Johnny smiled reflectively. "You know," he said slowly, "I have a mother sitting in Spain. If she thought for one minute that Jeannie—or a little boy—needed her, she'd be on the first airplane. And knowing my mother, if that flight was canceled, she'd start flapping her arms real hard. But she'd get here, one way or another. Nothing would stop her."

Mike got up to leave. "Well, don't do anything rash. And make certain you're both sure before you do anything. But if it works out with Ricky, let me know." He paused at the door. "Does anybody have any idea what kind of gift you send to congratulate the proud and happy new parents of a beautiful forty-five pound little boy?"

"Doctor Carrington. Doctor Michael Carrington."

Michael heard the page just as he was crossing the lobby to leave. Going back, he picked up the phone on the Admitting Desk, identified himself and was told there was a call for him from Emergency. The connection was made within a few moments.

"Doctor Carrington? Jeff Melburn here. I know you're not on call for us, but we have a gunshot wound of the leg. A policeman. He shot himself putting his gun in his holster. He's more embarrassed than seriously hurt," Jeff chuckled, "but I'd appreciate it if you could look at him."

"I'll be right there," Mike agreed quickly, and once again hurried down the short hall behind the Admitting Desk toward the swinging doors of the Emergency Room.

Epilogue

Susan Thomas stood in the doctors' parking lot of Marin Medical Center, leaning against the building, just to the right of the entrance door to the hospital. It was misting, and she wrapped her stylish gray leather raincoat more tightly about her, drawing the hood deep over her head. The modish white knee-high boots, trimmed in the same gray leather, protected her from the puddle that was forming at her feet, and as the mist turned to a light rain, she opened the matching, high-styled, long-handled French umbrella and waited patiently. From a distance, she looked every inch a fashion model who just stepped from the cover page of *Vogue* or *Harper's Bazaar*.

It had been almost a week since she had been discharged from the hospital. Before she had left, the electromyogram had confirmed her worst fears—the seventh nerve had been severed and the paralysis was permanent. Her face had not improved. Nor would it—ever. She avoided mirrors, but when inadvertently she happened upon her reflection, she was sickened. As each day passed, her bitter wretchedness and oppression burgeoned into utter hopelessness.

Frank Savage had upped his offer to ten thousand dollars. Susan knew she had settled cheaply—but what difference did it make? There wasn't money enough in the whole world to compensate for the agony and despair she was destined to endure for the remaining years of her life.

She was not working. She had no stomach for returning to her job in the hospital, and their vast relief at her decision had hurt. But she was getting used to hurt. Personnel had half-heartedly offered her a position in the medical records library where she would be buried—hidden from view. But she wanted no sympathy, no charity.

Susan had been home when she had called a cab about an hour before, directing the driver to deposit her at the doctors' entrance of the hospital, flinching at his sympathy as she paid the fare. He had murmured, "Good luck, Miss," and tears had sprung to her eyes as she realized that he assumed her visit there would alleviate the disfigurement. God, if it only could? She got out of the taxi—but she had not gone inside.

She stood, seemingly oblivious to the inclement weather, her thoughts on more important things. Through idle conversation with Mary the night before, Susan had determined that Dr. David Savage was due in surgery that morning, his last procedure scheduled for ten o'clock. It was almost noon. He should be finished soon. As she waited, several doctors entered and exited through the door a few feet away, and she deliberately held the umbrella low, ducking her head to avoid recognition.

It was another fifteen minutes before Dr. Savage emerged. Susan turned slightly so that her right side was closer to the building and quickly adjusted the hood to reveal the lovely features of the undamaged portion of her face. He was almost past her when she spoke.

"Why, David—hello," she said, feigning surprise, keeping her voice friendly, soft, almost provocative. He turned and stared at her for a moment.

"Susan?"

She nodded. "Hi. It's good to see you. How've you been?"

He glanced at her, unable to keep his eyes from appreciating what the tightly belted short raincoat and boots did for her figure and legs. She was really some-thing.

"Susan, how are you? What are you doing here?"

She forced a slight tone of frustration. "When Mary left the hospital this morning, she forgot her wallet, and since I was going to be in the neighborhood, I offered to drop it off. When I came back out, my car wouldn't start. Anyway, the garage just came and towed it away—a busted fuel line or something. I've called a cab to get home but," judging the angle carefully, she tilted her head and looked at the ominous, darkening sky, "in this kind of weather, I'm probably in for a long wait."

"I haven't seen you around," Dave said cautiously. "Are you working?"

She nodded brightly. "Modeling. It's kind of fun."

"Good." He paused and then said uncomfortably, "Susan, about that night—"

She shrugged and smiled. "Forget it, Dave. I proba-bly asked for it. Besides, no harm's done. If you ever have a spare moment and are in the mood, give me a call. "She turned away, casually dismissing him.

"Look," he said impulsively, "I'm going home, and the freeway takes me practically right by your apart-ment. I can drop you off. Let me give you a lift."

She pretended to consider. "Well, if it really isn't out of your way. I'm getting wetter by the minute—and I would appreciate it."

"Wait here," he urged. "I'll get the car."

She watched him hurry across the parking lot and as he returned with the Jaguar, she closed the umbrella, shook it to disperse the excess moisture, and slid into the car, still careful to keep her face slightly averted. The windshield wipers were beating a steady cadence as Dave turned from the lot, drove the two short blocks to the freeway and merged onto it. Although traffic was fairly light, a steady stream of evenly spaced vehicles prevented him from immediately slipping into one of the faster lanes. He kept his eyes on the sideview mir-ror, biding his time, waiting for an opportunity.

"So," he said easily, not looking at her, his attention

diverted, "what have you been doing besides modeling? You know, I'm glad you weren't seriously hurt. I was a little worried for a while. I heard rumors—"

"Rumors, Dave?" She twisted on the seat to face him squarely and pushed the hood back, allowing it to fall about her shoulders. Still engrossed in his effort to change lanes, he did not look at her for a moment. She simply waited. Staring at him. Finally, resigned to the fact that it would be some minutes before he could safely swing out, he glanced at her—and stiffened in horror as he saw the right side of her face for the first time. He could not tear his eyes away from the grotesque, drooping mask which was once her beautiful face.

"What kind of rumors did you hear, Dave?" she hissed. "That I was permanently disfigured? That no one can look at me without vomiting? That I'm a freak? Go ahead, Dave, tell me how beautiful I am. *Tell me!*" He could not keep the repugnance and disgust from his expression. He shuddered.

"What do you think, Dave?" she said softly, almost kindly. "You're a doctor. Let's have a diagnosis. What's your expert and learned opinion of my future?"

With a giant effort, he turned away.

"Nil, right?" Susan pressed. "*No* future! No future at all!" With a lightning movement, she thrust the fashionable umbrella between the spokes of the steering wheel, digging the sharp-pointed end deep into the luxurious carpeting of the Jaquar, leaning on it with all her weight, locking the wheel into a stationary position. At the same moment, she clamped her boot solidly over Dave's foot on the accelerator and pressed down with all her might. The car's sudden surge forward jolted him off balance for a moment. Then he began a silent, desperate struggle with her, scuffling to free the wheel and his foot. He glanced apprehensively at the freeway and saw the huge trailer truck laboriously chugging along in the slow lane in front of them, less than a half mile ahead.

Dave redoubled his efforts. Had there been more

time, his greater physical strength might have turned the tables, but their speed was now over eighty miles an hour—the Jaguar whizzing past cars in the adjoining lane and closing the gap between them and the trailer at express-train speed.

Dave made one final attempt to extricate the umbrella from the wheel and to slide his foot from under hers. But time had run out. He had only a second to glance at the cold, triumphant smile which made Susan's face even more grotesque and ugly before the sports car hurtled into the rear of the trailer with a deafening crash. The tremendous speed and impact caused it to skid halfway under the trailer bed, shearing off the top of the low-slung car—and the passengers inside.

For several moments there was the horrible sound of steel grating against steel, the sickening rasp and grind of tearing metal, the breaking of glass, and then— silence!

6